The Lies That Bind

Susan X Meagher

The Lies That Bind

ISBN (10) 09799254-2-8
ISBN (13) 978-0-9799254-2-9

THIS TRADE PAPERBACK ORIGINAL IS PUBLISHED BY BRISK PRESS, NEW YORK, NY 10011

COVER DESIGN BY CAROLYN NORMAN

FIRST PRINTING: OCTOBER 2008

Acknowledgments

Thanks to Jen Stamey for her very proficient editing. Any errors herein are solely my responsibility, since I kept changing things long after the "final" edit.

Dedication

I am forever bound in love to my partner Carrie.

By Susan X Meagher

Novels

The Lies That Bind
Girl Meets Girl
Cherry Grove
All That Matters
Arbor Vitae

Serial Novel

I Found My Heart in San Francisco:

Awakenings
Beginnings
Coalescence
Disclosures
Entwined
Fidelity
Getaway
Honesty

Anthologies

At First Blush
Infinite Pleasures
The Milk of Human Kindness
Telltale Kisses
Undercover Tales

To purchase these books go to

www.briskpress.com

Chapter One

The first day of October promised to be clear, cold, and clement. The leaves had been falling for weeks, but they hadn't turned the beautiful yellow, gold, and red that Erin so loved. Instead, they'd dropped to the ground after dimming to a muddy rust color.

She scanned the tall limbs that nearly formed a canopy over her street. It was almost seven, and the dawn hadn't broken yet, but there was just enough ambient light to see the plentiful leaves remaining. Erin's optimistic nature allowed her to assume that the elements required for a beautiful fall just hadn't coalesced yet, but would soon. She buttoned her faded, red barn jacket, surprised that the temperature was so low, hoping that the early cold meant an early snowfall.

As she crossed Main Street, a pair of headlights sliced through the dim predawn. The streetlights were off, so she had a hard time discerning whose car it was. While she was trying to solve what was, for Essex, a mystery, she heard an engine loudly and roughly come to life. There was no doubt whose engine it was. Darrell, the man who delivered the county newspaper, blindly backed out across both lanes and loudly crashed into the bumper on the driver's side of the mystery car, making the sickening sound of snapping plastic and bending metal.

Erin sprinted to reach the car, while Darrell jumped from his van as quickly as his frail, elderly bones would allow. He started complaining loudly, throwing his arms up in the air and addressing the driver. "Didn't you see me coming? It's not like I'm a little pipsqueak car."

Erin ran right past him, saw the driver's head bent over the wheel, and noted tan mittens that were covered with blood. She threw the door open and crouched down to take a better look. Touching the driver's shoulder, she spoke gently, "It's going to be okay. Let me take a look at your head."

The woman's voice was muffled, but Erin could clearly hear her say, "Fuck, fuck, fuck, fuck!"

With her hand still on the woman's shoulder, Erin said, "Do you feel any pain in your back or neck?"

"No. Just my head."

"Are you sure?"

"Yes!" she snapped, clearly annoyed. "Call an ambulance, will you?"

"Let me take a quick look at you. I'm a doctor."

The woman started to lift her head, and a cascade of pale red curls fell back against the headrest. She still held one mitten over her right temple, and blood was dripping down her face onto her coat. Her uncovered eye rotated in Erin's direction. "I think I'm really hurt."

"What's your name?"

"Katie," she said, her voice starting to break. "I'm afraid to take my hand away. I think my eye's gonna fall out."

Erin thought the chance of that was small, but there *was* an awful lot of blood. Darrell was still ranting, and she called him over. She reached into her coat pocket and tossed her keys to him, saying, "Go to my office, and get some gloves from the blue and white box in my exam room, and some towels. In the top drawer of the cabinet, there are some sterile pads. Grab a handful of them."

Once Darrell saw that the woman was injured, he started babbling incoherently. To get him to move, Erin said, "Everything's fine, Darrell. You didn't do anything wrong."

"The hell he didn't," Katie groused.

Still looking panicked, Darrell took the keys and started running as quickly as he could. "The accident was clearly his fault," Erin said. "Everybody in town knows to give him a wide berth. He's a little slow."

"Who gave him a fucking license?"

Erin couldn't help smiling. Her patient thought she might be losing her eye, but she still had the ability to cuss out a dimwitted stranger. "We can talk about him later. Let's take care of you first."

"Are you really a doctor? I can't see very well, but you don't look like you're old enough."

"Yeah, I am. I don't have my license with me, but it's in the office. I'll take you over there in a minute, and you can see it."

"If I still have two eyes," Katie complained, her voice merging equal parts annoyance and fear.

Erin reached across Katie and undid the seatbelt, her manner easy, calm, and self-assured. "Let me take a look."

With a timid, shaking voice, Katie said what would have been clear to anyone:

"I'm scared."

Erin could see that she was about to start crying. Her chest tightened in sympathy, but she didn't back off. She knew they'd both feel better once they knew the extent of Katie's injuries. "You don't need to be. I'm sure you're fine."

Firmly, Erin grasped Katie's hand and pulled it away from her face. To her relief, she saw nothing but swelling around the orbital bone and a laceration in the hairline, about an inch over the ear. She immediately smiled and lightened her tone. "You've got two very healthy-looking blue eyes, and they're both where they're supposed to be. All I see is a cut up in your hairline and a contusion just above your eye."

Katie yanked off her mitten and started to reach for her head, but Erin grasped her hand and held it. "Don't touch it. It's a clean-looking slice. You don't want to add any bacteria to it." She looked at the visor and saw a very large metal clip stuffed with receipts, notes, and all sorts of papers. It was an older style clip, probably made of steel. Erin touched it with her gloved hand. "This isn't a very good place to have something like this."

Looking at the clip malevolently, Katie said, "My mother always said being a pack rat would kill me one day." She swiped her hand across her cheek, looking perturbed at the blood flowing down it. "Did I cut an artery open?"

"No, but your scalp has a very rich blood supply. A wound there always looks worse than it is."

Katie took a long look at her bloody hand, and Erin saw her cheeks grow pale.

"Breathe normally," Erin said, reaching in to press Katie's shoulders against the seat and keep her from falling forward. She patted around the bottom of the seat and found a lever that lowered it. Erin's voice was soft and soothing. "You're a little lightheaded, but that's perfectly normal. You're going to be just fine. I guarantee it."

Darrell still hadn't returned, and a fine spray of hail started to hit Erin. "You'd better get into the car," Katie said, her voice soft and slower than it had been.

"I'm fine. I like the weather. An ice storm means we'll get some real snow soon."

Darrell finally chugged up alongside the car, carrying almost nothing that Erin had requested. He had remembered to bring some Steri-pads, and Erin opened a few of them, pressing them onto the laceration.

Katie hadn't said a word, and Erin suspected she was still feeling faint. "Think you're able to walk over to my office?"

Taking a surprisingly long time to answer, Katie asked, "How far?"

"Just across the square."

"What kinda office?"

Chuckling, Erin said, "I told you I'm a doctor. It's a doctor's office."

Katie's color had started to return, and she shrugged her shoulders. "Can't be too sure. I know an M.D. who builds sailboats."

"No sailboats. Just a nice, warm office with good lighting."

"I guess you can't carry me, huh?"

"No, but if you don't feel able to walk, I can call the emergency medical team."

Katie looked up at Erin and made a face. "No offense, but by the time somebody gets here from a real city, I'll have bled to death."

"No, you won't," Erin said, her tone surprisingly sharp. She touched Katie's belly, pressing her fingers into several spots. "Do you have any pain when I do this?" Her eyes were as sharp as flint, her manner brisk and cool.

"No," Katie said, slightly alarmed at the change in Erin's demeanor.

"Are you certain?" Erin pressed her breastbone, both clavicles and her belly again. "Anything?"

"No. Should I? I thought it was just a cut."

The stern look slowly disappeared. "It is. I just want to be careful."

"So, should I walk or wait for the ambulance? Will they go real fast and turn on the siren?"

"Doubtful. I could hit my office from here with a rock. By the time they turned on the siren, you'd be there."

Katie raised her seat and put a foot out. She accepted Erin's offered hand and stood up, her color now fine. "Then I guess I'll walk." They started to walk gingerly because of the ice.

"I'm surprised the EMS isn't here by now. They hear about accidents awfully quickly. You're lucky this is a Saturday. On a weekday, there'd be a reporter here, trying to interview you."

It was clear that Katie was feeling better. Her voice sounded strong and bore no trace of fear. "The reporters take the weekends off?"

"Reporter. Singular. He's a stringer for the county paper. And he doesn't really take the weekends off, but he doesn't go to the diner for coffee on Saturday. His wife makes him stay home for breakfast on the weekends."

"This place is amazing. Reminds me of the old saying, 'Any town too small to have one lawyer is big enough to have two.'"

"Are you a lawyer?"

"Yeah."

"Uh-oh." Erin paused. "Do you mind if I tell Darrell to leave town and never come back?"

Katie caught Erin's eye and smirked. "I can find him. Especially if he has good insurance."

When they entered the office, they stood face-to-face, with Erin putting her fingers under Katie's chin to hold her head still. She looked carefully at Katie's eyes and made sure her pupils were normal. "This is easy to do since you're my size," she commented, mostly to keep Katie's mind occupied while she looked her over. "You look perfectly fine."

"Why didn't my airbag explode?"

"You didn't hit Darrell hard enough."

"He hit me!"

"Right, right," Erin agreed, trying to get Katie to copy her calm tone. "You were only going a few miles an hour. If you hadn't had that clip there, you probably wouldn't have a scratch."

"I'm throwing all of my receipts out. Hell, if I haven't gotten reimbursed for all of this crap by now, it's too late."

"Maybe you could put the receipts in a box and go through them when you get home."

"No, if I'm going to get over my bad habit, I have to suffer. I hate to lose money because of my own stupidity."

"Maybe the clip was stupid enough," Erin said, smiling brightly. "How's that?"

"Not bad. You have potential."

⚬

Katie wasn't happy about having a small patch of hair shaved from her temple, but she proved to be a compliant patient. A late middle-aged woman burst into the office after they'd been there just a few minutes and exclaimed, "Darrell's telling everyone he killed a woman!"

The door to the exam room was open, and Erin called out, "Not even close. Everything is under control. It was just a fender-bender."

"Says you," Katie grumbled. "I'm gonna have to coach you to be a better witness."

The older woman walked into the room, and Erin said, "Madge, this is Katie. Katie, Madge is my receptionist."

"Goodness, look at all of this blood!" Madge walked over to Katie and inspected her carefully. "Thank God you didn't scar that beautiful face."

"Thanks. I can't tell what Erin's doing up there, but she swears it's not bad. Is she telling the truth?"

"Always. If Erin tells you something, you can take it to the bank."

"I don't know how secure your bank is." Katie chuckled at her own joke and watched, perplexed, as Madge took her parka, her scarf, and her gloves and promised to bring them back as soon as she'd gotten the blood out of them.

"When do Andy and Barney arrive to take the police report?" Katie queried.

"I suspect they'll be along soon," Erin answered, trying to affect a Mayberry accent. "I know Aunt Bee is putting up some preserves today, so Andy's probably busy helping out."

When Erin was finished, Katie stood up and walked to the mirror, looking at her haircut. "I'm glad you didn't go to beauty school. You're no Vidal Sassoon." She smiled, and Erin noted that Katie's entire face lit up when she did. "I've never had anyone use this glue on me before. Can I wash around it?"

"You need to be careful with it. It'll wear off on its own in about a week, and you don't want to do anything to compromise it. So, I'd just dab it with warm water. I was really glad the cut was clean, and I didn't have to put stitches in."

"Haven't practiced enough?"

Erin's smile was easy and warm. "No, I've had plenty of practice, but I'm wary about doing anything to an attorney that could cause a scar. If the cut had been worse, I might have put a butterfly bandage on it and sent you to a plastic surgeon."

"Thanks! Nobody wants to be nice to an attorney."

"I'm nice to everyone, but I'd have to really screw up to get anyone around here to sue me. I don't think a lawyer who doesn't know me would be as forgiving."

"I won't sue you. Besides, you probably have a Good Samaritan statute that would protect you from liability. That doesn't hold true for the jerk who hit me, though."

"I don't know if we have a Good Samaritan statute or not, and I don't know if those statutes protect doctors, anyway. I should look into that." Erin shrugged amiably. "Not that it would change the way I react in an emergency. If I see someone in trouble, I'm going to help."

The jingling bell over the door caused Erin to go into the main room. She saw the town's ruddy-cheeked, middle-aged police officer stomping around, trying to dislodge the ice from his boots. "Hi, Rich. The victim's still in the exam room, but I think she can make a statement." She called out, "Katie, do you want to talk to the police?"

Katie walked into the room. "What took you so long?" she asked good-naturedly.

"There are accidents all over town," the officer said, addressing Erin. "You'd think people around here would know how to drive on the ice. No other injuries, though."

"Good. Katie got a gash on her temple, but other than that and some bruising around her eye, she's just fine. I saw the accident, Rich, so I can make a statement."

Rich looked at Katie, and his expression was almost scolding. "When you see Darrell, you've got to stop, young lady. He's not all there, ya know."

She smiled thinly. "I know. Maybe you should put that on the 'Welcome to Essex' sign."

<hr>

Rich spent a long time taking her statement, and he was followed by Madge, who delivered sparkling-clean outer garments. Katie was still marveling over everyone's generosity after they'd left. "I never would have thought I'd come here, have an accident, and feel like I had to write a raft of thank-you notes."

"We're nice people."

"Does everyone like snow? Besides the nice people I can't think of many other reasons to live here. No offense," she said, grinning with a smile that didn't look sorry in the least.

"No, not everyone. I love to ski, though."

"I like to ski, too. I prefer boarding, but skiing's good."

"I can board, but downhill's my thing. I cross-country around town just for the exercise, but I'd ski every day if I lived closer and had a season pass."

Katie apprised Erin carefully. "You don't seem like the downhill type. You seem like a 'ski in a peaceful meadow and then have a picnic' kind of person."

Grinning, Erin said, "You seem like a 'snowboard with a hangover' kind of person."

Pointing her thumb at herself, Katie said, "Me? You got that from the little bit I've told you?"

"No, I got that from the fact that your cell phone has rung at least six times since you've been here, and you've told every person to bring some liquor." She was grinning like the Cheshire cat and looked very pleased with herself.

"It just so happens that I'm throwing a shower tonight for a friend who's getting married. I don't usually require people to bring liquor before they can enter my house."

"You don't live around here, do you?"

"No. I was just passing through, hoping to find someone to hit me. Thank God my luck held."

Ignoring her jibe about the accident, Erin said, "I figured you were from out of town."

"How'd you figure that?"

"Besides your accent?" Katie put on a scowl and Erin went on, "Around here, we have showers in the afternoon. And we serve punch and cookies."

"Remind me never to come to a shower around here. I've ordered a few deli trays, and I have a male stripper showing up at midnight."

"I don't think I've ever seen a male stripper." Erin thought for a moment and then laughed at herself. "I've never seen a female stripper, either, so I guess I don't have to qualify it."

"You've gotta get out more, Doctor…"

"Delancy, but most everyone calls me Erin."

They shook hands. "It's a deal. Now, how much do I owe you?"

Erin made a dismissive gesture with her hand. "No charge."

"What? You've got to be kidding. You just wasted three hours on me."

"No, I didn't. I had a nice day. You didn't interrupt anything important."

"Erin, you can't give your services away. You had to be doing something to be out so early."

"No, not really. I was up, so I thought I'd come by and finish up some paperwork I didn't get to yesterday."

"Fine," Katie said, exasperatedly. "But you still can't give your services away. How much do I owe?"

"Madge will bill your auto insurance. I'll have her call you."

"Why not use my health insurance?"

"What do you have?"

"I'm in an HMO."

"That's what I figured. I'd have to fill out a bunch of paperwork to get anything as an out-of-plan doctor. Even though it was an emergency, they'd give me a hard time about it."

"Then I'll just pay you."

"No, don't be silly. I'm not in a hurry."

Undeterred, Katie said, "How much will you bill my insurance company?"

"Oh, seventy-five dollars I suppose."

"For three hours?"

"No. That's what I'd charge for a short office visit. All I did was clean your wound and put some adhesive on it."

"Three hours ago!"

Her warm smile caused her dark eyes to sparkle. "Don't be so fixated on the time. We're not like that. I spent the time because I wanted to. I could have easily told you to wait at the diner."

"Yeah," Katie scoffed. "You look like you'd toss me out of here without a coat."

Erin's grin softened all of her features, making her look even younger than she was. "Well, I didn't say I would. I said I could. Just be glad I didn't take you to my house for lunch."

"You people are crazy! You wouldn't last a week in a big city. You'd be robbed blind."

"Good thing I'm here, then, huh?"

"I'm glad you were here, Erin. And you're going to get paid for your time today, one way or the other." As she walked out of the door she turned and added, "Your accent is stronger than mine." With a wink, she closed the door as a gust of wind blew a spray of ice inside.

⊚

Erin was nearly a block away from her house when she stopped and looked at it, almost as an outsider would have. The sun was high in the sky, crowning the chimney of the two-story clapboard, and Erin could nearly smell the scent of the place. Her house was unexceptional, and that was part of its charm. All of the houses on the block were built in the 1910s, and none of them had ever been remodeled significantly. Her exceptionally unexceptional home called to her, and she felt as though she might cry. She looked at her watch, mumbling to herself, "Yep. My period's due in three days."

Erin opened the unlocked front door and breathed in the smell of meatloaf. "I'm home!"

A pretty woman with ash-blonde hair emerged from the kitchen. "What in the world went on today? I heard more gossip in one day than I normally do in a year."

"Really?" Erin was grinning widely. She shrugged out of her coat and hung it on a hook.

"Yes. I was out raking leaves, and I finally had to come inside. Everyone who came by had to stop and ask what I knew."

"You should have called."

"Oh, I'd never do that. You're busy. But when I heard that Darrell had killed a woman, I was mighty tempted."

Erin's big brown eyes widened dramatically. "How does gossip travel that fast?"

"Don't hold out on me now! Tell me everything. You're the talk of the town."

Erin started to walk towards the kitchen. "Gee, Mom, the buildup is a lot better than the real story."

"I heard you saved a woman's life, honey. There has to be something exciting to tell."

Slumping down in a kitchen chair, Erin finger-combed her dark hair away from her face. "Not really. It was just a fender-bender. Darrell didn't look before pulling out, and he hit a woman's nice, new car."

"Oh, no," Gail Delancy moaned. "Darrell probably doesn't have insurance."

"No, he doesn't, but Rich smoothed everything over. The woman he hit won't sue him."

"Thank goodness. Who was she? No one seemed to know her car."

"I forgot to ask where she lives, but she's not local. She didn't sound like she was from New Hampshire. Different accent." She thought for a moment. "She looked like a city girl."

"Girl? Was she just a girl?"

Erin watched her mother go to the oven to serve their lunch. "She was older than me, but not by a lot." She unfolded her cloth napkin and neatly placed it across her lap, idly conjecturing, "She had a cosmopolitan air about her. Sophisticated, but not stuffy."

Gail placed a plate in front of her daughter and gently squeezed her shoulder. "Was she pretty?"

"Oh, yeah. Very," Erin said, before tucking into her meatloaf. "Mmm. Delicious."

"Was she single?" Gail asked, sitting down and arranging her own napkin.

"I have no idea." She smiled shyly and said, "I was at work, Mom."

"I'm just trying to keep my eyes open for you," Gail teased. "We don't get many single women coming through town."

"Don't remind me. I'm going to have to use a dating service."

"There's nothing wrong with that, Erin. You could meet a nice girl from Concord or Nashua or even Boston. There's a big world out there, and you can't wait for it to come to you."

Erin grinned, saying, "I know. Besides, everyone who comes to see me is sick or injured. I'd like a healthy woman."

"Then get busy! I want to have some grandchildren soon."

⸙

That evening, shortly after ten o'clock, Katie asked, in a loud voice, for a little quiet. Her friends, all women, ignored her at first, but they eventually quieted down and looked at her. "Did any of you guys invite anyone else?" she asked.

She received puzzled looks and a few head shakes. "Well, someone's about to knock my door down, and I don't think it's my neighbor." With a resigned sigh, she went to the front door and opened it to find six unapologetic men grinning at her. "Oh, no. No way." She started to close the door, but one of the men pushed back, easily negating her efforts. "No!" she whined as the men streamed past. "You guys will ruin the whole party."

The last man in line put his arm around her and escorted her back into the living room. He spoke in a calm, reasoned voice. "You know you like us better than the girls. And we brought our own beer."

Katie gave him a gentle elbow to the ribs, trying not to acknowledge that she wasn't upset. "This isn't a regular party, Tim. The whole point of a bridal shower is to grouse about men and warn the bride about the horrible mistake she's about to make."

The man put his hand over his heart. "Brutal!"

Katie squeezed him fondly. "You know you're a screw-up. Would you marry a guy like you?"

He leaned over a little and said quietly, "I wouldn't buy a guy like me a beer, but Jackie's just naïve enough to marry me. Besides, don't you think it's for the betterment of society to have someone keep a close eye on me?"

Impishly, she slapped him hard on the butt. "You have a point. I suppose it's better to sacrifice one woman than many. Now, go get that beer if you gorillas are gonna hang out."

He smiled happily and then paused to look at her. "Hey, what happened to you?"

"You're a very observant guy. You might even notice if I lost an arm. I had to run up to Essex today, and some centenarian ran into me."

Tim dramatically called out, "Clear the way. We've got a casualty." He put his hands on Katie's shoulders and guided her past their friends. "Mimi, can't you see this woman is injured? Give her your chair."

"Knock it off, Tim. I'm fine." But Mimi followed orders, and she took one of Katie's hands and helped her to sit. "Where was all of this help when I tore the tendons in my ankle?"

"That was just an ankle," Tim said. "You could have marred your beautiful face or your hair. Those are your greatest assets, you know."

Katie tried to kick him, but he jumped out of the way just in time. One of the other men said, "I talked to her when she was up there. I thought she was having hallucinations when she told me she couldn't leave because some woman was out washing her clothes."

"It's true, Gabelli. I thought I'd fallen through the rabbit hole."

Mimi said, "It's hilarious, guys. And she's got pictures. Show 'em, Katie."

"Oh, all right. I just happen to have downloaded them onto my computer." She got up and started to lead the way. "Come up to my office, and I'll show you."

All of the men and a couple of the women followed Katie up to her office. "Okay, here's the guy who hit me."

"Why did you take a picture with him?" one of the men asked. "And why are you both smiling?"

Katie moved to the next picture, that of a stocky, no-nonsense police officer. "Because this guy made me reassure the guy who hit me that everything was all right and I wasn't mad at him."

Amid remonstrations of surprise and outrage, Katie laughed and said, "I'm telling you, I passed through another dimension. A total stranger took my coat and gloves and washed them, leaving me stuck at the doctor's office for hours." She clicked her mouse, showing a picture of Erin. "Lobster, you're going to wanna move there. Check out the town doctor."

A tall, big-boned man pushed past the others to take a better look. "Holy mother of God. Look at that."

Katie clicked past four more pictures. "When I saw her, I thought she was just your type: young, fresh, pretty, innocent, smart, but naïve."

"You looked at a pretty girl and thought of me? That'll be the day."

Katie smiled up at him. "Well, you weren't exactly the *first* thing I thought of, but she seems like your type. Besides, she's geographically undesirable—even if she is gay—which I'm not at all sure of. I have a five-mile limit. I want to be able to walk home if I'm ever thrown out in the middle of the night."

"I can't see her breasts," Lobster said, leaning in close to the monitor. "How were they?"

"If you could get a girl like that, you wouldn't care if she was really a guy," Tim said. "She's got great hair, doesn't she?"

"So do I," Jackie warned.

"Oh, hers is only great. Yours is fantastic." Tim gave her a sincere-looking smile. "And she doesn't have pretty blue eyes like yours, honey."

"Hers look like a doll's eyes," Jackie said.

"Lifeless eyes," Tim said, affecting an exaggerated accent. "Black eyes. Like a doll's eyes."

"Please don't start doing your *Jaws* soliloquy," Katie begged. "Jackie, you should know you can never give him an opening like that."

"Well, they are," she insisted. "Her eyes are so dark you can hardly tell the pupil from the iris." She pointed at the monitor, underscoring her point.

"It must be the camera. They were a pretty brown. And her breasts were fine," Katie said to Lobster. Her brow furrowed as she thought. "Probably a 36B."

"Only a B?"

"I didn't weigh them. And even though the child-doctor is fascinating, isn't anyone going to ask me about the huge gash in my head or my once-beautiful car?"

Still staring at the pictures, Lobster asked, "Do you have any pictures taken from the rear? I'd like to see her ass before I drive all the way to Essex."

Katie answered by giving him a not-so-gentle slap to the back of the head.

Chapter Two

O n Sunday afternoon, Erin walked over to her office and found the contact information she'd taken from Katie. She dialed the home number and waited for her to answer, saying, "Hi, is this Katie?"

"Yep. Who's this?"

"Erin Delancy, from Essex. I'm calling to check up on you."

There was a pause, and Katie eventually said, "You're calling to check up on me? On a Sunday?"

"Yeah. You got hurt on a Saturday, so since Sunday is the next day…" Erin trailed off.

"Come on now. This is some kind of joke, right?"

"No, of course it isn't. You hit your head, and even though I'm sure you didn't suffer a concussion, I still wanted to check on you. I hope I'm not being a pest."

Warmly, Katie said, "You're not a pest at all. I think it's delightful. Unbelievable, but delightful."

"So, how are you?"

"I look a lot worse today, and it's not because I have a hangover. I was a teetotaler all night. And believe me…" She laughed. "My friends were stunned. They were all pretty sure I was hiding a fractured skull from them. They couldn't believe I was abstaining just because of a little bump."

Erin fought with her desire to ask Katie a series of questions to determine exactly how often she drank to excess, but she resisted, knowing that Katie was not going to be her patient long-term. "You don't have blood in your urine or any pain in your back or abdomen?"

"Uhm…I don't usually look at my urine. Do I need to?"

"Not if you feel well. I'm just being cautious. No blurred vision? No headache? No vertigo?"

"No, no, and no. I'm just fine."

"Did you learn to answer questions serially in law school?"

"Yes." Katie giggled. "And it's reinforced when you start practicing."

"What kind of law do you practice?"

"Real estate. It's not exciting, but I don't worry about my clients when I go home at night."

"I can see the allure. Worrying at night isn't as fun as it sounds."

"Oh, I've been there. I worked for a public interest firm after I graduated. I spent a lot of sleepless nights worrying about my clients and their problems. Now I work for people who can afford a lawyer, and I do a lot of pro bono work. Not Sonny Bono," she added teasingly. "That's lawyer talk for 'free.'"

"I think I've heard of that. I must've been reading a lawyer magazine."

"You know, I don't need pro bono medical care. I can pay you whether or not my HMO reimburses you."

"No need. We'll handle it. I'll have Madge call you."

"Okay. I need to thank her again for doing my laundry. I rarely get that service at my HMO."

"We aim to please in Essex. Make sure you have all of your accidents here."

"I hope that was my last, but if I have another, I can't imagine a better doctor to come to my aid."

∽∾

On Monday morning, Erin was in her office, making notes on the patient she'd just seen. "What's up?" she asked when Madge entered.

"You want me to submit a claim to her auto insurance for the girl from the accident? Why not her health insurance?"

"It wouldn't be worth it. She's with a big HMO that won't give us twenty-five dollars."

"Good. I hate to fill out those stupid forms for next to nothing. I assume you want to bill her for a short office visit?"

"You know me well," Erin said, showing her teeth when she grinned.

"She was a pretty girl, wasn't she?"

"Yeah, she was. She had great hair. I hated to have to cut off a hank of it."

"Oh, yes, she did." Madge sat down, and Erin knew this was going to take a few minutes. "What color would you call it?"

Erin tapped her nose with her pen. "Strawberry blonde? It looked red when we were outside, but it was more blonde in here. She had some curls, didn't she?"

"Adorable ones. I wish I could get my hair to curl. She had enough to go around."

"I don't think it works that way, Madge."

"She looked like Nicole Kidman to me."

Erin frowned, shaking her head. "Not to me. She had the curls and the coloring, but Katie's face is friendly. A little girl-next-doorish. Nicole looks icy."

"Nicole looks good with her hair Katie's color," Madge said thoughtfully. "I don't like it blonde. It looked better when she was with Tom Cruise."

"I'll bet Nicole thinks Katie has her color. I also like the length Katie has her hair. When you have really curly hair, it looks good at shoulder length. It gets too messy when it's longer."

"I think you're right."

Erin sat up and snapped some of her folders into order, subtly trying to get back to work.

"Why was she in town?" Madge asked, oblivious.

Erin let out a soft laugh. "I hate to disappoint you, but I didn't ask."

"Oh, Erin! An adorable girl comes to town, and you don't know if she's looking to move here? You know we need more single women. Is she married?"

"Don't know." Erin held up her hands, looking a little guilty. "I don't know why, but she looked single to me."

"Because she was thin. Everyone gains weight after marriage. She was very thin."

"Not just thin," Erin said thoughtfully. "She was slight. Small-boned. We were the same height, but I bet she weighs ten pounds less."

"Fifteen or twenty," Madge said. "You're sturdy."

"Thanks."

After waiting a few seconds to see if she could wring any more conversation out of her, Madge reluctantly got up to go back to work.

⌘

The next day Erin finished a very long, fairly trying consultation with one of her difficult patients, Hilda Lubansky. After they finished, Erin opened the door to the exam room. Mrs. Lubansky gasped with delight and darted into the main office. "Dr. Worrell!" The woman launched herself into the man's arms and hugged him energetically. "It's so good to see you again!"

"It's good to be seen." His voice was firm and clear, with just a trace of a sibilant *s*. He was sitting on the edge of Madge's desk, and when he stood, his posture was erect and sure. "There's my girl." He extended both hands toward Erin, and she noted that the tremor in his left hand was greatly improved.

Erin walked right into the older doctor's arms and accepted a fond hug. "It's good to see you."

"I thought we were going to lose him, didn't you, Erin? I just thought we were going to lose him." Mrs. Lubansky was tsking and clicking her teeth. "My brother Ernest had a stroke that wasn't half as bad, and he was dead within an hour." She looked from Madge to Erin, commenting once again, "I thought we were going to lose him."

Erin stepped back and clapped the doctor on the shoulder. "We were all worried, Mrs. Lubansky, but Doc showed us all what he was made of. That's some hearty New Hampshire stock here."

"I'm just too ornery to die, and that's the truth. How's everything going, Hilda?"

The woman batted her eyes at the doctor. "Oh, Erin is such a dream. I never thought we'd find anyone to replace you." Obviously hearing herself, Mrs. Lubansky shifted her gaze from Dr. Worrell to Erin. "Not that anyone could replace you, but Erin's wonderful."

"I'm very glad to hear that, Hilda. She's sure the best-looking doctor in New Hampshire. It's almost unfair that she's talented."

Erin rolled her eyes at his gentle teasing and then quickly shifted the focus back to Mrs. Lubansky. "Call me in a few days and let me know how the new blood pressure medication is working. I gave you enough samples to last for a week. Once we see how it goes, I'll give you a prescription. Do you have any more questions?"

"How could she?" Dr. Worrell teased. "I've had two cups of coffee and heard all of Madge's gossip during the time you two were in there."

Mrs. Lubansky giggled and then took Erin's hand, squeezing it. "I'll call you, honey." She pinched Dr. Worrell's cheek and clicked her teeth as she walked to the door, softly saying, "I thought we were going to lose him."

Erin waited until she was certain the woman had cleared the doorway. Then she sat down on a chair in the waiting room and wiped her brow dramatically. "I'm thinking about having a cardboard cutout of myself put in the exam room. As long as I have it say 'uh-huh' every ten minutes, most of my patients wouldn't know the difference."

"Now, Erin—" Dr. Worrell began in a chiding voice.

Madge interrupted, "After twenty years, I know that tone. I'm taking off." She went to the coat hook, took her jacket, slid into it, and waved goodbye to both doctors. "Don't forget to lock up."

"It's nice to see some things never change," Dr. Worrell said. "Madge still runs for the hills when she thinks I'm mad."

Erin laughed, nodding. "You have quite the reputation, Doc. I've never understood it, but people seem to think you're quite abrupt." She got up and walked over to him. "Are you just out for your walk?"

"Yes. Betsy won't let me back in the house unless I'm gone for an hour."

"She's too smart for you."

"I've known that since I met her." He put his hand on her shoulder and looked into her eyes. "I don't like to meddle in your business, but I'm going to have to give you a lecture. It took me many years of experience to learn that you have to train your patients to fit your schedule. You can't spend hours with the lonely old biddies who come in here just to have something to do. And you, little pup, still haven't taken that advice seriously."

"I'm trying to. It's just hard to change my personality."

Gently, the older doctor put his other hand on Erin's shoulder and pulled her close. "This is what you're not getting. You can't change your personality, but you can change how you treat people. I know you haven't learned this yet, and maybe you have to learn it on your own. I just wish I could convince you to change before they wear you down."

Laughing, Erin said, "You make them sound like rushing water and me like a rock."

"That's it exactly. It won't happen in a day or week or a year, but inexorably, they will wear you down. If you don't put a stop to it now, you might never be able to."

Erin held out her hands, looking completely puzzled. "I don't understand how my style is harmful. Everybody seems happy. My mom tells me that people stop by the library just to praise me."

He leaned back and looked at her, his arms crossed over his chest, and he considered her for several moments. "I've tiptoed around this Erin, but I'm going to give it to you short and sweet. If everyone is happy with you, you're doing something wrong."

"What?"

"You heard me. They're taking advantage of you. I've heard people talking, too. They try to tell me in their not-so-subtle ways that they're finally getting the medical care they deserve."

Outraged, Erin let out a squawk. "How dare they!"

Sagely, he nodded his head. "You're treating them better than I did."

"That's ridiculous. You're ten times the doctor I am."

He chuckled, smiling at her. "I don't know if that's true, but I know I was a damned fine doctor. When I say you're treating them better, I don't mean medically. You're spending more time with them, you're listening to more of their complaints, and you let them vent more. They feel more comfortable with you."

"Everyone loved you, Doc."

"Some did, and some didn't, but I hope everyone respected me. I did my best to make sure they respected me *and* my time. That's where you're falling short." The computer was still running, and he pulled up her appointment calendar. He pointed at that day's events, shaking his head slowly. "You had an hour free between three and four o'clock. That can happen. But it's ridiculous to allow it to happen on a day you see your first patient at seven a.m."

"I have to see the farmers that early. It's hard for them to get away once they start their day."

"Let's say that's true. I can see wanting to start early in the day to help those guys out. So, quit work at three o'clock to make up for coming in so early."

Looking a little sheepish, Erin shrugged and fiddled with the end of her stethoscope. "I don't want kids to have to miss school."

"And you don't want people to have to leave work early, and you don't want people to take a shorter nap, and you want to make sure the guys at the tavern finish a game of darts and that the women have time to get their hair cut and…"

"Okay!" Erin held up her hands in submission. "My schedule is a little out of control. I'm still trying to figure out how to come up with a schedule that's convenient for everybody."

Dr. Worrell reached out and rapped Erin's head with his knuckles. "I know you're smarter than you're acting. I'm trying to tell you, child, that you can't please everyone. You set a schedule that works for you and gives you enough free time to have a fulfilling life. The way you're set up, you're going to spend ten years here as a virtual slave, and at the end, you're going to hate your job and everybody in this damned town."

"I don't feel enslaved. I'm thankful that the town paid for my education. Not having a gigantic loan payment every month is a huge benefit."

"You're a smart girl, Erin. I know you talk to people you went to med school with, and I know you know how much they earn."

"I'm making about the same as most of them, but I'm the only one who isn't still in a residency program."

"Don't remind me. I still feel guilty about that."

Erin put her arm around the older doctor's shoulders. "Well, next time you have a stroke, you could be a little more thoughtful about everybody else's predicament."

He looked up at her and smiled. "I know, I know. It would've been a hell of a lot better for me to have worked a few more years. And it would've been a lot better for you to work with me for a few years. I would have toughened you up, you little softy."

"I have to find my own way, Doc." She giggled guiltily. "Even at the risk of driving you batty."

"And working Madge to death." His gaze wasn't benign now.

"Doc, I swear I tell her not to come in until nine a.m. She won't listen to me."

"That's another issue, pup. I knew it would be hard, your having grown up here. It's gonna be much harder for you to earn everyone's respect. You'll get that over time. I just pray that you're not hiding in your office cursing your fate before you get it."

❧

Erin sat at dinner that night, telling her mother about Dr. Worrell's visit.

"Well, you've come to the wrong place if you want me to tell you he's wrong," Gail said. "You know how I feel about your schedule."

"I have to do what feels right to me, Mom. Ever since I was a kid, people in town have been complaining about how hard it is to get in to see the doctor."

"I know, dear, but Tom's right. You can't please everyone. He saw everyone who needed to be seen and still had time to develop a fantastic golf game."

Erin sighed. She stood up and started to clear the table. Gail said, "You've had a hard day, sweetheart. Why don't you go relax?"

Pausing for just a second, Erin gave in. "All right. I've got a book I'm interested in starting." She kissed her mom on the cheek and headed for the staircase. When she reached her room, Erin took off her clothes and put on a long T-shirt, then flopped down onto the bed and pulled a book from her nightstand. After about twenty minutes, she let the book fall onto her chest. She stared up at the ceiling, thinking for a while. Checking her watch, she saw that it was only nine o'clock. Erin found her phone and dialed her friend Kim.

"Hey, Kim. What's going on?"

"Erin! It seems like it's been months. What have you been up to, other than saving accident victims from certain death?"

"Oh, no, you heard about that?"

"That was big news, woman. All of the kids from Essex were running around school that Monday acting like big shots. It's rare that the kids from the smallest town have anything to add to the gossip page."

"We're in trouble when a fender-bender is the big story at the county high school."

"It was a slow news day," Kim teased. "So, you didn't really use your hands like the Jaws of Life to drag a woman from a burning car, did you?"

"No, but my adrenaline was really pumping. It was pretty exciting—for two or three minutes. But once I saw it was only a little cut and that my heart was still beating quickly, I realized it was because my patient was totally cute." She giggled like a teenager.

"Dr. Delancy! You let yourself look at a patient like a real woman?"

"Yeah. I'm human, Kim. She was very, very cute, but I don't think she was gay. At least, she didn't look it."

"Ack! You'd kill me if I said that!"

"I didn't mean it like…I'm not sure how I meant it," she admitted. "I guess I'm saying I got a little bit of a vibe from her, but nothing specific."

"Well, the fact that your libido woke up for a few minutes is an accomplishment. Keep it going, girl."

"I know I've been neglecting my social life, but it's clear I'll never find a girl here. Besides, I've been working too many hours to do anything fun. How about you?"

"Same thing. I stupidly assigned a ten-page paper to my freshmen. When will I learn?"

"Freshmen today seem a lot dumber than we were, don't they?" Erin laughed, and Kim joined her.

"We were never that young."

"I was thinking about going hiking this weekend. Would you like to go with me?"

"Ooh, I'd love to, but I'm sure I'm going to be grading papers. How about the week after?"

"Sure. Any time. How's Henry doing?"

"He's good. He said to remind you to come out and see the football team before the season's over."

"I'll try. My mom and I go out for dinner and a movie on Fridays, but we could probably handle a football game instead."

"Good. I'd like to see you. Rumor has it that you're working some crazy hours. Are you still having trouble getting a fixed schedule?"

"Yeah, I am. I can't get it just right, but it's not for lack of trying."

"You're tenacious. You'll figure it out. My mom was lamenting the fact that we finally have a doctor who'll see her after work, but you're the doctor."

"I'd have fifty more patients if my friends' parents would come see me, but I understand it's hard to trust a doctor you've seen playing with dolls."

"You and I have the same issue to different degrees. My students' parents think of me as Holly, Jimmy, and Stacy's little sister."

"That sounds familiar," Erin said, laughing. "We should have moved to a different town, Kim."

"It's not in us, buddy. We're hometown honeys."

"Yeah, I guess we are. Will I see you at church on Sunday?"

"Of course. Maybe we could have brunch after the service."

"Maybe. My mom and I usually go wild and venture out to Concord or Manchester after church to add some excitement to our lives. Would you be up for that?"

"I'm always up for a change of pace. Maybe Henry will let me drag him to church if I promise a nice brunch afterwards."

Sanctimoniously, Erin said, "Tell Henry that saving his soul should be enough of a lure."

"Yeah. Right. How often did you go to church when you were in school?"

"I was saving lives, Kim. That's what Jesus prefers."

"I think Jesus prefers for you to go to church even when your mom doesn't make you."

"My mother doesn't make me go," Erin said, trying to sound indignant. "She just gets me up an hour beforehand and tells me to hurry up and eat my breakfast so I'm not late."

"I'd make fun of you if my mom didn't call me at seven-thirty every Sunday morning to make sure I'm up."

⚯

October the fifteenth bestowed the first snowfall of the season upon the town. A light white blanket crunched under her feet when Erin crossed the town square. The clock struck seven p.m. as Erin cut through City Hall to go into the library through the back door. Her mother wasn't in her office, so Erin walked along the corridor and saw her at the front counter. As she approached, she paused to take in the scene. Her mother was talking to a big, sturdy, redheaded man—a man Erin had never seen before. That alone was a little odd, but more puzzling was Gail's posture and expression.

Erin had never seen her mother flirt, but even from a distance, Erin could tell that's what she was doing. Her instinct was to go back the way she'd come, but her mother turned and saw her in the middle of her quandary. "Erin," she said, her voice full of surprise and embarrassment.

"Hi," Erin said, waving. "I thought you'd be closing up."

"Oh, my," Gail said, looking at her watch. "Is it that time already?" Nonplussed, Gail looked at her watch again, as though it were incorrect. "I can't guess where this day has gone. I always think I'll get more done on our late day, but that never seems to be true."

"I've been taking up too much of your time," the man said. "I'll let you get going."

"No, no, I love to talk about books." Gail gave Erin a tight smile and said, "This is Dan Tierney. He's taken over the Jackson place out on highway 128. He's planting blackberries and raspberries."

Erin extended her hand. "That's good news. We can use more farmers. I'm Erin. Good to meet you."

"Erin..." Dan asked, looking a little confused.

"Erin Delancy," she said, her puzzled gaze going from Gail to Dan and back again.

"Delancy? Are you Gail's..."

"Daughter," Erin said, trying not to shoot her mother a perturbed look for not introducing her properly.

"Daughter?" Dan's wide eyes settled on Gail. "No way! You couldn't be over thirty-five."

"Oh, I could be," Gail demurred. She put her arm around Erin's waist and hugged her. "This is my pride and joy."

"Are you in school...around here?" Dan asked, clearly trying to fit the pieces of their story together.

Chuckling, Erin said, "We both look younger than we are. I'm a doctor."

"A doctor? A medical doctor?"

"Yes. I'm the town's only doctor."

"Get out!" he said, clearly flabbergasted. "I knew there was a lady doctor here, but I had no idea..." He looked at first Gail and then Erin, shaking his head. "I'd say you two look like sisters, but you don't resemble each other at all."

"No, Erin takes after her father," Gail said, now seeming like her normal self.

"Your...husband?" Dan asked tentatively.

"My late husband," Gail said, to Dan's mildly relieved expression.

"I was going to pay you a visit," Dan said to Erin. "I need my allergy prescription refilled."

"Mmm," Erin said pensively. "I'd love to have you as a patient, but I'm not in the habit of writing a prescription for someone I don't know."

He made a face, and she added, "If you want a quick scrip, go over to the Redi-Doc in Nashua. You can make an appointment and not have to wait. They're more than happy to see patients for a single complaint."

"But not you."

"No. I practice community medicine. I want to know my patients. That's how the town likes to be taken care of."

"She's a wonderful doctor," Gail said. "We're very lucky to have her."

"Well," Dan said, stretching his muscular arms out. "I'll get this one thing out of the way and maybe make an appointment when I have time."

"Don't give it another thought," Erin said. "You can use the group in Nashua for a lot of things."

Dan looked at Gail and mused aloud, "You're lucky to have your daughter close by. I wish I could have retired in Boston, so I could be close to my son and my grandkids, but I'd been wanting to run my own business for years and now was the perfect time."

"The whole town benefits from having Erin here," Gail said, smiling at her daughter. "But I benefit the most."

Dan must've realized he was staring in Gail's direction because he seemed to snap out of his reverie, looking a little discomfited. "Well, I'll let you get back to closing up or whatever."

"Come by any time," Gail said, a little too enthusiastically for Erin's taste. "I can get anything you want from interlibrary loan."

"Will do. See you around."

After turning off the lights and locking up, Gail and Erin started to walk home. "How long has Dan been in town?" Erin asked, breaking the silence.

"A month or two, I think. I'm surprised you don't know about him."

"No, I haven't heard a thing. That's quite a Boston accent he has, eh?"

"It was pretty strong. He sounded like one of the carpenters on that PBS home repair show. He said he's from Southie. I suppose that's a neighborhood in Boston."

Erin shrugged. "I couldn't say, but he looked like he could handle his own in a fight."

"A fight? He didn't look like a fighter to me," Gail said, sounding girlish. "He looked like a big, cuddly teddy bear. His hair is cut so short in the back it almost looked like fur."

Erin studied her mother carefully, seeing, even with the dim streetlight, a sparkle of excitement that was new and odd.

⁂

The next day, Erin was between appointments when Madge walked into her office. Erin asked, "Have you heard about the guy who took over the Jackson place?"

"Of course. He's all anyone has been talking about."

Erin leaned back in her chair, shaking her head. "Why do I never hear any gossip?"

Madge sat down, clearly thrilled at the opportunity to lecture the young woman she viewed as her "project." "The answer is so simple that I shouldn't have to explain it to you."

"But you will," Erin allowed.

"It's because you don't *give* any gossip. You aren't in any clubs. You don't play cards. You don't volunteer. You don't even have many friends, and the ones you have are just like you." Madge's chin tilted up as she crossed her arms over her chest, looking satisfied with herself.

Erin considered her points for a few moments. "Then I guess I'll have to get used to not knowing any gossip." She chuckled at Madge's disappointed scowl. "I'm sorry," she said, "but I don't want to give any gossip. And I don't like to play cards, and I'm happy with my friends."

"Well, you should do some volunteer work. The town doctor should be more involved in the town. Doc was on the school board, and he did a lot for the Boy Scouts."

"That was Doc. This is me." Erin held her palms out. "I'm a mass of deficiencies."

Madge stood up and leaned over the desk, playfully slapping the side of Erin's head. "You're hardheaded. Just like your father. He was a loner, just like you."

Smiling contentedly, Erin said, "I can think of worse people to be like."

"You should at least think about doing some charitable work. It doesn't look right to have you not be more involved."

Erin briefly considered Madge's suggestion, but she didn't respond. Her sixty-plus hours of work were all she was willing to give to the town, but she thought it impolite to say so. "I'll take that under advisement," she said, shifting her eyes and her attention back to her paperwork.

⁂

A few evenings later, Erin walked into her house and called out, "I'm home." She expected a reply from the kitchen, but her mother's voice floated down from the second floor.

"Your dinner's in the oven, honey. I've got plans."

Erin mentally considered what day of the week it was, but couldn't figure out which of her mother's many activities occurred on a Thursday. She carefully washed her hands and then pulled out a tasty-looking dish from the oven. She idly read the paper while she ate and was almost finished when her mother dashed through the living room, calling out, "I'm running late, honey. Have a good evening. I'll see you in the morning, if not later tonight."

"Where…" Erin began, but the front door was opened and closed before she could finish her sentence.

At ten o'clock, Erin started to get ready for bed. She'd had a long day, but she had a little trouble falling asleep. There was a part of her brain that couldn't fully relax while her mom was out. She knew it was silly of her to have any worries about her mother's safety. There hadn't been a violent crime in Essex in Erin's memory, and the few serious matters the police investigated were always domestic. Still, she was a creature of habit, and it was hard for her to unwind knowing that her mom was not home.

⸙

The sound of an unfamiliar engine woke her, and Erin reached over to her window to push the sheer curtain aside and look out. A large, muscular pickup truck was idling in the driveway, and that made Erin wake up fully. She sat up to take a better look and was just about to go downstairs to investigate, when the driver's door opened and Dan Tierney stepped out. He jogged around to the passenger's side and opened the door for Gail, whom he then helped step down from the unnaturally high seat. Erin goggled the pair, searching her mind for any indication that her mom was going to go on a date with the newcomer.

Erin lay back down, her cheeks flushed, her body throwing off heat. She was incensed. Not that her mother had accepted a date; that was something she'd long wanted her to do. The more she thought about it, the more she realized her mother had orchestrated the evening to preclude telling Erin about the date at all, and that was both insulting and irritating.

She lay there for a good ten minutes, stewing over the situation, until she heard Gail open the door, close it, and come up the staircase. Erin's door was open, and she sensed her mother poke her head into the room, but she closed her eyes and acted as though she were asleep. If her mother didn't want to talk about it, she certainly wasn't going to ask.

⸙

The next morning, Erin woke to a silent house. It was still dark out, so she turned over to fall back to sleep. A few moments later, she heard her mother call out, "Erin, it's time to wake up, honey."

She focused and looked at her clock, saw that it was almost seven o'clock, and jumped out of bed. Erin grumbled to herself while she took a remarkably quick shower, jumped into her clothes, and ran downstairs. She knew it was childish of her to blame her mother for waking her up late, but this was part of their routine, and she was irked to have it upset.

Gail, looking chagrined, handed her a toasted bagel with peanut butter and an apple. "I'm sorry for not getting you up on time," she said, her blonde hair sticking out at odd angles. "I must not have set my alarm last night."

"It's all right," Erin said. "I think I'm old enough to get myself up on time. I shouldn't rely on you for that."

"I like it when you rely on me." Gail gave her a quick but fond hug. "Have a good day, sweetheart."

"I will. You, too, Mom."

As Erin walked down the street, munching on her bagel, she tried not to let her mind conjecture about whether or not her mother had purposefully gotten her up late to avoid questions about her evening. That was the kind of thinking that made women mad, and she didn't like to invite anger into her life.

❧

Erin arrived home after seven o'clock that night, having been held up seeing a child through an asthma attack. She walked up the stairs to her home with one of her mother's card-playing friends. "Hi, Mrs. Merkel. Is it Mom's turn to host bridge?"

"Yes, it is, honey. Do you think you might join us tonight?"

"No, I don't think so. I'll eat my dinner and turn in early."

"You work too hard for a young girl. My James is just like you. All he does is work."

Erin opened the door for Mrs. Merkel. "How is James? Other than overworked."

"I think he's fine. He keeps asking his father and me to come visit him in New York, but I don't like going to big cities."

Erin caught her mother's eye and waved. "Tell him I asked after him." She handed Mrs. Merkel off to her mother, put her own coat on the hook, and slipped into the kitchen. She peeked into the oven, saw her dinner waiting for her, draped a tea towel around the edge of the hot plate, and made a beeline for the stairs, trying to hide before six more of her mother's friends arrived.

❧

Katie Quinn tossed her head, trying to keep her curls from tumbling into her eyes. She pressed herself against her date, a woman she'd been out with twice. Erica had a very inviting pair of lips, and they were calling to Katie. She leaned into her a little more heavily, but Erica put her hand between them and straightened her silk blouse, obviously trying not to wrinkle it.

Pulling away, Katie repositioned herself and went in for a kiss. The invitation Erica's lips gave off was warmer than the reality, but the experience was still more than pleasant. They kissed gently for a few minutes, with Katie holding back to see if Erica tried to escalate, but the escalator was not in working order. Erica seemed more than content to let Katie kiss her, but it seemed as though she would just as gladly stop. Mentally pondering her next move, Katie's attention was distracted by the ringing telephone. She made it a habit never to answer her phone when she was doing something fun, but the name on the caller ID made her break that rule. "I'm sorry," she said to Erica, "but I need to get this."

She picked up the receiver, saying, "Hello?"

"Is this Katie?"

"It is. Is this Dr. Delancy?"

Chuckling, Erin said, "You must have caller ID."

"I do. And I've never known a doctor who doesn't turn it off. Aren't you worried that some patient will come to your house in the middle of the night, complaining about a sore throat?"

"They all know where I live." After a short laugh, she added, "I'm sure they all know when I go to bed. Probably when I wake up, too."

"That's a frightening proposition." Katie looked at her date, who seemed a little perturbed. She put her hand over the receiver and said, "It's my doctor."

Erin, having heard Katie say something, asked, "Is this a good time? I don't want to disturb you."

"It's fine," Katie said, watching Erica's eyes narrow. "What's up? Did you get bad results from my tests?"

"I didn't take any tests, but I'm sure you would've passed them all. No, I called to tell you that your insurance company paid me in full."

"You're kidding."

"No, no, they paid right on time. No problem."

"I meant that you're kidding about calling to tell me that." She laughed, thinking of the earnest young doctor doing her billing at nine o'clock at night.

"I didn't mean to bother you at home…"

"No, not at all. You're not bothering me in the least. I just can't believe that you do your own billing." Erica picked up a magazine, found a pen, and scrawled in large letters: *"Are you going to be long?!?"*

Katie looked at the woman, noted the anger in her eyes, saw that her silk blouse was still in perfect condition, and realized that the date was over. Once again, she put her hand over the receiver and said, "I think I might be. Do you mind?"

"No, I don't mind. You can talk as long as you want to." Erica marched to the door, picked up her coat, and exited, slamming the door loudly on her way out.

Erin cleared her throat. "I think I'm disturbing you. That's really all I had to say."

Katie kicked off her shoes, put her feet up on the sofa, and then started to unbutton her blouse and lower the zipper on her slacks. "Are you in a rush? Someone was here, but I'm alone now."

"Are you sure?"

"Yep. Now, tell me about your accounting degree. Did you get it at the same time as your medical degree?"

Erin chuckled, fully aware that she was being teased.

A few nights later, Gail passed by Erin's room on her way to bed. She saw her sitting at her computer and entered to stand behind her. Gathering a lock of Erin's hair in her fingers, she twisted it into a tight curl and then let it go. "Your hair is losing a lot of its wave now that it's longer. Even though I love it short, it looks good like this."

"Yeah, I like it. It's nice to be able to pull it back when I'm fishing."

"I'm glad you got your father's dark eyes and hair. And I'm very glad it isn't getting prematurely gray like mine did."

"I don't recall your hair ever being different than it is now. Even in my earliest memories, it was ash-blonde."

"I started coloring it not long after you were born, and even though you've always been stunningly bright, I don't think you can remember back to when you were a month old."

"No, that's a stretch. I've always rather liked it that you and I didn't look very much alike. It was nice to have one bit of individuation in town." Erin laughed, showing her sunny grin.

"Well, I'm glad you look like your dad. He was a handsome man, and you're a very beautiful young woman."

Looking slightly embarrassed, Erin turned her chair back around and started to shut down her computer. "I should get to sleep."

Gail lightly put her hand on Erin's shoulder. She was still standing behind her, making Erin unable to turn around to face her. Threading her hand into Erin's hair, Gail began to give her a gentle massage. "Dan Tierney and I went out the other night. I didn't have a chance to talk to you about it beforehand."

"Mmm. Did you have fun?"

"Yes." Gail continued to play with Erin's hair. It was clear she was nervous, but

Erin didn't try to allay her skittishness. "Do you like him, honey?"

"Uhm, sure. I don't know him at all, but I have no reason not to like him."

"I like him," Gail said, sounding decisive. "How do you feel about that?"

Erin composed her face and turned around. "How do I feel? I feel fine. How do you feel?"

"Good. I feel very good." Gail cupped Erin's cheek and looked into her eyes. "You'd tell me if you didn't approve, wouldn't you?"

"Do you mean if Dan confided in me that he struggles to control his homicidal rages?"

Gail grasped a fistful of Erin's hair and tugged on it. "You know exactly what I mean."

Erin told the unvarnished truth. "I wish you would've been going out for the past ten years, Mom. You're a fantastic catch, and he's lucky you're available."

"He's a pretty good catch, too, honey. Every single woman in the county who still has her teeth is talking about him."

Erin got up and gave her mother a hug. "I still say he's the lucky one."

"Do you mind if I go out with him on Friday? Could you and I do dinner and a movie on Saturday instead of our usual end-of-week blowout?"

Erin's stomach tensed appreciably. "Sure. That's fine. Kim's been after me to go to a football game. This will be a good opportunity."

"If you're sure." Gail met and held her daughter's gaze.

"I'm sure. Really." Her mother kissed her head and left the room. For a few minutes, Erin tried to sort out the slight upset she felt in her gut. She always felt stress in her stomach, and she knew her mother's news was upsetting her body, but her mind was nearly blank. She finally decided the novelty of the whole thing was getting to her, and she tried to reassure herself that a little change to their routine could be a blessing.

In the year she'd been in practice, her week had become stunningly predictable; only her outings with Kim broke the pattern. However, she was uneasy about her mother being the one to branch out and do something radically different. That wasn't something she had ever stopped to consider, and she wasn't in the mood to consider it now.

Chapter Three

On Friday evening, Erin carefully composed her expression into a pleasant smile and opened the door. Dan Tierney stood in the yellow glow of the porch light, his mouth gaping open. "Do you live here?"

Erin stepped back, holding the door open wide. "Sure do. I have since they brought me home from the hospital." Dan entered, looking uncomfortable and puzzled. "I mean when I was born," she added, trying to inject some levity into the tension. "Not last week."

He looked at her, and then his eyes darted to the living room and back. "I don't know why I'm so surprised, but I am." He scratched at the back of his head, looking puzzled. "I guess I assume young people want to live alone...or with a boyfriend or..." He trailed off, clearly irked at his inarticulateness.

"I like it here, and even if I didn't, there aren't any decent apartments close to my office. And I'm a long way from being able to afford my own house."

"Really?" He looked at her curiously. "A doctor can't afford a house?"

"No, I can't. Besides, as I said, I like living at home. My mom's a great cook."

"Now that's a good reason to live at home. Both of my brothers lived at home until they were over thirty, and our mother couldn't cook to save her life."

Erin detected some motion, and she looked up the stairs to see her mother descending. "You look great, Mom."

Dan watched Gail move, echoing Erin's sentiment. "Great indeed." Taking a quick look at Erin, his gaze went back to Gail. "You and Erin are both beautiful women, but as I said before, you look almost nothing alike."

"We were just talking about that the other night," Gail said. "Erin's a Delancy through and through." Gail walked between the pair and went to the mantle. She picked up a photograph and gently wiped the glass with the sleeve of her sweater. "She looks just like her grandmother." Dan walked over to her and accepted the frame when Gail held it out.

"That's remarkable," he said. He looked at Erin and then back at the photograph. "How old was your grandmother in this picture?"

"I'm not sure. Mom?"

"It was before she was married, so she was younger than you are now, Erin. I'll have to ask her."

Looking a little surprised, Dan asked, "She's still alive?"

"Oh, yes. She's hale and healthy. Erin's grandfather is, too. He still works part-time."

Dan chuckled. "A flinty New Englander."

"No," Gail said. "Rather immoderate Montréalers. They were obviously blessed with good genes, since they both violate every rule a prudent doctor would lay down." She smiled at Erin and patted her cheek. "And I hope my girl takes after them in every way. Well, not the smoking, but in every other way."

"Smoking has never appealed to me, Mom. I can keep up with them at the dinner table, though."

"This is true, but they can drink you under the table without even trying."

Dan laughed. "Those sound like my kind of grandparents. All I can remember getting from my grandmother is a mint she'd pull out of her pocket. There was always so much lint on it that it looked more like a caterpillar than a piece of candy."

Gail smiled up at him, her pale blue eyes twinkling. "I bet you do a terrific job with your grandsons."

"You'll meet them soon, and you can decide for yourself," he said, looking at her as if he'd forgotten Erin was in the room.

Erin felt her stomach roil at witnessing this small intimacy. "You two don't mind if I start my dinner, do you?" she asked. "I've got to get over to the high school."

"Oh, no, honey," Gail said. "You must be starved."

Erin was backing up, heading for the kitchen. "No, nothing that severe, but I'd better get started." She waved, even though she felt foolish doing so. "Have a good time."

She pushed through the door to the kitchen, hearing Dan and her mother say in unison, "We will."

Once on the other side of the door, Erin leaned against the oak, letting the substantial, familiar door reassure her that nothing had, or would, change.

❧

Three hours later, Dan and Gail stood on her front porch, where she babbled uncharacteristically. "I had such a nice time tonight. I don't get down to Boston often enough. The last time I went to Boston on a date was when I went to hear Arthur Fiedler and the Boston Pops at the Bicentennial Celebration."

"No kidding? I worked that detail. You didn't get arrested for drunk and disorderly, did you? We might have met."

She giggled and then cringed at how immature it sounded. "No, I was well behaved. Like I always am."

He assessed her, his clear blue eyes roaming boldly up and down her body. Nodding, he said, "There's nothing wrong with being well behaved. After thirty years of police work, I've had my fill of bad actors. There's something very appealing about people who know how to behave."

Gail laughed nervously. "Then you're going to love me." A look of horror came over her when she realized what she'd just said. "Goodness, that came out all wrong."

Dan leaned over and brushed her cheek with his lips. He looked directly into her eyes, and as a half-smile settled onto his face, he said, "Maybe not."

~

Several days later, Gail was getting ready for another date with Dan, her second that week. "Why won't you come with us, honey?"

"No offense, Mom, but I never wanted you to come on one of my dates. I can't imagine you or Dan need a third wheel. Besides, I think I've seen enough Thanksgiving pageants to last a lifetime."

"Well, I think the town doctor should go to all of these cultural events." Gail chuckled. "Some day, I want to have some grandchildren singing off-key and missing their cues. I'm just staying in shape."

"I'd like that, too, but I'm not in a rush. Thank goodness," she said, laughing ruefully.

"You're lucky, honey. I was the only one who could have a baby when your father and I married. You might be able to talk your partner into being the one to experience the joys of childbirth."

"I have to talk someone into going out with me first. I don't think it's wise to bring up childbirth until the second date."

"You're very prudent," Gail said, bending to kiss her daughter goodbye. "Maybe you should be less prudent and a little more reckless. There has to be a woman out there who would love to marry a beautiful doctor. You just have to get busy and find her, and I'm sure she's not in Essex, so you'd better get out more."

"I'll get around to it." She leaned back in her chair and took a long look at her mother, smiling as she did. "Are you ready for the fallout you'll get from taking Dan to a big, public event?"

Gail rolled her eyes. "Everyone knows. The old ladies keep coming into the library just to look at me."

"You *do* look happy, but it's not a huge change."

"I don't think I look any different, but people are treating me differently. Snagging an eligible bachelor has cast me in a whole new light. Older men practically wink at me!"

Erin laughed hard, imagining some of the more straight-laced old men doing just that. "I think they should be winking at Dan. He's the lucky one."

With a thoughtful look, Gail said, "Not having dated all these years must have made people think I was…well, I don't even know."

"I think people have assumed you weren't interested. Refusing every offer you've ever gotten probably cemented that reputation."

"I've been interested for years," Gail said, grinning playfully. "But I wasn't going to go out with a local divorced man. I wouldn't think of hearing how I was buying someone's damaged goods. No, if Dan hadn't moved here, I'd still be happily going about my life."

Erin nodded, even as the thought flitted through her brain that having people talk was a thin reason to stay at home. "You seem happy, so I'm glad Dan came to town. I know you don't like to be the main topic of gossip, but that'll pass."

"Goodness, I hope so. Is it wrong to hope that Jimmy Edgar falls off the wagon and starts cheating on his poor wife again?"

Erin got up and hugged her mother, sharing a laugh. "Yes, Mom. It's wrong. You've got to tough it out."

⟅⟆

After Gail left, Erin was feeling antsy, so she drove over to Nashua to see a movie. She chose the multiplex closest to her home and lucked out, finding an action-adventure movie that was scheduled to start soon. She bought a large popcorn and instructed the young woman to put extra butter on it, even though she knew the yellow grease had little to do, then or ever, with butter.

Two hours later, she was feeling much better. The movie had gotten her blood flowing, and the junk food gave her some much needed sinister pleasure. She was feeling so happy about her popcorn indulgence that she bought a candy bar the size of a paperback book to munch on as she walked to her car. When she got home, her mother was still out, so she picked up the phone and called her friend Kim. "Hey, Kimbo. Any news?"

"None," Kim said desultorily. "You?"

"No, no news, but I do have a question. Remember that woman who was in the fender-bender with Darrell?"

"How could I forget? You saved her life."

"Right," Erin agreed, chuckling. "Well, I called her the other night to tell her that her insurance company paid the bill, and she seemed kinda…I don't know…interested in talking to me."

"Oh, Erin. Sometimes I forget how hard it is for you, having had so little dating experience."

"I have experience," Erin said, sounding insulted.

"No, you don't. You didn't experience the whole 'Does he like me? Will he ask me to the dance? Will you ask your friend if his friend says he likes me?' stuff most of us straight girls go through."

"Hey, I had my first date before you did."

"That was your first date with a boy, and we now know, in retrospect, why you never seemed to care if you had a date or not. You were never invested like the rest of us were. You didn't spend every waking moment wondering if Nathan Jones was really looking at you in biology class or just staring into space."

"Were you really like that?"

"Yes, of course I was. I thought you were just above it all or didn't have to worry since the boys always loved you."

"No, you're right. I didn't care. Do you really think I missed out on a lot?"

"I'm sure you did. If you'd cared more then, you'd have better instincts about whether or not this woman is interested in you."

"So, what do I do?"

"Ask her out."

"Oh, no, no, no. I couldn't do that."

"Why not?"

"I'm not sure if she thinks she's my patient or what. If she thinks this is a professional relationship, then that's what it should be."

"What if she asked you out?"

"I'd be thrilled, but I think I have to wait and see."

"Why don't you call her again, just to chat?"

"I feel like I have to have an excuse. She already thinks I'm a little crazy for calling to tell her that her bill was paid."

"Do you normally do that?"

"Gosh, no. I used it as an excuse; that's why I'm out of them."

"Well, I don't think it's unprofessional to ask her out, but I know you're very persnickety about things like that."

"You think I'm persnickety about everything. Admit it," she said, laughing.

"Just most things. Like ninety-nine percent of things. But that's part of what makes you you, and I like you just the way you are."

⁓

Talking to Kim hadn't improved Erin's mood. She still felt restless and agitated, so she sat at her desk and started to write. She had been working on one particular story for about a month. Even though it wasn't the proper chronological time for it to happen between the characters, she spent a solid hour writing the most erotic sex scene she could conjure up. By the time she was finished, she could have grabbed the first warm body walking down the street and pulled her into the house. But very few people walked down her street at night, so she had to satisfy herself in the usual solitary way.

⁓

Erin was back at her desk writing when her mother came home. "Hi, Mom!" she called out through her closed door. "Did you have a good night?"

Gail knocked politely, then walked into the bedroom and kissed the top of her daughter's head. "Yes, I did. Dan took me to a new restaurant he'd heard about in Nashua. We had a real feast."

Turning in her chair, Erin said, "A feast, huh?" She spent a moment assessing her mother's expression. "You don't look like a woman who just had a great time. Is something wrong?"

Gail went over to Erin's bed and sat down. "I'm a…I suppose I'm a little down. Have I told you that Dan goes to Florida for the winter?"

"No, you haven't. How can he do that when he's trying to start his business?"

"He says there's really nothing to do with the land over the winter, and as long as he has his laptop with him, he can take care of everything no matter where he is. He's leaving in two weeks." She sighed, and Erin could practically see the longing in her eyes.

"He'll come back."

Chuckling soundlessly, Gail nodded. "I know, and I feel silly mooning over it. I just feel…I feel like we were really starting to click, and I hate to have that stop. You were right, you know."

Erin walked over and sat down next to her mom. She put an arm around her shoulders and rested her head against her mother's cheek. "About what?"

"You were right to tell me that I should get out and meet someone. I hadn't realized how much I missed being with a man." Erin's body stiffened, and Gail backtracked. "Oh, I didn't mean that like it sounded. You know what I mean, don't you?"

"I'm not sure," Erin said hesitantly.

Patting Erin's leg, Gail said, "Of course you do. There's a spark, a level of excitement that you get when you spend time with someone you're interested in romantically. It's a feeling you don't get from friends and family. I've missed it." She wrapped her arms around her daughter and hugged her tightly. "I know you miss it, too, sweetheart, and I pray every night that you find someone. Life's too short not to have someone to love."

Erin smiled shyly. "I was thinking about getting a cat…"

Gail caught her daughter's nose between her fingers and pinched it. "A cat is no substitute, but if you really want a cat, you can get one—as soon as you get your own house."

"When is *your* tomcat coming home?"

"Very funny. He thinks he'll stay through February."

"Maybe we can see him when we go down. Speaking of which, we haven't made any plans. I know you had to drag me to Florida last year, but I think your idea of going on a winter break every year is a good one. I could really use a few days off."

Gail hesitated, looking uncertain, as if she wanted to avoid the topic. "I'm not ready to make any plans yet. Let's see how things stand in a month or so."

"Mom, you're the one who started planning last year's vacation while we were still swimming in the lake. You told me there's nothing good left after November."

"That's not true. I'm sure there are plenty of places. But don't let me hold you up. If you're ready to make winter vacation plans, don't let my indecision stop you."

"Stop me?" Erin's confusion showed in her eyes. "You're the one who craves the warmth just when it's getting good here."

"You're just like your father. It must be the Canadian in you. And if you need to get away, you should go."

It finally dawned on Erin that her mother wanted her to make her own plans— alone. Feeling foolish, she said, "Well, things were pretty slow in December last year. I expect the same this year. Maybe I'll go up and see Grandmother and Grandfather for a few days."

"Oh, that would be wonderful. I know they'd love to see you, and I know you'd love to see their snow." Gail stood up and walked toward the door.

"I love them more than I love snow, Mom. Well, I love them equally as well as I love snow." She watched her mother walk down the hall, wondering if Gail had already made plans that she wasn't willing to share.

◈

On Saturday morning, Erin drove through the square, spotting Katie's relatively unique boxy orange car. She pulled up alongside and honked. Katie rolled down her window and said, "I was driving by to see if you were open. You look like the kind of woman who works Saturdays."

"No, I'm going running. I'm as happy as a bug in a rug now that it's cold."

"Can you stop for a minute? I have something for you."

"Sure." Erin pointed at the corner diner. "I'll buy you a cocoa."

Katie parked and dashed inside, patting her arms dramatically. "Damn, it's cold!"

"Yeah. Cool, huh?"

"I like the cold, too, so don't think you're tougher than a Boston girl. We get the wind off the ocean, you know."

"I do. I've been to Boston. I love it in the summer, but you can't cross-country ski five minutes from your house like I can here."

They sat down at the counter, and the waitress approached. "What's up, Doc?"

Erin smiled back, even though she'd heard the lame joke nearly every day since she'd returned to town. "I'd like some cocoa, Judy. Katie?"

"The same." Judy left to get their drinks, and Katie pulled her curly blonde-red hair back, showing her temple to Erin. "You did a good job."

With a tender touch, Erin ran her finger over the slightly raised, pale pink scar. "Not bad. Are you using that scar cream I recommended?"

"No. I put it on for a week, but I got bored. I kinda like having a few scars. Especially when you can't see them from across the room."

"You have to be close to see yours," Erin said, gazing at it thoughtfully. "When the lock of hair I had to cut gets to the same length, you won't be able to see it at all."

"Hey, I meant to ask who's following up with Darrell?"

"Rich made sure he got insurance. He didn't know he needed it. He's…a little slow."

"So I've heard." Katie put her chin on her hand and looked Erin over. "What's a young doctor like you doing in a place like this?"

"I like the cocoa," Erin said, smiling when Judy put their drinks down. They each took a sip, and Erin waited for another question, but one wasn't forthcoming. Instead, Katie was gazing at her, clearly waiting for Erin to speak. So, Erin answered the question she'd teasingly ignored. "This is where I'm from. I moved back after school to take care of the town and my mother."

"Oh," Katie said, looking concerned. "Is she…ill?"

"No, not at all. She's probably in better shape than I am. But we're really close, and I didn't want to move too far away."

"Hmm. Interesting." Katie's eyes narrowed slightly, as she picked up her cup and blew across the liquid to cool it.

"You put a funny emphasis on 'interesting.' Do you mean 'loser'?"

"You don't look like a loser. Not at all." Her bright blue eyes scanned Erin slowly. "You look like a very bright, very attractive, very young woman." She cocked her head a little, still assessing. "Are you sweet on someone in town?"

Erin knew she was blushing, but she tried to act like she wasn't embarrassed. "No. I wish I were, but there's not much to choose from."

"Oh, come on," Katie scoffed. "You're an hour from Boston when traffic's good and only what…twenty minutes from Nashua? There are little towns all over the place. Someone must have a cousin or a co-worker they'd like to fix you up with. You're far too good-looking to be single if you don't want to be."

"Are you single?" Erin asked, desperately trying to get the focus off herself.

"Yeah." Katie grinned, one eye closing a little, her chin lifting, making her look as if she were keeping a very interesting secret. "But I want to be. You sound like you don't."

"I guess I don't." Erin contemplatively took a sip of her cocoa. "I think I'm better when I'm in a relationship."

"Mmm, I've had some trouble in that department." Katie's eyes were dancing with impish good humor. "But I'm not unwilling to keep trying until I get it right."

"Do you date a lot?"

Nodding, Katie said, "A whole lot. How about you?"

"Not at all. I haven't had a date since I got back to town." She looked a little glum, and Katie gazed at her profile for a few moments.

"Are you incredibly particular?"

"No, not incredibly so."

"Then why no dates?"

Erin shrugged. "There really isn't much to choose from. This is a very small town."

"So, you need to go outside of your town. Why not ask your friends to hook you up with someone from Concord or Manchester?"

Looking uncomfortable, Erin said, "Not many people have offered."

"Are you shy?"

"No, not very. But I guess I'm…maybe lazy? My mom keeps telling me to find someone online, but that seems like a lot of work."

Katie gazed at Erin for another few seconds, trying to get a bead on her.

"Isn't it worth some work if it's important to you? Strangers don't come to my door asking me out. I work hard to meet new people." She put her head on the counter, sighing dramatically. "I'm pooped!"

"Yeah, yeah," Erin agreed. She sipped at her cocoa, looking both uncomfortable and anxious. "I guess I'd do it if I were ready." She turned to Katie and said, "Maybe I'm shyer than I think I am."

"Maybe you are," Katie agreed, still having no idea what the young doctor was looking for or even if she herself knew.

❧

That night, Katie worked the room at a Boston GLASS Community Center fundraiser. She caught an old friend's eye and made her way across the room. "Hi, Naomi," she said, hugging the woman.

"How are you, Katie? I haven't seen you since the barbeque at Jake's house out on the Cape. Are you still dating that woman you were with?"

"Uhm, who was I with? Was she a tall blonde?"

"No," Naomi said. "She was a short Latina."

"Oh, right! Nice, nice woman. but she liked to play the field as much as I do. I think she was a little too young for me." She laughed and added, "Maybe that's the wrong adjective. I think she was a couple of years older than me."

"That's refreshing to hear. Most of the women I talk to seem to want a much younger girlfriend."

"I guess I wouldn't mind a young woman," Katie said, "but they're hard to pin down. I have a little crush on a woman from New Hampshire, but I can't even find out if she's gay. And I will never again go out with someone who's ambivalent or uncomfortable with her sexual orientation."

"Have you been burned?"

"Haven't we all?" Katie sighed.

❧

Erin ran into Dan the day before he left for Florida. They stood in front of the post office, with Erin trying to think of something interesting to say. "My mom tells me you'll be out of town for quite a while. Is there anything we can do to keep an eye on your place?"

Dan squinted a little, looking at Erin for a few seconds. "Your mom's right, you know. You're a damned nice girl."

Grinning at him, Erin said, "I'm sure she didn't say that. At least, I've never heard her say the word 'damn.'"

"Well, words to that effect. Your mom's a real lady."

"She is. And she's a very good person, too."

"You're both good people. But you don't have to worry about my place. My boy is going to come take care of it. It'll give him a chance to get out of the city."

"Well, give him our number just in case. We'd be glad to help out if he needs anything."

Out of the blue, Madge was at Erin's side. "My husband is a very good mechanic," she said. "If anything at the house breaks, tell your son to call us."

"I swear I've met more people here than I knew in fifty years in Boston. And every one of them is nice."

Erin and Madge giggled conspiratorially. "He hasn't been here long enough to know the dark side," Erin said. "The kooks tend to come out at night when the nice people are asleep."

That night, Gail sat on Dan's lap at his home, trying to impart with her kisses the way she felt about his leaving. "I'm going to miss you," she whispered into his flushed ear. "I'll miss this, too." She kissed him again, longer and sweeter this time.

"How much will you miss me?" He pulled away and looked deeply into her eyes. "Are you sure you don't want to…" He slipped his hand between their bodies and played with the top button of her blouse.

Her smile was warm and welcoming, but her words made her position clear. "It's too soon, sweetheart. I know you want more, but I'm not willing to have casual sex."

"There's nothing casual about the way I feel. Nothing." Dan's blue eyes gleamed with intensity.

Gail stroked his cheek and soothed, "I know that, and I didn't mean to diminish your feelings. But I've made it clear that I don't feel comfortable having sex until we're further along."

Frustrated, but still good-natured, he said, "What happened to the free love generation?"

"I never joined that movement, and they're not taking memberships any longer. Plenty of other women are in the club, though."

"You've got me hooked, and you know it. It's a waste of time to go to Florida this year. I won't even want to look at the girls in the bikinis."

"Now I know you're lying." Gail slid off his lap and kissed the top of his head. "I promise to call you every other day just to remind you of what you've left behind."

He got up and took her hand. "And I'll call you every day that you don't call me, but I won't need to be reminded. You're on my mind all day now, and I get to see you most evenings. It's going to be much worse when we're a thousand miles away."

They hugged, and she said, "Maybe absence will make our hearts grow fonder."

"There's a fondness limit, and I'm nearly there."

The next Saturday morning, Erin was walking down Main Street, enjoying the snow flurries that were still blowing through town. A good blanket had dropped on them the night before, and she was going to get her cross-country skis and head for the hills outside of town as soon as she picked up her dry cleaning. A honking horn made her turn to see Katie's orange car. Erin waved, and Katie pulled over. "Buy you a cocoa, Doc?"

"Sure. Meet you at the diner if you can find a parking spot." There were probably ten spots available right of front of her, and Katie smiled at Erin's sense of humor.

A few minutes later, they both stomped the snow off their boots and took stools at the counter. Rich, the police officer who took the report on the accident, entered the diner just then and waved to Erin. He spent a second staring at Katie and then walked over. "Hey, you're the girl who had the accident."

She extended her hand, and he shook it. "Boston police don't remember the murders, much less the fender-benders. You people are well cared for around here."

"Well, we try. Are you up here for business?" Rich asked.

"Not really. My brother was supposed to come up and clear my father's driveway, but he got called in to work, and he told me I had to come." She made a face. "I get to do it on the day it's two degrees."

"Your father? Does he live around here?"

"Yeah. Dan Tierney. Do you know him?"

"Tierney? I thought your name was—"

"Quinn," Katie said.

Not the most tactful soul, Rich said, "I didn't know he had a girl."

"I'm a little past the girl stage, but I take it you know he has a boy," Katie said dryly.

"Yeah. And three grandsons."

"I'm sure he'll get to me sooner or later. Probably later."

Katie turned to Erin and noted how uncomfortable she looked. "Don't tell me you're dating him," she said, looking pained.

"No! I'm not dating him."

"Her mom is," Rich supplied helpfully.

Now both Katie and Erin looked uncomfortable. Almost in unison, they said, "I'm sorry."

Katie cocked her head and asked, "What do you have to be sorry about?"

"Nothing. I just…I don't know," Erin said, embarrassed. "I don't want to make you uncomfortable."

"It's okay with me if he goes on dates. He and my mom are long divorced."

"He's divorced?" Erin and Rich asked, again, in unison.

"Are you two related?" Katie asked. "Yes, he's divorced. He didn't tell everyone he's a widower, did he?"

"No," Erin said. "I guess I just assumed he was."

"Don't people get divorced around here?"

Erin laughed a little hesitantly. "No, people get divorced. Not very often," she added. "But they do."

"Your mom's not divorced?"

"No. My dad's dead."

"I'm sorry to hear that. I hope my dad's been nice to her."

"I think he has," Erin said, still looking unsure of herself. "My mom seems to like him."

Katie laughed. "Oh, women like him. He's very likable."

"Did you do the drive yet?" Rich asked.

"No. I was just coming into town. I stopped to see Erin."

"I'll do it for you. Do you have the keys?"

Stunned, Katie stared at the officer. "Are you kidding?"

"No. A young lady shouldn't be doing that kind of work. You probably don't even know how to lower the plow on the little utility vehicle he has, do you?"

"Well, no, I don't, but my brother said it's simple. I'm supposed to call him and have him walk me through it."

"Give me the keys," Rich said. "I'll be done and back in no time."

"Really? Are you sure?" She was already reaching for her pocket while she spoke.

"I'm sure." He took the keys, put his hat on, and lowered the earflaps. "Don't go anywhere."

Katie's mouth was still agape when Erin said, "Andy takes real fine care of us now that Barney's retired. He was always getting into some kind of trouble."

"That was freaky."

"We're nice people. Hasn't your dad told you that?"

"He and I don't talk a lot, but he does seem to like it here." She gave Erin a suggestive glance. "Maybe that's because of your mom." Erin blushed, making Katie laugh. "Damn, I didn't mean to embarrass you. Is this something new for you? Having your mom date, I mean."

"Yeah. Brand-new."

"Has she been widowed long?"

"Uh-huh. I assumed she'd never date. This caught me by surprise, but your dad seems like a good guy."

"He has his good points," Katie said rather noncommittally. "We're just not very close."

"But you're close enough to drive all the way out here to help him out. That shows something."

"Just that I'm a sucker," Katie said, showing that half-grin. "Why aren't you out enjoying the snow?"

"I was planning on going as soon as I run a quick errand."

"I don't want to hold you up."

"We'll have snow for another five months. I can wait a few minutes. Besides, I don't get to talk to too many people who have their clothes on." She heard how her words had come out and blushed again, her already pink cheeks becoming darker. "I didn't mean that like it sounded…"

"It's okay." Katie patted Erin's arm. "You're a delicate little thing, aren't you? Are you *sure* you're old enough to be a doctor? Did you skip nine or ten years ahead?"

"No, but I was young to start school. My mom pulled some strings and got me enrolled a little early. That's all of the skipping I've done."

"So, you're just a sweet-cheeked country girl, huh?" Katie was grinning rather evilly, and it was clear that she was enjoying the taunting and teasing.

"I suppose I am, but I'll toughen up over time."

Katie fixed her with a sober gaze, once again touching her arm lightly. "Don't get too tough. Gentle people are a rarity. Just get hardened enough so you don't blush every time you make a vaguely suggestive joke. You'll burst something."

"I'm pretty sure there isn't anything that can burst from being gentle, but I'll keep an eye on myself just to be sure."

"I feel kinda bad having Rich do my work for me. I think I'll go help."

"Can I go with you?" Erin asked, surprising herself with her forthrightness.

"Sure, if you want. I can't promise excitement, but I'd love the company."

They got into Katie's car and drove out to Dan's farm. Rich was already finished with the drive, and he handed Katie's keys back and left before she was able to slather him with thanks. "He's a sweetheart," Katie said.

"Yeah, he is. One of our nicest."

"How many do you have?"

"Four."

Shaking her head in amusement, Katie said, "That's a small class to be at the top of." They were at the side door and Katie opened it. "I have to check on a few things. Come on in."

"Uhm, maybe I'll stay outside. I hate to go into someone's house when he's not home."

Katie put her hands on her hips. "Why did you come all the way out here?"

"I don't know." She looked down at the damp ground. "I thought you might need help."

"Well, I do, but you have to come in to help me."

Erin looked up and met Katie's penetrating gaze. "Okay." She walked in, managing to avoid looking at almost everything.

"You're an odd one," Katie said. "You act like we're going to go through his underwear drawer."

"I know." Erin was clearly embarrassed. "I'm funny about a lot of things. I've got a real fixation about privacy."

Katie grasped the sleeve of Erin's coat and pulled her to a chair. "Sit." Erin followed the order, sitting primly on the edge of the seat. "Now, take off your coat." Once again, Erin did as she was told.

Removing her own coat, Katie sat on the sofa and said, "What's the deal with you?"

"Deal?"

Katie regarded her for a few seconds. "I can't figure you out. I could see living here because you were in love with someone local, but you said that wasn't true."

Erin shook her head. "No. No love life. No prospects."

"So, that must mean you love small-time medicine with a passion. What is it that appeals to you so much?"

Scrunching her eyes into slits, Erin thought for a minute. She finally said, "I like being part of the community, and I get to see all kinds of issues. Not that most of them are very unique…" she said, trailing off. Another minute of silence followed, with Katie looking at her carefully. "People rely on me. That can be nice, but it also puts a lot of pressure on me." She shrugged. "I get to spend a lot of time with my mom."

"And she's your best friend."

Bristling, Erin said, "I'm not ashamed to be close to my mom."

"You shouldn't be, but you could be close to her and work in Nashua or Manchester or even Boston."

"Yeah, I could have, but the town needs me. It's really hard to find a doctor for a town this small. There's not much money here, and most doctors want to specialize. That's where you can make some real cash."

"What's the worst thing about your job?"

"Oh, that's easy. Watching someone you can't help slowly deteriorate, knowing you're going to lose them. That's the worst. By far."

"But isn't that the point of small-town medicine? It's a birth-to-death kind of thing, isn't it? Being there for people as they breathe their last?"

"I hate that part," Erin said, looking at the floor. "I truly hate it."

"What part do you like?"

Erin grinned guiltily. "Honestly? The best days I've had have been accidents. Cars, threshers, combines, people falling off ladders. When someone comes running into my office, dripping blood, I get that adrenaline burst I had when I was doing my rotation in the emergency room. I never knew what would happen next." She sighed happily and relaxed into her chair.

"Are you sure you've thought this through? You don't get too many accident victims, do you?"

Erin laughed hard, her dark eyes nearly closing. "I'm gonna buy Darrell a faster van."

"I'm serious, Erin."

"I know you are. And to be honest, I'd like a more exciting life, but you can't have everything. I'm just going to have to figure out how to add some excitement here. I don't want to leave my mom."

"Would she mind if you left?"

Looking sheepish, Erin said, "Probably not. I didn't say it made sense, but that's why I came home. It seemed like the right thing to do when it came to making my decision."

"Do you still think it was the right thing?" Katie was staring at her so intently that Erin was thankful she'd never be on the other side of a court case from her.

Feeling terribly uncomfortable, Erin held up her hands. "I'm not sure. Things were really good at first, but now…" She looked at Katie, seeing sympathy and understanding in her gaze, even though Erin wasn't at all sure her situation demanded sympathy.

"You didn't plan on your mom getting involved with someone, did you?"

"No, I didn't." For the first time since Dan had appeared, Erin felt like crying about the whole situation. The warmth in Katie's eyes made Erin feel, for just a moment, as if she could pour everything out. Tell her how lonely she was. How hard it was to be a young professional in a blue-collar town. Tell her how she doubted she'd ever find a partner here. Most of all, ask her if she'd mind if Erin called her once in a while—just to have someone she could vent to. But she didn't, and Katie didn't continue her line of questioning.

Katie gazed at her for another minute and then gentled her voice, asking, "Do you mind if I ask about your dad?"

"No." Erin's body language closed immediately. She drew her arms across her chest and crossed her legs. Her head even dropped a little, and she looked at Katie through hooded eyes. "What do you want to know?"

"How long has he been dead?"

"He died when I was twelve."

"Ow." Katie made a face. "You were so young. Was he sick?"

"No. He was teaching my brother how to drive, and they were hit by a truck that skidded on the ice."

Katie's eyes widened, and she blanched. "And your brother?"

"They both died. My dad died that day, and my brother died the next." She blinked a few times and added, "I'm not sure about my dad, but my brother would have lived if he'd gotten to a trauma center faster."

"Oh, damn, Erin. That must have been horrific."

"It was." She nodded slowly, looking almost confused. Her visage brightened when she said, "But it made me and my mom much closer, and that's been really nice."

"Did your mom ask you to stay here to practice?"

"Oh, no. She never expressed an opinion about that. She wants me to do what makes me happy."

"Interesting," Katie said, nodding.

"Hey, when did this become a cross-examination?"

"Common rookie error. When I question you as my witness, that's a direct examination. Cross is when the opposing side questions you."

"Thank you for clearing that up. What's it called when you avoid my question?"

"Standard operating procedure."

Erin stood. "Let's do what we need to do. If you want to question me more, we could go to the diner."

"You really want to get out of here, don't you?"

"Yeah." She hung her head guiltily. "I feel like I'm trespassing."

"You're a whack job," she said, looking at Erin curiously. She shrugged in what looked like submission. "Okay, let's go."

After they finished checking the heat and making sure the basement was dry, they went out to the car. Katie drove back to Main Street without saying much, and Erin felt too discomfited to talk. "I'll let you go," Katie said when she pulled up to the diner. "I've got to get home. Big party tomorrow."

"Really? Another party?"

"That's two. The shower and the Clash of the Titans, as we've been calling it."

"Clash of the…"

"The Pats and Indianapolis are both undefeated. I'm having a party to watch the game."

"Wow, a party just to watch a game. That must be nice."

"Well, I have a lot of friends. You must, too. You're probably friends with the whole town."

Erin shrugged. "I'm friendly with most everyone, but it's been hard to continue to be friends with a lot of the people I knew in school. This is a working-class town, and if a person goes to college, they usually don't come back."

"And you went to a lot of college," Katie said, getting the point.

"Yeah. Most of my good friends left, and the few who didn't leave don't seem interested in hanging out." She looked a little puzzled. "I guess their lives went in a different direction."

"You've gotta get out more. Do you ever come to Boston?"

"Not much. I don't know anyone there. I go down for a ball game a couple of times a year…"

"Red Sox nation!" Katie held up her hand, and Erin slapped it.

"Yeah. Big fan."

"Bigger," Katie insisted. "Much bigger."

"We'll have to…watch a game sometime."

"Sure. That'd be fun." Katie expectantly looked at the door. "I'd better get going. I've got to clean my house, so my friends can trash it."

"You sound like you're still in college," Erin said, sounding wistful even to her own ears.

"I had my fifteen-year reunion last year. I'm just immature." Erin opened the door and got out, and Katie rolled down the passenger window. "Take care of yourself, and try to do something exciting."

"I will," Erin said. She waved as Katie drove away, continuing to talk to her. "Have fun with your cool city friends. Don't worry about us poor country bumpkins. I'll go down to the bakery tomorrow during the game and watch the bread rise."

❧

Erin ran home after getting her dry cleaning, surprising her mother when she burst into the house. "Guess who I just spent a little time with."

"I can't imagine. Who?"

Erin locked eyes with her mother and said, "Katie Quinn."

Gail's gaze shifted from her daughter to the kitchen and back again. "That's a surprise." She got up and said, "I've got something in the oven."

Erin followed her. "Do you know who Katie Quinn is?"

"Yes. That's Dan's daughter."

"You knew he had a daughter?"

"Yes, of course I did. He has a son, too."

"I know, Mom. Everyone in town knows about Danny and the grandchildren, but I'd never heard about Katie."

"Really?" Gail busied herself at the sink. "I've never mentioned her?"

"No, you haven't." Erin didn't speak for a few moments while she watched her mother work. Gail was uncharacteristically clumsy, dropping a knife onto the floor, then nicking her finger with a vegetable peeler. Erin finally spoke. "Why didn't you tell me about Katie?"

Gail looked at her for a moment and then once again turned away as soon as Erin's eyes met hers. "I don't know what you mean. Dan's told me a lot of things I haven't talked to you about. I didn't know you were that interested in him."

"Having two kids versus one is pretty basic information. She has a different last name, too. Is Katie some sort of black sheep?"

Gail was busily adjusting the burner under a pan. "I don't think so. I mean, Dan's very close to his son and the grandkids. You know how grandparents are. He's always talking about something one of the boys did. You probably haven't been around when he talks about his daughter."

Erin sat at one of the kitchen chairs, still regarding her mother curiously. "What does he say about her?"

Gail's hands flitted nervously. "Oh, I don't know. He mentioned that she took her mother's name after the divorce. She's an attorney."

"Yeah, I know. Anything else?"

"She lives in Boston, I think."

"Yeah, she does," Erin said. "She's also got a little scar across her temple. Did you know she was the woman Darrell backed into?"

"Not at the time." She turned away, washing her hands needlessly.

"But you knew later."

"Well, yes, Dan mentioned it."

"That would have been a good time to mention it to me, don't you think?"

With more annoyance than she usually exhibited, Gail said, "Goodness, why are you grilling me about this? You've never asked one question about Dan's farm or his career or his likes and dislikes. It seems odd to me that you're so focused on the fact that you didn't know about his daughter."

"It seems odd to me that you didn't tell me." Erin hadn't changed the tone or volume of her voice, but her mother was clearly uncomfortable to be under her level, calm gaze.

"I didn't think it was important!"

A little stunned by the force of the reply, Erin stepped back a bit. "I didn't mean to upset you."

"I'm not upset," she said, even though it was obvious that she was. "It would just be nice if you were as interested in Dan as you are in his daughter."

Erin pursed her lips and rolled her eyes slightly. "I think we've reached an impasse. I'll try to show more interest in Dan, since it's clear you're serious about him."

"That would be nice," Gail said. "I *am* interested in him. And I've asked you to join us several times. I'd like it if you'd get to know him better."

"You're right. I'll tag along sometime after he gets back."

Neither of them spoke for the next few minutes, and Erin reluctantly went upstairs to change clothes. She didn't have any idea why her mother was so skittish about Katie, but she was certain she wasn't going to find out today.

Chapter Four

On Sunday night, Katie called Erin on her home number. "Hi," she said when Erin answered. "This is Katie Quinn, lawyer and stalker."

"Hello. I didn't expect to hear from you."

"You don't mind that I'm calling, do you? I got your number from directory assistance."

"No, of course not. What's up?"

"I've been up there two times, and each time, I forgot to give you the cookies I bought for you and Madge."

"Oh. Well, you could bring them the next time you visit your dad's place."

"Yeah, I could, but he won't be back until spring. Maybe I'll head up there sometime and spend the weekend. It might be nice to get out of the city."

"Don't waste a trip up here just for Madge and me, but if you like peace and quiet, Essex is the place to be."

There was a lengthy pause. Erin wondered if she was supposed to say something, but she was fairly certain it was Katie's turn to talk. She was proven correct when Katie said, "What do *you* do for fun on a weekend?"

"Nothing much. I love to be outside, and I love the cold, so I ski and snowshoe. I love to fish, too, but I reserve winter for winter sports."

"Fishing sucks, but I love winter sports, too."

"I can't imagine why people live around here when they don't like to be outside. The lure of warmer climates would pull me away if I hated snow as much as some do."

"What about nightlife?"

Erin chuckled. "The library is open until seven on Thursday, and the diner's open until nine Monday through Saturday. They close at three on Sunday, though, so don't expect much action on the Sabbath."

"Whew! How do you keep up with it all?"

"It's not easy. I've learned to pace myself."

"Do the people around there know how lucky they are? I thought they stopped making doctors like you fifty years ago."

"There are plenty of doctors like me. A lot of small towns have done what Essex did."

"Which is what?"

"They paid for me to go to medical school, and in return, they own me." Erin laughed, but her laugh didn't sound very jolly. "I'm just kidding. I don't feel owned, but I do have a contract that spells out how the town wants me to practice medicine. And one of the things that's important is to have a lot of personal contact with my patients."

"And not take money for that contact."

"I take money," Erin demurred. "I just try not to take more than people have."

Abruptly, Katie switched topics. "So, tell me more about your mother."

"I didn't tell you *anything* about my mother."

"Old lawyer trick. I learned it from an old lawyer. Sometimes I can get somebody to tell me something if they think they're just adding on to what they've already said."

"You don't have to trick me into talking about my mom. She's great. She seems to like your dad, but to be honest, we haven't talked about him or her dating him much. We're both a little uncomfortable about it, I think."

"So, she really hasn't dated much, huh?"

"No, she hasn't. I don't know if this is fair to ask, but you don't think your dad is going to hurt her, do you? She's pretty inexperienced."

"Honestly? I don't know. He's dated a lot of women, but I don't know how serious he's been about any of them."

"You've given me the impression that you don't see each other a lot. How do you know about the women he's dated?"

"We don't see each other a lot," Katie admitted. "We don't see eye to eye on most things. And I know about the women because he'll almost always have a date for family functions. As I said, I don't know a lot about them. So, I don't know if he's broken hearts all over Boston or if the women were as casual as he was."

"I don't know how serious my mom is, but it would kill me to see her heartbroken."

"I wish I could reassure you, but I can't. All I know is that he broke my mom's heart, and that sure as hell didn't make me happy. I know what it's like to feel protective of your mom."

"We're protective of each other."

"I guess that's true of my mom, too. We had some tough times, but just the usual growing-up issues. She's always got my back."

"I guess we'll just have to see how this all plays out, but it sure is odd. I always urged my mom to go out on dates, but I never took it to the next level—what I'd do if she found someone she loved."

"I guess we'll both find out. But you seem like you'd be a good stepsister." She chuckled softly.

"Oh, my! That sounds so…"

"'Oh, my'? You say, 'oh, my'?"

"Profanity is for people with poor vocabularies," Erin said archly, clearly teasing. "My mother told me that, and she'd never lie."

"My mom's biggest piece of advice was to wear clean underwear in case I was in an accident. That's never paid off."

Erin nearly made a joke connecting that comment to Katie's car accident, but she stopped herself, deciding that would be too familiar. "Keep doing it, just in case. It couldn't hurt."

"Well, I guess I'll see you around."

"Yeah. Stop by next time you're in town if you have time. Madge and I would love to see you."

Katie waited a few seconds before responding, "I might. I'd hate to disappoint Madge. Take care."

After hanging up, Erin spent a few moments staring at the phone. She felt like she'd been a half-step off during the entire conversation, but she wasn't sure what she was missing.

⁂

The weather grew unseasonably warm in mid-December, and Erin's mood fell as the temperatures rose. "The snow's all melted," she said glumly one Saturday morning. "I guess I'm going to have to go running to get any exercise."

"I'll go with you," Gail suggested. "Give me just a few minutes to get ready."

An hour later, they were running down a well-kept path along the Nashua River. They usually ran closer to home, but Gail suggested they do some shopping or see a movie after their run and make it an outing.

They chatted about the weather for a while, and then Gail said, "How would you feel if I went to Florida for a little vacation?"

Erin looked at her, puzzled. "You? Instead of us?"

"That's not how I'd put it, honey. This is a new opportunity." Erin could see her swallow and noted the tense set of her mouth.

The light slowly dawned. "Oh. You want to go see Dan."

"He invited me, and since we didn't have any plans, I thought it might be fun to go."

Erin didn't say that they didn't have plans because her mother hadn't wanted to make any. "Whatever you want. When would you go?"

"I found a great fare if I left on Christmas Day. I could stay until the third of January. Then I wouldn't have to take as many vacation days."

"Oh. Okay." She was quiet for a few beats. "I guess it would be good to travel on Christmas Day. Not as many people."

Gail kept sneaking glances at her daughter, but Erin's face was relatively expressionless. "Do you mind if I go?"

"No." Erin's voice was more certain when she repeated. "No. I'll go have Christmas in Montréal. I haven't done that in years."

"Are you sure?"

"Sure I am. I'll call grandmother later and let her know. I'll drive up on Friday after work."

Gail looked puzzled. "You'll leave on the twenty-third?"

"Yeah. You know they have their big gathering on Christmas Eve. I'll be able to see everyone at once."

"That's true." She was quiet for a moment, only their soft footfalls piercing the silence. "We've never been apart on Christmas."

"No, we haven't," Erin said. "We'll have it early. Maybe on Wednesday or Thursday of that week."

Gail didn't reply. They settled into their own thoughts, neither speaking for the duration of their run.

❧

It was almost bedtime when Erin and Gail returned home. As soon as they said their goodnights, Gail went to her room and put in a call to Dan. "Hi," she said when he answered. "I'm not disturbing you, am I?"

"Of course not. You've never disturbed me. Did you have a good time with Erin today? Was it good running weather?"

"Yes, we had fun, but I feel like I've handled my plans for my trip poorly."

"What's wrong, honey? You sound sad."

"I am. I'm never really sure what Erin's thinking. When you tell me about the fights you've had with your daughter, it sounds so alien to me. I don't think we've ever had a real argument. Erin and I are so alike in so many ways, you'd think we'd be better at communicating."

Dan chuckled softly. "I wouldn't recommend starting to fight. That's not a very good way to communicate, either."

"No, I suppose not."

"Come on now, tell me what's going on."

Gail sighed heavily. "I kept putting off talking to her until I was sure I could schedule the time off. It's hard to make sure I have coverage when I can't afford to hire anyone. So, I have to have a backup for each volunteer."

"They're lucky to have you, honey."

"I'm lucky to have them. I'd be working the third shift at the factory if Mrs. Fillmore hadn't stayed on for an additional two years while I got my master's degree in library science. This town has kept us afloat more times than I can count."

"And you pay them back. I wouldn't be able to hire migrant workers this summer with what they pay you."

"Oh, you can't think of it like that. This is my home, Dan. It's like an extended family."

"I know," he said, his voice warm and tender. "I'm just grateful you were there for me to find. Now, tell me about Erin."

"Well, I told you about the great airfare I found, but it's for Christmas Day. I didn't think that would be so terrible because it's late in the evening, and we always open our presents and go to church on Christmas Eve. But as soon as I told her I was going to leave on Christmas Day, she said she'd go see her grandparents."

"Well, that sounds good. I know you were worried about leaving her."

"It *is* good," Gail said, sounding like she was on the verge of tears. "But she wants to leave on Friday. I can't tell if she's leaving early to get back at me or if that's really what she wants to do. She's so hard to read."

"I know what you mean. She looks at you with those big dark eyes, and you can never really see what she's thinking. I like her an awful lot, but I honestly don't know her at all."

"I was so worried about it when she decided to move back here. I love her so much, Dan, but this just doesn't seem like the right atmosphere for her. She doesn't have many friends, and even though I know she loves all of her outdoor activities, that doesn't seem like it's enough for her."

"I think she's just a small-town girl, Gail. And everyone I talk to loves her as a doctor."

"I know she's good at her job, but I can't help thinking she'd be happier in a bigger town. Maybe I'm projecting my feelings onto her. I dreaded the thought of living in a town no bigger than the one I grew up in. But Richard was offered a good job here, and I eventually became part of the fabric of the town. Maybe this *is* enough for her. I just wish I were more certain of that."

"I don't know why it's so darned hard to talk to your kids. The only thing Danny and I talk about is work. Thank God he became a cop, or we wouldn't even have that. I assume he and Stacy are happy, but it's just that—an assumption."

"I don't want you to get the wrong impression, Dan. I love my girl, and it's so nice to have her close. I never dreamed I'd be able to see her every day. But I worry about her. She's such a closed book."

"Maybe she just needs someone to help her open up."

"Maybe so. I wish I could do it for her, but I honestly don't have the first idea how to do that."

On a bright, clear Sunday afternoon, Erin went to pick her mother up at the Manchester airport. Gail's flight was right on time, and she looked healthy and happy when Erin spotted her at the baggage carousel. "Someone had good weather," Erin said, kissing her cheek. "Did you use sunblock?"

"Yes, doctor." Gail gave Erin a long hug. "But we were outside every minute. I picked a wonderful week to go. The temperature was in the seventies, and there wasn't a cloud in the sky."

"I was checking the weather when I was in Montréal. We were all a little jealous." She amended, "I wasn't, since there was snow in Montréal, but everyone else was."

"I missed you, honey. My vacation would have been perfect if you'd been there."

Erin smiled stiffly, thinking that her mother was either lying or disconnected from reality. She was certain that the last thing her mother and Dan would want was a third wheel, and she had to admit that she had no interest at all in being that wheel.

On the way home, Gail talked at length about the weather in Florida. Erin was beginning to wonder if her mother was taking up meteorology, when it dawned on her that Gail didn't want to share the details of her trip. So, Erin talked about her relatives in Montréal, filling Gail in on all of the details of the extended Delancy family.

In late January, Katie dropped by the office on a Saturday morning. Erin was with a patient, and when she emerged from the exam room, she found Katie drinking a cup of coffee and eating cookies with Madge. "Hey there, Erin," Katie said. "It took me a while, but I finally brought a little thank-you gift for you and Madge."

Erin bid goodbye to her patient and then walked over to Madge's desk. "Ooh, cookies. We love cookies, don't we, Madge?"

"We sure do. These are great, Katie."

"I got them fresh this morning from an Italian deli near my apartment."

Erin went back into the exam room and washed her hands. Madge rolled her eyes. "She thinks the world is covered in germs."

"It is," Erin said, laughing as she emerged, drying her hands on a paper towel. "I haven't caught a cold since I've been here, so don't knock it." She took a white, fluffy-looking cookie and bit into it. "Mmm, these are great."

"I had to check on the house again, so I thought I'd drop by."

Erin started to nibble on the next cookie that caught her attention. "I don't understand why you and your brother have to come out here. I offered to look after the place for your dad."

"Oh, he probably didn't want to impose—on you," she added, chuckling. "He doesn't mind imposing on us."

"I'm sure my mom offered, too."

"He probably thought it'd be too much work for her."

Madge laughed. "Gail's probably in better shape than your dad is, honey. She lifts weights and swims and runs."

"She does?" Katie blinked in surprise. "My mom's kinda sedentary, and I'm sure she wouldn't have a clue how to drive that little utility vehicle. I just assumed…"

"My mom can drive a big tractor," Erin said. "She grew up on a farm in Maine."

"She did?" Katie scowled. "Then why in the hell am I driving up here on Super Bowl weekend? I've got a million things to do before my party."

"Ooo, a Super Bowl party," Madge said. "Those are fun. What are you doing for the big game, Erin?"

"Nothing much. I'd love to watch the game, but I don't have a TV…"

Erin waited just a second or two, wondering if Katie would do the polite thing and invite her. But when her visitor seemed fully involved in picking out a cookie Erin tried to pick the conversation up where they'd left it. "Your dad must not have wanted to ask my mom to help. Maybe he thinks you like coming up here."

"Doubtful," Katie said, smirking. "I mean it's nice here and all, but I'm plenty busy at home."

Madge giggled at Katie's pink cheeks. "He's got things figured out. He goes to Florida, has you do the work around here, and gets to have his girlfriend visit him and lie in the sun. You girls didn't get the best end of that deal."

Katie turned to Erin and raised an eyebrow. "Your mother went to visit him?"

"Uhm, yeah, she did."

"Maybe they *are* serious, huh?"

Erin looked sheepish. "I guess so, but I really don't know. We barely talk about it."

"Oh, they're serious," Madge declared. "You don't go to Florida to visit a man if you're not serious."

"That's probably true," Katie agreed, "but my dad stays with his brother Willie. They had chaperones. And my uncle has four bedrooms, so they probably—"

Erin put her fingers in her ears and started humming a loud, directionless tune.

Laughing, Katie pulled one of Erin's hands away. "I think she's skittish about sex, Madge. What do you think?"

"She must be because she sure doesn't have any," Madge chortled.

"Hey, hey, when did this become pick on Erin day?"

"As soon as it became fun," Katie said.

"Well, the fun's over. Let's just eat some cookies in silence."

"Aw, I think we pissed her off, Madge."

"Oh, she never gets angry. Erin's the most even-tempered girl in the world."

"I'm not mad," Erin agreed. "I just like to keep some things private. Like my life."

"She doesn't like to gossip, either," Madge told Katie. "I have to find out everything the hard way."

"By snooping," Erin said, scowling playfully.

"You leave me no choice. Everyone in town expects me to keep them up-to-date."

"And those same people don't want me to tell anyone about their health issues," Erin reminded her.

"Well, I'd love to stay here and chat, but I've got to get out to my dad's place and act like the hired hand...who doesn't get paid."

"You should go with her, Erin," Madge said.

"I would, but I have a patient due in a half-hour. Maybe it'll be someone with a complex diagnosis," she said, her smile filled with longing.

"Well, if you get finished early, come on by," Katie said. "It's not very exciting, though."

"It's as exciting as going home to her mother," Madge said, giggling.

Katie stared at Erin. "You live with your mom?"

"Yeah." Erin looked a little embarrassed. "There aren't any nice apartments close to town."

"Wow. I love my mom, but we'd strangle each other if we lived together."

"Gail's the second most even-tempered woman," Madge declared. "Neither one of them ever complains about the other. It's very strange."

"That is strange," Katie agreed. "Well, I'll see you two around. Take care."

Katie walked out the door, and Erin looked at her calendar. "I wonder how long Mrs. Russell will take. I'd like to run out to Dan's if I have time."

"Miracles can happen," Madge said.

※

As Madge predicted, Mrs. Russell took up quite a bit of time. Erin scrambled to get out to Dan's, but Katie was already gone by the time she pulled into the drive. It was cold and blustery, but Erin got out of her car and walked around the property, just wasting time. After a long while, she got into her car and went home, depressed at the thought of another night working on her computer.

※

Erin stopped in her tracks on the way home on February 14. Dan's truck was parked in front of her house, and she considered turning around and going to the diner, but she knew her mother was expecting her, so she dutifully continued on her way.

Dan, in a blazer and a tie, was sitting on the sofa, and her mother slid away from him as the front door opened. Gail looked flustered, and she began to speak quickly and enthusiastically, as one would to a child. "Look who's here!"

"Hi, Dan," Erin said, crossing the room and removing her glove to shake his hand. "This is a nice surprise."

"I was planning on coming back the first of March, but then I thought 'Why not spend Valentine's Day with the prettiest girl in New Hampshire?'"

While she was taking off her coat, Erin noted the lavish display of red roses on the coffee table. "Nice flowers."

"Aren't they beautiful?" Gail was positively glowing, and Erin desperately wanted to make herself scarce.

"They really are." Erin sniffed at the blossoms, finding they lacked any scent whatsoever. "They're lovely."

"You don't mind if I take your mother out to dinner, do you?" Dan asked.

"Of course not," Erin said, relieved that she wouldn't have to watch her mother swoon over Dan the entire evening.

"Dan wants to go to Boston," Gail said. "He has a favorite restaurant."

"Wow, you haven't been there in a while."

"Not for months." Gail was practically bouncing in her seat.

"You'd better get going," Erin said. "It's six o'clock."

"I have to change." Gail was wearing a blue cable-knit sweater over a turtleneck, along with tan wool slacks, and she looked perfectly fine to Erin. "Entertain Dan while I'm gone."

"Happy to." Erin stood in front of the sofa, feeling ungainly. "Can I get you something to drink?"

"Sure. What do you have?"

"Probably orange juice, cranberry, sparkling water. Or I can make you coffee or tea or cocoa."

"Do you have anything a little stronger?"

"Strong…oh! Yes, I think we have some wine." She headed for the breakfront in the dining room.

"No, that's okay. I was thinking of scotch or whiskey. Sparkling water is fine."

"Okay. Coming right up." Erin returned with two glasses of water, and said, "How was Florida?"

"Great, just great. My brother has a boat, and we went out almost every day, but your mom probably told you about that."

Erin nodded, not mentioning that her mother had said almost nothing about the trip other than it had been wonderful. The way she'd moped around the house for almost two weeks after her return told Erin more than she wanted to know.

"I caught a tarpon the week after your mom was there." He smiled and leaned back in his seat, looking very pleased. "I wish she would have been there. It's nice to share something like that, you know?"

"Oh, yeah. That would have been memorable." Erin knew that her mother was almost antagonistic towards sport fishing, but she decided she'd let Dan find that out for himself.

Gail came down the stairs, dressed in a slim-fitting, stylish, dark grey dress that Erin had never seen before. Dan stood up and whistled softly. "You look fantastic."

Erin saw his eyes light up with delight, and she had to look away. "You look great, Mom. Really nice."

"Thank you." Gail went to the hall closet and took out a black wool coat that she only wore for special occasions. Her down coat was much warmer, but the wool made her look tall and elegant. Dan helped her into the coat and watched her add a thin, silk, paisley scarf, making the coat look even classier.

"I guess we're off," he said, pulling on his own topcoat. "Don't wait up," he said, winking at Erin.

"I didn't start dinner, honey, but I bought some nice lamb chops. You can broil a couple for yourself, can't you?"

"Yes, Mom." Erin rolled her eyes, feeling about fifteen. She kissed Gail on the cheek and said, "Have a great time."

"We will," the couple said in unison. A blast of cold air entered the room when they opened the storm door. Erin walked over to the sofa and plopped down, considering her options. She knew Kim would be having dinner with her husband, and she couldn't think of anyone else she knew who was single and available. But she was antsy to do something, to go somewhere. So, she washed her hands and put her coat back on. A few minutes later, she was sitting at the counter in the diner, chatting with Thelma, the evening waitress, about her bunions.

The birds chirping outside her window woke Erin the next morning. She was wearing her pajamas, but she wasn't between the sheets. She'd obviously pulled the comforter from its moorings during the night, as it was covering parts of her in a piecemeal fashion. The edges of a book bit into her arm, and her bedside light burned brightly. "What in the heck?" She sat up and tried to recall her evening, and then it dawned on her that her mother must not have come home. Her heart started beating fast and heavy, and she jumped from the bed to confirm what she knew. Gail's bed was neatly made, and her blue sweater and turtleneck were lying right where she'd put them when she was rushing to get ready.

"Oh, no," she said aloud. Her stomach was gripped with the too-familiar intensity that came upon her whenever she worried about her mother. It was the same sickening feeling she'd felt sixteen years earlier—the feeling of impotence and loss. She saw her mother's cell phone lying on the dresser and had the overpowering desire to take it and throw it against the wall. They'd made a pact years before to always carry a cell phone when they left town, and she was instantly furious that Gail had broken her vow.

She didn't know Dan's cell number, an oversight she cursed herself for. Without showering or combing her hair, she threw on her clothing from the day before and went to her car. It was cold and damp, and the engine was a little balky, but it finally turned over, and she headed for the one place that would resolve or confirm her fears: Dan's house.

It took about fifteen minutes to get there, and she flipped between praying that his car was there and making plans for what she'd do if it wasn't.

When she reached the house, her stomach clenched painfully when she didn't see his truck, but he had a huge garage in which he probably parked. She shouted a joy-filled cry when she saw lights on in the house and noted some movement behind the sheer curtains. She continued down the highway a short distance and then pulled over to the shoulder to collect herself.

Relief was flooding through her body, and she realized she was sweating despite the bitter cold. After she stopped shaking, the next wave of emotion hit her, and this time it was anger. Explosive, raw anger that she hadn't felt in years, if ever. The kind of anger that made her want to go into Dan's house, grab her mother, and shake her, screaming at her for worrying her so horribly.

After a few minutes, she began to calm down, and the anger was replaced by the dull, empty feeling that signaled her clear loss of status. She was no longer the person that her mother thought of first. She was one down now, with Dan clearly standing at the top of the heap.

❧

Even though she and Gail stopped work at the same time that day, Erin didn't go to the library as she had nearly every Thursday night since she'd begun her practice. She wasn't ready to act as if nothing had happened, and she didn't want to hear her mother's embarrassed excuse for why she hadn't come home. So, she called the house, knowing her mother wasn't home yet, and left a message, saying she was going out to dinner. She didn't know where to go, but she found her car headed east, as if it were being pulled in that direction.

An hour later, she found herself in Durham, where she'd spent her undergraduate years at the University of New Hampshire. She found a parking space downtown and walked around for hours, stopping for a slice of pizza at one of her old haunts and then getting a hot fudge sundae at another spot to top it off. She sat in her favorite bookstore until closing time, but still wasn't ready to leave. So, she walked around until the stores closed one by one. The small throngs of pedestrians thinned out and slowed to a trickle, and Erin had to choose between going to a bar and heading back to her car. She opted for the car and started the long drive home.

To Erin's relief, the house was dark save for a light in her room. She went in, smelled the scent of a home-cooked dinner, went upstairs, and found a note on her bed:

I hope you had a nice night out, honey. I turned in early. See you at breakfast. Love, Mom.

❧

Erin slept soundly, tired from her long day. When she woke up the next morning and went down to breakfast, her mother greeted her enthusiastically, hugging her tightly. "I have news," she said, her green eyes gleaming with excitement.

"Okay," Erin said warily, sitting down. "What is it?"

Gail extended her left hand, revealing a glittering diamond ring. "Dan asked me to marry him."

Erin thought she might faint. In seconds, she saw her plans for the life she'd built disappear. She felt like a complete fool, as if she'd inserted herself into a plan that was of no interest to her mother. She knew she had to speak, to offer enthusiastic congratulations, but she was unable to say a word. Luckily, Gail seemed to take her silence as a sign of surprise or shock. She leaned over, and Erin hugged her so hard she distinctly felt her mother's ribs. Tears came to her eyes, and she sniffled a little. "I'm happy for you, Mom. I think Dan's a very, very lucky guy."

Chapter Five

*T*hat weekend, Gail and Dan drove up to Oxford, Maine, to meet Gail's parents and her sisters, both of whom lived within an hour's drive of Oxford. They'd invited Erin to go with them, but even though she hadn't seen her relatives since Thanksgiving, she declined. She knew she wouldn't be able to put on a happy face for the whole weekend, so she thought it best to stay home.

She did very little, finding she didn't have much energy. She considered that she'd caught a bug of some sort, but she had no other symptoms, so she dismissed that idea. Chalking her malaise up to overwork, she lay on the sofa and read, finishing two books by the time she went to church on Sunday.

Erin had to accept congratulations from nearly every person in the congregation, which she did with good humor. Betsy Worrell, always perceptive, came over to her and said, "You look a little lonely today, Erin. Come home with us and have lunch."

Erin practically leapt at the invitation. The Worrells had invited the minister and his wife, as well, and the five of them had a nice meal. It wasn't until Erin was leaving that she stopped to consider that having lunch with the pastor and the former town doctor had not only been the highlight of her weekend, it was probably going to be the highlight of her week, too.

Dan planned a big family party for the first Sunday in March. Erin wasn't particularly looking forward to it, but it was something different, so she agreed to help with the preparation. Besides, her mother was very excited about meeting more of Dan's family and friends, and her excitement was partially contagious. After church, Erin and Gail made a few batches of cookies, and they headed over early to help him get ready.

When they arrived, Dan looked harried. "I've never had a big party before," he said, cheeks flushed. "It's a lot of work."

"Dan lived in an apartment in Boston," Gail told Erin. "He didn't have space to entertain."

"My ex-wife got the house," Dan added, resentment coloring his tone. "As usual."

"She probably got the kids to go with it," Erin surprised herself by saying.

Dan blinked at her. "Just my daughter. Danny came to live with me. In a one-bedroom apartment," he added with a touch of bitterness. "I slept on a pullout couch until he went to college."

"How old was Danny when you divorced?"

Partially closing one eye, Dan thought for a second. "Six, I think. He was in first grade, and Katie was in sixth."

"Wow, that's young," Erin said.

"Yeah. My mother was alive at the time, and she watched him when I was at work." He stared into space for a moment, looking uncharacteristically thoughtful. "It probably would have been better for the kids if we'd stayed together, but you never know. It's hard to know what to do when it's happening."

"I'm sure it is," Gail said, her expression full of sympathy and understanding. "I hate to change the subject, but we'd better get ready. We've got plenty to do."

⤞⤝

The house was filled by two o'clock: some of Dan's policeman friends, his brother, two sisters with their spouses and kids, Katie, Danny and his wife Stacy and their sons, and dozens of people from town. It was too cold to enjoy being outdoors, but a few smokers braved the elements to indulge.

Gail was serving as an unofficial hostess, and Erin helped as well. She spent most of the afternoon making small talk with the locals and refilling drinks. She kept trying to find some time to chat with Katie, but every time Erin was free, Katie was involved in one game or another with her nephews. Erin found it funny that Katie was the only adult who got down on the floor and played with the kids, especially since Danny and Stacy were younger than Katie was. The boys seemed crazy about Katie, and Erin wished she could have gotten down on the floor and played with them, too. However, she was always conscious of her job, and she tried to act older than her years. So, she acted like an adult even though her heart sometimes wasn't in it.

At around four, Erin saw Katie walking around the room saying goodbye. When Katie made her way over to Erin, she said, "I'm gonna take off. Sorry we didn't get to chat, but the little guys keep me busy."

"Yeah, I'm sorry we didn't get to talk, too. I'd much rather talk to somebody

I haven't known my whole life, but people love to have a few minutes with me to talk about little things that they don't think are important enough for an appointment."

Katie gazed at her for a few seconds, and Erin had the uncomfortable feeling she always got when Katie looked at her intently. It was as though Katie was studying some unique creature, and it made Erin want to hide. Finally, Katie spoke. "You can't give yourself away. When people try to get free legal advice from me, I give them my card and tell them I'd love to talk about it. Most of them don't want to talk at all when they have to pay."

"I guess you're right, but it's different when you're a doctor."

"Why?" Again, the blue eyes bore into her.

"Well, it's their health. They're worried about something, and it doesn't cost me anything—"

"Yes, it does. You just said you wanted to talk to me but couldn't. Isn't that a cost?" She tilted her head, and her curls settled on her shoulder, looking a lovely shade of blonde against her blue sweater.

"No one was forcing me," Erin said, finding herself laughing nervously.

Katie's unblinking gaze focused on Erin for a few seconds. "Exactly."

Erin knew it was her turn to speak, and she knew she should use that opportunity to make it clear that losing the chance to talk to Katie was, indeed, a cost. For the first time since they'd met, she found herself looking—really looking—at Katie as a woman. There was something in the way the late-afternoon sun lit her face that made her ethereally beautiful. Her features were fine and delicate, and the light illuminated the classic lines as though she were a fine sculpture.

Tongue-tied, Erin realized she'd fouled things up dreadfully. She was monstrously attracted to this woman, and she had only herself to blame for not being more forthright. She felt like slapping herself for the way she acted around Katie, but in the midst of her internal diatribe, she noticed Dan approach from the side. Katie clearly saw him as well, since, without a word, she headed for the door, grabbing her coat as she went. Dan followed right behind her, and Erin moved over to one of the big windows that overlooked the drive. Dan had his hand on the door of Katie's car, and he seemed to be either lecturing or yelling at her. He was in just his shirtsleeves, and his breath came out in white puffs of air. His face was pink, but Erin couldn't tell if that was from anger or the cold. When he didn't stop talking for a solid minute, Erin decided it was anger.

⸘⸘

The warm air blew out of Dan's lungs like puffs of smoke. "I don't care if you like it or not. This is my house, and I'm the one who decides who's welcome."

"You don't even know her."

"And I doubt you do either," he snapped. "If you want to bring a woman to a party, I want it to be someone who's going to be around for a while. Not one of your one-night stands."

"I don't remember the names of any of the bimbos you've brought to family parties, but if I want to bring someone, she has to be wearing an engagement ring!"

"I didn't say that, and you know it. I just want to make sure the boys aren't confused."

"By what?" Her face was bright pink, and she threw her hands up into the air. "By having another stranger in the house? They didn't know a third of the people in there, and I didn't see them biting their nails over it. You're a homophobe! Admit it!"

"Goddamn it, I am not! If I disagree with you on one issue, I'm a homophobe! That's total bullshit!"

"You probably haven't even told Gail that I'm gay," she said, eyes burning.

"The whole town's going to know every bit of your business if you don't lower your voice. Why do you have to make a scene every single time I see you?"

"Lower yours! You're the one who started this. I just wanted to bring a date to your stupid party. I shouldn't have come at all."

"Now you're just being a baby. I always want you to visit, but half the time, you make me regret it. You just can't give me a break."

"The same goes for you! You act like I'm some sort of freak."

"Goddamn it, I do not! You're just a girl who won't grow up. I don't want the boys to imitate you and think it's cool to have dozens of girlfriends."

"You did!"

Dan took in a breath, wishing he could spank his daughter and send her to her room, but knowing he was thirty years too late for that.

⁂

Erin put aside her confused thoughts about her interaction with Katie to focus on the fight right outside the window. Katie looked like she was giving as good as she was getting, a situation Erin could barely comprehend. She couldn't imagine what it must feel like to yell at your father, much less what it felt like to be yelled at.

It looked like Katie was pointing her finger at Dan, but since she was wearing mittens, her whole hand jutted in the air. Erin watched them go at it, unable to turn away. This was the first time she'd seen them together, and she began to compare them, finding little that was similar.

Dan was very sturdy, almost stocky, and he looked younger than his fifty-six years. He didn't have a bit of gray in his short-cropped, brick-colored hair, and the lines on his face all seemed like they were from laughter. Katie's hair was red in the sun, but it was a completely different shade than Dan's. Dan's was straight and coarse, where Katie's was curly and fine. Her hair was probably her most attractive feature, Erin thought, although her blue eyes were very expressive. Actually, everything about Katie was expressive. Erin was sure she'd be able to tell her mood just from looking at her face, but anyone would've been able to tell Katie's mood at the moment. She was very angry, and Dan was the same.

Katie wasn't a small woman, but she had none of her father's raw-boned stockiness. Nonetheless, she didn't look intimidated by Dan in the least. Erin knew she should move away from the window. She hated to spy on people, but part of her was afraid Dan and Katie would come to blows, and she wanted to be ready to intercede if things got out of hand.

After a few more minutes, Dan had finally had enough. He stormed away, but he didn't come back inside immediately. Katie got into her car and pulled away, leaving a hail of gravel in her wake. It took almost fifteen minutes for Dan to come back in, and when he did, he seemed his normal self. He was laughing and joking just as he had been earlier. Erin didn't know Dan well enough to talk to him about the fight or to see if he was all right, but she decided she'd call Katie as soon as she got the chance.

⬬⬬

As soon as Erin got home, she put in a call to Katie's house. There was no answer, and even though she had Katie's cell phone number, she decided not to use it. Instead, she decided to call again later and try to catch her at home.

It took until Tuesday night to find Katie at home. "Hi, Katie," Erin said when she answered. "It's Erin. I wanted to call and see how you were doing."

"I'm fine. Why do you ask?"

The almost businesslike tone she used caught Erin by surprise, and she wished she hadn't called. "Well, I saw you and your father having words in the driveway on Sunday. If you don't want to talk about it, that's fine, but if you do, I'm a good listener."

"Oh, I hate to air our dirty laundry. It's just our sucky family dynamics. I just hope he's more even-tempered with your mom."

Erin jumped in, wanting to extricate herself from the conversation. "Okay. No problem. I just wanted to lend an ear if you needed one."

Katie didn't respond immediately. When she did, she said, "I can say this. My dad has very strong ideas about most things, and sometimes, he and I don't see eye to eye."

Erin let out a short laugh. If you were a little taller, you would have been eye to eye. If you'd both been men, I think you would've been swinging at each other."

Katie laughed as well, and when she spoke, she sounded warmer and more relaxed. "My being a girl has probably prevented me from being pummeled by him dozens of times. I really get under his skin." She sounded strangely pleased with herself at this declaration.

"Do he and your brother argue?"

"Not very often. They've had their problems, but they seem to understand each other very well. Plus, they're cut from the same cloth. I think my brother would be very happy to mimic my dad in almost everything."

"But you wouldn't."

"No, not in most things. If I had to choose, I'd rather be like my mom."

"I haven't met her, so I can't tell if you're meeting your goal."

"She's nice. You'd like her. But my dad will never have her anywhere near Essex, so you'll probably never get to meet her."

"Well, I don't wanna keep you. You're probably busy."

Her voice warmed up further, and she said, "Not very. What have you been up to?"

"Nothing interesting. I have a patient who's near death, and I've been trying to go see her as often as I can."

"Oh, that must be hard."

"Yeah, this is my first one. I hope it's my last."

"You haven't lost a patient yet?"

"Not someone I know. It's different. It's really getting to me."

"I hate to say it, but you're gonna have to get used to people dying, unless you have some plan to get rid of all your patients who seem really sick."

"I wish I did," Erin admitted sheepishly.

"I'm kind of surprised that you haven't lost patients before. I figure you've been in practice one or two years."

"How do you figure that?"

"I saw the diploma in your office, and I did the math. I just don't know if you need to have a one-year or two-year residency in New Hampshire."

"You have to have two years. I was actually in a three-year program for family medicine, but I dropped out when the town doctor had a stroke."

"Wow. So, you aren't certified in a specialty."

"No, I'm not, but that won't hurt me here."

"I don't feel the love, Dr. Delancy."

Erin chuckled. "What love is that?"

"I don't feel the small-town doc vibe from you. You look the type, and you act the type, but there's something missing." Erin could hear a clicking or tapping sound from Katie's end, and she decided it must be a pen clicking against her teeth. "I think," Katie said thoughtfully, "that your placid demeanor conceals a risk taker. I bet you like roller coasters."

"I love them. And don't tell my mom, but I went skydiving on my twenty-first birthday." Erin giggled girlishly. "I have a few little secrets, even from my best friend."

"Any more good ones?"

"No, I tell her everything important. And I've been really lucky. She's always been supportive, even of things I thought she'd have a hard time with."

"I've always found it best not to talk to parents about politics, religion, sex, and…well, just about anything interesting, to be honest. The weather's always safe."

"I've talked to my mom about all those things. Not in detail, of course, but I don't hide big things from her."

"To hear Madge tell it, you don't have anything to talk about on the sexual front."

"Madge doesn't know everything, but in this case, she's right."

"How long has it been?"

"This is March, so…gosh, it's been eighteen months. I think all of my potential dates moved to bigger towns as soon as they were able. But I'm gonna have to find a way to import some attractive and willing, or even just willing, women into town."

A pause went on longer than Erin was comfortable with. Then Katie spoke, her voice filled with mirth. "Dr. Delancy, are you implying that you're a lesbian?"

"No, I'm not implying. I'm stating it. That doesn't bother you, does it?"

Katie laughed. "I'd have serious double-standard issues if it did."

"Really?" Erin's heart started to beat quicker, and she felt a little tongue-tied. "I was kinda wondering…"

"It doesn't bother *you*, does it?"

Erin wasn't about to admit that it bothered her in a way she didn't feel comfortable expressing. She also wasn't about to admit that she tingled all over. "No, of course not. Are you out to—"

Katie interrupted. "Everyone. From the first. How about you?"

"I tell on a need-to-know basis. Everyone I'm close to knows."

"What about Madge?"

Chuckling, Erin said, "She doesn't know."

"Why? Aren't you close?"

"She's never been to my house for dinner. That's the test. Besides, if I told Madge, I'd be telling the county. I'm going to wait until I have a girlfriend to make a general announcement."

"Is that wise? Why not get it over with so you don't have to hide?"

"I don't hide," Erin scoffed. "I just like to have some privacy here in town. Hiding means you're ashamed of something. I'm not. I just don't want my female patients wondering if I'm looking at them funny. It's better if your patients don't know too much about you."

"Uhm, how will waiting until you have a girlfriend help with that?"

There was a significant pause. "I never thought about that. I guess I'll figure that out when the time comes."

"I'm sure you know what works best for you. Is your mom cool with it?"

"Yeah. No problems. I told her right away. She wasn't thrilled, but she was fine."

"That's good news. Hey, now that I know you'll understand, I can tell you what my dad and I were fighting about."

"I can't wait to see how that all fits together."

"He doesn't like me to bring dates to family functions. He thinks it sets a bad example for the boys. As you can tell, I disagree." She chuckled, and Erin could hear that touch of pleasure that colored her voice when she talked about upsetting her father.

"You can't bring a date because you're gay?"

"*I* think that's the real reason, but he denies it. He claims it's because I never have a steady girlfriend. He says it would upset the kids to see me with different women, but I don't think he'd feel that way if I were dating men. Of course, we'll never be able to find out."

"Yeah, he's got you there. Unless you're flexible."

"I'm flexible about a lot of things, but not about the sexuality of the people I sleep with. How about you? Are you flexible?"

"No, I'm pretty set in my ways. I wonder what your dad thinks about me. I take it he didn't mention to you that I'm gay."

"No, he hasn't said a thing. Well, that's not true. I keep hearing the 'Why can't you be more like Erin?' rant, but I ignore that."

"Does he really say that?"

"Not in so many words. But he loves the relationship you have with your mom, and he loves how respectful you are of her. Of course, I have a great relationship with my mom, and I'm very respectful of her. So, he gets his way, but he doesn't see it like that."

"Gosh, it's a shame you don't get along better. I'd really like it if you and I could be friends."

"Yeah," Katie said, a little noncommittal for Erin's tastes. "But what *you* really need is a date. I'll see if I can come up with somebody who'd like to move to Essex."

Stung by the clear rejection, Erin fought through her discomfort to ask, "Are you serious with someone now?"

"According to my father, I've never been serious about anyone. I hate to admit it, but he's not terribly wrong."

"Really? No one?"

"No, that's not true. I was pretty serious about my first two girlfriends, but that's been almost twenty years." She giggled again, sounding happy about her status.

"So, you're not serious about the woman you wanted to bring to the party?"

"Not yet. It's a little too early to tell. We'll have to see how that goes. Now as for you…" There was a beat, and Katie continued, "I bet you're the type to fall in love with the right person and be slavishly faithful."

"You know me pretty well for not knowing me. Things haven't worked out like that, but that's my goal."

"How close have you gotten?"

"I thought I was there, but the woman I was in love with wasn't in love with Essex. And she didn't think I was making the right choice for my career."

"She didn't want to be with a doctor?"

"No, that's not it. She's a doctor, too. She's in Chicago in the third year of a seven-year residency, and we finally stopped trying to make it work. I'm sure she'd never move here, and I don't, or I didn't, want to leave."

"Not even for the love of your life?"

Erin was quiet for a minute. "She probably wasn't the love of my life, but I don't know how to judge that at this point."

"Well, I don't think you need to rush to find the love of your life, but if you don't get a date soon, you're going to explode."

"I think I'll be fine. I'd love to meet someone, but I haven't spent a lot of time on my social life. I'll get to it, though."

"You're gonna waste away in Essex if you don't get something going. Let me know if you need help. I have a lot of friends."

Even though she knew she'd rather be alone than ask for help, Erin said, "I will."

"I've got to get going. I've got some things to do before I go to bed. Take care, okay?"

"I will. You, too." She hung up and crossed her arms over her chest, feeling discomfited by the entire conversation. She was almost sure that Katie had gone out of her way to say she didn't particularly want to be friends, and her offer to find Erin a date was insulting in almost every way. She'd been uncertain about Katie's sexual orientation, but now she was certain her attraction for her would grow. However, Katie was clearly not on the same plane, and that made Erin feel like crawling into bed and hoping for a brighter day. First, though, she had to speak with her mother. As soon as possible.

∼

As soon as Katie hung up, she called her brother. He was at work, but he answered his cell phone promptly. "Hey, Lieutenant Tierney. What's going on?"

"Not much. I'm doing paperwork. What's up?"

"I've got news from New Hampshire."

"Really?" Danny chuckled. "Are the primaries this soon?"

"Don't think so. I just talked to Erin Delancy. Turns out she's gay."

"No shit?"

"No shit. Did Dad ever mention that to you?"

"No, never. I wonder if he knows."

"Hell, no. He would have said something. Something like, 'Remember that woman I was engaged to?'"

"Aw, give him a break, will you? He wouldn't stop seeing Gail because of her daughter. He's not the world's biggest jerk."

"I agree, Danny, but he's not Mr. Wonderful, either. And I know it would make him mental to know Gail's daughter was a daughter of Sappho." She giggled gleefully.

"What difference would it make to him? I don't think he's as hung up on this stuff as you do."

"That's because you haven't ever been a member of a group that's on his shit list."

Danny started to whistle quietly, making his phone emit a sharp whine. "I can't hear you," he said, starting to whistle again.

"Stop it!"

"I'll stop when you stop acting like he's a dictator. He's not the asshole you make him out to be."

"Well, whatever kind of asshole he is, I have a feeling Gail's going to finally see the part of our dear father that I know and dislike."

⌁

Gail was out with her bridge club, and Erin paced around the house, waiting for her to return. As soon as she turned the knob, Erin was in the entryway.

Gail blinked in surprise. "What's wrong?"

"Nothing," Erin said, showing her impatience. "Did you know that Dan's daughter is gay?"

"Goodness, honey. Let me get my coat off. Why are you so agitated?"

"Why aren't you answering my very simple question?"

Gail stopped in the middle of removing her coat. Gently but pointedly, she said, "Erin, please go sit down. I don't like being assaulted the moment I walk in the door."

Erin turned and walked toward the couch, feeling like a scolded child. She couldn't remember the last time her mother had spoken to her sharply, but she also couldn't remember the last time she'd been abrupt with her mom.

Gail took longer than normal to remove her coat and scarf, and Erin recognized the tactic from years of use. Her mother's sole form of discipline had always been to encourage good behavior and ignore bad. The three minutes that Erin waited seemed like a much longer time, and for the first time since she'd been back in town, she regretted her decision to move back in with her mother.

Finally, Gail sat on the couch. "Now, tell me what has you so upset."

Erin took in and slowly let out a deep breath. Trying to keep the rancor from her voice, she said, "I asked you a simple question. After you answer it, I'll tell you why I'm agitated." Her expressive mouth was pulled into a tight circle, making her look as if she'd just tasted something very sour.

"I don't understand why you can't tell me what's going on, but I'll do it your way. Yes, I know that Katie is gay."

"How long have you known?"

"I'm not sure, but it's been a while. Why? What is the problem?"

"Why didn't you tell me?"

"Tell *you*? Why would I tell you?"

"I don't know, Mom. That's what I'm trying to find out. First, you didn't tell me about her existence. After I'd told you that we'd met, that would've been the perfect time to tell me a little bit about her. Our sharing a sexual orientation is the kind of thing I would expect you to mention."

Looking flustered, Gail said, "Dan has told me a lot of things about Danny and Katie, and I haven't shared them with you. I've gotten the distinct impression that you aren't interested in learning about Dan. So, why would I assume you'd want to learn about his children?"

Erin didn't buy the excuse, but she didn't have the nerve to accuse her mother of lying. "Okay, I can understand that. When did you tell Dan that I was gay?"

Gail looked like she wanted to jump up and run. "I haven't."

Willing the tears she could feel welling up not to escape, Erin controlled her voice and asked, "Why?"

Softly and gently, Gail said, "I try to respect your privacy. I've watched how you deal with the issue, and I model you."

"What in the heck does that mean?"

"Honey, I can see that you're upset, but you don't have any reason to be. I've never heard anyone in town talk about your sexual preference. As far as I know, everyone assumes you're heterosexual. *I'm* not going to be the one to tell something that you haven't told."

"Dan's not some local you're gossiping with. From what Katie says, he has a real problem with her sexuality. I'd think you'd want to know if he's anti-gay before you got married."

Gail's hand went to her throat, and she looked truly offended. "You don't know him. He's a very nice man. Granted, he has some very strong opinions about certain things, but he's not a bigot. He's always been nice to you."

"He doesn't know I'm gay! What if he doesn't want me around? Will you cut me off?"

Gail stared at her, dumbstruck. "I can't imagine what has you so upset. No one in the world could make me stop seeing you. I'm amazed that you can even suggest—"

Erin stood up and turned away right in the middle of her mother's sentence. She felt tired, depressed, and lonely. Strikingly lonely. Heading for the stairs, she said, "You have my explicit permission to tell Dan that I'm gay. Also, for the record, I'm interested in hearing anything you want to tell me about Dan or your feelings or anything else."

Gail jumped up and intercepted her. She put her arms around Erin and held her tightly. "I'm sorry. I'm so sorry that I've hurt you. I never meant to."

Erin felt more embarrassed than comforted, and she realized that she was too old for this type of interaction. She pulled away and tried to compose herself. "I'm sorry I made such a big deal out of this. I've got a bad case of PMS this month."

Gail's hands dropped, and she looked as uncomfortable as Erin did. "You were upset, honey. I want you to be able to talk to me when something's bothering you."

"I am. Able to, that is. This was just a bad day. I'm going to turn in. Goodnight, Mom."

The expression on Gail's face showed she was at a loss for how to resolve their spat. Eventually she sighed and said, "Goodnight, sweetheart. Sleep in a little bit if you can."

"Okay." Erin walked up to her room, kicked off her shoes, and lay on her bed without undressing or getting under the covers. She pulled the comforter over her feet and went to sleep, dropping off quickly and dreamlessly.

Chapter Six

*K*atie stood on the steps of her brother's house, trying to convince her nephew Cooper to let go of her leg and go back inside. The woman she'd been dating, Melanie, stood next to her, watching the interaction.

"Go on, Cooper. It's too cold out here for you. I've got to go home, buddy."

"No, Aunt Katie," the boy whined. "Stay and play."

Katie met Melanie's eyes, and she could tell that Melanie didn't think the scene was funny or cute. She seemed like she was tired of being around the boys and ready to go to the car.

"I've got to go, Coop." Katie squatted and kissed her youngest nephew noisily and then picked him up, handing him to her sister-in-law. Cooper started to cry, and Katie peppered his face with kisses until he started to giggle and push her away. "I'll come see you this weekend, bucko." She blew an air-kiss to Stacy and said, "Sorry if I wound them up too much."

"Don't worry about it. They'll be asleep in minutes." Stacy turned to Melanie. "It was nice to meet you."

"You, too. Thanks very much for dinner."

They walked to Melanie's car, and she opened the doors of her BMW with the remote. When they were inside, Katie said, "The boys are a handful, aren't they?"

"Yes, they are," Melanie said, not elaborating.

Curious, Katie probed, "How do you feel about having kids?"

Melanie started the car and fastened her seatbelt. "I'm a little old to consider it. It seems selfish to me to have a child when you know you're in a high-risk group."

"Lots of women have kids when they're your age."

"Lots of women do lots of things I'm not going to do. Having kids is one of them."

"Well, how did you feel ten years ago?"

"Mmm, it didn't ever seem like something I needed to do." She looked at Katie, her smile warm and gentle. "It seems like an awful lot of work if you're not desperate to do it."

"It is," Katie agreed. "It has to be a life goal. It really has to be."

<hr>

Erin walked down the street on Wednesday night, going back into town to the diner after getting home and finding her mother gone to Dan's house. She was still a block away when she spotted Katie's car coming down the street. Waving, she found herself smiling as Katie rolled down her window and said, "Where do you think you're going?"

"To the diner for dinner. Why are you in town?"

"Get in, will you? I don't want another crazy Essexite to run into me."

Erin did, then sat quietly in the warm car, looking at Katie expectantly.

"You look funny. Like depressed or something. Are you?"

Suddenly shy, Erin shrugged. "Maybe a little. I had a good day, but I don't have anyone to share it with." She looked down, feeling more emotional than she knew she should have. "I'm feeling a little sorry for myself."

Katie looked straight ahead for a few moments and then turned and looked directly into Erin's eyes. "Let's have dinner."

Erin looked at her with a slight sparkle in her eyes. "Really? You haven't eaten?"

"I had a snack, but I'm hungry again."

"What are you here for?"

"I brought Cooper, my youngest nephew, to see his grandpa. He's the only one who isn't in some form of school, and he gets lonely with just the babysitter."

A bright grin broke out over Erin's face. "That's nice of you. Did you take a day off to do that?"

"Yeah. It's the weekdays he needs the attention."

Erin's grin was luminous. "That's really cool. You're a good aunt." She smiled shyly. "When we were at your father's party, I wanted to get down on the floor and play with you and the boys."

Katie leaned back in her seat and regarded Erin with suspicion. "Why didn't you?"

"I don't know. I guess I'm always thinking about how things look. I want people to respect me and think I'm old enough to trust."

Katie shook her head, looking mildly perturbed. "Erin, who are you living your life for?"

"I'm part of something here. It's not just about me."

Shrugging, Katie said, "Whatever. So, how about dinner?"

"Great. The diner's food is as good as its cocoa."

"No way. We're going someplace nice."

"Really?" The innocent joy on Erin's face was touching. "Where are we going?"

"Anywhere you'd like. I'm treating."

"You don't have to do that."

"I want to. You decide where to go."

"Let's go somewhere halfway between here and Boston, so you don't have to drive far after dinner."

"You're ridiculously thoughtful, not that that doesn't have some appeal."

"Would you mind if I went home and changed?"

Katie looked at Erin's worn jeans and blue fleece top, partially hidden by her silver ski jacket. "You look fine to me, but I have time to wait."

When they reached the house, Erin ran up to her bedroom and picked out some clothes that roughly matched Katie's slightly more sophisticated look. Then she went into the bathroom, washed her face, brushed her teeth, combed her hair, and put on some blush and lipstick. She put on the clothes she'd selected, but then thought better of the sweater. So, she chose another one and gave herself a critical look, now happier with her selection. She was just about to polish her shoes when Katie called up, "While we're young!" Erin started to walk down the stairs, with Katie asking, "Have you decided where you want to go to dinner?"

"I really don't know any place. When I want to go someplace nice, I go to Manchester or Nashua, but that's not in the right direction for you."

"I only know places in Boston. Could we get on the Internet and look up something?"

"Sure. Come on up to my room." She reversed course and went to her room to turn on her computer.

"Does that line work on most of your dates?"

Erin laughed. "I'll let you know."

Katie stopped at the top of the stairs and smiled. "You look good," she said, her eyes darting up and down Erin's body. "Red's a good color for you."

"Thanks." Erin wanted to give herself a high-five for choosing the right look, but thought that might seem a little odd. She opened up her browser. "Do you want to do this?"

"Yeah." Katie sat down at the computer and started typing away, talking the whole time. "I'm glad you have a PC. The kids have Macs, and they drive me nuts."

"You really like spending time with your nephews, don't you?"

"Oh, yeah. I'm getting near the end of my reproductive life, but I'm still thinking about having kids."

Erin watched her fingers fly over the keys, as Katie sorted through one dining guide after another.

"What's stopped you from taking the leap?"

"I didn't want to do it alone. I want somebody to pawn off all the work onto." She didn't smile, but Erin was getting to know her well enough to realize that she often kept a straight face when she was making a joke.

"What about the woman you've been dating? Is she a suitable pawn?"

"Woman? What woman?" Katie's blue eyes glowed from the light of the computer screen.

"You told me you were dating someone."

"Me? Dating someone? You must be mistaken. I'm just sitting around waiting for the right woman."

Erin's grin grew as Katie finished her sentence. Her heart started beating a little more rapidly, and she wiped her damp palms on her gray slacks. "Hurry up there. I'm about to starve."

"A few more minutes won't hurt you. Sometimes, you've got to wait for the right opportunity." There was no particular inflection in Katie's voice and no change in her expression, but something about the way she talked made Erin's heart start to race. She just hoped that Katie hadn't heard her gulp.

❦

They decided on a place right on the Massachusetts-New Hampshire border. Neither of them had been to the restaurant, but they got lucky. It was small, friendly, and quiet with unhurried service.

Erin ordered a glass of wine, and Katie went with a winter lager. They tapped the edges of their glasses together, and Katie toasted, "To good medical care."

"I can't argue with that." Erin took a sip of her wine and nodded her satisfaction. "This is nice."

"So," Katie said, narrowing her gaze, "tell me more about you."

"You know, every time we've spoken, I've done all of the talking. So, it's your turn. Tell me about this endless round of parties you have."

Katie smiled. "It's not endless, but I do entertain a lot. I have a backyard."

"That must be pretty rare in Boston."

"It is. That's why I'm entertainment central."

"Where'd you get all of these friends? I couldn't put together enough people to have a poker game."

"Really?" Katie looked genuinely puzzled. "I keep in touch with people. I've got friends from high school and college and law school. I pick people up along the way and hold on to them. You don't do that?"

"No, I guess I don't. Are most of your friends lesbians?"

"I've got a big mix of friends. I went to Boston College for undergrad and law school, so most of my friends are from there. We tailgate at football games and stuff like that. Some of the people have done really well for themselves and have summer places out on the Cape or on a lake. We have big parties in the summer. Hundreds of people."

"Gosh, that sounds cool," Erin said wistfully.

Katie giggled. "I don't mean to laugh, but it's funny to hear somebody your age say 'gosh.'"

Looking a little embarrassed, Erin said, "I never got into the habit of using foul language. My mom wouldn't approve. Neither would my grandparents. My maternal grandparents, that is. If you never start using it, you don't have to clean up when the adults are around."

"Damn, you're young enough to have grandparents still alive?"

"Yeah. All four of them. My dad's parents live outside Montréal, and my mom's parents are farmers in Maine. They're all really active and healthy. Actually, my great-grandmother died just a couple of years ago, and she wasn't ill. She slipped on the ice and died from a brain hemorrhage." She chuckled softly. "She probably would have survived that, but she wouldn't go to the hospital even though she had a splitting headache."

"That's remarkable! You'll probably have seventy or eighty more years to blow through. I figure you're around thirty."

"That's about right. I'll be twenty-eight in May."

"Really? I'm the seventeenth."

Erin grinned. "I'm the fifteenth. We're practically twins."

"Almost. Except for the nine-year age gap. You probably still get carded."

Nodding, Erin said, "All of the time. I don't mind looking young, but sometimes new patients have a problem with it."

"So, what's happening on the Essex medical front? Tell me about this good day."

Erin took a sip of her wine, showing a good-natured smile. "Do you really want to know? You don't have to give in to my whining."

"Oh, honey, you don't know the first thing about whining if you think that's what it is. And yes, I'm interested."

"Well, you probably won't think it's exciting, but it made my week. Maybe my month." She sat back in her chair and rolled her eyes. "I never imagined something like this would be the highlight of my month."

Katie reached out and grasped Erin's arm, shaking it roughly. "Get on with it."

Showing a shy grin, Erin said, "I saw a patient who'd been to three different doctors, and none of them made the proper diagnosis."

"Go on," Katie encouraged

Erin made a face, her eyes almost closing. "That's kind of it."

"There has to be more. Did you save your patient's life?"

"No, nothing that dramatic, but I did determine that she had something that could cause her serious trouble if it developed further." It looked as though the starch was leaving her sails. "I gave her the same advice the previous doctors had, but I think she'll listen to me and actually do what we all suggested. Sometimes having a name for your pain makes all the difference."

Katie was gazing at Erin intently. "There's more to this. Don't shrug it off. Tell me why this made you proud of yourself because I know it did."

That shy grin showed itself again, and Erin's head dipped down a little bit. "Yeah, I was proud of myself. This woman had been in an awful lot of pain, and she was frantic. Desperate, really. Nobody had taken her seriously."

"That alone is a lot."

"I know, but what I'm proud of was my ability to make a quick diagnosis. I think that's one of my best attributes as a doctor, and it's definitely the thing I most enjoy. Three different people missed something big with this patient, and they missed it because it didn't fit with the train of thought they were on. I think that's nearly inexcusable, especially for a doctor in emergency medicine. You don't get another chance at most people you see, and shuffling them off without looking at the whole picture is wrong."

As she spoke, Erin's voice grew louder and more emphatic. The candle on the table cast a golden glow to her brown eyes that made them dance with emotion. Katie sat back and let her eyes rove over Erin's face and posture. "There's a fire to you when you talk about emergency medicine. Is that what you really want to do?"

Erin looked almost frightened. "Do I really look different? That's not a good thing. I don't want people, especially my patients, to think I'm not happy."

"But you're not, are you?"

Their server brought their appetizers, and Katie asked for another beer, even though she still had half a glass left. When the waiter brought the refill, Katie nodded when he asked if he should take the first beer away. Erin watched, wondering why she'd throw half away and buy another.

She was thinking about this when Katie said, "Your turn. I'm waiting to hear whether you're happy or not."

"Oh. Uhm, I'm not unhappy. I'd say I'm content. I live in a nice place, I'm surrounded by people who care for me, and I do something that interests and challenges me. Most people can't say that."

Katie took a bite of her salad, chewed thoughtfully, and then offered a bite to Erin. "This is really good. I love blue cheese."

Erin took the bite, freeing the lettuce from the fork with her teeth. "That *is* good. Would you like one of my oysters?"

"Sure. Load one up with horseradish for me." She ate the oyster, smiling with contentment. "As fresh as the sea." She took another bite of her salad and said, "Don't you think you're a little young to settle for contentment? Isn't this the time in your life to try and get the most you can possibly get and then settle for contentment when you realize you can't have it?" She chuckled wryly.

"I guess, but that's not how things have worked out for me. You're not the first to tell me I'm doing this the wrong way. My ex-girlfriend shares your view."

"Is that why she's your ex?"

"If I have to be completely honest, yes. She didn't want to live here, but it was more than that. She didn't think I had enough drive or ambition."

"There's nothing wrong with not wanting to be the doctor of the year. Maybe you're just the kind of person who likes a less stressful life."

"I wish I could say that was true, but Suzy was with me in medical school. She knows I got off on the emergency medicine and surgery rotations."

"So, she thought you were settling for something that wasn't right for you?"

Erin ate another of her oysters, slowly chewing and considering her answer. "It was worse than that. She thought I let the town and my mom put pressure on me to do something I didn't want to do. She never believed this was entirely my choice."

"That seems strange."

"Not really. Her parents put a lot of pressure on her and tried to manipulate her into doing exactly what they wanted. I don't think she believed my mom was the saint I made her out to be." She giggled girlishly. "I'm sure she isn't the saint I make her out to be, but she's pretty great."

Katie gazed at her for a few moments, and Erin felt her heart start to race as those penetrating blue eyes passed over her face slowly. "Sometimes, you seem so young, but then you say something that's so remarkably mature. You're an interesting critter, Erin. Very interesting. I'd like to see you open up and let go."

Erin's eyes lit up. "Then let's head to Killington while they're still making snow. The craziest I ever get is on the slopes."

"It's a date," Katie said, and Erin's palms got wet at the thought that Katie might have meant it literally.

⌘

Erin was just starting to work on her entree when Katie asked, "Other than Suzy, how many other women have you been with?"

Erin popped a fried shrimp into her mouth and pointed at herself, indicating she couldn't answer because her mouth was full. She pointed back at Katie and raised her eyebrows in question.

"I can wait," Katie said, smiling sweetly.

Erin finished and said, "You're too quick for me. It's not fair."

"Lawyers are never fair. Confess."

"Oh, all right. Just Suzy."

"Really? How long were you together?"

"We met at UNH at the end of our sophomore year. It was probably around Thanksgiving in our junior year when we started dating, if you can call it dating. We basically fell in love immediately."

Katie looked surprised. "What did you do between spring and fall?"

With a sheepish grin, Erin said, "I didn't know that I was gay, and Suzy didn't tell me I was until it became clear I wasn't going to ever figure it out for myself."

"Are you a slow learner or what?"

Slightly insulted, Erin said, "I've never been called slow. It just didn't occur to me."

"So, you were with men for a while, right?"

Erin picked up another shrimp and bit into it. She was clearly considering her answer, and she finally said, "I dated boys in high school and college, but I was never in love before Suzy."

Narrowing her eyes, Katie said, "You're evading the question."

"Yes, I am. I don't like to talk about the past very much. I like to look to the future."

"Okay. I like to dissect things into the smallest possible particles, but I'll respect your boundaries."

"Thanks." Erin gave her a warm smile. "I appreciate that. But I'd love to hear about your history, since you like to talk about it."

"Maybe another time. I don't like to spill too much if I don't get details in return. You can sneak up on me sometime when I'm not aware that you're not sharing."

"It's a deal."

⊷

While they were waiting for Erin's dessert to be delivered, Katie said, "Have you heard the news about the wedding? All I get are generalities about 'some time in the future.'"

"Pretty much the same for me."

"I guess we'll have to wait until we get our invitations in the mail."

Erin made a face that made Katie laugh. "Ick," was all she said.

⊷

They stayed at the restaurant until Katie noticed their server sitting on a chair by the cashier, looking like she was about to fall asleep. She glanced at her watch and gasped, "It's eleven o'clock!"

"Gosh, it is. We'd better get going." Erin reached for her wallet, but Katie put out a restraining hand.

"I've got this one. I think I should buy you a lift ticket to Killington, too. I checked with one of my doctor friends in Boston, and you gave me a very sweet deal. Apparently, most doctors don't take accident victims into their offices on their days off and patch them up for next to nothing."

"My contract is for a fixed salary, no matter how much I bring in. So, I set my own prices."

Katie shook her head. "I think Suzy might've been on to something. Maybe somebody implanted a chip in your head that made you strike a crazy bargain to be an indentured servant."

"No, I volunteered, and I'd do it again in the same set of circumstances."

"But not in this set of circumstances?"

"Mmm, no comment. I prefer not to analyze decisions that can't be changed."

⊷

Even though the snowfall for the year was negligible, it was still very cold. Katie and Erin stood in the parking lot for a minute, rubbing their arms and moving briskly to keep warm.

"That's a very cute coat you have there. And you're the only person I've ever seen wear a hat like that and not look like a dunce."

"Is that a compliment?"

Katie laughed, her eyes crinkling up when she did. "Yes, it was a compliment, but I sure as heck didn't frame it very well. It's just that I see a lot of women try to wear a hat like yours, and they usually look awful in it. Like Elmer Fudd."

"And I don't?" Erin tilted her head, her brown eyes looking for confirmation.

"I'm not doing very well here. Yes, you don't look like Elmer Fudd." She giggled at her own ineptitude at extending a compliment. "Is that rabbit fur? I thought you'd be a 'no fur' kind of girl."

Surprised but charmed that Katie considered her choices, Erin said, "I think of rabbit like beef. We eat them, why not use the fur?"

"Well, the bunny gave his life for a good cause. The fur looks nice against your dark hair. Not many people can wear a white, knee-length, down coat, either, but you look great in it."

"My grandmother bought the coat and hat for me when I was up in Montréal for Christmas. She's kind of a clotheshorse. I let her dress me up any way she wants. It makes her happy."

"Montréal, huh?"

"Yeah. I went up there when my mom visited your dad."

"Oh. I didn't realize they'd been together at Christmas. No wonder he didn't come home like he usually does. The boys really missed him, but I'll be nice and not tell them their grandpa chose a woman over them." Katie jumped up and down, trying to get some feeling back into her feet. "I'd better go."

Erin was rather frantically trying to decide if she should hug Katie goodbye, but before she could make up her mind, Katie said, "I'll call you about Killington, okay?"

"Yeah. Do you still have my number?"

"No, but directory assistance still does." She grinned, wrinkling her nose when she did. Then she got into her car and turned the engine over. Erin waved goodbye and got into her own car, where she spent the drive home wondering if the trip to Killington was really going to be a date and, if it wasn't, how she could make it into one.

❧

Erin was whistling a happy tune when she opened the door to her home. She was surprised to see that her mom was home and became puzzled when Gail, who was sitting on the sofa, stood and said, "Where have you been? I've been worried sick about you!"

"Pardon?" Erin stood in the entryway for a moment, her hands poised to remove her coat.

"I didn't know you were going out. You didn't even leave a note." Gail's voice was high and thin, nearly a whine.

Erin took off her coat and walked over to the sofa. "I didn't think you were coming home. I knew you were at Dan's, helping out with Cooper. I assumed you'd stay overnight."

"How did you know about Cooper?"

Even more confused, Erin said, "Because of Katie. She saw me walking to the diner and offered to buy me dinner."

"She had dinner with us." There was something snippy about her tone, and Erin didn't let it pass.

"Is there a problem?"

"Were you out with her?"

"Is…there…a…problem?" Erin stared at her mother, unblinking, her jaw set.

"Yes, Erin, there is a problem. For one thing, I don't like your attitude. And for another, you've always told me when you're going to be out for the evening. When you don't do that, it worries me."

Erin could feel the flush creeping up her cheeks. The words started to pour out of her before she could stop them. "How do you think I felt the first time you stayed out with Dan? I don't recall getting a note or a phone call, and you didn't take your cell phone so I couldn't call you. I woke up the next morning and drove over there before dawn just to make sure you hadn't been in an accident."

Gail's mouth opened and closed. She said, "I didn't know. Why didn't you say something?"

Letting out a derisive snort, Erin said, "What was I supposed to say? You were either embarrassed to call, or it didn't occur to you. Either way, the damage had been done."

"Damage?" Gail's eyes were wide, and she looked like she might cry. "Did I really hurt you, honey?"

"Yes. Yes, you did. A lot."

"Oh, my. Erin, I never meant to hurt you. But I was…carried away. I didn't plan on staying over, but that was the first…" Her cheeks were flushed, and she was clearly at a loss for words.

"I got over it, Mom. Now I assume you're with Dan when you don't come home. I've stopped worrying."

Gail sighed heavily, and she looked weary and frustrated. "I'm sorry. I can't express how sorry I am."

"It's all right. I'm okay with it now, but you can't expect me to keep you apprised of my schedule when you don't do the same for me." She broke eye contact and looked down. "It's not fair."

"You're right," Gail said. "I was…I suppose I was uncomfortable talking about being with Dan…in that way." She swallowed. "I still am."

"Nobody wants to talk about things like that, and I don't want to hear about them. It's too personal."

"I agree, but I should have been more thoughtful. It was insensitive of me not to get up and…" She trailed off, her skin coloring. "I was too embarrassed the next day to even face you."

"It's over and done with. Let's drop it."

Eagerly, Gail said, "We probably should."

"You haven't answered my question about Katie, though, and I don't want to drop that. You seemed unhappy to think I spent the evening with her."

"Not unhappy," Gail said, her eyes flitting across Erin's face. "I was surprised. I assumed she was going home. I don't know why she needed another dinner."

"It was more than that, Mom."

"Oh, honey." Gail scrubbed her face with her hands. "Don't read too much into things. If you want to be friends with Katie, I certainly don't have any objections." She looked at Erin and added, "It *is* just friendship, isn't it?"

"For now it is, but I'd like it to be more."

Gail blanched noticeably. "You're interested in her?"

"I'm not *uninterested*. She's nice and funny and quick and…well, you've seen her, so you know how pretty she is."

"Yes, she's very pretty. I think her looks have made her very…popular." There was a touch of censure in her expression.

"I wouldn't mind being more popular, in any sense of the word."

"Oh, Erin, you're not that type of girl."

"What type of girl?" She was clearly annoyed, and her cheeks were growing pink again. "Just say something if you have something to say."

Gail waved her hand. "I don't have anything to say. I just want you to be careful. Katie has a lot more experience than you do."

"She's nine years older. She *should* have more experience. And I have a lot less experience than most women my age. I have no lesbian friends and only one good straight friend in town. I'd love to just meet some people through Katie, but if something more comes of it, I expect you to support my decisions just like I've supported yours."

With a tight, plastic smile, Gail said, "Of course I will. I trust you to make the right decisions, Erin. You always have."

⟠

Erin waited impatiently for Katie to call. She was finally rewarded four days after their dinner when the phone rang while she was sitting at her computer, working on a story. "Hello?"

"Hi. It's Katie. Still up for a ski trip?"

"Yeah. Yeah, definitely. We need to get going while it's still cold."

"Do you think you can wait until Saturday?"

"This Saturday?"

"Yeah. Does that work for you?"

"Sure. I mean, that's fine."

"I'll come pick you up. I can put a double rack on my roof."

"Are you sure? I could meet you there."

"Erin, I want to go skiing with you because I like you. Since I like you, I want to spend time with you. Spending time with you includes time in the car. So, being in the—"

"Got it! I've got it," Erin repeated, laughing. "I'd love to have you pick me up. I just didn't want to inconvenience you."

"Well, what's most convenient is for me to sit on my butt in my pajamas all weekend. Does that work for you, or would you rather go skiing?"

Chuckling softly, Erin said, "I'm not that considerate. I'd rather go skiing."

"Finally! Ask for what you want, 'cause most people only think of themselves. You'll get trampled if you're too considerate."

"You're probably right, but I think it's too late to change the big things. I guess I just have to hope I can jump out of the way."

"We'll see how you do on the slopes. I have to take a good look to make sure you're agile enough."

⟡

On Saturday morning, Erin was up early, getting her gear ready for Killington. Gail made breakfast for her, but was nearly nonverbal. Erin was bubbling with anticipation, looking as forward to seeing Katie as she was to skiing.

The doorbell rang, and Erin jumped up to answer it. When she opened it, she stood there for a second, trying not to stare. But she had obviously revealed her interest because Katie grinned and said, "This is a really cute sweater, isn't it."

"Yeah. Really cute." Erin took the comment as permission to look at Katie without trying to act like she wasn't. There was nothing remarkable, per se, about the sweater. It was a mint green hoodie, but it was made of a knit that looked soft and strokeable, and it fit Katie's trim body snugly. "The color is…" Erin's eyes kept darting back to Katie's breasts, which the sweater displayed to perfection. "Great."

"Thank you." Katie bowed and took a long look at Erin. "You look pretty good yourself. Pale blue is a good color for you. It brings out the pink in your dewy cheeks."

Giggling, Erin said, "What does that even mean?"

"I have no idea." Katie walked inside. "I used to hear it on commercials. Are you ready?"

"Yeah. Just about."

Gail walked into the room and smiled. "Hi, Katie. You must be an early bird to get up here so early."

"Only for fun. You can hardly dynamite me out of bed to get to work early."

"I hope you two aren't wasting a trip. I can't imagine they have any snow in Killington. There certainly isn't any here, and that's very rare for March."

"I looked on their web site, Mom. They're making snow. It's still cold enough for the base to stay firm."

"Well, I hope so. I assume you'll be home pretty late, right?"

"We're coming back tomorrow," Katie said. She looked at Erin. "Didn't I mention that?"

"No, I don't think you did, but it's a good idea. This is the last gasp for the slopes. We'd better eat 'em up while we can."

"You're staying overnight?" Gail asked, her voice a little high and tremulous.

"There were plenty of rooms," Katie said. "I got a good deal. We'll be back tomorrow afternoon or early evening."

Erin picked up her skis and started for the car, stopping and giving Katie a dirty look. "You brought skis *and* a board?"

"You can rent a board if you want."

"I've got one." Erin sighed and made a show of having to go get her gear.

Gail stood near the car, watching Katie organize things to make room for Erin's skis and board. "Do you like winter sports?" she asked.

"Oh, yeah. I like just about anything in snow: skiing, boarding, snowshoeing, tobogganing."

"That sounds like Erin. I think she'd live in the Arctic if she could."

"Boston's close enough to the Arctic circle for me. I like summer things, too, especially waterskiing."

"So does Erin," Gail said, not looking particularly happy about the shared interest. "I hope I'm not interfering in family matters, but I wanted to let you know that I felt very bad about the fight you and your dad had at his party."

Katie paused and looked at Gail, who seemed to pull back from the intense assessment she was receiving. "Do you know what the fight was about?"

"Yes. He told me after the party was over."

"Well," Katie said, focusing her attention back on her car, "he's not the most open-minded guy in the world. He thinks you're either with him or against him."

"Is that how you see him?" Gail asked, a furrow of concern showing between her brows.

"Yeah, but he probably feels the same way about me. He's not going to march in the gay pride parade with me, and I'm not going to march in the St. Patrick's Day parade with the Irish cops."

"Do you march in the gay parade?"

Katie grinned. "Sure. It's a great party."

"You might not believe this, but he's never said a negative word to me about your being gay."

Fixing her with that penetrating stare, Katie said, "Has he ever said a positive word?"

"Well, no, but he's never said a positive word about your brother being straight."

Katie crossed her arms over her chest and looked at Gail with an expression somewhere between amusement and mockery. "Of course he has. He talks about my sister-in-law and how great he thinks she is. He talks about what a good mom she is, and he talks about what a great cop wife she is. I know he does."

"I'm sure he'd do the same for you if you were in the same position. Maybe you and the woman you've been dating should get together with him. I'm sure he'd feel different about her if he knew her better."

Katie turned back to her car and opened the back door. She looked up at Erin, who was just closing the front door to the house, then turned back to Gail and said, "He missed his chance. We're not seeing each other anymore." Her eyes darted towards Erin, and she followed her progress down the stairs and across the lawn. Katie wasn't ogling her, but she seemed to forget that she and Gail were in the middle of a conversation. As she watched, her smile grew until her eyes met Erin's. "That's a nice-looking board you have there. Good boots, too. Those are my favorites."

Gail looked very discomfited. She slowly backed up and was just about to reach the porch when she heard a car stop. All three women looked up to see Dan park in front of the house. He turned off his engine, but didn't get out immediately. When he did open his door, he looked thoroughly puzzled. "Katie? What are you doing here?"

"I came by to pick up Erin. We're going skiing."

His eyes darted from Katie to Erin and back again. "Are you going, Gail?"

"No, I'm not. Just the girls."

He scratched at the back of his head, a sign all three women recognized as his habit when he was confused or annoyed. "Did you just now decide this?" He must have heard how silly the question sounded because he recanted. "I mean, when did you decide this?"

Erin could see that Dan was flummoxed, but she didn't know why. "We decided a few days ago. We both like to ski, and this is probably our last chance this season."

Dan's puzzlement was slowly morphing into pique, and all assembled could see that it was directed at Katie. "Call me when you get home," he said, his tone gruff and demanding.

"Sure," Katie said, a smile playing at the corners of her mouth. "We'd better get going. I hate to waste getting up early. See you two." She waved at Dan and Gail and got into the car.

Erin looked a little puzzled, but she hugged her mom and nodded goodbye to Dan. "See you later."

"Have fun," Gail said unenthusiastically.

Katie started the car and pulled out of the driveway, sneaking a look back as she drove down the street. She giggled with adolescent glee. "Daddy doesn't look happy."

"Then why do *you* look so happy? I don't like it when my mom's angry."

Shrugging her shoulders, Katie said, "You're more mature than I am. I take guilty pleasure in tweaking him when I can."

Erin reached out and touched Katie's arm. In a tone that brooked no dissension, she said, "Would you pull over, please?"

Katie shot her a quick look and then followed directions. She pulled over to the curb, put the car in park, and turned off the engine. "What's the matter?"

Erin looked like she was on the verge of crying. "Are you hanging out with me just to aggravate your father?"

Loudly, Katie said, "What?"

"I don't want to be a pawn between you and your dad. I've only spent a little time with you, but this isn't the first time I've seen you look happy to annoy him. It's none of my business what kind of relationship you two have, but if you're spending time with me to get between him and my mom or some other reason—"

"Stop!" Katie held up her hand. "There is only one reason I want to hang with you." She stopped and started again. "I want to see you because I like you."

"Are you sure that's true?" Erin searched Katie's eyes, looking for any sign of evasiveness or dissembling.

"I'm positive. I won't lie to you; I do like to piss my dad off. But I'd never use another person to do that. Especially one as nice as you are."

"I need to be sure of that. Are you certain you understand your motives for wanting to hang out with me?"

Katie smiled sexily, and her gaze lingered on Erin's lips for a few moments. "Believe me," she said, "my dad has nothing to do with it. I'd like you even if my dad had never met you. Annoying him is just a bonus I'll try not to revel in." She gave Erin such a sincere but devilish smile that there was nothing to do but smile back.

Chapter Seven

*D*an stood at the window of the Delancy house, his thickly muscled arms crossed over his chest. "Why didn't you tell me Erin and Katie were going skiing together?" he asked, not turning to look at Gail

She sat on the sofa, trying to compose her thoughts and her expression. "Erin just mentioned it to me last night."

Turning, Dan looked at Gail for a few moments, his head tilted in question. "There's more. I can tell you're holding something back. What is it?" He was almost glaring at her, and she shrank a little under his inspection.

"I didn't think you'd like it," she said, her voice quavering. "They had dinner together the day Katie brought Cooper up here. I think it was just a fluke that they ran into each other, but they did go to dinner."

"There aren't many flukes where Katie's involved. She's very calculating." He watched Gail carefully, clearly bothered by her affect. "You don't seem bothered by them being away together."

"I suppose I'm not. I'm glad Erin's doing something besides sitting at home."

"She'd be better off at home," Dan said, scowling. "I'm sure Katie wouldn't force herself on her, but Erin seems like a very impressionable girl. She probably doesn't have much experience being around lesbians. She might do something she'll regret." He looked at Gail sharply. "She doesn't drink much, does she?"

"No, hardly at all." She swallowed nervously. "I haven't mentioned this, honey, but, uhm, Erin has had a lesbian experience."

"What?" His eyebrows rose. "What do you mean by that?"

"She's been with a woman."

"When did this happen? Recently?"

"No, not recently."

"When? Was she a girl?"

"It happened when she was in college."

"College, huh?" He scowled at her. "That's not uncommon. Nothing up until then?"

"No, I don't think…no," she shook her head decisively. "That was the first time."

"Did she just have one…what do you call it…incident?"

"Well, uhm, I suppose that depends on what you mean."

Clearly frustrated, Dan said, "This isn't a difficult question."

Looking resigned, she said, "She met a woman and fell in love with her."

"Love? She fell in love?"

Gail nodded, not looking up.

"So, she was in a relationship." It wasn't a question.

"Yes." Her head was still tilted down, and she looked like she was waiting to be scolded.

He walked over to her and sat down heavily, making the sofa squeak in protest. "Why didn't you say anything?"

"I don't like to talk about her personal life. That's for her to do."

"Well, is she a lesbian?"

"Probably." She hesitated. "That's the assumption I've made, but I'm not entirely sure. I thought she might have just come under this particular woman's sway, but she hasn't been out with a man since this happened."

"Jesus, Gail, don't you know her at all?" His face was red, and his eyebrows were arched dramatically. "I thought you two were so close."

"We are," she said, a little defensive. "But she's a private girl. She always has been. She doesn't share a lot of her personal thoughts."

"Have you asked her if she's a lesbian?"

"No, not directly. It's just been assumed. She was with this woman she met in college for a while."

"A while? Could you define that a little better?"

"It was quite a while," she admitted. "Through medical school and most of her residency."

"Oh, God." He rubbed his eyes with his fists. "So, this weekend could be a date. They could be sleeping together."

"I suppose they could be, but that doesn't sound like Erin."

"Well, it sure as hell sounds like Katie. She's only interested in putting notches on her belt. She'd break a kid like Erin's heart in no time." He got up and went to the window again, staring out at the dark night. "I'm not happy about this. Not happy at all."

"I can see that."

He turned to face her. "And I'm not happy that you didn't tell me about Erin. You intentionally kept that information from me."

"I didn't—"

"Yes, you did. I told you Katie was gay, and the normal response would have been to tell me about Erin. Whether you thought she was just experimenting—for a significant portion of her life—or whatever, you should have told me." He stared at Gail for a full minute, and she looked like she wanted to crawl into a hole. "We can't have a marriage filled with secrets."

⚬

They were barely out of town when Katie said, "I like how direct you are. You really are astoundingly mature."

"Yeah, I am in a lot of ways. But I'm immature, or at least inexperienced, in a lot of things, too. I guess that's true for all of us."

Katie gave her a quick look. "What would you have done if I'd said that I liked you partly to annoy my dad?"

"I would have asked you to take me home."

"I'm glad." Katie nodded, looking thoughtful. "I wouldn't want to spend time with someone who didn't have some self-respect. I'm really glad you asked your question and got it out of the way." After another quick look at Erin, she asked, "Are we good?"

"We're good." Erin winked at her when Katie snuck another look her way.

⚬

Dan opened the door to Gail's house and stomped his feet a few times, as much to get the feeling back in them as to clean them. He hung up his scarf, his hat, and his coat, and then walked through the living room into the kitchen. He opened one of the beers he'd bought during the walk he'd taken to cool off, poured it into a glass, and went back into the living room.

Neither he nor Gail spoke while he deliberately drank a little of his beer. "There's something here that doesn't make sense. I've thought about it six ways to Sunday, and it doesn't make sense that you wouldn't tell me about Erin."

"I can see that, but I don't have any better way to explain myself. I don't like to talk about Erin's private life. That's for her to do when and if she chooses."

His face started to turn pink again, and he looked as though he were trying hard to control his temper. "I'm not some guy checking out a book at the library. You and I are going to be married, Gail. You might not like the fact that Erin's gay, but it's not something you should hide from me of all people."

Gail was leaning on the far arm of the sofa, looking like she wanted to be as far away from Dan as possible. "I'm not hiding anything. There are all sorts of things about Erin I haven't told you. I don't understand why this is so important. It's not who she is; it's what she does."

Clearly astonished, he opened and closed his mouth twice before he spoke. "Who in the hell told you that? It *is* who she is."

Slightly defensive, Gail said, "That's not how I view it. To be honest, it annoys me when people use gay as a noun."

"I don't give a good Goddamn if it's a noun, an adverb, or a preposition. Your kid is gay, and you didn't tell me."

Gail changed her position and leaned toward Dan, looking him right in the eye. "Now you know why I don't like to talk about this. People act as though this is *the* defining element of who Erin is, and I think that's ridiculous. I'm so sick of hearing everyone in town talk about Richard, the gay florist. Why does it matter? No one talks about Orville, the angry insurance salesman. And believe me, his anger makes up a bigger part of his personality than Erin's sexual preference. I'm sure Erin hasn't had sex in a year, but Orville is probably throwing a fit right this minute."

"What kind of mixed-up logic is that?"

"You don't know what it's like here. You haven't lived here very long, Dan. You don't know how people talk."

He pointed at himself with his finger. "I don't know? I don't? You can go down to South Boston tomorrow and ask anybody there the name of the cop who has the dyke daughter. Since she was sixteen years old, she's made it her business to let everybody know she's gay. So, don't you dare tell me I don't know what it's like."

"It's more than that," Gail said, her voice rising. "Boston's a big city. You can blend in better. It's not like that here. It's been bad enough trying to keep everybody in town out of my relationship with you. I don't want to have to go through that with Erin."

"Are you serious? It's only a matter of time until she dates someone. Have you given any thought to that?"

She dropped her head, looking disconsolate. "I know, I know. I don't like to think about it, but of course you're right."

"Do you think not thinking about it is going to make it not happen?" His face had continued to color, and it was now close to the color of his hair.

She looked like a child trying to convince herself of the existence of the Easter Bunny. "It's been well over a year, and she hasn't shown any interest..."

The veins in his temples visibly throbbed. "Are you serious?"

"Yes...well, no. I suppose that was wishful thinking." The room was deathly silent, and she tried to order her thoughts. "There's such a big part of me that wants her here, but I'm not ready to deal with the consequences of her lifestyle. I just wish she would have moved to Chicago, but she was intent on living here."

"Chicago? Why would you want her in Chicago?"

"That's where her girlfriend moved. They broke up because Erin didn't want to leave Essex."

He stared at her, plainly stunned. "She stayed here rather than go with someone she was in love with?"

"That's why I keep thinking she might not be serious about being a lesbian. I drop hints about her finding someone, but she hasn't seemed interested in dating or anything…gay."

"Well, hold on to your hat because knowing Katie, she'll have Erin marching in a little gay pride parade right down Main Street."

⟨⟩

The runs were open, but the conditions were as bad as Erin had ever seen them. True to her word, Katie suggested they try skiing first and resort to boarding if they weren't having fun.

They had to go far up the mountain to find decent conditions, but Erin liked that only knowledgeable skiers were on the hill. They reached the summit and clicked their boots into their bindings. "I'm gonna take it slow for a while to get comfortable," Erin said.

"I'm not!" Katie let out a whoop as she propelled herself down the hill with abandon.

Erin couldn't let Katie dust her, so she followed behind, looking for a spot to overtake her. She found it on the last turn before the end of the run. Recklessly, she carved her way across the turn, slipping beneath Katie and spraying her in the face with snow as she sped by. "You can ski!" Erin enthused, panting at the bottom of the hill.

"You kicked my ass, you sneak!" She playfully slapped Erin's pink cheek. "I thought you might be tentative out here. You surprised the hell out of me when you tried to break your neck to beat me."

Erin pushed her goggles up and tilted her head in question. "Really? Why?"

"You just seem pretty…the word isn't mellow, but I'm having trouble thinking of the right one. Maybe cautious?"

"Only in some things. I'm confident about my skiing, so I let 'er rip."

"Interesting," Katie said. She gave Erin an inscrutable smile. "We'll have to do more things you're confident about."

Erin watched Katie head for the lift, wondering exactly what she meant by that.

                          ❧

They skied non-stop for over an hour, and Erin's thighs were beginning to cramp, but Katie wanted one more run before lunch. She took off first and was about halfway down the hill, when her lead ski slid on the icy run and her legs flew out from under her. She landed flat on her back in some manmade powder. Her bindings had released, and her skis lay under her, pointing down the hill. Erin had to cut hard to come to a stop. "Katie! Are you all right?" Erin got out of her skis, her eyes darting up and down Katie's body, looking for signs of trauma. "Katie!" she said again, her heart thudding in her chest when she got no response. She bent her knees to get closer and shrieked when Katie grabbed her by the shoulders and pulled her to the ground.

"What in the heck?" Erin was lying on her back, spitting snow out of her mouth and trying to blink away the crystals that covered her lashes. "I can't believe you tricked me!"

Laughing, Katie said, "I can't believe it took me this long. Too bad I almost had to break my neck to get the chance. A day on the slopes isn't complete without some hijinks."

Spluttering, Erin made a face. "This snow is half dirt. I think we'd better switch to boarding. At least there I can keep an eye on you."

"Won't help." Katie got up and then pulled Erin to her feet. "I'm the merry prankster."

                          ❧

They were both a little sluggish and tired after lunch, so they sat in the lodge for a while, sipping cocoa. "Why do you think your dad was upset about us going skiing?" Erin asked thoughtfully.

"He probably thinks I'm a bad influence. I've told you that he isn't very gay friendly."

"Did you tell me that? I don't remember if you said it that way."

"Maybe I didn't say it exactly like that. I was probably trying not to color your judgment of him."

Erin smiled. "That was nice of you, but I tend to make up my own mind about people. I know that everyone has a point of view that skews her opinion."

"Mature, mature, mature," Katie teased, wrinkling her nose. "What did he say when he found out you were gay?"

Erin shrugged. "I don't know. My mom doesn't tell me much, and I don't ask many questions."

"That's why you two get along."

Erin nodded, smiling. "You might be right. We do things together and talk about a lot of things, but we don't bare our souls." She shook her head. "We never have."

"I'd get along with everyone if we didn't talk about important issues and emotions."

"Maybe that's why we haven't had many things to argue about until now."

"Now? Why now?"

"Oh, I don't know." Erin let out a deep breath. "I guess it's hard for both of us to have this big change. We're probably just going through an adjustment period."

"Well, I hope my dad's homophobia doesn't scare your mom away."

Erin's eyebrows crept up a half-inch. "He's that bad?"

"Yeah. I mean it in the true sense of the word. I think he fears gay people. He's really squeamish about gay men, and he doesn't understand lesbianism in any way. He's one of those guys who thinks a woman can't be satisfied sexually without a man."

Erin's eyes nearly bugged out. "He's told you that?"

Waving her hand, Katie dismissed the question. "Not per se, but it's clear that's what he thinks. And I know he's freaked out by gay men. He used to carry one of those CPR kits so he wouldn't ever have to put his mouth on another man's mouth. It skeeves him out."

"That's a public safety practice," Erin said, looking distracted. "Still…I wonder what he said when my mom told him I was a lesbian."

"Maybe she didn't tell him," Katie said, looking at Erin inscrutably over her mug.

"Nah. I told her she had my permission to tell him. I made it really clear."

"She didn't tell him you and I were going skiing," Katie said, her eyes dancing with the satisfaction she seemed to get from proving her father to be flawed.

"No, I guess she didn't." Erin held up her hands. "Maybe it just didn't come up."

"It came up today," Katie said. "I bet it's still coming up."

⁂

Erin bounced on the balls of her feet as they waited in line to check into the lodge. They'd been too early to check in when they'd first arrived, and Katie suggested they get it out of the way during their break.

"You still have a lot of energy," Katie said, watching Erin fidget.

"Oh! Oh, yeah, I do. I can't wait to get back out there."

"What do you want to do?"

"Whatever. I'm up for anything."

The clerk smiled and asked, "May I help you?"

"Yes. Reservation for Quinn."

He looked at his computer. "Kathleen Quinn?"

"That's me."

"I didn't know your name was Kathleen," Erin said, after the man went to print something off.

"Yep. Katie isn't a saint's name."

"You have to be named after a saint?"

Looking at her quizzically, Katie said, "Of course. Weren't you baptized?"

"Yeah, but I didn't think there was a name requirement."

"Aren't you Catholic?"

"No."

"Aren't you Irish?"

"No. Mostly French Canadian."

"Why's your name Erin?"

"I guess because my parents liked the name."

"They named you after Ireland, and you're not Irish?"

"What's 'Erin' got to do with Ireland?" Erin asked, clearly puzzled.

"Faith and begorrah! You don't know a thing about Ireland. I was just going to ask you to come to my St. Patrick's Day party."

Erin grinned at Katie's dismay. "I thought everyone was Irish on St. Patrick's Day."

Exaggeratedly rolling her eyes, Katie said, "I suppose that's true. Do you want to come?"

"Sure. When is it?"

"Next Thursday."

Erin scrunched her mouth into a small circle. "No, I can't do that. I have to work on Friday."

"Could you come on Friday night?"

Cocking her head, Erin said, "Yeah, but how does that help?"

The clerk returned, and Katie signed the registration forms. He handed her two keys, and she gave one to Erin. "We're next door to each other," she said, smiling brightly. "We can pass notes under the door."

Erin's heart sank when she saw that they wouldn't be sharing a room. "Can I give you a check for my room?"

Katie put her hand on Erin's arm and led her away from the counter. "No, don't be silly. You didn't even know we were staying over. My treat."

"Gee, Katie, you don't have to do that."

"I know I don't have to. I want to. And if you'll come, I'll move the party to Friday."

Stunned, Erin stared at her. "You will? Won't that inconvenience people?"

"Maybe, but it will convenience you." She touched the center of Erin's chest with her finger and batted her blue eyes. "Everybody can't be happy. It's my party, so I get to play favorites."

Puzzled but pleased, Erin tried to figure out what was going on. She followed Katie outside, more confused about the trajectory of their relationship than she had been the day before.

⁕

A half-hour later, they were in line for a very steep snow tube run. The tube would ostensibly hold two, but Erin couldn't figure out how they'd ride it. "I see four handles, but where do we sit?"

"I'll show you. I'm not good at explaining things in space. I'm a hands-on person."

"That must add to your popularity," Erin said, blushing a little before the words were out.

"Why, Erin! That was positively bawdy coming from you." She seemed to take great delight in the teasing, and the more Erin's color turned, the more she laughed.

"I'm not a prude," Erin said rather defensively.

"The jury's still out on that." They were up next, and Katie sat on the edge of the tube. "Now you sit opposite me." Erin stood there, perplexed, trying to figure out where to put her legs. "Sit down," Katie said again. Erin did, and as soon as her feet were in the air, Katie took them and pulled them until they bracketed her hips. "See? All cozy." She put her legs on top of Erin's. "Now, you hold on to the handles, and I'll put my feet here." She wedged them between Erin's hands and her body. "Give us a push," she called out before Erin had time to blink.

"Darn it!" Erin cried as they began to fly down the slope. "Can't you give me a little warning?"

"Don't you ever cuss?" Katie cried, laughing demonically.

Erin tried to keep from biting her tongue off as they bounced into the air and crashed back to earth time and again. "YEOOOW!!!" she cried after one hellacious leap into the air.

Katie was hooting the entire time, her head thrown back in glee.

They finally skidded to a stop, and Erin took in great gulps of air. "Wow! Let's go again!"

"That's the spirit!" Katie said. "How much do you weigh?"

"About 135 or 140. Why?"

"You're on the bottom next time."

"The bottom?"

"Trust me, you'll love it."

Once again, Erin followed Katie up the hill, wondering what in the world she was getting herself into. Katie refused to give any more information until it was their turn. When it was time, she said, "Lie down."

"Lie down? Like how?"

"Face first." Erin didn't hop to it, and Katie said, "Trust me. It's fun."

Warily, Erin ignored the laughter from the young men who were there to assist them. She lay down and gulped when Katie climbed on top of her and grasped a set of handles. Katie's face was right next to her ear, and she almost purred when she said, "Hang on tight."

The young men gave them a hearty push, and Erin's heart leapt to her throat. She had to work to keep her head up, given that Katie was atop her, but she wasn't about to let nature direct them. She used every bit of her strength and dexterity to guide the tube. They both screamed all the way down, and Katie clapped her hard on the back when they rolled off. "Great job! I crashed the first ten times I did that."

"Some instruction might have been nice."

"Instruction's for wimps. Let's go again!"

❧

Before the afternoon was out, they'd been down the hill in every conceivable position. Erin's favorite was when they both sat up on the tube with Katie behind her. Erin got quite a nice little thrill when Katie's thighs surrounded her, and she debated asking if they could do that again the next day. She was idly thinking about how it would feel to do that in the nude when Katie asked, "Hungry for dinner?"

"Oh! Yeah, I'm starving."

"We can eat here or go to a place I know not too far away. Your choice."

"No, your choice. I'm a follower…so I've discovered," Erin said, chuckling abashedly.

❧

Erin started to work on her Chicken Parmesan, while Katie took a careful spoonful of her minestrone soup. She blew across the spoon and then tipped it into her mouth. Smiling happily, she said, "Delicious. The vegetables aren't mushy. Don't you hate mushy vegetables?"

"If left to my own devices, I don't think I'd ever eat a complex carbohydrate." She smiled somewhat guiltily. "My mom cooks healthfully, so you'd think that's what I'd crave. No such luck."

"So, when your mom's not home, you have to go to the diner, huh?"

"I don't have to, since she always has plenty of food in the freezer, but I'm pretty fond of the cheeseburger-chocolate malt combo at the diner."

"Ah. So, you're both lazy and unhealthy."

Unrepentantly, Erin smiled and nodded. "That's me. I only have to temper my desires if there are kids there or a patient who I've been after to improve their diet."

Clearly amazed, Katie squinted at Erin for a minute. "You order differently if there are kids there?"

"Sure. I have to set a good example. It's not fair to the parents to have me talk about healthy eating and then have the kids see me snarfing down two thousand empty calories."

"Interesting. Very interesting. You don't care about your own health; you just care that people think you're healthy. Very wily, Dr. Delancy. When you drop dead of a heart attack, no one will have a clue."

"There's a chance of that, but the odds are with me. Eating healthfully can help, but there's nothing like a good set of genes."

"My genes aren't so great, so I'd better keep an eye on my diet."

Erin's eyes slid up and down Katie's body, taking in her trim form. "Whatever you're doing is working just fine."

⟨⟩

By the time they returned to the lodge, both women were so tired it was comical. "I'd love to go sit in the whirlpool, but I can't summon the strength," Erin said as they rode the elevator to their floor.

"I'm going to take a hot bath and try not to drown."

"Good idea. If I drown, tell my mother I died a happy death."

"Damn it, now I'll worry about you." Katie slapped weakly at Erin's arm. "Let me know when you get out of the tub."

"I'll knock on our shared door."

"Don't forget," Katie said, leaning against her door, finding it hard even to pull her key out of her pocket. "I had fun today."

"Me, too. Best time I've had in a long time."

"Stick with me, kid," Katie said, trying to imitate some long-dead Hollywood type. "I'll show you the bright lights of the big city."

"If you don't kill me first."

"No guarantees," Katie said. She put her key in the door and stumbled inside, sticking her fingers out for a quick wave before she closed the door.

❧

About a half-hour later, Erin knocked on their joint door. "What's up?" Katie called.

Erin's reply was faint and muffled.

"What?" Katie asked. Again, she couldn't make out exactly what Erin was saying. She unlatched the lock and opened the door, getting a big, fluffy snowball right in the face.

"G'night," Erin said sweetly, giggling like a girl when she closed and locked her side of the door.

"Beware, Delancy. Your days are numbered!"

❧

When Erin got home late Sunday afternoon, she was bubbling with energy. So, she called her friend Kim and started to babble. "Hey, I just got home, and I had to tell you all about the weekend. It was really great, but I'm more confused than ever. You've gotta help me figure all of this out because—"

"Hey, hey! Slow down. Gosh, I haven't heard you this wired since you drank all of that coffee so you could stay up and study for that history final in high school."

"See?" Erin said, triumphantly. "That's the kind of thing that's wild for me. I could never keep up with her!"

"Erin, slow down and tell me what's going on in that head of yours."

"All right." She took a breath. "Katie and I spent the weekend at Killington."

"Ooh…the weekend. I thought you were just going for the day."

"So did I. I swear she didn't tell me we were staying over, but she made reservations for us."

"Cool. Did you sleep together?"

"No. She reserved two rooms, but she paid for mine."

"Interesting. That sounds like a date."

"That's what I thought, but maybe she's just polite. She really didn't tell me in advance."

"Hmm, that could be."

"But if it was a date, wouldn't she want to share a room?"

"No," Kim laughed. "That's kinda forward, Erin."

"Oh. I thought that meant something. What, I didn't know, but I'm grasping for straws."

"Well, what happened?"

"Not a lot. She's a great skier by the way, but we just skied and hung out. But she kept saying little things that were kinda suggestive."

"Suggestive to anyone or to you?"

"Hey!"

"Oh, come on. You know you aren't the wildest girl around. She might just be friendly. Give me an example."

"I can't think of any. I'm not good at remembering little things like that. I just get a feeling that I can't explain. And I got that feeling a bunch of times."

"Well, that sounds good if you want to strike something up with her. Do you?"

"Yeah, I think I do, but she's very different from me."

"Different can be good. You don't want someone too much like you. You need someone to stir you up."

"Oh, she'd do that. She's wild."

Excitedly, Kim said, "That's great. So, what's the problem?"

"I'm not sure," Erin said thoughtfully. "I get the impression she parties a lot. And I think she dates…a lot. I'm not sure she's the kind of woman who's ready to settle down."

"So? Maybe you could have a fling with her. That wouldn't hurt you a bit if you knew that's what you were in for."

"Right, but I'm looking for a girlfriend."

"I know you are, but you could also use some dating experience. You're practically a virgin."

"I am not," Erin said, offended. "Suzy and I had sex."

"Not very often."

"Darn it! I should never have told you any details. I'm keeping my big mouth shut from now on."

"Oh, don't whine. You have one of the smallest mouths in the state. You told me almost nothing. All I know is that you didn't do much and you didn't do it often. I still don't know why you two didn't have any spark."

"We…I…well, it's over now, so it doesn't matter. And I dated a lot in high school and college, so I'm not totally naive."

"Yeah, but you never really liked any of the guys you went out with. It doesn't count if you're not invested."

"You're right there, but I didn't know I was gay. I thought kissing was supposed to be boring."

"Did you kiss Katie?"

"No," she said, sounding dejected. "I don't know if she's interested in me in that way."

"There's one way to find out. Kiss her and see if she slaps you."

"Oh, you're a lot of help."

"I mean it. You can't play it so safe. You've gotta take a risk."

"Mmm, I don't like those kinds of risks. I'll just see if she makes a move. God knows she isn't shy."

"If she does, will you go for it?"

"I'm not sure, Kim. I don't want to get involved with Katie and find out she's got an alcohol problem or that she just wants to have sex."

"Yeah, that'd be awful," Kim said, sarcasm dripping. "Sex is such a waste of time."

"I don't think that," Erin said, raising her voice. "And I wouldn't mind just having sex if our parents weren't together. But they are, and I don't want to get hung up on her if she doesn't want to be in a relationship. It would be a big mess."

"You've got a point. Are you going to see her again?"

"Yeah," Erin said, sounding very pleased. "She's moving her St. Patrick's Day party to Friday so I can come."

"Well, well, well. That sounds promising."

"Yeah, I think it does. Maybe I'll have a better idea of what's on her mind after that."

"Good. I hope there's something there for you, Erin. If not, I'm going to set you up with someone."

Erin was quiet for a few seconds. "Who?" she finally asked, a definite challenge in her voice.

"There's…someone around here. There has to be."

"You're all talk, Kimbo. I'm the only lesbian you know."

"Not true, not true. It just so happens that I work with a genuine lesbian."

"You do? You've never mentioned that."

"I don't share things like that unless I know the person doesn't mind. But we were having a chat in the teacher's lounge the other day and Bett, that's my authentic lesbian's name, said that she was out to the administration. So I figure it can't hurt to tell you."

"Interesting. It would be pretty cool to have a girlfriend in state."

"Oh, you could do a lot worse. Bett's probably the best looking teacher in the high school. She's about your height, with dark hair and dark eyes. Actually, she looks a little bit like you. But hotter." Kim laughed, sounding so pleased with herself that Erin couldn't help but join her.

"If this doesn't work out with Katie, you'll have to fix us up."

"Don't think so. She wouldn't be interested."

"What?" Erin squawked. "She's that much hotter?"

"Well, frankly, yeah." Kim laughed again, but this time Erin didn't find it so funny. "But that's not why. She's got a partner, Suzan. They're rock-solid, buddy. But they might have friends who are more on your level."

"Great. Just great." She sounded a little grouchy, but her mood picked up and her voice filled with excitement when she said, "Oh, I forgot to tell you about what happened when Katie came by to pick me up yesterday. We were getting ready, and Dan came by…"

⁂

Gail didn't return home until late that evening. She looked tired, and when she went upstairs, she sighed softly as she kissed Erin, who was working at her computer. "Hi, there. Did you have a good time?"

Erin smiled up at her and said, "Excellent. The skiing wasn't great, but we didn't let that stop us. I'm going to need a crane to get out of bed in the morning, though."

"You?" Gail sat down on the bed. "That'll be the day."

"Wait and see. You'll hear me moaning from your room." Erin closed the document she was working on and turned to face her mother. "How was your weekend?"

"It was all right." She got up, looking relieved. As she walked past, she stroked Erin's head and said, "I'll see you in the morning, honey."

"Mom?"

Gail stopped and turned. "Yes?"

"It's only nine. Do you need to go to bed right now?"

Looking longingly at her bedroom, Gail said, "I'm tired, but I can stay up for a bit if you need me to."

"Well, it's not a need, but I'd like to talk for a while."

With a pained smile, Gail said, "What would you like to talk about?"

"I think you know." Erin made eye contact and wouldn't relinquish it. "Why did Dan look so upset yesterday?"

Surprisingly, Gail looked relieved. "I think he was upset about a few things. He was quite perturbed with me for not telling him you and Katie were becoming friends."

"Why didn't you?"

"I don't feel comfortable being in the middle. I don't want to tell you what Dan tells me, and I don't want to tell Dan what you tell me. I don't understand why you both want me to be the postman."

"Gosh, Mom, I don't think I've done that."

"Yes, you have," Gail said briskly. "I think you should talk to Dan if you want to know how he feels about things."

Stung, Erin leaned back in her chair. "Fine. I'll call him." She'd put his number into her cell phone, and she started to scroll through the numbers when her mother put a hand on her shoulder.

"I'm sorry I snapped at you. I really *am* tired."

Looking at her for a few moments, Erin said, "You act like you're angry with me. Did I do something?"

Gail nearly trudged back to the bed. She sat down heavily and said, "No, of course you didn't. I'm just being selfish."

"Selfish?"

"Yes." Gail sighed and brushed a few locks of hair from her eyes. "It would be much easier if you and Katie weren't striking up this…friendship."

"Why? What's up with those two? How does Dan really feel about her?"

Shaking her head even before the question was finished, Gail said, "I can't talk about things Dan tells me. It's not fair."

"Then how am I supposed to find out what's going on? Katie's view of him is very negative, Mom. I'm trying to keep an open mind, but she doesn't give him many props."

"Props?"

"She doesn't speak highly of his views on a lot of things. Specifically lesbianism."

Gail's color rose along with her voice. "Why is this such a big issue for everyone? Why can't sex be a private thing between two people?"

"It can be," Erin said slowly. "It *should* be. So, I'll go about my business, and you go about yours. No questions asked," she added pointedly.

Gail stood and started to walk, but she stopped for a moment and touched Erin's shoulder. "I think that's best, for a while at least."

"Fine. Sleep well."

"You, too, honey."

She left the room, and Erin closed the door behind her. She waited until she heard her mother close her own door before she dialed Katie's number. "Hi, Katie?"

"Hi. What's up?"

"I've got a question for you."

"No, I'm not moving my party again. I just got off the phone calling a boatload of people."

Erin chuckled. "No, that isn't my question. I'm looking forward to it. I just wondered if you'd talked to your dad."

"Ugh. Don't remind me. I'm in the process of drinking him out of my head."

"Do you really…" Erin stopped herself and changed the question. "Find that works?"

"Not with one beer, no. But I did talk to him…at length."

"Why was he upset with you yesterday?"

"Just as I thought. He thinks you're some sweet, innocent little thing and that I'm out to corrupt you."

"I could use a little corrupting," Erin admitted, "but I haven't gotten the impression you're a bad influence."

"Well, I don't know if you want to hear this, but he didn't know you were gay. That added a little fuel to the fire."

"Are you kidding?"

"No, Erin, I wouldn't kid about that. He was really angry with your mom because she hadn't told him. Didn't she tell you?"

"No, she didn't, and I gave her every opportunity. Darn it," she said, thumping the desk with her fist.

Katie sounded thoroughly amazed. "You really don't curse, do you?"

"No, I don't. It's just a habit, you know. My 'darn it' is the same as something more colorful."

"You must think I sound like a sailor with a nasty rash."

Erin laughed. "No, I don't. I don't think I'm morally superior or anything. I just never got into the habit. My choice."

Katie sounded unsure of herself, a rarity for her. "Are you sure? I could try to clean it up if it makes you uncomfortable."

"Katie, I've never noticed your language. It doesn't register with me."

"Well, fuck, I must not be on my game."

"That's better. I might start cursing when I bring this up with my mom."

"Ooh, don't tell her I ratted her out. My dad will be even angrier with me. He thinks I'm a child molester as it is."

"A child molester? Oh. Because of our age difference?"

"No," she said dryly. "Because I hang out by the grade school and drool. Of course it's because of our age difference. He acts like you're the Virgin Mary's purer sister."

"I'm not," she said, but then realized how silly that sounded.

"My dad just loves to assume I'm going to do the worst possible thing. He actually asked me if I pushed you to have sex."

"Are you serious? That's awful!"

"I know, but that's what he thinks lesbians are like. He makes me so fucking mad!"

"What did you tell him?"

"I told him what I do is none of his business. He can think what he wants. Next time you see him, you should start crying when he asks if you had fun when we went skiing." She laughed lustily, making Erin shake her head in dismay.

"I'm not going to get in the middle. Besides, I've got my hands full with my mother. What am I supposed to do? Just act like everything's normal?"

"I do that all of the time. I'm not going to take a call from my dad for a week or two. I don't invite trouble."

"That's gonna be hard to do at the breakfast table."

"That's why God intended people to go away to school and never ever return. He told me that during one of my trances."

Even though she was miffed, Erin couldn't help but smile. "You've cheered me up. Thanks."

"You're welcome. Now, rest up so you can party all night long on Friday."

"I've been on duty all night more times than I can count. I should be able to summon some of my stamina for a party."

"Have you ever been up all night just for fun?"

"No. Not even close."

"Girl, you've got a lot of living to do. I hate to admit my dad's right about anything, but you do need a little corrupting."

"I leave myself in your capable hands. See you Friday."

Chapter Eight

Gail had obviously decided that she didn't want Erin to be tempted to question her because she was gone by dawn. A nice, healthy breakfast was waiting along with a note that wished Erin a good day.

Erin crumpled the note and tossed it across the room, where it landed on the floor, missing the wastebasket by a foot. Boldly, she left it lying there and then put her healthy cereal back in the box. She gulped down a cup of coffee and left the dishes on the table, not feeling guilty in the least. Then she walked down the street and picked up a couple of donuts from the diner, wishing she could add a cup of coffee to go. Unfortunately, Madge believed Erin didn't drink coffee, and Erin would never let her know the truth—or drink Madge's horrible coffee.

⸻

When Erin got home that night, she played the message on their home answering machine:

"I'm going to help Dan with some planting this week, honey, so I might not get home much. Call me if you need anything. I have four or five different meals set up for you in the freezer. Just take a container out and put it in the microwave."

"They'll still be here when you get home," Erin said, putting her coat back on to walk back to the diner, where she'd become a nightly fixture.

⸻

Erin arranged to leave work by quarter past six on Thursday, knowing her mother had to be at the library until seven. Gail was the only paid employee, so she had to be there to lock up.

A high school student was at the desk, checking out a pile of books for an older man. "Hi, Sierra…Mr. Duncan," Erin said as she walked past.

"Hi, Doctor Delancy," the young woman said. "Your mom's in her office."

"Leaving work so early, Erin?" the man asked.

"Yes, I am." Erin gave him the smallest of smiles and kept moving. She found that she'd grown prickly over comments about her schedule, even if they were made in a joking manner.

Gail was on the phone when Erin entered the office. A look of near panic crossed her face, and Erin could feel her irritation start to rise. It was a business call, so Erin sat down and entertained herself by looking at a stack of magazines that had obviously just come in. She blinked in surprise when her mother passed her a note saying that she wasn't going to be going home for dinner if that's why Erin had stopped by. Erin read the note twice, crumpled it into a ball, and tossed it across the room, missing the wastebasket. She didn't make eye contact with her mother again, quietly stewing. Gail hung up and didn't say a word.

Erin reached behind her chair and closed the door. "Why didn't you tell Dan I'm gay?"

Unexpectedly, Gail took the offensive. "What have I done to merit such rude behavior? You don't even say hello to me?"

Immediately, Erin reverted into her "respectful child" mode. "I'm sorry. That was rude of me, but it feels like you're avoiding me, and I'm angry about that."

"Erin, I don't know when this started to happen, but you seem to think that I'm accountable to you."

Erin felt like she'd been slapped. "I don't think that!"

"I think you do. You come in here filled with attitude, demanding to know what I have or haven't talked to Dan about. Frankly, our conversations are none of your business."

Erin stood, on the verge of telling her mother off for the first time in her life. In the end, she wasn't able to break a life's worth of polite respect. "I apologize for bothering you. I hope you have a good evening. Goodnight." She practically sprinted from the library, ignoring the goodbye from the young woman at the front desk. As soon as she was outside, she bellowed a yell, her voice reverberating off the two-story brick buildings in the square. She kicked the granite step, still enough in control to make sure she didn't hurt her foot.

Even though it was cold, she was so hot she took off her coat, letting the brisk wind cool her skin. When she got home, she took a big pillow from the sofa and beat it against the wall until her muscles were tired. She stood there for a few moments, trying to decide how to vent. After throwing out all of the choices that most appealed to her, she decided to go for a run.

Sprinting through the dark, quiet streets of Essex made her feel worse, rather than better, but she kept going. Every landmark she passed was etched into her brain. She could identify the owner of each house and could relate a few details about each. It was all so crushingly familiar that she wanted to scream. Instead, she ran until her side hurt, and then she walked until the pain passed and ran again. By the time she returned home, she was sweaty and tired, and after two bowls of cereal, she went to bed, knowing the next day would bring some blessed relief from the monotony that was Essex.

⁂

When Erin was getting ready for work the next day, she saw the light on the answering machine blinking. She hit the button and heard the computerized voice announce a call from the night before. Her mother's voice said, "I'm so sorry for being rude to you. I don't know what's come over me, honey. Maybe menopause is hitting me hard right now, but even if that's it, I had no right to be so curt with you. Call me if you feel like talking. I love you."

She looked at the phone for a moment, but then decided against making the call. She knew it was a little small-minded, but she didn't want to hear another lame excuse for her mother's behavior or more declarations of her neutrality in the Tierney-Quinn feud.

⁂

Erin wasn't able to leave work until five o'clock that afternoon, but the traffic into Boston wasn't as bad as the traffic leaving. She reached Katie's neighborhood at around seven and spent a good fifteen minutes looking for parking, lucking out when, on her fifth trip around the block, someone left a legal space.

She was nervous and had been all day. She still wasn't sure what her or Katie's intentions were, but she had the kind of butterflies in her stomach that she'd experienced when she and Suzy had first gotten together.

It wasn't hard to find Katie's apartment. The row house wasn't exactly bulging with people, but it looked like a few more bodies could well make the walls bend. The entrance was up a small flight of stairs, decorated with strings of green lights, and there was an inflatable leprechaun swaying in the light breeze. The front door was open, and people stood in the doorway and on the stairs looking like they wanted to move in, but couldn't find space.

A knot of people stood on the sidewalk, smoking cigarettes. They each had a beer in hand, and several men invited Erin in—even though they didn't know she'd been invited. They were very enthusiastic when she indicated she would come inside, and she spent the few moments it took her to get in wondering about the guest list. She'd assumed that Katie's friends would be mostly gay, but the guys smoking looked and acted very straight. There were also several baby strollers next to the stairs, and some of the women near the door were in their fifties or better.

One of the women peered at Erin over the top of a pair of reading glasses. She was a merry-looking sort, and her wavy blonde hair reminded Erin of a more relaxed variety of Katie's. "Are you Erin?"

"Yes. Are you Katie's mom?"

"How could you tell?" She laughed throatily, her eyes crinkling up in a very attractive manner. Her accent was more thickly Bostonian than Katie's, and she smiled even broader than her daughter did. "I've been waiting for you. Katie put me on duty an hour ago. Now that you're here, I can get a refill." She held out an empty green plastic cup. "Do you drink beer, sweetie?"

"Uhm, sure. I can have one."

Laughing at the joke Erin didn't know she'd made, Katie's mom said, "One. That's funny." She looked at the woman standing next to her and said, "How many times have we heard that? Oh! Where are my manners? I'm Betty Quinn. This is my sister Eileen." She winked. "That was a movie a hundred years ago. Did ya see it?"

"No, I don't think I did," Erin said, having no idea what the woman was talking about.

"Well, Eileen usually likes to meet people first, so I can't use my line, but I beat her to it this time. Just my luck you don't know the movie."

Eileen stuck her hand out. "Katie's told us all about you. Are you keeping an eye on that bonehead father of hers?"

"Yes, I'm…well, my mom…" She fumbled, not quite knowing how to reply.

"Stupidest thing he ever did was divorce my sister," Eileen confided loudly, her volume reflecting her inebriation. "I hear he's dating your mother. Is she some youngster?" She squinted at Erin for a moment. "Are you out of high school?"

"Yes, I am. Uhm, she's fifty-four." Erin found it odd that they referred to them as dating. She couldn't imagine that Katie hadn't told her mother about the engagement, but she knew she wasn't going to be the one to break the news.

"Huh. Did ya hear that, Betty? He's dating someone your age. Go figure. There must not be any thirty-year-olds in that town desperate for a man."

"Katie told us all about her," Betty said, rolling her eyes. "Leave the girl alone. She doesn't wanna get involved with all our crap." Betty put her arm around Erin's shoulders, even though it was a stretch for the diminutive woman. "My sister's never forgiven Dan for leaving us, but to tell you the God's honest truth, we were better off without him. No more fights. Don't you hate to listen to people fight?"

"Yes, I guess I do."

"Her father's been dead for a long time," Eileen said, leaning her head in Erin's direction. "And her mother's been single all that time. The kid probably hasn't been around much fighting."

"That's true," Erin said, trying to join in the conversation about her. "And my parents didn't fight when my father was alive. They were both pretty calm people."

"Katie says you're not Irish," Betty said. "Why'd they name you Erin?"

Shrugging, Erin said, "I meant to ask my mom, but I keep forgetting. I think they just liked the name."

"Funny," Betty said. "It's like naming you France or Holland." She nodded thoughtfully. "Holland's a nice name for a girl, but France doesn't make it."

"There was France New-something," Eileen chimed in. "What was her name?"

"Nuyen. France Nuyen. South Pacific." Betty turned to Erin. "Wasn't she in South Pacific?"

"Gosh, I don't know…"

"Where's Katie? Katie?" Betty called out. "Was France Nuyen in South Pacific?"

Miraculously, Katie appeared through the crowd. "I've got the DVD in the TV thing, Mom. Go take a look." She nodded at Erin and grinned. "Come in out of the rain."

"It's not raining," Erin said, wondering if everyone was drunk or just odd.

"That's an expression. Don't take me so seriously."

"That's a good habit," Eileen said. "She's always kidding, Katie is. Is Danny gone?"

"Yeah. They snuck out the back a little while ago. The boys were getting cranky."

"Oh, your brother was here?"

"Do you know Danny?" Eileen asked.

"Yes," Erin said. "I met him at Dan's house."

"Like peas in a pod, those two. I guess everyone's going up to New Hampshire now, huh? They'll need a special highway just for the crowds."

Katie put her arm around her aunt and kissed the top of her head, which was, conveniently, right at the level of Katie's mouth. "There's nothing at the farm but twigs in bare dirt, Aunt Eileen. You haven't missed a thing."

"I wouldn't go up to that place for love nor money," the woman said, looking like she could go on with her harangue for quite some time.

"Come on, you." Katie grasped Erin's hand and pulled her into the house, forcing Erin to bump into several people on her way. Erin had never been in a row house, and she was surprised at how small the interior was. They walked through a parlor, past a half-bath, and into the kitchen, the only three rooms on the floor.

They wound up near a keg of beer that had been set in a nook in the surprisingly spacious, modern kitchen. "Feel free to ignore my family. They might have had a little too much to drink." She grinned at Erin, using her best bad-little-girl look. "I'll show you how to have fun and not look like a Mormon."

"A Mormon?" Erin felt like she was lagging behind in a conversation that was covering too many topics simultaneously.

"This is the secret to near-sobriety," Katie said. "I take a cup." She held one up. "And fill it with maybe an inch of beer." She did just that. "Then I take a big sip. Mmm, there's nothing better than the first sip of a cold beer." She wiped the foam from her lips. "Then I carry the cup around with me until I want another sip. I come back in here, throw the dregs away, and pour another inch. I can go the whole night and not have more than one or two beers, but it looks like I'm keeping up with everyone, so no one tries to force more on me." She grinned, her eyes dancing. "Smart, huh?"

"Yeah. Very smart if people try to make you drink more." Her confusion showed. "Does that happen?"

"All the time. Don't you go to parties?"

"Yeah, mostly med school parties, though. Med students can be a pretty tame bunch."

"Tame we ain't. You'd better protect yourself."

"Okay. Mind if I copy you?"

"No, be my guest. I've gotta warn you about my friends. Every straight single guy and some of the women will hit on you. Don't be afraid to be rude if you have to be. Some of them may have been over-served." She wrinkled her nose when she grinned, looking so much like her mother it was amazing.

"Boy, you don't have to guess how you'll look when you're a little older, do you?"

"Nope. Luckily, everyone says my mom's adorable, so I'm not worried."

"She is adorable. That's quite an act she and her sister have."

"Oh, yes. They're always looking for an audience. They've got another sister in Brookline. When the three of them are together, it's like the Marx Brothers. Just don't let them get you involved in their movie trivia. You'll never get away from them."

"I'm not much help," Erin admitted. "I don't know much about movies. I can't remember half of the ones I've seen in the last year, much less older ones."

"Just play along and agree with them. All they want is to think they're right."

Erin smiled, delighted to have Katie seem so interested in her acclimating with the family. "That's all most people want, isn't it?"

"Maybe so. I'll have to think on that. For now, let me introduce you around." She guided Erin by the elbow and started to make the rounds. After they spoke to a few people in the parlor, Katie led her to the staircase that took up a good portion of the first floor. They ascended the stairs to a beautiful double-parlor with a big bow window that looked over the tree-lined street.

"This is lovely," Erin said, stunned at the care that Katie had put into decorating her home. The place was fairly spare, but every piece looked like it had been carefully chosen. The furniture wasn't exactly modern, but it was clean and contemporary and looked wonderful against the wooden floors. "How long have you lived here?"

"Mmm…" Katie flapped her lips in thought. "Seven years, I guess. I really lucked out."

"How's that?"

"Well…" she said, leaning in close so that Erin could hear her over the noise. "A buddy of mine told me the developer of this place was going belly-up."

"Developer? The building looks really old."

"It is. It was built in 1883, but it was a rat hole when the developer bought it. He spent a ton fixing the plumbing, electrical, and heating systems, but he was overextended and couldn't get the loans he needed to do the interiors the way he wanted to. So, a couple of friends and I bought it from him at a steal." She wiggled her eyebrows, showing her pleasure in her good fortune. "I kept the best apartment, and we sold the others. I love it here."

"I can see why. I've never been in one of these houses, but I've seen them on TV."

"Don't even think of buying one now." Katie rolled her eyes and let her head bobble about. "They're crazy expensive. We got in during a pretty good dip in the market. Timing is everything in real estate."

"I think that's true in all parts of life."

They'd been chatting with their heads close together, and Katie pulled away and gave Erin a look that Erin had seen before, but had never been able to figure out just what it meant. "I think you're right. Being in the right space at the right time is half of the game."

⁂

"You weren't kidding when you said you had friends from all over," Erin said when they paused for another beer-sip stop.

"I like different kinds of people, and once I meet someone I like, I do my best to hold on to them."

"I couldn't believe there's someone here who went to kindergarten with you. I think that's amazing."

"How far back do you go with your oldest friend?"

Erin froze for a second and then started to laugh. "Kindergarten. But it's different in a small town. I've known almost everyone in Essex forever."

"Every town's the same in some ways. It's hard to hold on to friends, but in my view, it's well worth it."

"I like your view," Erin said. "Hey, if you have things to do, you can cut me loose. I can mingle. I'm not shy."

Katie gave her the little grin that Erin was growing to love. Her eyes closed a little bit, and she looked like she knew a very interesting secret. "No, I think I'll keep close tabs on you. Are you ready to meet some of my exes?"

"Sure. I've always admired women who could maintain good relations with ex-lovers."

"I didn't say they all liked me. The beer *is* free, you know."

Erin met so many women that she was certain Katie couldn't have been in love with each of them. However, she was a little afraid to ask for details, and Katie didn't provide many. She just introduced Erin, telling people that she lived in Essex and that she was a physician. The people who knew Dan asked how she thought he was doing in town, and she gave about the same answer to all of them. They walked near Betty and Eileen, and Eileen said, "I bet Erin knows. Erin, was Julie Christie or Faye Dunaway in *Doctor Zhivago*?"

Erin couldn't guess why Eileen thought she'd know that, and as she was trying to recall if she'd even seen it, Katie leaned close and said, "I've got to make a pit stop. Just try to agree with Eileen. It's much easier."

Erin nodded and tried to think of a way to agree when she didn't know either of the actresses Eileen was talking about. "Describe Julie…" she trailed off, already forgetting the woman's last name.

"You know," Eileen said. "*Shampoo, McCabe and Mrs. Miller, Bullitt, Bonnie and Clyde*. Real tall, statuesque blonde."

"You know her from *Doctor Zhivago*," Betty said. "And *Shampoo*. But she wasn't in *Bonnie and Clyde* or *McCabe and Mrs. Miller*. That was Faye Dunaway."

"Right," Erin said, trying to look like she was thinking. "I'm not sure, but I think she might have been in *Bonnie and Clyde*."

"Ha! Ha!" Eileen did a little jig. "I told you she was in *Bonnie and Clyde*! Time for a refill!" She reached up and pinched Erin's cheeks. "I knew I liked you."

Erin blinked in surprise, watching Eileen weave through the guests, stopping to chat with almost everyone. "She's a pip, isn't she?" Betty asked.

"Sure," Erin said, not exactly sure if being a pip was a compliment. "I haven't been to Katie's house before. It's awfully nice."

"Yeah, it's really nice. The kid's in the chips. This place is lots nicer than where I live…where Katie grew up."

"Really?" Erin's expression was full of concern.

"Yeah. We didn't have two nickels to rub together when we got married. We probably could have afforded to move when the kids were older, but then we got divorced. And no matter what anyone tells you, nobody makes out during a divorce. I had to go to work for the first time in my adult life."

With a sympathetic nod, Erin said, "My mom had to go to work after having been a homemaker. It was really tough for her. I can imagine it was awful to have your family broken apart and have to change careers."

"Damned straight," Betty said, tipping her cup in Erin's direction. "Being a good mom and taking care of the house is a career. Most people don't believe that. Dan didn't," she added bitterly.

"Oh, I do. I was old enough to be able to share responsibilities with my mom, but it took a lot out of her."

Betty touched Erin's arm and looked into her eyes. "Katie told me about your dad and your brother, honey. I'm really sorry you had to go through that."

"Thank you. It was…very hard."

"And don't listen to Eileen. Dan's not so horrible. Your mother could do worse."

With a partially relieved smile, Erin said, "That's very nice of you to say. I don't know Dan well, but my mother seems…very fond of him."

"We were just too young and too stupid to get married. You know how it is. You have a couple of kids, and before too long, you don't have any idea why you're together."

"I think my mom's a pretty good judge of character, but I've got to admit I'm a little worried. Katie doesn't seem to think her dad's a great catch."

"Oh, she's so blind about some things." Betty laughed hard, with the same expression Katie often had when she found something particularly funny. "She's so much like him it's crazy."

"Really?" Stunned, Erin said, "But she and Eileen say Danny's just like him."

"No, no, Danny's like me. Katie's like her dad. And if you ask me, the main reason those two don't get along is because he's jealous of her."

"Jealous? Of what?"

"Honey, he didn't want to be a cop. He wanted to go to law school. But you know how babies can turn up when you don't expect them…"

"Oh." Erin nodded. "And he had to give up on his plans?"

"Yeah. He just had two years of junior college finished. He was going to transfer to BU or BC, depending on what kind of financial aid he could get. But with Katie on the way, we decided to get married. It was probably stupid, but that's what you did back then."

"I'm sure it was for the best," Erin said, even though she wasn't sure of that at all.

"Eh, maybe. Who the hell knows? He joined the force, just like his father and his older brother." She shook her head. "His younger brother got to go to law school, and it just killed Dan."

"So, you really think Katie's like Dan? I don't see it."

"They're both hardheaded, loyal to a fault, smart as a whip, and the women love them."

Erin smiled. "Well, all of the women in Essex talked about Dan like he was…I can't even think of anyone to compare him with."

"That must be a very small town," Betty said, a sardonic smile on her expressive face.

❦

A little after one o'clock in the morning, Katie put her feet up on an overstuffed footstool and slowly kicked off her loafers, showing bright green socks with golden shamrocks decorating them. "Whew! I'm beat. How about you?"

"Yeah," Erin agreed, laughing softly as she spied Katie's socks. She sank into the cushy leather sofa and let her head rest on the back. "I started at six a.m."

"Was it worth it? Did you have fun?"

"A ton," she said, lifting her head and grinning happily. "I really liked your friends, and your mom and your aunt are great."

"Good." Katie slapped her hands together. "I asked around, and you got a pass from everyone, including the family."

"A pass? What's a pass?"

"Everyone likes you. That's good."

"Uhm, yeah, that *is* good," Erin said, looking a little puzzled. "Well, you're a great host. I appreciated how you introduced me to everyone."

Katie cocked her head. "I'm not such a great host. I don't do that for everyone. Just for the women I'm dating."

Stunned, Erin's eyes opened wide despite her fatigue. "We're dating?"

"Hell, yes, we're dating. What do you think we're doing?"

"Well, I, uhm, thought you might just want to be friends."

"Did you see how many people passed through here tonight? Does it look like I need more friends?"

"I guess not," Erin admitted, "but you haven't made it clear that we're dating."

Nearly squinting, Katie studied Erin for a few moments. "I know you're bright, but you're the slowest bright woman I've ever met."

"Hey!" Indignantly, Erin said, "You weren't clear. You didn't even try to kiss me."

Lackadaisically, Katie shrugged her shoulders, smiling cheekily. "I have a timetable."

"Weird." Erin, now wide awake, sat on the edge of the sofa, looking as confused as she felt. "Uhm, was Killington a date?"

"Yes," Katie said, her voice low and sexy. "A very good date. I got to see how much fun you could be. You boosted your score way up on that one. Way, way up."

"The night we went to dinner?"

"Yep. It wasn't a planned date, you know. I just saw you walking down the street, and I had a real need to spend some time with you."

Erin beamed. "Really?"

"Yeah. I'd given up on you by then, but you looked so cute walking down the street I couldn't help myself."

"What?"

Ignoring her outraged squawk, Katie said, "You did well there, too. You're very smooth and gracious in public. You know how to order, you have good manners, and you're polite to the waitstaff. Two thumbs up."

"I'm glad I did well."

Her befuddlement was comic, but Katie didn't laugh. She just smiled, looking very happy. "I couldn't stop looking at you when we were outside after dinner. You looked fantastic in that hat and coat. Your cheeks were so pink, and your hair looked so dark and full." She fanned herself dramatically. "I was a stuttering idiot, and I expected you to tell me to snap out of it."

"I had no idea. How about your dad's party?"

"No, don't be silly. I was going to bring a date, remember?"

"Uhm, yeah, but when I asked you if you were dating someone, you denied it. It's hard to get a straight story out of you."

Katie closed her eyes halfway and chomped her teeth together noisily. "I'm a lawyer. I've been trained to blow smoke."

"Do you mind talking about why you stopped dating her?"

"Oh, it was a sad case." She gave Erin a pitiful look. "She had a lot going for her. She was doing really well in a lot of areas, but she flunked the friends test. Barely got 50 percent."

"You honestly let your friends rank your dates?"

"Sure. They're a big part of my life. And they aren't blinded by…other things that can muddle my thinking. And she had a couple of…" She put her hands in front of her and acted like she was hefting a heavy object in each. "Things that muddled me thoroughly."

"So, your friends didn't like this woman, and you stopped seeing her." Erin's expression showed just how odd she found this.

"No, I'm not that rash. Even though she flunked the friends test, I decided to go to the next level and take her to meet the parents. That's why I was going to take her to Essex."

"To meet your dad, whose opinion you don't respect."

"Don't try to figure out the game. You're years behind."

"Okay…so, you didn't take her to Essex."

"No, my dad put the hammer down on that. So, I took her to dinner over at my brother's place. That's when she struck out. Didn't even take the bat off her shoulder." She imitated a baseball player watching strikes go by.

"What happened?"

"She didn't like the boys. She didn't say she didn't like them, but she didn't talk to them or play with them or show any interest whatsoever. That's a big no-no because I spend a lot of time with them. And she admitted she didn't plan on having kids. She was a veteran, and I figured it was too late to change her mind on that, so I had to cut her loose." She shook her head sadly. "It was a damned shame. She had potential, but she couldn't make it in the big show."

"But I'm still on the roster, huh?" Erin asked, grinning. "Am I a veteran?"

"You've gotta be kidding! You're a raw rookie, but at this rate, you're set to make the starting lineup. You've got heart, kid."

Erin got up and sat on the footstool, moving Katie's feet into her lap. "So, what's next? How can I impress the manager?"

"Hey, I can't do everything for you. You've gotta have a little initiative. I need a playmaker on my team." Grinning wickedly, Erin put her hands under Katie's thighs and pulled her onto her lap, surprising Katie thoroughly. "Damn! You're strong." They were face-to-face and as close as they'd ever been.

"Isn't this funny?" Erin asked softly, her eyes scanning Katie's face and then settling on her eyes.

"What's funny?" Katie tilted her head, some of her red-blonde curls slipping across her face. Erin reached up with gentle fingers and tucked them behind her ear.

"Once you admit you're interested in someone, the physical barriers start to fall. I find that fascinating." With a look of wonder on her face, she delicately traced along Katie's features, smoothing her pale eyebrows, following the straight line of her nose, over her subtle cheekbones, along her defined jaw line. "I would never have touched you this way before this moment, but now   now I feel like I have to…" She leaned over and kissed Katie's forehead. "Kiss your beautiful face." Erin slipped her hands along smooth cheeks that were beginning to color. She held Katie's face in her hands, and their eyes met for several heartbeats. "Remember this," Erin whispered. Their lips met and paused just a second before softening to relish their first intimate touch. Erin deepened the kiss, feeling the supple softness of Katie's warm mouth.

Suddenly, Katie's arms were around her, and their bodies pressed together firmly. "Mmm," Erin sighed. "You have the most beautiful mouth I've ever kissed."

Katie smiled through another gentle, deliciously soft kiss. "Your mouth is absolutely lovely." She put her finger on Erin's lips and traced all around her mouth. "Your kiss is so gentle and sweet. I knew it would be like that. I just knew it."

"You've been thinking about kissing me?" Erin was clearly charmed.

"Uh-huh. I've thought about it a lot. I like you a lot."

"I like you, too." They leaned their heads together, their breathing joined. "Am I going home?"

"No, you're staying here." Katie's breath was warm, and it caressed Erin's face. "I need to know you better."

"Okay." Sighing heavily, Erin asked, "Do we sleep together?"

"No, not yet."

"No?" Erin tilted her chin and kissed Katie once again, keeping her touch light and tender. "Too soon?"

"Mmm-hmm." It felt like they were in a little cocoon. All that existed was the sound of their breathing and their fascination with the sensation of holding each other. Katie turned her head and snuggled her face into Erin's neck. They stayed just like that for a long time, feeling each other's heartbeats slowly become syncopated.

"I'm so tired, but this feels wonderful. I could stay like this all night."

"Me, too." Katie shifted a little, and Erin nearly grew dizzy just from feeling her body press against hers in a new, glorious way. "Can we lie down and kiss for a while? I want to get used to your body."

Erin's deep chuckle made both of them vibrate. "I'd love to have you get used to my body."

Katie lifted her head and placed a sweet kiss on Erin's lips. "Come on," she said. "Follow me." She disentangled herself from Erin's lap and held a hand out for her. Erin took it, and Katie pulled her to her feet. They stood in place and held each other for a few minutes, neither in a hurry to progress. Then Katie dropped her arms and took Erin's hand again, leading her upstairs to a bedroom. She lit large candles on either side of the double bed and then sat down, pulling Erin down next to her. "Is this okay?"

"Yeah," Erin said, her voice a little rough. "This is very, very good." Erin put her arms around Katie and pulled her down with her until they were both lying down. "So many sensations," she said. "All of them good."

Katie burrowed into her, touching from head to toe. She ran her hand along Erin's body. "You're strong," she said when she felt along her shoulder and upper arm. "And soft." Her hand brushed the side of Erin's breast and traveled down to her hip. "Womanly. Soft and feminine."

Erin's fingers tangled in Katie's fine hair. "You're so pretty," she whispered. "Such soft, beautiful hair. Like an angel's."

"I like yours," Katie said, threading her fingers into Erin's. "Thick and silky. I could get lost in it."

"This is so nice. So relaxing. I feel good with you."

Katie rolled onto her side and covered Erin with an arm and a leg, cuddling up tightly against her. Their breasts pressed firmly together, bellies softly compressed, hips touching hips. "Oh, you're nice to snuggle with."

Erin tucked her arm around Katie's back and stroked her hair with her hand. "Perfect."

Neither spoke for a few minutes, each concentrating on the sound and feel of the other's heartbeat. "Will you sleep with me?" Katie's soft voice asked.

"Sleep?" Erin waited a beat. "Just sleep?"

"Yeah." Katie rose up and rested on one elbow. "No good?"

"I kinda…think that might be a little too…" Erin struggled to find the right word. "Hard for me."

"Too intimate?"

"No, I love being intimate, but I like to keep going. You know," she said, shifting her eyes to the bed.

"Oh." Katie cupped her cheek and looked into Erin's eyes. "I'm not ready for that. I'm surprised you are. Shocked, actually."

Grinning, Erin said, "I was ready the night we had dinner together."

A surprised, yet pleased smile settled onto Katie's face. "Nice. That's nice to know. You could have fooled me, but that's nice to know." She placed another gentle kiss on Erin's cheek. "I'm very attracted to you, but I'm not ready to have sex. We don't know each other well enough."

"That's okay. Why don't we just sleep? That can be a first step."

"No cuddling?" Katie asked, looking at her with big blue eyes.

"You have your limits. I have mine."

That earned Erin a bright, wide smile. "I like a woman with limits."

Chapter Nine

*E*rin slowly opened her eyes, trying to figure out why things didn't seem normal. Her eyes snapped open when she saw an oddly placed window and unfamiliar furnishings. A soft voice caught her attention, and she saw Katie gazing at her from a foot away. "You're a very beautiful woman, Erin Delancy."

A big yawn preceded a shy smile. "Am I?"

"Like you don't know it." Katie put her hand on Erin's cheek and stroked it tenderly. "Everybody but my mom was checking you out last night. That's the real reason I was on you like a dog on a bone. I didn't want anyone to claim you."

"Even your aunt?" Erin teased, making her eyes wide with feigned alarm.

"I've always had my suspicions about her. She's never been married, you know."

Katie's expression was completely serious, but Erin had learned that didn't necessarily mean that her message was. "Well, your aunt is cute, but you're cuter. And I'm only interested in a woman's beauty. I'm extremely shallow, you know."

"Cool! Me, too. We should get along great."

"I think we're getting along pretty well. I really enjoyed knocking down some barriers last night." She put her hand on Katie's waist and gave her a scratch. "I'm ready to knock more down whenever you're ready."

"Ooh, you are *quite* forward once you get started. Maybe you're not the shy little country girl I have you pegged as."

"I'm not very shy. I can be quiet, and I don't usually take the lead, but I'm not shy. I'm pretty confident when I'm in my element."

"Interesting. I'll have to think about that."

Erin slid her hand into Katie's hair and tried to slip her fingers along its length, but she didn't get far before she was locked in a mass of tangles. "Uh-oh. I'm stuck."

Katie disentangled her, saying, "You're going to have to learn the rules for curly hair. You have to start at the ends to get through it if I've slept on it."

Scooting over to be able to get a better angle, Erin took a hank of curls and methodically separated them. Her eyes were intently focused, and there was a little tension between her brows.

"I like a woman who has patience. You're very good at that."

"Well, I made the mess." She finished and patted the bottom of the set of curls. "It doesn't bounce into little spirals like it normally does."

"You've ruined the magic." Katie took her hand and kissed it. "The curls set when it's wet. If you screw around with them once they're dry, God knows what will happen."

"I love them," Erin said, pulling on a tightly coiled group and letting them spring back. "Your hair is fascinating. Beautiful and fascinating."

"Thanks. I've had my ups and downs with it, but I like it now."

Scooting closer still, Erin put her hand on Katie's hip and pulled her towards her body. "I like you." She leaned in and started to kiss Katie's face, slowly lavishing her fair skin with sensual affection. "Your skin is so beautiful."

Katie sighed and tossed both an arm and a leg over Erin's body. "Cuddle me. I was lonely not being able to touch you all night."

"Oh…" Erin held her close, gently kissing her face and hair. "Poor thing."

Katie luxuriated under Erin's touch for a while, then pulled back and stared at her with a perplexed gaze. "I can't tell you how surprised I am by how physical you are. I can *feel* the sexual energy rolling off you."

"Is that bad? I thought you wanted me to be honest. You're always telling me to stand up for myself and say what I want."

Katie smoothed the little wrinkle that had formed on Erin's forehead. "I do want that. That's what's best for you." She kissed her lips, stroking her back gently when she did. "You say what you want, and I do the same." She touched Erin's face, looking into her eyes. "I'm not hurting your confidence, am I?"

"No, I don't think so. I can tell you're just not ready. It'd be different if I thought you'd never be ready."

"Then we're making progress. And you shouldn't worry about me never being ready. We just have to let the process work."

"There's a process?"

"Of course. I have an evaluation process for almost everything that's important."

"What exactly am I being evaluated for?"

Katie gave her a pinch, rather like an elderly aunt would bestow. "I'm looking for the first, and hopefully the last, Mrs. Kathleen Rose Quinn."

Erin blinked slowly and repeatedly. "You're looking for a wife?"

"Yes. I'm only interested in marriage. My days of dating for kicks are over."

Erin rolled onto her side and brushed her hair over her shoulder. "I'm surprised at that. How do you know that's what *I* want?"

"You already told me so." She tapped the tip of Erin's nose with each word. "You said you were looking for a partner. So, I knew you were onboard from the start."

"Gosh, I should watch my words. Who knows what else I've signed up for?"

With a flash of concern, Katie gently stroked Erin's cheek and moved closer to her. She gazed into her eyes for a few moments, searching them carefully. "I'm not wrong, am I?"

Grinning widely, Erin said, "No, you're not wrong at all, but I think 'Doctor and Mrs. Erin Delancy' has more cache."

"Ooh, big word. A doctor with a big vocabulary. No wonder my mom liked you. How about 'Doctor and Mrs. Quinn-Delancy, J.D.'?"

"Don't think I didn't notice that Quinn comes first, even though Delancy is higher up in the alphabet." Erin tugged on Katie's nose and then slid over and kissed her forehead. "Other than worrying about our monogrammed towels, what's on your agenda? I know you have one."

"Sure do, and you're more than halfway home. You've done well on the absolute requirements." She started to tick them off on her fingers. "You're very down-to-earth. You're a regular girl—no 'I'm a cool doctor who went to an Ivy League med school' attitude."

"How do you know where I went to med school?"

"Diploma. Office." She shook her head. "I'm paying attention, Erin. This is my life we're talking about."

"Right. I keep forgetting we're talking about *you* here."

"Maybe *us*. Stay in line, and you might hit the big time. Now, where was I?" She held up her hand and stuck her index finger up. "Next item, you're bright and clever. Three, you're kind, and you care about people. Four, you're not obsessed with money and things."

"How do you know that? I might have millions in offshore bank accounts."

"I've seen your house and your room and your car. You're moderate. You don't wear an expensive watch, and you don't spend a lot on clothes—even though you dress very nicely. I think you're a Gap, Banana Republic, and J. Crew girl."

"Only end-of-season sales at J. Crew, but add some L.L. Bean in there, and you've got me."

"See? I know a lot about you."

"You clearly do. And most of what you know you figured out for yourself."

"That's the only way to trust it," she said seriously. "I'm looking for a wife. This is important."

"I can see that. Is there anything else on your 'must have' list?"

"Yeah. You have a good sense of humor, and you're playful—once you open up a little bit. I was very, very worried about that."

"Whew!" Erin wiped her forehead. "I'm glad we went skiing."

"That's *why* we went skiing. I had no interest in going up there to ski on ice and dirt. But you said you loved it, and I thought it was important to go somewhere you loved. That seemed like the only way to put you in your comfort zone."

"You're serious?" Erin looked stunned.

"Completely. I wouldn't have asked you out again if you'd been too reserved. I need someone who'll play with me. That's why I didn't kiss you until I'd had time to think things over and decide that we could really work. I didn't even want to put a toe into the water until I was confident about you."

"Wow. I'm really amazed. There was this whole process going on that I completely missed."

Smiling, Katie said, "I'm glad you missed it because I was sure you weren't for me that day we went to my dad's house. I was *sure*," she said, emphasizing the word.

"Gosh, I almost took myself out of the lineup before I knew I was in the game!"

"You're always being judged by someone. Fact of life."

"That's why my mother told me never to curse," Erin said, smiling sweetly.

"Well, you were out of the game after that fiasco. You acted like you were a ten-year-old snooping in the neighbor's house."

"How did I climb out of the hole?"

Smiling, Katie said, "I'm not sure. I hate to admit it, but it's partly because you're so damned pretty." She pinched Erin's cheek again. "And you're such a nice person. Those are hard to find. I'm really glad our parents being together has allowed us to see each other a few extra times, or I would have put you on the reject pile a long time ago."

"Darn, you're awfully honest!"

"Yeah, I am." She looked at Erin for a few moments, utterly serious. "I'm not playing around. I'm looking for a spouse, and I want to have kids. I don't want to waste months with someone who isn't after the same thing."

Erin nodded, her brow creased in thought. "I understand. I'm not in a hurry, obviously, but I want the same thing you want."

"Excellent." She kissed Erin and then continued with her list. "You like kids, which is a must. Now, if you don't want to have them, we've got problems. But I think you do."

"I do. Adoption would be fine, but I want to raise some kids."

"I'm not picky about how I get them, but I'd *like* three," Katie said. "I'm flexible about the number."

"Clearly."

"Sarcasm is allowed. So, you're good on all of the required items I can check at this point. We're on to the options page."

"There are other required items?"

With a wickedly sexy grin, Katie reached behind Erin and grabbed a handful of her ass, giving it a firm squeeze. "What do you think? I'm not going to marry someone who can't rock me."

"Oh, great, not too much pressure."

"You have time to work on it if that's a problem."

"I don't think it's a problem, but I suppose we'll see, eh?"

"We will. We have to spend time together and talk. It's highly unlikely, but you might not want to go forward with *me*, you know."

"Highly unlikely," Erin agreed, grinning.

"I'm very serious about this. Very serious."

Erin nodded somberly. "I can see that."

"About five years ago, I decided I was ready to settle down. Since then, I've only dated women who I thought I could be interested in as a partner."

"You told me last night that you were going to introduce me to your ex-lovers. All of those women we talked to weren't on that list, were they?"

"Of being an ex-lover?"

Erin nodded.

"No, no. And a lot of them didn't know they were in the running." She tapped Erin on the nose again. "Kinda like you. Some people are really slow."

"Is someone an ex-lover if you went out with her once or twice?"

"Someone I dated for a short time is an *x*, as in crossed off the list. But as I said, some of them didn't know we were dating."

Erin's amazement was visible. "I'm sure I've never met anybody who has a process like this. You might be unique in the entire world."

"No way. There are lots of nerds in the world. One of them has to be as crazy as I am." She moved still closer and put her arm around Erin's waist. "You must have a list, too. Tell me about it."

Looking a little embarrassed, Erin said, "I hope this doesn't sound awful, but you're the first woman I've even been mildly interested in since Suzy and I broke up. I've spent the last year figuring out how to run my practice and trying to fit in, which sounds kind of funny for a woman who grew up in the town."

"Not to me. I couldn't move back to South Boston." She shook her head, looking like she was trying to dislodge some bad memories. "I don't know how you do it. And I hope that 'mildly interested' comment wasn't intentional."

"Of course not. I'm just trying to be honest about my frame of mind. I wasn't looking for a girlfriend, but not because I didn't want one. I just thought it wasn't possible right now."

"When did you first realize you were interested in me?"

"Pretty soon. Sooner than I felt comfortable with. It was really odd for me to be attracted to someone I was dealing with professionally."

"You liked me right away? Really?" she asked, looking very pleased.

"Yeah, I did, but I decided I couldn't make the first move since I'd seen you professionally."

"Damn, you are the most passive doctor I've met in my entire life! I was giving you so many clues that it was embarrassing, but you didn't seem to pick up on them. I kept thinking you were a possible, but then you'd act like you had no interest in me. The worst was the day I offered to come up and see you for a weekend, and you told me not to bother just for you and Madge. That was cruel!"

Erin covered her face with her hands. "I'm so sorry, but you hurt my feelings when you pointedly didn't ask me to your football party. I was sure you didn't like me."

"I *didn't* when you seemed so passive about your life. It worried me that you were the type to let things happen rather than take charge."

"Once I know something's possible, I focus on it, and I work hard until I get it. But I have to admit that I don't look for challenges. If you hadn't told me we were dating, I wouldn't have ever told you I was interested in you romantically. I'm cautious."

Her expression softening, Katie moved back toward Erin. She put her arm around her and pulled her close. "It's okay. Don't look so anxious. This is why we're dating. We have to find out if we click."

"I want to click," Erin murmured into the fabric of Katie's blouse. "I really like you, and I think we could be good together. You're just the kind of woman that I didn't know I wanted."

Katie shook her roughly. "I like honesty, but this is too much!"

Erin rolled onto her back, laughing softly. "I just mean that I didn't know I needed someone feisty. I thought I'd hook up with someone kind of like me: quiet, reserved, reflective. Content to spend the day fishing in a pond and then reading a good book."

"Don't take this the wrong way, but I'd rather poke out my eyes with a rusty ice pick than fish and read. I do read, of course. That's what I do when there's nothing fun to do."

"That's what I mean," Erin said excitedly. "I've let my passive side take over, but I didn't realize that until I met you. I had such a good time last night. I loved meeting all of your friends and your family. It reminded me of being in college. I really, really miss being social, but I haven't let myself think about that."

"You don't even think about it?" Katie asked tenderly, looking into Erin's eyes.

"No, I don't do that." She said this very matter-of-factly, as though her style was the common one.

"Uhm, don't take offense, but that's pretty odd."

Surprised, Erin looked at Katie, her head cocked in question.

"Most people want things they can't have and think about things that aren't likely. Damn, if I only flirted with women who I knew were gay, I'd…well, I'd bat my eyes a lot less often. It amazes me that you just shut down on the idea of being social. That's a damned big thing to let go of."

"Yeah," she said, seeming like she was thinking about it for the first time. "Every time I've been with you, I feel like a new person. I feel younger and happier and more alive. I guess it didn't dawn on me that I missed that me."

"Why do you think you let that all go?"

"Mmm, medical school, my residency, and then starting my practice. I've worked really hard since I got out of college. I haven't had time to have fun."

"There's always time for that," Katie said. She was gazing into Erin's eyes, and her voice was soft and low. "You can't wait for someone to give you permission to have fun. What's life for if not to be happy?"

"I've…maybe I've got my priorities mixed up."

"Maybe you do. It's something to think about at least." Katie started to sit up. "Are you ready to get up?"

"It feels like we never went to bed. We're fully clothed and didn't get under the covers."

"Hey, what happened to the candles? I thought they'd burn down."

"I blew them out as soon as you fell asleep," Erin admitted. "I couldn't relax until I did."

Katie grabbed two handfuls of her hair. "Arghhh!"

"What would you rather have? The house burn down or me being a little cautious?"

Sliding to the floor, Katie said, "I'll get back to you on that."

⟨⟨⟨⟩⟩⟩

Erin followed Katie to her bedroom, stopping in the doorway to marvel at the room laid out before her eyes. "Gosh, you have a great house. It was hard to tell last night, since your place was so jammed full of people, but it's really, really nice. This room is so calming. I love this window." Erin went to the bow window that looked onto the street. "This is fantastic."

"Thanks. I love it, too. My sister-in-law helped me decorate since I don't know much about the whole thing."

"The light green color is perfect for a bedroom. This is one of my favorite colors."

"I think this was called…oh, who knows? I like it, too. That's all that matters." Katie went into her bathroom and produced a new toothbrush. "There's some face soap, a comb, brush, and clean towels in the guest bath. Go take care of your morning business, and I'll find something for you to wear." Erin took the brush and went back down the hall.

When she returned, Katie's hair was neat, and she was looking through a large dresser. "I'm trying to find something you can wear." She looked Erin over carefully. "I think my Super Bowl pants will fit you."

"Super Bowl?"

"That sounds nicer than 'fat pants,' doesn't it?" She grinned at Erin and held up a pair of chinos.

"I'm not fat!"

"I know that, but you're bigger than I am. I'd bet just one size. These should work for you."

"I can just go home…"

Katie looked at her with absolutely no hint of her feelings showing. "What do you want to do?"

Erin shrugged. "Stay here until you throw me out."

"Then say so! Damn it, Erin, ask for what you want."

"I'm irritating you, aren't I?" Erin walked over to her and put her hands on Katie's shoulders. "You seemed like you were about to tell me our dating period was over when I told you I'd blown out the candles."

Clearly frustrated, Katie looked up at the ceiling and then took in and let out a breath. "You're so close! You're almost my perfect woman." She grasped Erin and shook her. "It's so frustrating when you do something so...I don't even know what to call it."

"Stiff?"

"No, not stiff."

"Unimaginative?"

Katie shook her head. "No, not that. It might just be that you're very cautious or tentative." She stared at Erin, looking like she was trying to see inside her soul. "You seem like you try to leave a very small footprint."

"Footprint?"

"Yeah. Like you don't want to upset anyone. Anyone on earth. I'm not sure what to call how you are, but it makes me want to scream."

"You can scream if you like. It won't bother me."

"You're driving me nuts. Positively nuts." She wrapped her arms around Erin and whined, "Do you have any idea how hard it is to find a woman who has all of the requirements?"

"Uhm, no, I guess I don't. Suzy found me. I just had to say 'yes.'"

"Well, trust me, it's a bitch."

"There are some important items on your list you're not telling me about, aren't there?" Erin looked abashed. "You look like my organic chemistry prof did when I was barely pulling a C. Like there's little hope, but you're afraid to tell me."

Katie sat down on the king-size bed and patted it. "Come here." Erin did, sitting down next to her and looking at her with a somber, attentive expression. "I made a mistake. I never should have told you about my system. Now if we don't click, you're going to think you screwed up."

"Well, won't that be true?"

"No! You should only want to be with me if we really bring out the best in each other. This shouldn't only be me rating you. You should be rating me, too."

"You're great," Erin said, her big brown eyes looking remarkably earnest. "You're smart and funny and kind and clever and energetic. And you're fantastic-looking. You have just the kind of look that knocks me off my feet." Erin put her hand on Katie's thigh and stroked along it. Her voice grew softer and a little deeper. "And your body is...wow," she said, her eyes fluttering. She leaned over and delicately nibbled on Katie's ear. "Even though I didn't know we were dating, I've been dreaming about making love to you. If you're half as feisty in bed as you are just walking around..." She took Katie's face in her hands and tilted it up, then covered her mouth with her own and started to kiss her. She held her head firmly, moving it where and when she wanted.

Erin's tongue slid into Katie's mouth the second her lips parted, making her gasp in surprise, but Erin didn't let up. She gently pushed Katie onto her back and pinned her to the bed with her leg, holding her still.

Katie's surprise slowly ebbed, and she started to respond. Her arms slid around Erin's back, and she pulled her close, pressing their breasts together before she shifted her shoulders, rubbing Erin's body into her own.

Erin lifted her hips, sliding further onto Katie's body, continuing to hold her head still while she relentlessly nibbled and sucked on her full lips. Katie moaned under her and held her tighter as she began gently pumping her hips against Erin's. After another few minutes of escalating passion, she pressed into Erin, trying to push her onto her back, but Erin held her in place, moving even more of her weight onto her.

Katie responded with a satisfied purr, and she moaned throatily when Erin straddled her and rested her upper body fully on Katie. Erin growled when Katie's hand found her ass and started to massage the muscular flesh, but when Erin's hand slid between them and started to unfasten buttons, Katie grasped her hand and held it. "Stop," she got out, her voice weak and high.

"I want you," Erin murmured, her lips touching Katie's as she spoke. "Let me show you how much."

"*Now* you ask for what you want," Katie moaned. "Damn, that was…" She looked into Erin's fiery eyes and kissed her hard. "Excellent." Dropping her head to the bed, she once again tried to push Erin off, finding the job very easy this time. Erin lay next to her, gazing at her so intently that Katie had to break eye contact. "Damn it, Erin. I can't say 'no' when you look at me like that. You look like you're going to eat me alive."

"I'd love to."

Katie snuck another look at her, finally giggling and putting her hand over Erin's eyes. "Stop it!"

"Okay, okay. I'll calm down." Erin turned her head and looked up at the ceiling, taking in and expelling several long breaths. "I couldn't help myself. I started thinking about what I'd like to do to you…what I've dreamed about doing to you…what I *will* do to you…and I couldn't wait to get started."

"When do you start work on Monday?"

"Huh?"

"When do you—"

"I heard you. I'm just wondering where that wicked non sequitur came from."

"Answer the question."

"I think I have an eight o'clock. Why?"

"Could you leave here at six and get there on time?"

Erin turned, grinning. "Yeah, I think so."

"You're mine 'til Monday. I need to know you better. Much better. I can't figure you out for the life of me, but I'm gonna die trying."

⤲⤳

They went to a local spot for breakfast, walking along the quiet, neat streets in the cool breeze. They were nearly back home when Erin said, "I forgot to mention this, but it was obvious your mom and your aunt don't know our parents are engaged. Afraid to tell them?" She had a mischievous grin on her face, and Katie reached over and patted her cheek.

"Yes, as a matter of fact, I am. If my father wasn't going to invite anyone from the neighborhood, I'd never tell them."

"Really? Will your mom be hurt or angry or what?"

"I think my mom will have a short, bitter moment. It'll last for an hour or so, and then she'll be mildly upset around the big day. My aunt, however, will be a whole different case." She rolled her eyes dramatically.

"She seems pretty antagonistic to your dad in general."

"Yep. I was young when my parents divorced, but my memories are of all three of them arguing." She laughed, seeming a little melancholy. "It must have been hard for my dad, moving in and getting two Quinn women when he barely wanted one."

"Your aunt lived with them?"

"Yeah. He moved into their family home. And I bet he wanted to move right back out."

"Now, you don't know that." Erin took Katie's hand. "Is this okay?" she asked, holding up their joined hands.

"Of course. I'll never live somewhere where I can't hold my lover's hand."

"That's a good vow. One I should seriously consider."

⤲⤳

When they reached the house, they went out through the big French doors that led to the backyard. It didn't get much sun, but the high walls protected it from wind, and it was warm and calm.

Katie had an off-white upholstered loveseat and two chairs outside. She sat down on the loveseat, pulling Erin down with her. She put her arm around Erin and positioned her face so it was an inch away. "What do you want to do for the rest of the day?"

"Kiss you," Erin said, looking dreamy-eyed.

"No more of that. You get too carried away, young lady. You almost compromised my virtue this morning."

"Never," Erin said softly, gazing into Katie's eyes. "You're virtuous on your own merits. I just want to show you how beautiful I think you are and how you make me feel."

Leaning back, Katie asked, "How *do* I make you feel? Other than horny."

Erin puzzled over the question for a few moments, finally giving up. "I'm not very good at expressing things like that. I just know how I feel."

"And that is?"

"Like I'm really attracted to you, and I want to get to know you a lot better."

"That's it? That's really all you have?" Katie's laugh was just short of derisive.

Erin nodded. "Yeah. That's it."

"So, you'd like to have sex, but you're not sure I'm your soul's desire?"

"You might be," she said, smiling charmingly. "Maybe we'd know after we had sex."

Katie ran her hand along Erin's thigh and then briskly patted between her legs. "I'm not sure your drive is all about me. It seems like it might fire in any receptive woman's direction. That worries me."

Looking crestfallen, Erin said, "I don't think that's true, but I can't be sure. I *am* pretty desperate for contact."

Smiling warmly, Katie cupped Erin's cheek and looked into her eyes. "I love that you're being honest with me. Keep doing that, and we'll really get somewhere."

"I'll try, but it's pretty hard for me to express myself off-the-cuff. I'm better at putting my thoughts down on paper."

"So, you want to what…write to me?"

"No, that's silly. I…" She looked away and shifted her position, looking uncomfortable. "I write. I mean, I write stories. It's the main way I get my feelings out."

"You keep a diary?"

"No, no. I write fiction, but I put things in the stories that perplex me or are hard for me to express in person. I've already written about…" She thought for a second. "Six stories about the things that are happening between me and you."

"Six? You just found out we were dating."

"I know," Erin said, grinning guiltily. "I told you I'd been fantasizing about you. One of the ways I do that is in stories."

"Fascinating. Truly fascinating. Would you share any of your writing with me?"

"I never have," Erin said immediately. "I've never even told anyone I write."

"Not even your mom?"

"No one."

"I'm stunned. Truly stunned. You have this vent that means a lot to you, but your mom doesn't know about it? I can't figure you two out."

Shrugging, Erin said, "We're close, but we don't talk about emotions very much. We both have our secrets. That makes living together easier."

"Easier and less fulfilling."

"Maybe. I don't know. I'll have to write about that and see what I think."

"Oh, you're going to be a tough nut to crack." Katie hugged her hard. "But I love a challenge."

"I guess I could show you one of my stories. You have to promise not to make fun of it, though," she said, looking very young and very earnest. "I couldn't handle that."

Katie took her hand and brought it to her lips for a kiss. "I would never make fun of you, Erin." She wrapped her in a hug and gently stroked her back. "I hope you know that I plan on teasing you constantly, but never about anything that has any emotional significance."

"I figured that's what you meant," Erin said, breathing in Katie's scent. "I like it when you hold me."

"Well, I like holding you. You feel really good in my arms." She continued to stroke Erin's back and moved her head just enough to brush their cheeks together. "You're a very sweet woman. There's an innocence about you that really touches me."

"And annoys you."

"Yeah," Katie said softly. "But just a tiny bit. Mostly it's adorable."

"What else do you like about me?"

Katie pulled back and placed a soft, lingering kiss on Erin's lips. "You have an extraordinary mouth," she said, adding a nibble or two. "And you're very, very pretty. Your body feels amazing when I put my hands on you. You have such womanly curves. You're not all bones and muscle. I bet you're gorgeous when you're naked."

"I'd be glad to show you…"

"I know," Katie said soothingly, petting her again. "Your vote has been counted."

"It's okay," Erin said. She snuggled up against Katie again, resting her head on her shoulder. "Tell me more about me."

Katie's soft chuckle made both their bodies vibrate for a few seconds. "Okay.

I like your kindness and your loyalty. I love how you care so much about your mom and the people in your town. And I've already told you how bright you seem."

"Any more about me?"

"Let's see. I like your body, your mind, your morals…what's left?"

"My madcap, wild, unpredictable nature?"

"Hey, stability and predictability can be very good things. I can be wild enough for both of us."

Erin pulled away and looked into Katie's eyes. "Your eyes are almost the same color as the new leaves on your tree." She shook her head. "Focus, focus. I was trying to ask if you really think that's true."

"Yeah, I do. I usually hook up with fiery women, and we burn out really quickly. Maybe it makes more sense to be with someone who can ground me a little. We'll have to see. What about you? Who've you chosen in the past?"

"I told you I've only been with one woman, and Suzy was almost exactly like me. Our friends called us the twins. We didn't fight, didn't disagree on most things, and we were in the same field."

"Sounds a little narcissistic to me."

"Maybe. I've never thought about it like that, but maybe we were too much alike to have enough spark."

"How was your sex life?"

Erin pulled away, her eyes wide with shock. "That's private. And I'd never ask you about yours either."

"Are you serious? You aren't interested in the women I've been with?"

"Yes and no. I'm interested, but I'll never ask. Your past doesn't apply to our present."

"You really don't want to know my history?"

"No. I definitely *don't* want to know your history."

"Well, this will be a first. I've never had a girlfriend who didn't want to examine every facet of my life."

"I want to examine every facet of you," Erin said, running her hand up Katie's side. "Just you. Just now."

"See?" Katie said, giving her a quick kiss. "This is another part of you that's just wonderful. You have this remarkably mature side that's terrifically appealing. It might not be as exciting as a woman who grills me and then throws things at me when she finds out I slept with her sister, but that gets old fast."

Erin grinned at her placidly. "I'm not going to ask if that's true, so you're going to have to try to taunt me in another way."

"Are you ticklish?" Katie asked, digging her hands into Erin's sides.

Without flinching, Erin said, "Not a bit."

"Damn, I'm going to have to stay up nights thinking of ways to torture you."

"Torture me in bed," Erin said, taking Katie in her arms and kissing her hard and fast.

⁓

Erin drove back to Essex on Monday morning, the events of the weekend playing in her head on a nonstop loop. She had a packed schedule, and by the time she left the office, the library had been closed for an hour. She was a block away when she saw lights on in her house, and her heart started to beat a little quickly when she saw her mother's car in the drive. Given the fact that Gail came home so infrequently, Erin assumed this particular visit was only to find out what had happened during the weekend.

To her surprise, the scent of a home-cooked dinner made Erin's anxiety start to evaporate as soon as she opened the door. "I'm home," she called out.

"Erin." Her mom poked her head out of the kitchen. "How are you, honey? Did you have a tough day?"

Erin put her coat away and went into the kitchen where she hugged and kissed Gail. "Not too tough. Busy, though. How about you?"

"Nothing epic. How was your weekend?"

"It was good. I had a lot of fun." She went to the sink and washed her hands. "Yours?"

"Good." Gail smiled at her, looking stiff. She finished doing a few little things, but paused after a minute. When she said, "We can't tiptoe around each other like this. We've got to clear the air," she sounded anxious and frustrated.

"Okay." Erin sat down and gazed up at her mother. "Do you want to talk or listen?"

Gail ran her hand over Erin's hair. "You're probably starving. I shouldn't jump on you the minute you walk in the house. Let's eat."

Relieved, Erin nodded. "I am hungry. And I don't like to be jumped on, but we can still talk. I can do two things at once."

Gail put their plates on the table and took her seat. "All right. I'll talk." She fidgeted a little and then took a bite of her salmon, wasting a little more time. "I didn't have a particularly nice weekend."

Erin's eyebrows went up questioningly. "Why?"

"Well," Gail said, her eyes roving around the area near, but never lighting on, Erin's face, "I told Dan you were going to Katie's party."

Waiting for more, Erin finally said, "And that hurt your weekend?"

"No, of course there's more."

"I can't guess what's on your mind."

"It doesn't seem like it should be that hard for you. You know there's some tension there."

Erin ignored her first instinct, which was to snap off a sharp reply. Instead, she took a bite of her food and thought about what she wanted to say. "You haven't ever confirmed that Dan has negative feelings about Katie. Everything seems like it's such a secret."

"This is hard!" Gail said, the emotion in her voice surprising Erin. "You know how close Dan and I are, but you're my daughter."

"Yes," Erin said slowly. "Why is that a problem?"

"Because I don't want you to get hurt, but I truly hate being in the middle. Dan was so frustrated with me this weekend. He can't understand why I haven't interrogated you about Katie."

Smiling, Erin said, "I don't think you've ever interrogated me about anything. That's not how we are."

"I know." Gail rested her head on her hand and poked her food around on her plate listlessly. "He and I have very different styles when it comes to parenting."

"I don't know what his is, but I like yours better."

Gail smiled, her blue eyes twinkling a little when they shifted in Erin's direction. "How do you know that?"

"Because I know how I feel about you, and I have a pretty good sense of how Katie feels about Dan."

"She doesn't give him a chance! She blames him for everything, and that's not fair."

Erin's voice was cool and soft, and it sounded even softer compared with Gail's uncharacteristically emotional comments. "I'm not sure what you're talking about, but I'm certain their relationship is more complex than you or I know. I don't think it's a good idea to get too involved."

"How do I avoid it?"

"I don't know, but I try not to get into it with Katie. I don't really want to know what's gone on between her and her father, but I'm more than willing to listen to her feelings."

Gail stared at Erin for a few seconds, seemingly on the verge of asking a question. She finally did. "*Do* you care about her? As more than a friend?"

Erin had decided to be honest with her mother, and she wasn't willing to compromise on that decision, even though the thought was tempting. "Yes. We're dating."

"Oh, honey." Gail closed her eyes briefly. "Are you sure that's wise?"

"No." She laughed, but it wasn't a particularly joyful one. "It's never wise to date someone. It's much smarter to stay home with your mom, but my mom's engaged. She's hardly ever home."

"Are you…are you saying you're dating her just to have something to do?"

"No, of course not, but I was happy just hanging out and getting my practice in order. I hadn't given any serious thought to finding someone to date."

"Then why date Katie? Maybe you should trust your instincts. I mean, if you don't think you're ready—"

Erin put her hand up, and Gail stopped mid-sentence. "I wasn't motivated. I was content when you and I were spending time together, but I would have jumped at the chance to date her if she'd come along last week or the week after Suzy and I broke up."

Gail's face was lined with worry, and she speared another bite of her dinner. Erin watched her eat, having decided to wait and see if Gail would comment. It took a while, but she finally said, "I feel like my being with Dan is pushing you to do something you're not ready for." Their eyes met. "It worries me."

Erin couldn't help but laugh. "Mom, I'm dating a woman I really like. It's not like I joined the Army because you were ignoring me. You're being kind of silly about this."

Gail's cheeks colored when she said, "I don't feel like I'm being silly. I'm honestly worried that you're not doing this for the right reasons."

Erin's dark eyes searched her mother's. "What are the right reasons? I'm really attracted to her, she's a kind and generous woman, and she's a lot of fun. Aren't those enough reasons to date someone?"

"Yes, I suppose they are, but I don't think that's everything. I think you're lonely, and you might be feeling like you'll never find anyone around here."

"I won't! I've always assumed I'd have to go to a bigger town to meet women, but that's not the issue. The issue is that I wasn't looking forward to the search. I was content enough and busy enough that I was just biding my time."

"I worry that you've had so few opportunities, Erin. There might be someone who's a much better fit for you, but you haven't taken the time to look. I think the same thing happened with Suzy. You fell into that relationship. You've as much as admitted that, I'm worried that you're doing the same thing because you haven't had any other offers."

Erin put her fork down and leaned forward, resting her forearms on the edge of the table. "I've had opportunities. I knew a lot of people at Dartmouth, and when word got around that Suzy and I had broken up, I heard from quite a few people. Some of them wanted to go out; some wanted to fix me up. But I didn't want to be fixed up, and I wasn't interested in the women who wanted to go out with me. I'm interested in Katie, so I'm going to go out with her. I know what I'm doing." Her last sentence was delivered with calm, precise diction, as though she wanted to make sure her mother understood every word.

"All right." Gail's reply was quiet and almost meek.

Erin could see that she'd been too harsh, and she tried to lighten the exchange. "What I'm trying to say is that it's always risky to open yourself up to someone. It's scary. Things were much simpler when you and I had dinner and went for a long walk in the evening. Remember how nice it was last summer? It wasn't exciting, but it was nice."

"It *was* nice. And it was wonderful getting to know you as an adult. You're so mature, Erin. You're nothing like the girl I sent off to college so long ago."

"I'm still wet behind the ears in a lot of areas. Katie pointed that out many times this weekend."

"You're so much younger than she is and so much less experienced. It must be odd to go out with someone who's not in the same place you are."

"Not really. Katie challenges me. And no matter what Dan says about her, she's a really good person. She is," she said emphatically.

"I'm sure you think that, honey, but how can you be sure?"

"The same way you're sure of Dan. You talk a lot and try to keep your perspective. You can't do it quickly. It takes time."

Gail reached over and took Erin's hand, rubbing her thumb over the back of it. "Please be careful. I don't want you to get your heart broken."

"Who wants that? I don't want that to happen to you, either, Mom, but I can't stop it from happening. I've got to trust that you know how to protect yourself. I think you should do the same for me."

"I want to," Gail said emphatically, "but I know how kindhearted you are. And you're so trusting. You don't know how callous people can be."

"Mom! You act like I've been sitting in my room for the last ten years. I've seen some awful things since I've been in school. I've treated liars, schemers, alcoholics, drug addicts, severely mentally ill people, and your average lowlifes. I know people can be awful, but they can be wonderful, too. And I think Katie's wonderful." Her jaw was set in a defiant pose.

"Take it slowly," Gail said. "Please, honey, don't rush into anything."

"I'm taking it very slowly," Erin said, not adding that the speed of their progress was entirely in Katie's hands.

"It's hard sometimes, watching you grow up and knowing I can't protect you from a lot of things."

"I can understand that. Really, I can. But you have to let me go, Mom."

Gail reached over and took Erin's hand, squeezing it tightly. "I'm very sorry about the way I spoke to you the other night at the library. I just get so anxious. I feel like I'm being pulled in two different directions."

"By me and Dan?"

Gail nodded. "You both want me to do things I'm not comfortable with, and I'm not good at being in the middle."

"I don't want to do that, but I'm involved in some of the things that happen between you and Dan."

"That's true. But if you and Dan had a better relationship, he'd talk to you instead of me. I think that would be better for all of us."

Erin didn't reply. She took a bite of her dinner, trying to recall if her mother had always been so conflict-averse or if it had gotten worse since Dan had come on the scene.

❧

It was a warm, dry night, so after dinner, Gail and Erin went out for a long walk. Erin told her mom all about Katie's home and her mom and aunt. Gail, for the first time, talked about the little details of her weekend with Dan. She didn't say anything particularly important, but just talking about the meals they'd had and a movie they'd rented seemed to make both Delancy women more at ease with each other.

It was almost ten when they got home, and when Erin kissed her mother goodnight, she said, "I'm glad we talked tonight. I feel better about things."

"Me, too. We have to work on our relationship instead of focusing too much on these Bostonians."

"Absolutely. You can't neglect your girlfriends when you get involved with someone. And neither of us should try to be like Dan and Katie. They're both pretty feisty, and we're not like that."

"No, we're not. And frankly, I don't want to be that way. I like our relationship. I don't want to argue like they do."

"I don't either, Mom. We have to make them accommodate to our style a little bit. We can't let them push us around."

"Goodness knows Dan wants to."

"Katie wouldn't mind either," Erin admitted, smiling. "But I'm going to stand my ground."

"I'll try, too. I'll never be happy if I try to imitate him."

Gail gave Erin another hug and left her room. Seconds later, Erin called Kim.

"Is it too late?" she asked when Kim answered.

"For…"

"For me to call you?"

"That'll be the day. I bet you've never voluntarily been up later than I have. How did your party go?"

"Great. I got home this morning."

"Erin Delancy! What a little slut you are!"

"I wish," Erin said, giggling. "I practically begged her to go to bed with me. Actually, I *did* beg her to go to bed, but she wouldn't bite."

"You tried to force yourself on someone who wasn't interested? You?"

"She's interested, Kim. She's very interested. As a matter of fact, we've been dating for weeks."

"Ha! I knew she was hot for you. So, why didn't she want to have sex?"

"She doesn't want to go too far too fast. She wants to be in love before we get too involved."

Kim was silent for a few seconds. "Are you serious?"

"Yeah. Completely."

"Damn, Erin, being with women couldn't be more different than being with men. Don't ever ask me for advice because we're operating in different worlds."

"I could have used some advice this weekend. My stock was up and down so fast my head was spinning."

"Really? Why?"

"Well, Katie likes me a lot, but I also seem to drive her crazy."

"That doesn't sound promising. This is pretty early to be at the 'you bug me' stage."

"I know, but I think that's because she has this list of requirements she wants in a girlfriend. I met all of the big ones, but I was sketchy on a lot of the little ones. Every time I'd do something that she didn't like, she'd get all agitated, like she desperately wanted me to do well but I just wasn't performing."

"Erin, don't take this the wrong way, but she sounds crazy."

"She is a little bit. Okay, she's pretty nutty. But she's a lot of fun, and smart, and I'm really, really attracted to her. She's ridiculously pretty and her body is…"

"Enough! I don't need to know what nasty little thoughts go on in your head."

"You know I wouldn't tell you my nasty thoughts. I only do that with people I'm being nasty with."

"I hope you get to be nasty with Katie if that's what you want. She sounds interesting, that's for sure."

"She is. And really, really hot."

Kim laughed. "I had no idea you were so shallow. I thought you'd be the one with the list."

"No, I'm not like that, thank goodness. We'd have to have an independent set of auditors come in to analyze our requirements. And I don't think I'm shallow. I just know when I feel a spark, and I feel a whole lot of sparks with Katie."

"God knows that's important. Do you think she feels the same about you?"

"Yeah, she does. I can tell she's really attracted to me, and she likes some parts of me better than others."

"Like?"

"I figured out that she particularly likes it when I'm forceful and confident. So when she seemed perturbed at me I turned the tables on her and acted kinda pushy. I'm gonna focus on being that way as much as I can."

"Erin, you can't put on an act."

"I'm not acting. There's a big part of my personality that's forceful. That's the part I have to show. I'll keep the sniveling weakling part hidden until she's in love with me."

"I can tell you've got this well under control. It's thinking like this that got you into Dartmouth med school."

"My rockin' GPA got me into Dartmouth, but my confidence is going to get me into Katie's heart."

❦

Even though it was late, Erin took one of her recent stories and read it thoroughly, making a few changes to polish it up. Agreeing to share her writing was harder than she could have imagined, but she took a deep breath and sent the story to Katie, feeling sick to her stomach as her mail program digested her words.

Chapter Ten

When Erin got home the next night, it was almost nine o'clock. Her mom wasn't home, and even though she hadn't eaten, she didn't even bother to look in the refrigerator. She was just going to brush her teeth and go to bed, but she turned on her computer to check her email, an obsessive habit.

A small smile curled the corner of her mouth when she saw a reply to her message to Katie. It didn't say much, but she followed directions and called her at home. "Hi, it's Erin."

"I've been waiting all night. How long will it take you to get here? I don't care if we're in love or not. I want you to do exactly what you enumerated on page six to me as soon as possible."

Erin laughed, but the laugh was weak and short. "I think I'm going to have to take a rain check. I had a tough day."

"Hey, what's wrong? You sound awful."

"I am," Erin said, suddenly overcome. "I lost a patient tonight." She tried to hold them in, but the tears finally escaped. "I'm sorry. This is so hard for me."

"Oh, Erin," Katie said, her voice filled with sympathy. "You poor thing."

"No, not me. My patient was the poor one. She was all alone. If I hadn't been there, she would have died just like she lived—all alone." She let out a rough grunt. "Not that having me there was any great thing. It's not like we were friends."

"But you were there," Katie said softly. "That was all you could do, right?"

"Yeah. I couldn't do anything for her health. She was in terrible shape."

"Was she elderly?"

"No, not really. She was a recluse. Maybe even mentally ill. No one really knew her, even though she's lived here for sixty years." She sniffed, her breathing shaky and rough. "It just makes me so sad to see someone go downhill like she did, especially since I know she didn't really live her life to the fullest. Such a waste," she said, sighing heavily.

"Did you get to know her when she was failing?"

"Yeah. I spent a lot of time with her."

"How often did you see her?"

"I called every day, and I went two or three times a week."

"How did you manage? I know how long you stay at the office."

"I went early in the morning if I could, or I'd go by after dinner. It's only about a twenty-minute drive. And then I went on the weekends."

"Erin…" Katie's voice was so gentle and loving that it felt like a caress. "You did so much for her. Even though you couldn't save her, you showed you cared. That's so much. That's all that anyone wants. Someone to care."

"I did care," Erin sobbed. "It drove me crazy not to be able to help her. I honestly thought about her throughout the day—every day. I knew she was too far gone to arrest her disease, but I kept thinking about her."

"You've got to let go. I know it's hard, but she's gone now. You did what you could. Hell, you did two thousand percent more than any doctor I've ever met would do. I can hear how sad you are, but this is what being a family doctor is all about—doing your best for your patients from the cradle to the grave, right?"

"I don't want this," Erin gasped before dissolving into huge, wracking sobs. "I don't want this!"

"Sweetheart, shh, shh, it's all right. Now, take a few deep breaths. Come on. Take a few and talk to me. Tell me what you mean."

"I don't want to do this," Erin moaned. "I want to see them, patch them up, and send them on. I don't want to have relationships with them. I don't, Katie. I don't."

"You've had a terrible time with this patient. You're doubting yourself now, but you'll feel better in a few days."

"No, I won't. I won't. I've felt like this since the day I started."

"What?" The shock in Katie's voice was poorly disguised. "Since the first?"

"Yes."

Erin sounded so disgusted with herself that Katie hardly knew how to respond. "Have you…what…what can you do?"

"Nothing. I'm locked in. I made a promise to my town. They paid for me to go to school, and I promised to be their doctor. I just have to learn how to toughen up."

"Is that it? Is this something you can get over?"

"I'm going to have to. I don't know how, but I'm going to have to. If I don't, I'll lose my mind."

"Okay," Katie said, sounding like she had some control of the situation. "Here's what I want you to do. Go take a long shower. Scrub yourself really well so you smell fresh and clean."

"All right," Erin said slowly.

"Then I want you to sit down and think about how few options you had with this patient. But don't think about your career or anything like that. Just think about this particular patient and how you didn't have any other viable choices. You know that, I know you do. You feel shitty about it, but you know it. I know you well enough to know that you did everything you could have."

"All right. I can do that."

"Then get into bed and let yourself feel how tired you are. I can hear it in your voice. You sound absolutely exhausted."

"I am." Erin tried to hold in a yawn, but was only partially successful. "I'm beat."

"And there's one thing you have to promise me."

"What's that?"

"That if you can't sleep or you wake up in the middle of the night, you'll call me. It doesn't matter what time. I want you to promise me, Erin. On your honor."

"I promise," she said, starting to cry again. "Thank you. Thanks for caring about me."

"I care about you very much. Even more than I did when you called. Now, go get busy. And keep your promise."

"I will. G'night."

"Goodnight, Erin. Imagine I'm holding you tightly."

"Okay," she said, her voice breaking again. "Bye."

She hung up and rested her head on her desk for a few minutes, letting herself cry it out. Then she got up and followed Katie's instructions to the letter. A half-hour later, she was in bed and, a short time after that, fast asleep.

<hr>

Around eleven o'clock the next morning, Erin looked up when her office door closed. Katie stood leaning against the door, motioning for Erin to approach. "What are you doing here?"

"Shh." Katie held her arms open, and Erin nearly leapt into them. "You sounded so sad," she whispered. "I had to see you."

Lifting her head, Erin asked, "You came all the way up here just for me?"

Kissing her forehead tenderly, Katie said, "I'd go a lot farther than one little state for you. How are you?"

"Shaky. I would have cancelled my appointments for today, but I had a particularly demanding patient first thing, and I knew I'd hear about it for ten years if I cancelled." Her eyes had none of their usual sparkle, and her cheeks bore none of their customary healthy hue.

"Well, you're finished now. Get your coat. We're going to spend the day together."

"Katie, I can't do that."

"Yes, you can. I called Madge early this morning and told her you'd had a tough night. She called all of your patients and rescheduled them." Laughing, she added, "She wouldn't call the mean one, though, so you had to see him."

Erin put her head on Katie's shoulder and soaked up the care and concern so fully offered. "What am I going to do? I see my life stretch out in front of me, and it makes me want to leave town and never look back."

"Oh, no, you don't. I don't let my girlfriends get away so easily. Come on," she said. "Get your coat, and let's get out of here."

"No arguments." Erin kissed Katie repeatedly, each kiss soft and gentle. "Thank you."

<hr>

When Erin opened the door to the office, Madge practically ran over to hug her. "Why didn't you tell me about that poor woman dying?"

Erin shrugged, looking small and young. "I didn't want to talk about it."

"Well, you're lucky your future stepsister is such a nice person." Madge beamed at Katie. "It's so nice to see you taking care of our Erin."

Katie gave her a remarkably sincere smile. "I've always wanted a sister."

"Do you want me to make you two some soup for lunch?"

"No, thanks, Madge. I think Erin needs some quiet. Is that true?" She looked at Erin and received a nod in confirmation.

"Yeah. I'm not hungry right now. We'll get something later."

They started for the door, with Madge saying, "Call me if you need anything. Promise?"

"I promise." Erin gave her another hug, and she and Katie walked out, leaving Madge to lock up. "Well, that was odd," Erin said when they were on the street. "It didn't occur to me that people would think we'd see ourselves as sisters."

"Essex is weird in many ways. You're just too close to see it." They started to walk to Erin's house, but hadn't gotten more than a block when her cell phone rang. She looked a little panicked, but answered it immediately. "Oh, hi, Mom," she said. "Yeah, it was tough. I'm taking the afternoon off." She paused, listening, and they continued walking. "I'm all right. Katie's here." Another pause. "No,

I didn't ask her to come." She turned her head and gave Katie a sweet smile. "She's a very caring person." Another pause. "I'm sorry I didn't call you, but I didn't feel like talking about it last night." She nodded, looking like she was anxious to hang up. "I know. I know." Still another pause. "No, you don't have to come home tonight. Katie will probably hang around." She looked at Katie, who nodded emphatically. "I love you, too. Thanks." She snapped the phone shut. "My mom."

"I guessed that." Katie put her hand around Erin's arm, but then pulled it away. "I guess I shouldn't do that, right?"

"What?"

"Touch you in public."

With a derisive snort, Erin took Katie's hand and pulled it to her chest. "I have nothing to hide."

They walked the rest of the way in silence, holding hands in the early spring chill. The day was gloomy, and the cloud cover nearly reached the steeple on the Methodist Church in the square. Erin's house was silent, and it stayed that way for a few minutes. Katie took off her coat and then took Erin's, hanging them on the coat tree in the hall. They went to the sofa and collapsed into each other's arms. Katie sat in the corner of the sofa, and Erin rested her head just above Katie's breast. Her body grew more relaxed as Katie stroked her hair and hummed a soothing tune.

They stayed just that way for a very long time. Neither was in a hurry to talk, and they slowly reached a kind of altered state where they were deeply concentrating on each other, almost unaware of the rest of the world. Neither heard Gail ascend the front stairs and stop when she looked in through the glass in the door. Nor did they hear her leave after being unable to resist staring at them for a full minute.

Erin finally spoke. "How do I learn to care less?"

"I wish I knew. I had to stop working at a job I loved because I couldn't do it."

Looking up, Erin said, "You did?"

"Yeah. I went to law school on a scholarship BC has for people who commit to practicing public interest law. I did it for five years and finally quit when I had to start taking anti-depressants."

"That sounds horrible. What kind of law was it?"

Katie chuckled. "That's the most embarrassing part. It was just housing law. Nobody was dying or losing a job or anything really terrible, but I got to where I couldn't stand to show up in the morning. Every day, I was fighting a losing battle against landlords and the city and Housing and Urban Development and…ugh!" She dropped her head against the back of the sofa. "I cared too much. I got personally involved in my clients' problems. I lent people money. I begged my friends for furniture, clothing, food. No one wanted to take my calls." She shook her head, looking chagrined. "My mother wanted to have me committed when I took a Columbian woman into my house."

"Why'd you do that?"

"She was hiding from the guys who lent her the money to hire coyotes to bring her into the country. My mom was sure I was going to be murdered."

"You could have been!"

"You feel indestructible when you're young. I felt really bad for this woman. She was living in a basement, and the city got a tip about the illegal rental and tossed her and four other people out. She was only about nineteen, and her story broke my heart."

"How long did she live with you?"

"Until I found her a new place." Katie hedged for a moment. "Six months."

"Six months!"

"Yeah. That's when my mom wanted me locked up. Not long after that, I started having a hard time getting out of bed in the morning. I thought I was sick, but my doctor eliminated any physical issue and prescribed anti-depressants."

"They can really help," Erin said, sitting up and looking at Katie with concern.

"This was almost ten years ago. I started to take Prozac, but it destroyed my sex drive and that's one drive I refuse to lose." She grinned impishly. "So, I took a month off and started feeling better as soon as I knew I didn't have to go to work the next day. That was a clue that my depression wasn't…what do they call it?"

"Real?" Erin asked, grinning.

"Yeah. That's it. It wasn't real." Katie pinched the tip of Erin's nose. "Thanks for the second opinion. You're quite a doctor."

"So, what did you do? Just quit?"

"It wasn't that easy, but that's what I did eventually. I didn't think I could make myself care less." She gently stroked Erin's face with her fingertips, looking into her soulful, dark brown eyes. "That might be true for you, too."

Erin started shaking her head before Katie finished speaking. "I don't have the luxury of being able to quit. I tease about being an indentured servant, but in essence, that's what I am."

"There has to be a way out of your contract. It's illegal to force someone to do a job they don't want to do."

"But it would cost me…" She shook her head, looking dizzy. "I don't even know how much. But a lot more than they gave me."

"Let's not talk about details right now. Let's talk about what you really want. Did you always want to be a doctor?"

"No. I wanted to be a writer. From the time I could read, I knew that's what I wanted."

"I don't want to get off on a side issue, but that story you sent me made me melt." She fanned herself dramatically. "You could've had me six ways to Sunday if you'd been in Boston last night."

Erin grinned shyly. "I don't know what that means, but it sounds good. I wish I had been in Boston last night, but then I'd feel guilty about not being with my patient when she died."

"The story was sizzling hot, you little minx. If I would have read that before last weekend, I wouldn't have been so surprised when you tried to get my pants off."

"It was a big deal for me to send you that one. I was really tense."

"Uhm, not to mention the obvious, but how can you be a writer if you don't share your stuff?"

"Oh, if I were writing for public consumption, I'd write about normal stuff. I just write about sex for myself. It gets lonely in Essex," she said, smiling so charmingly that Katie was unable to resist the urge to kiss her. Their lips met, and before she knew what had happened, she was pressed against the back of the sofa, with Erin holding her head in her hands, making her whole body feel like it was ablaze.

"Good God, you don't know how to go the speed limit," Katie panted. "Do you drive like you kiss?"

"I don't know. You'll have to tell me after we've driven together." She grasped Katie's head firmly and was about to dive in for more when Katie regretfully called a halt.

"Slow down now," she soothed. "I want to talk to you." She gave her a quick kiss. "Even though certain parts of me would much rather keep kissing."

"You came up here to cheer me up," Erin said, her face just an inch or so from Katie's. "I'm very cheerful when I kiss."

Smiling at her perseverance, Katie said, "You're goddamned giddy, but I still want to talk. Tell me how an aspiring writer wound up in medical school."

"Oh." Erin's smile left, and she sat up and straightened her hair. Katie watched as her whole demeanor changed in the blink of an eye. "After…the accident, I was obsessed with figuring out why my brother died."

Seeing the flat, almost expressionless set of her face made Katie wrap her arms around Erin and hold her tightly. It took a few minutes, but Erin finally continued, her voice soft, but more inflected with feeling.

"My dad died almost immediately, and he probably couldn't have been saved. But after talking to my mom and to the doctors at the hospital and to our local doctor, it became clear that Brad died of internal bleeding because we didn't have a trauma center. We still don't," she said with a look of disgust.

"Weren't you just a kid? I'm surprised you got involved in trying to figure all of that out."

"I was fairly young, but I wasn't a kid. I've always been interested in why things happen. I…well, no one seemed to…" She shook her head. "No, that's not true. I'm sure other people cared about the details." She met Katie's eyes, and the intensity of Erin's gaze was stunning. "I *had* to know. I wouldn't stop asking questions until I knew what happened and why. And once I knew that Brad could have been saved but wasn't…" She took in a deep breath. "I had to do that. My plans changed that day, and I never thought of being a writer again."

"That's amazing," Katie said, feeling the raw energy that practically poured from Erin.

"No, not really. I was good in science, and it came easily to me. Dr. Worrell, our local guy, encouraged me and guided me through high school and college. He's the one who convinced the city to send me to medical school. He knew it would be almost impossible to lure a young doctor here once he retired."

"Why does your town want a doctor? Aren't there plenty of them in Nashua?"

Erin shrugged. "People here don't like change. They've always had a town doctor, and they wanted to keep one. The men on the town council are very influential. They run the town they way they want it, and they want a doctor."

"That seems weird to me, but knowing you, I can see why you made the decision to stay. But if you don't like being a doctor—"

"No! No! I love being a doctor. If I were a writer, I'd be too much in my head. Being a doctor makes me come out of my shell and interact with people."

"But you don't want to care for them when they're terminally ill?"

"No, it's more than that. I want to be an emergency medicine doctor. That's everything I like. You have to make a quick diagnosis, you have to think on your feet, everything comes at you a mile a minute, and they live or die right there. There's no nursing them through a chronic illness and watching them fall apart before your eyes. It's none of this glacier-paced medicine that I hate with a passion."

Looking stunned, Katie said, "Did you know this when you agreed to live here?"

"Of course not. I knew my favorite parts of medical school and my internship were my rotations in surgery and in the ER, but I didn't know I'd hate family practice as much as I do. It's like watching grass grow most of the time, but every once in a while someone dies, and you feel like you've died a little bit yourself."

Katie wrapped Erin in a strong, but tender hug. "Is that how you feel?"

"Yeah. I was thinking about it today when I had a few minutes. I was thinking that being the town doctor might be like being an air traffic controller. Every little blip on your radar screen is critically important, but you take them for granted and just make sure they're on the right path. It must be boring beyond belief most of the time. But if you make a mistake or somebody else makes a mistake or something awful happens, you can lose three hundred people in the blink of an eye. Those people must never get over that. The responsibility must be grinding."

"So, why is it less responsibility to have people on the edge of life and death? I'd think emergency medicine would be worse. You'd lose a lot more patients."

"I know that. But you don't build a relationship with them. I was able to divorce myself emotionally when I was in the ER. Not completely, of course. I still cared deeply, but I didn't have to watch anybody die over a period of months. I didn't have to sit there day after day, cursing my impotence while a life slipped away." She burrowed her face into Katie and started to cry. For a long time, Katie just held her and tried to soothe her. "I hate it more than I can say."

"Then we have to figure out a way to get you out of your contract."

Erin looked up at her, her eyes filled with sadness. "There's just no way."

"There's always a way. It might not be pleasant, but there's a way."

❦

An hour later, Erin paced behind Katie, who was leisurely reading Erin's contract with the City of Essex. Katie made an occasional notation with a pencil, making Erin stop to look over her shoulder, but she didn't work any faster, going at her own pace until she was finished. "Well," she said when she was done, "I would have tried to strike a better bargain for you. This is pretty tough." She slapped the bunch of papers onto the desk.

"I can only get out if I buy my way out, right?"

"Right. I'm sure you know the important provisions. I understand why they stuck a 50 percent default penalty on you, but that's really tough. You started out with a debt of $150,000, and they'll tack on $75,000 if you quit. They're only charging you interest on the $150,000, which is nice, and the rate is low. But given that you've only knocked off one year of your ten-year commitment, you owe them…a fuckload."

"Could I take out a loan?"

"Sure. If you know anyone who'll give you $200,000 unsecured. They've really got you by the short hairs. You can't get that kind of loan, and even if you could, the interest rate would be ridiculous."

"If I could get the loan, how much would my monthly payments be?"

Katie blew out a long breath, flapping her lips as the air escaped. "I really don't think you could get the money. A bank would want repayment in no more than five years. I can't do the math in my head, but it could be $4,000 or $5,000 a month."

"A month! That's $60,000 a year!"

"I know," Katie said glumly. "You'd have to make $100,000 just to pay the loan."

"Fat chance of that. I don't have a specialty. I'd be lucky to make $100,000 working at an HMO in Manchester or Nashua. And I'd still be doing family practice."

"We'll have to keep thinking. There's a way out."

Erin went to her bed and flopped down on it. "I think the way out is to hope the next nine years fly by."

Katie lay next to her, and they shifted around until she was snuggled up against Erin's side. "That's not an option. You're a great-looking woman. We could probably pimp you out for a few thousand bucks a pop."

Erin laughed half-heartedly. "I can't even get out of the deal by losing my license, so there goes the lure of developing a drug habit."

"Nope. If you lose your license or they fire you for cause, the due date is accelerated. We've got to figure out a way to get the money. That's our only option."

"I can't tell you how much better it makes me feel to have you say 'our' and 'we.' Even though it's my problem, it feels so good to know I have your support."

Katie kissed her cheek. "You have more than that. When I say 'we,' I mean it. We're going to figure this out, and you're going to get out of this contract. I can't stand by and watch someone I care about get beaten down. And that's what will happen if you stay here."

"I know that now. I just wish this hadn't happened for a few years. I could have struggled through. But losing this patient has made me see that I can't take it much longer."

"The other thing you have to think of is your duty to the town."

"Like I don't think of that? It's on my mind constantly!"

Katie gently patted her belly, trying to soothe her. "No, not your commitment to stay. Your commitment to provide good medical care. You can't do that if your heart isn't in it."

"That's not true. I can still be a good doctor. I'll just have to figure out some way to dull my feelings."

"Erin." Katie sat up and gazed at her. "That's what *makes* you a good doctor. You can't be empathetic and caring and connected to your patients if you're dulling your feelings. And how will you do that? Drugs? Alcohol?"

"Sex?" Erin suggested, a very faint smile on her lips.

"If it would help, I'd gladly devote an hour or two a day to keeping a smile on your face."

Erin looked positively charmed. Her smile was luminous. "Would you really? Even though you're not ready?"

"Hey, don't think I don't want to have sex with you right now. I'm being prudent only because I think it'll be easier on both of us if things don't work out. But I'd take one for the team if it would keep you sane." She gave Erin a soft kiss, lingering right above her lips for a moment when she broke the kiss. "Besides, I'd love an excuse to be imprudent."

"I could probably come up with a few excuses, but I don't want to rush things. I want to make sure we nurture this. Having a relationship with you is worth more than having sex."

"Good answer." Katie kissed Erin again, pressing their bodies tightly together. "I hate to deny pleasure, but it's a good answer."

⁂

They drove over to Nashua for dinner, and when they returned, they lingered on the front porch for a few moments. "Can you stay overnight and go home in the morning?" Erin had her arms around Katie's waist and was idly considering the beautiful color of her hair in the golden porch light.

"I could, and I will if you need me to, but I despise getting up really early."

"Are you awake enough to drive home?"

"I'm fine. It's only nine o'clock."

"I'll walk you down to your car." As before, they held hands on the short walk.

"This morning, I thought maybe you were trying to get the town to fire you by being an obvious lesbian, but now it seems like you're comfortable being a little affectionate."

Erin stopped, put her arms around Katie, and then kissed her with abandon.

"I'm comfortable being very affectionate," she whispered. "I'm confident about my sexuality. Of course, if they'd like to fire me and forgive my debt…"

"I knew you had an ulterior motive!"

"I do," Erin said. "I want as many kisses as I can get. I'm a very hungry woman."

⁂

The next morning Erin woke to a clattering coming from downstairs. Essex was so small and peaceful she didn't for a moment worry that her house was being burgled. She got up and went to the landing, calling out, "Mom?"

"Hi, honey. I'm making you breakfast."

"Wow, that's a treat. I'll be right down." She put on her robe and slippers and dashed down the stairs, greeting her mother with a quick hug. But Gail wasn't satisfied with that. She turned and wrapped her arms around her daughter, holding her tightly.

"I've been neglecting you terribly. I feel like such an awful mother."

Erin patted her and sat down at the table. "Don't be silly. You're just living your life. I know what it's like when you're getting close with someone. It's perfectly understandable that you want to spend all of your time with Dan."

"I've been acting like a girl in high school, and even though I appreciate your trying to relieve my guilt, I think it's justified."

"I don't think so. The only way it works for us to live together is if we're more friends than mother and daughter. We should treat each other more like roommates."

Gail didn't say anything for a moment. She finished the egg-white omelet she'd made and placed it in front of Erin.

"Oh, this looks good. Mushrooms and tomatoes…my favorites. I think I'll add some salsa." She started to get up, but Gail stopped her.

"I'm already up. I'll get it for you." She put the jar of hot salsa in front of her daughter and sat down to eat her own breakfast. Several times she looked like she was about to say something, but she'd take a bite of her breakfast instead. Erin watched her, seeing the indecision, but not wanting to push her. After a few minutes of silence, Gail said, "Did you and I ever discuss how our relationship was going to change when you moved back home?"

Erin's brows knit together. "I don't think we talked about it in so many words. Do you…is there a problem?"

"I think there might be," Gail said, looking intently at her breakfast.

"You want to add a little to that?"

"I was very happy with the way our relationship was before you decided to return to Essex. I don't see the need to change that. I don't want to be your roommate. I want to be your mom, and I want you to be my girl. I like taking care of you. When you hurt, I hurt. That's not how roommates are."

"Well, I guess you're right, but things have changed between us. I know you feel it."

"I do, and some of the changes aren't working for me."

"Like?"

"I want to know what's going on with you. I want to know how you feel about Katie and how you feel about Dan and me. We used to talk about things like this, Erin. You used to come to me for advice and guidance."

"I don't need much advice anymore."

"I don't think that's true. As soon as Dan came on the scene, you stopped doing that, and that's one of the reasons I didn't know how involved you were with this patient. Madge told me some things yesterday that just about broke my heart."

"You've been gone a lot. I'm not going to call you over at Dan's to tell you about a patient who's worrying me."

Gail put her fork down forcefully, the ringing echoing through the quiet kitchen. "Why not?"

Flinching from her mother's glare, Erin said, "I wouldn't feel comfortable doing that. I wouldn't want to intrude."

"On what? I don't know what you think goes on, but our evenings together are very mundane."

"I just feel uncomfortable. I wouldn't call a friend of mine if I knew she was out on a date."

"This is part of the difference between a friend and a mother, honey. No matter what I'm doing, it's never more important than you are. Dan is very important to me, but you're my flesh and blood. There will never be anyone in this world as important to me as you are." She picked up her napkin and dabbed at her eyes. With her voice breaking, she said, "We're drifting apart, and I can't stand it."

Erin slid her hand across the table and grasped her mother's. She squeezed it and said, "This is just a rough patch. It'll be fine."

"I don't think it will. I've let it slide because it's clear to me that you're uncomfortable, but Dan is part of my life, and I have to integrate him into our family."

"I know," Erin said, her head down and her eyes cast to the ground. "But you seem uncomfortable, too."

"I am, or I was, but I'm better now. But Dan still seems to be off-limits. You've made it clear that you don't want to talk about my relationship with him. I've respected that, but I think that was a mistake. I think you'd like him if you got to know him better. I want to normalize things so that we're all more comfortable with one another."

"How do you intend to do that?"

"I can't do it alone. Things will only get better if you're willing to bring Dan in. I'd like to have him come here for dinner, and I'd like you to come over to his house. I'm under no illusion that you'll think of him in any sort of familial role, but I'd love it if we were all comfortable enough to spend time together."

Erin gazed at her mother for quite a long time. With a challenging tone, she asked, "Will you do the same for Katie?"

"Yes. I can't speak for Dan, but I'd like to spend time with her." She took Erin's hand in hers and placed it over her heart. "I miss you."

Erin's eyes began to mist up. "I miss you, too, Mom. I miss talking to you."

"Let's start now. I want you to tell me all about your patient and how you're feeling about everything that happened."

By the time they'd finished talking, Erin had to rush to get ready for work. When she came back downstairs, Gail asked, "Would you mind if I had Dan over for dinner tonight?"

Trying her best, Erin smiled and said, "That would be great. I might have to work a little late to make up for the appointments I missed yesterday, but I should be home by seven."

"That's just fine. I'll make one of your favorites. And Erin? I think you should talk to Dr. Worrell about how you're feeling. No one knows better what it's like to try to attend to this unruly flock."

"I'll do that, Mom. Maybe I can get some time tomorrow."

Gail hugged her tightly and kissed her cheek. "I hope you have a good day. You deserve one."

Chapter Eleven

*E*rin carved a few minutes out of her busy day to respond to a text message from Katie that asked, "Are you smiling today?"

She dialed Katie's direct office number and said, "I left that text message on my phone, and every time I look at it, I smile."

"Hello, Erin." Katie's voice was smooth and sultry. "I've been thinking about you all day. Remember the first time you kissed me?"

"Of course I do. It was only a couple of days ago."

"You said 'remember this' when you did, and I thought that might have been a line."

"But now?"

"You're not the kind of girl to use a line. I think you're just a romantic."

"Since you're the second girl I've kissed, even my lines wouldn't have been used very often. But you're right. That wasn't one. I looked into your eyes that night, and I was saying that to myself. I didn't even realize I was speaking until I heard the words, but I knew I'd want to remember."

"You're a darling woman. And I hope you're smiling more often than just the few chances you have to look at your cell phone."

"Not many more. This is a really busy day. And at the end of it, I'm having dinner with your father."

"By choice?"

"Yes. My mother's." She chuckled, saying, "She came home this morning to make me breakfast. We had a nice talk."

"How did she take the news that you'd like to get out of your contract?"

"We didn't get that far. We talked mostly about our relationship and how it's suffered since she's been seeing your dad. We both agreed that we're going to try to be more open with each other."

"Maybe you should start with the fact that you want to get out of your contract," Katie persisted.

"I'll get there. My mom suggested I talk to Dr. Worrell, my predecessor, about how I'm dealing with my patient's death. I think that was good advice. I'm going to try to feel him out about the contract issue."

"Just don't let it drag on. The sooner you talk about it, the sooner we can all put our heads together to figure out a way to make you happy."

Erin laughed, her eyes almost closing with the effort. "I don't know that it's everyone's priority, but it would be nice."

"It's my priority, and it should be yours, too."

Erin had to hustle just to get home by seven-thirty. She burst in through the front door, calling out, "I'm finally home."

Dan came out of the kitchen, holding a drink in his hand. "I'm glad you made it. Would you like a cocktail?"

"Oh, no, thanks. I don't want to hold dinner up any longer." She walked into the kitchen and gave her mom a hug. "Sorry I'm so late, but everyone from yesterday showed up today."

"Don't worry about it. I made beef stroganoff because I knew it held well."

"Mmm, one of my favorites." Erin went to the sink and washed her hands thoroughly. "Did both of you have good days?"

Dan said, "Mine was just fine. Our mild weather has let me do a lot of work I didn't think I'd be able to get to yet."

"My day was good, too," Gail said. "I'm going to go help Dan tomorrow, since it's my day off."

"I'd be glad to come help some weekend," Erin said.

Dan grasped her shoulder and said, "I'd be grateful for the help. Maybe you can get my girl out here to lend a hand."

Erin smiled tightly. "I can ask her."

Gail bustled around the roomy kitchen, putting dinner on the table. They all sat down, and before anyone had taken a bite, Dan said, "I hope you don't mind me being direct, but I don't like to tiptoe around things."

"You don't look like the kind of guy who likes to tiptoe," Erin said.

Dan laughed and took another sip of his drink. "Your mom told me about you being interested in Katie."

Gail interrupted, "You being interested in each other."

"Right, right," Dan said. "I just want you to know that it's fine with me. Katie and I don't always get along, but she's a good kid." He smiled, and it looked genuine and affectionate to Erin. "She's a very good friend to about half of

Boston, and she's loyal to a fault. You can't say that about a lot of people. She's the kind of girl who'd find money on a bus and go out of her way to turn it in."

"I believe that about her," Erin said.

"She'd do that even though the practical part of her knows that the person she turns it in to is gonna steal it." He laughed again, shaking his head. "She's the definition of a bleeding-heart liberal. I don't know where she got it from."

Erin didn't comment, thinking it best not to defend Katie and her motivations.

"I barely know her," Gail said. "We'll need to have some family dinners."

"You're not picking out china patterns yet, are you, Erin?" Dan asked. There was something almost snarky about his expression, but Erin didn't rise to the bait.

"No, we're not."

"I didn't think so. She's a tough one to pin down. She has a million friends, but I bet she doesn't have one close one." He nodded to himself as he picked up his fork and took a bite of dinner.

<hr />

After dinner, Dan and Erin went into the living room while Gail stayed in the kitchen to make coffee.

Dan smiled at Erin and said, "I think it's good for Katie to go out with someone like you. Being around a mature person might help her finally grow up."

"She doesn't seem like she needs any help from me. I think I can learn a lot from her."

"I don't think you need to learn the lessons Katie can teach you. You seem like a very levelheaded woman. Not that Katie's dumb or anything. She just doesn't always seem to think first."

Erin was itching to tell Dan she wasn't interested in his observations, but she thought it wiser to let him talk. "If things work out between us, I'm sure we'll both benefit from each other's background and knowledge. I'm not worried about it."

"No doubt about it. Experience is the best teacher, and Katie's got an awful lot of experience. An awful lot."

Gail came into the room carrying cups of coffee for herself and Dan. "Are you sure you don't want any, Erin? It's decaf."

"No, thanks, Mom. I really enjoyed dinner. It's been a long time since we had stroganoff."

"Your mom is a great cook. Did you learn all of her secrets?"

Shaking her head, Erin said, "No. I've never cooked. I had an apartment when

I was a resident, but I was hardly ever at home. I was very good at ordering pizza, though."

"I'd be happy to teach you anything you want to learn," Gail said. "You just let me know."

"I will, Mom. You won't think me rude if I go to bed now, will you? It's been a very long day."

"You go right ahead," Dan said. "I should get going myself."

"You're not staying over?" Erin asked.

Gail looked from her daughter to Dan and back again. "I thought…we thought that wasn't appropriate." She looked horribly embarrassed, and even Dan looked uncomfortable.

Erin went over to her mother and gave her a hug and a kiss. "You should do whatever feels right to you. You don't have to stand on ceremony for me."

"We'll think about that for the future. Goodnight, honey."

"Goodnight, Erin."

"I had a nice time tonight. You're welcome to come anytime, Dan." She walked up the stairs to her room, hoping he didn't take her too literally.

⁂

Erin heard the front door close, and she looked out her window to see her mother and Dan get into his truck. She shook her head, a little perturbed that Gail hadn't admitted she was leaving with him. She started to get undressed while she tucked the phone under her chin and called Katie. "Hi," she said, her mood lifting just to hear her voice.

"Hi, there. Hold on a sec, will you? I've got some people over."

For some reason, Erin tensed up when Katie said that. Her stomach was knotted with anxiety when Katie came back on the line. "Hi," she said, the ambient noise much reduced. "Some of my buddies came over to watch the Sox."

"Oh. I didn't know they were on TV."

"I hate to admit this, but I pay extra to get all of the games, even spring training." She chuckled, saying, "I'm such a baseball groupie it's not even funny. If I'd invested all of the money I've spent on the Sox through the years, I wouldn't have to work."

"How many people are watching with you?" Even as she asked, Erin knew it was none of her business. "I mean, you said buddies. Is that, uhm, guys or… girls…" she trailed off weakly.

Katie's tone was friendly, but there was a hint of warning in it. "Jealous already?"

"No, no, I'm just interested. I want to know what your life is like."

She laughed wryly. "It's like the life of every other adult who pays to watch people exercise. Pathetic."

"That's not pathetic. You exercise, too. You couldn't slide down a hill the way you do if you weren't in shape. I love the Sox, too, you know, and I don't think my life is pathetic."

"You sound…" There was a significant pause. "Less than happy tonight. What's going on?"

"Mmm, not much. I am a little glum. I worked awfully hard today, and then I had to be a good hostess for your father when I wanted to just go to bed."

"Right. I forgot about that. How'd it go?"

"Fine, I guess. My mom was pretty anxious. I see how much she wants us to get along, and that makes it harder. But it was all right."

"I'm sure he brought me up. He can't resist."

Erin tried to stop herself, but she started talking before she could. "Do you like fussing and fighting with your dad? It seems like you get pleasure out of it."

"Erin," Katie said, her voice low with warning. "This isn't a good direction to go in. I understand if you're feeling out-of-sorts, but don't pick on me."

"I apologize," Erin said stiffly. "Maybe we'd better talk later."

"Your call. I'm here for you if you want to talk."

"You've got people over there. You probably don't have time."

"I'm a big girl. If I don't have time, I'll say so. You don't have to think for me."

"Darn it!" Erin snapped. "I can't say anything right. You've got so many darned rules! I'm going to hang up before I make any more mistakes."

"If that's what you want."

"I don't know what I want," Erin admitted, sounding calmer. "I'm just grouchy. I think I'll go to bed."

"I hope you sleep well. Can I give you a kiss?"

Erin smiled and let out a little laugh. "Please."

Katie made a loud smack into the phone. "You don't have to be in a good mood to call me. I just have some boundaries that I don't let people cross. Don't think I'm a bitch, okay?"

"I don't think you're anything other than a nice woman who has a lot of rules."

"Damn, I can't even trick you into saying 'bitch'? You're righteous."

"Goodnight, Katie. Have fun with your friends."

"You mean supermodels. A baker's dozen of them. All hot and naïve and loose—"

"Bye-bye." Erin hung up and got into bed without bothering to brush or floss. She was trying to decide if she was irritated or hurt when the phone rang. She got up and picked up her cell, not surprised to see Katie's number. "Hi. Miss me?"

"No," Katie said, chuckling. "I was trying to be funny, but I shouldn't do that when you're grumpy. My bad."

"It's okay. I think I'm a little lonely. That can make me grouchy."

"Lonely?"

"Yeah. I miss you. It feels like you're so far away."

"Is my dad still there?"

"No. He and my mom snuck out of here like a pair of teenagers. I told them I didn't mind if your dad stayed over, but my mom said they didn't think that was appropriate, whatever that means. So, as soon as I came upstairs, they ducked out."

"That's love. When you can't stand to be apart even when it makes you look dumb, that's a sure sign."

"Oh, yeah. They've as much as moved in together."

"Living in sin, huh?"

"I never would have guessed it for her. She's pretty traditional. But she's different now."

"Well, you'd have your own place if she officially moved out. It might be nice to have some privacy."

"I don't need privacy," Erin said, trying not to whine. "And I don't need a whole house just for myself. If she moves out, I might try to find an apartment."

"Are there any?"

"Yeah. The room over the drugstore has been vacant for a while."

"The room over the drugstore? Erin!"

"What? I don't need much. It'd be even closer to work."

"When you say 'room,' do you mean that it's just a room?"

"Yeah. Bathroom at the end of the hall. No kitchen."

"Are you stealing from your drug supply? That's like living in a garage. I sue landlords to improve places like that."

"I don't have much money."

"You have more than that! Are you really saying you'd rather your mom sell your home than live in it alone?"

"Oh, darn," Erin said, letting out a heavy breath. "No, I don't want her to sell the house. It's got too many memories." She started to cry softly. "I must be getting my period. I've got to check the calendar."

"Maybe you're just sad. That's allowed, you know."

"Are you sure? That's not against the rules?"

"I do have a lot of rules," Katie admitted, sounding a little hurt. "But I don't think they're too onerous. I've got boundaries. Hard-earned ones."

"I understand. I could use some myself."

"Yes, you could. I'm sure you don't want my dad sleeping over. Why did you offer that?"

"I don't know," Erin said glumly. "I was just trying to be accommodating. It's what my mom wants."

"I bet your mom doesn't want you to be uncomfortable. I think she wants you to be genuine."

Erin chuckled softly. "Nobody wants that. They want you to put up a good front."

"I don't. I want you to be honest and genuine. That's how I'll be with you."

"I'll try. I genuinely care for you, Katie. I'm very honest about that."

"I care for you, too."

"Do you mind telling me who's at your house? I guess I am a little jealous. Not because I think you're dating other women, which I know you're allowed to do, but because I'm jealous that other people are with you and I'm not."

"I don't mind a bit. I never mind answering questions. I just don't like innuendo. That's what made me snap at you. I apologize for that."

"It's okay. So, who's there?"

"Matt and Mary Connelly, Tony Giarmo, and Rick Matthews. Rick's girlfriend is supposed to come, but she hasn't shown yet."

"Did I meet all of them?"

"Yep. Every one of them. They're my main BoSox buddies."

"I want to be there. I want to be a BoSox buddy."

"Aw, you sound like a little girl."

"I'm sorry—"

"Don't apologize for being adorable. I like little girls. Don't take that literally, by the way. I like big girls who have a little bit of little girl left in them."

"I try to hide mine most of the time. I don't like to have people see me acting like a kid."

"If you want to be my girlfriend, and I think you do," Katie added sexily, "you won't try to hide parts of yourself. You'll open up to me. That's the key. Opening up."

"Will you open up to me, too?"

"That's the only way it works. It's got to be mutual."

"I'll try, Katie. I really will try."

"Oh, I can hear how little you are today. You didn't make a sex joke, and I gave you a huge opening."

"I guess I'm not feeling sexy tonight."

"Damn! I gave you an even bigger one, and you didn't bite. You need some sleep. Here's a big kiss. Now go to bed and feel all better in the morning, okay?"

"I'll try. Here's a kiss back." Erin made a smooching sound. "I'll call you later in the week."

"Not soon enough. Call me tomorrow. I miss you, too."

Erin hung up, and by the time she lay down, she was smiling.

❧

The next afternoon, Erin finished with her last patient and walked into her office to find Doctor Worrell sitting at her chair. "Change the nameplate on the desk, and it's yours," she said, hugging him as he stood up.

"No, this one's all yours now." He patted the desk fondly. "If I examine the corners, I might find your teeth marks on it. I seem to recall you being a chewer."

"I have no memories of that period, but if you think so, it's probably true." She took off her white coat and hung it up. "Did you know I was going to call you today?"

"No, but Madge did." He chuckled. "She's maddening, isn't she?"

Erin sat down in her chair, and Dr. Worrell took the chair opposite her desk. "She's my lifeline. Her annoying traits don't come close to equaling her good ones. I just pray she never wants to retire."

"She'll probably outlast you. She'd have to volunteer at her church to get half the gossip she gets here. She might as well get paid for it."

Erin laughed, nodding her agreement. "I assume Madge called you to come over and help me put death into perspective."

"That sounds like more than I'm capable of, but she mentioned something along those lines. Having a tough time, pup?"

"Yeah." She put her hands on her desk and clasped them together. "Very tough."

"I thought you'd be prepared for your patient's death," he said, gazing at her curiously. "You've had a long time to realize it was inevitable."

"Yes, I did. It's not that it caught me by surprise. It's just that I…I'm having a very hard time getting past it. I'm going to her memorial service tonight."

"Just pay your respects and leave. That's your job. Keep it simple."

"I'll try. It's just really hard for me."

"Did you know her a lot better than the rest of us did? Did you spend a lot of time talking?"

"No, not really. We only talked about her pain."

Doctor Worrell stood up and walked over to the window, looking out on the people strolling down Main Street. "I don't want to have to beat this out of you, Erin. It wouldn't look good."

She chuckled softly. "There's nothing to beat. It just wore me down to visit her and watch her die. I don't have any other way to explain it."

"But that's your job," he said, turning to face her. "That's almost the essence of it. The only reason the town decided to hire you was so we could hold on to that old style of medicine. Supporting a patient as she dies is something you can't get from some HMO over in Nashua."

Erin dropped her head into her hands and rubbed at her eyes roughly. "I know that, and I'm doing what I'm supposed to be doing. It's just hard for me."

"I think you're getting too involved, pup. You've got to be able to step back and have some distance."

"I'm sure you're right. Now I have to figure out how to do that. I can't seem to find the 'off' switch for my emotions."

Doctor Worrell sat down heavily. "I don't know how to tell you to do that. It wasn't that hard for me. Of course, back in my day, we were pretty sure we were gods by the time we got out of school. I had to work on being emotionally connected." He pursed his lips thoughtfully. "That took me quite a few years."

"I'll be in my narcotics safe if I can't get some distance soon. Miss Blake's heart is failing fast."

"Did she teach you?"

"First grade," Erin said sadly. "I was crazy about her. I wanted to be just like her when I grew up."

"Some little girl will feel the same way about you. That's part of the thread that holds us all together."

"I suppose. I just hope that little girl doesn't want to be just like Dr. Delancy, now serving ten years for writing fake prescriptions."

Doctor Worrell looked at her carefully, his expression somber. "I've never known you to tease about things like this."

"I'm not teasing." She shook her head. "I am, in a way, of course. You know I'd never abuse drugs. But I'm not teasing about how I feel. I'm just using gallows humor."

"You shouldn't feel that your job is a gallows, Erin. You're going to have it for forty years if you're lucky."

"That's not something I'm able to contemplate right now. I'm just going to try to get through the week." She stood up, and he rose with her. "I appreciate that you came by. I've got to run to get over to the funeral home. They're only having visitation for an hour." She went to get her coat, adding, "I think that speaks of the poor woman's popularity."

"I'm worried about you," Doctor Worrell said, grasping Erin by the shoulders and looking into her eyes. "Call me in a few days."

"I will. Or maybe I'll stop by on Saturday. I go see Miss Blake most Saturday mornings, and she's just a block from you."

"Do that," he said, gazing at her worriedly as she left the office.

❧

As Erin pulled out of the parking lot at the funeral home, she dialed her home, getting no answer. Determined to be more interactive, she dialed her mother's cell phone, which was answered in four rings. "Hi, honey," Gail said.

"Hi, Mom. I'm getting ready to go home, and I wanted to see if you were there."

"No, I'm over at Dan's. Do you need something? I can be home in twenty minutes."

"No, I don't need anything. I haven't had dinner yet, so if you weren't cooking, I was going to stop some place around here."

"Around…oh, I forgot you had to go to the service tonight. How was it?"

"Not too bad. My attendance increased the crowd by 25 percent, so I'm really glad I went. My patient wasn't close to her relatives, but it's got to be awful to bury someone and have only one non-relative come."

"One besides you?"

"No. Just me."

"Oh, Erin, are you sure you don't want me to come home and make you something? Or you could come by here, and I'd have you fixed up in minutes. Why don't you do that?"

"No, I think I'll stop here. I've got a book with me that can keep me company. I'm starving, to be honest. I want to eat soon."

"You don't think about yourself until you have a free minute. You've got to learn how to be more selfish, even though I know that doesn't come easily for you."

"I can be selfish. I just don't want to make a habit of it," she added, laughing tiredly.

"Get a little bite to eat and go home and rest. You're working too hard."

"I'm fine, Mom. I just wanted to check in with you."

"Thank you, Erin. You're a good daughter and a good doctor. I'm proud of you, sweetheart. I know it wasn't easy for you to go tonight."

"It was okay. That's my job, Mom. For better or worse."

❧

Erin was just finishing her dinner when her cell phone rang. She tried to keep from rolling her eyes at the thought that it was a patient, knowing that wasn't a good habit to get into. A smile lit her face when she saw it was Katie calling. "Hi," she said.

"How was the 'event'?"

"Not too bad. I can hardly hear you. Is that your TV?"

"No, I'm out with some friends. I just wanted to make sure I talked to you before you went to bed. I know the sandman comes to your house early."

"Aw, you're nice. Are you having fun?"

"If I wasn't having fun, I'd go home." Katie paused for a moment and said, "Were you trying to ask me what I was doing?"

"Yeah. Do I have to be explicit all the time?"

"No, you don't. My bad. My bad. I've just gone out with women who were pretty clingy. I need to remind myself that isn't how you are."

"I'm just interested," Erin said, sounding offended. "I'm not clingy."

"I know that. I'll try to cut you a break."

"Thanks."

"We're out at a club listening to a band some of us like. I'll take you to hear them the next time they're playing on the weekend."

"Okay," Erin said, perking up. "What kind of music?"

"Rock and jazz, I guess. I'm not that knowledgeable about music. I just like them."

"I'd like to go to a club with you."

"And stay up late?"

"I can manage. I've got to drive home now, so I'd better go."

"Where are you?"

Erin laughed quietly. "Are you being clingy?"

"Not in my bag of tricks."

"It doesn't have to be. You know that I haven't had a date in years, and I don't notice when women are checking me out. I'm not the kind of woman you have to keep a close eye on."

"Oh, yes, you are. I want to keep my eye on you. Both eyes."

"I like that. Can I put my eyes on you this weekend?"

"You sure can. Come over on Friday night."

"Oh, I can't. I have to go see a patient on Saturday."

"Want me to come to see you?"

Erin sounded flabbergasted. "Would you?"

"Of course! You're my girlfriend."

"I thought we were just casually dating."

"Hmm. You must have gotten a promotion because you're my girlfriend, Erin Delancy, and don't try to weasel out of it."

❧

Katie called Erin on Thursday evening, greeting her with, "When do you want me, Slick?"

"Slick?" Erin asked, laughing. "No one has ever called me Slick. Where did that come from?"

"Who knows? I've been trying to think of a good nickname for you, so I'm trying some out."

"Does Slick have any meaning?"

"Not yet. I'm not crazy about it, to tell you the truth, but you don't have any traits that jump out at me."

"Not one?" Erin asked, sounding offended.

"Well, there's beautiful and lovely and pretty and smart and clever and thoughtful and sweet, but those aren't good nicknames. I'm looking for something like Curly or Stumpy or One-Eye. Something obvious."

"How about Doc?"

"Oh, Erin, I can see you have no aptitude in the nickname game. That's too obvious."

"More obvious than One-Eye?"

"Well, maybe not One-Eye, but Doc isn't colorful enough. Unless you weren't a doctor, that is. If you gave medical advice all of the time, but didn't know what you were talking about, you might earn Doc."

"I agree with you."

"About what?"

"I have no aptitude in the nickname game. What's yours?"

"You didn't hear anyone call me by my nickname when you were at my house?"

"No, I don't think so."

"Then you have to wait. You'll know soon enough."

"How about tomorrow?"

"Mmm, probably not tomorrow. It might take a while. You're not terribly quick at this, you know."

"No, that's when I'd like you to come over. Can you make it?"

"That all depends. How long do you want me to stay?"

"As long as you want."

"Answer the question, Slick. How long?"

"Until Sunday night. Or longer."

"Okay, you're getting the hang of this. I want an honest answer when I ask a question like this. I don't want to come for just the evening if you'd like me there the whole time or show up with a suitcase when you want me to have a cup of tea and take off."

"Katie, you can assume that I want you to show up with a suitcase. Or a moving van."

"Ack! The lesbian second date!"

"Just kidding. But since I'm your girlfriend, I need to spend time with you to cement my position."

"I'll clear my calendar. I probably won't get out of the city until latish. Is that okay?"

"Sure. How latish?"

"I have dinner plans for tomorrow, and I don't like to cancel this late. So, probably ten, maybe eleven."

"Okay. I'll take a nap when I get home. Call me if you're going to be much later than eleven, so I don't worry."

"Well done. Ask and you shall receive."

"Ha! I've been turned down for something I've asked for a couple of times already."

"Maybe that should be 'ask for something that I don't think will hurt our relationship' and you shall receive. How's that?"

"That's good. I like that you're taking care of our relationship."

"And you."

"That's the best part, as long as I can take care of you."

"That's the deal, Slick. I'm a giver, but I don't give to a taker."

⟐

Katie arrived at ten minutes until eleven on Friday night. Erin had been too agitated to sleep, so she'd taken a long bath while she waited. She'd had a glass of red wine as well, so she was relaxed by the time she heard footsteps on the porch.

Erin opened the door right before Katie knocked. "Well," Katie said as she raked her eyes over Erin. "You look like a juicy peach."

"I took a bath and decided to put on my robe."

Katie lifted her chin to allow for the difference in their heights created by the threshold. "Kiss?"

Replying with a soft, sweet kiss, Erin said, "Come on in. Can I get you something?"

"Beer?"

"I bought some just for you," Erin said proudly. "Of course, I had to explain why I was buying beer, since everyone at the store knows that neither my mother nor I ever buy any."

Katie set her overnight bag on the floor and took off her anorak. "I'd be up in the bell tower picking people off with an AK-47 if I lived here. I don't like it that the people at my local coffee shop know my order. They're always so proud of the fact that they've memorized it that I hate to change it even when I want something different."

"The day I got my first period, the pharmacist congratulated me when I walked by his store." Erin put her hands around her neck and feigned throttling herself. "If you want privacy, this ain't the place."

They walked into the kitchen hand in hand. "I like privacy, but I could probably get used to a small town. I was just teasing about going nuts if I lived in a place like this. I'd just have to leave town to buy sex toys and crack."

"Sex toys definitely. You could probably find crack fairly easily." Erin took a beer from the refrigerator. "You'd have to go to the bad part of town, though."

"There's a bad part?"

"Well, it's a bad street. It's over by the factory, just next to the train tracks. We can drive over there this weekend—if you're brave enough."

Katie took a sip. "Mmm, the first sip is the best. Want one?"

"Sure." Erin took a healthy swig. "That really is good."

"But you don't like it enough to buy any?"

"No. I like wine. It's good for your heart, you know, according to some studies that often conflict."

"An honest doctor. What a find." Katie took Erin's hand and led her back into the living room. "Are our parents out for the night?"

"Yep. My mom came home and cooked dinner for me, but she left at around nine."

Katie snuggled up against Erin, who put her arm around Katie's shoulders. "Wanna make out?"

"Yes." With a devilish smile on her face, Erin shifted and kissed Katie longingly. Then kissed her again. She was about to pull away when she had to have another, this one longer and softer and sweeter than the last. "I like to make out."

Katie's voice took on a decided purr. She stroked Erin's cheek with her fingers, while looking into her eyes. "You really are a beautiful woman. I think you have the sexiest eyes I've ever seen." She touched the edge of an eyelid. "They're so dark and expressive. I can see little squalls roll through them when you're upset or sad. But when you're happy…" She sighed deeply. "They're the most welcoming things on earth. So warm and peaceful."

Erin dipped her head and kissed Katie again, sighing when arms draped around her neck and pulled her close. They kissed gently and tenderly, not escalating the tiny fire that burned between them whenever they were close. "Let's do this every Friday night. This is the perfect end to a not-so-perfect week."

Leaning her head on the sofa, Katie continued to touch Erin's face. "I've been looking forward to this weekend. I was worried when I didn't hear from you by Thursday. I thought you might not have time to see me."

Eyes opening wide, Erin said, "Was I supposed to call?"

"Yes," Katie purred. "You invited me to your house. You needed to tell me when to arrive."

"Oops. I thought I'd made it clear that you were welcome anytime. I assumed you'd tell me when you were available."

"Well, I normally would have waited you out, but you've gotten under my skin, Peaches. I'm off my game."

"Peaches?" Erin asked weakly. "That's not a great one. It sounds like a cat's name."

"It is." Katie playfully stroked Erin's hair. "You don't mind if I pet you, do you?"

"Not a bit."

She tickled under Erin's chin. "How about this?"

"That's gooood."

"Scratch your belly?"

"Anytime." Erin straightened up, presenting her midsection to Katie's fingers.

"Comb your pretty hair?"

"I'd be yours forever. I love to have my hair combed."

"What will you do if I scratch right above your tail?" Katie's eyes were filled with daring.

"Uhm, I'm not sure, but I bet I'd love it."

Playfully patting both of Erin's cheeks, Katie asked, "Have you ever had a cat?"

"No. Never."

"Well, let me give you a little tip. If you scratch a cat right above her tail, she'll shake it like it's electrified. My next question was going to be about pulling on the skin over your shoulder blades. A male bites right there when he's going to mount her. Sometimes, a cat will bite and snap at you when you scratch her there."

With a sexy smile playing at her mouth, Erin said, "I promise never to snap at you when you mount me. I'm sure I'd purr, though. And if the mood strikes me, I might bite, but I don't think you'll mind." She leaned forward and nibbled on Katie's neck, making her squeal and try to wrench away. Erin held her tightly, continuing to nibble and lick until Katie was shrieking for her to stop. "I guess you're ticklish, huh?" Erin asked, not looking sorry in the least.

"Not very!" Katie pulled her shirt down and pushed her hair from her eyes. "But that was fantastic foreplay. Make a note."

"I don't need a note. I want to kiss and lick and touch every part of you. No one has to remind me of that." Her voice was low and soft, and the sexual vibes pouring from Erin made Katie squirm.

She gently pushed Erin away and took several deep breaths. "You're not shy, are you?"

"I told you I wasn't." Erin's head hadn't moved, and her gaze was nearly burning.

Katie turned away, giggling. "You can't look at me that way, Erin! You make me want to climb into your lap and have my way with you."

"Who's stopping you?"

Taking Erin's head in her hands, Katie turned it so there was no chance of eye contact. "I'm stopping me. Just barely, I might add."

Looking straight ahead, Erin leaned over and rested her torso on Katie. "How about a little push?"

"Not just yet." She wrapped her arms around Erin's shoulders and pulled her down into her lap. "I don't know what you do, but it's very hard to stay on track when you touch me like you do. You're very dangerous."

"May I ask a question?"

"Yesss," Katie replied, drawing out the *s*.

"Why do you have your 'no sex' rule?"

"I told you. Once I start having sex, I get very invested. It's so much harder if things don't work out. I've had more experience in this area, and trust me, it sucks to break up when you think you could've fallen in love."

"I know that, even though it's only happened to me once."

"So, you get my point?"

"No." Erin disentangled herself from Katie's grip and sat up to face her. "It would be very hard for me if you decided not to see me anymore. I'm sure it would be harder and harder the longer we're together, but I don't think having sex would make it that much worse. Actually, I think sex can help us know we're right for each other."

"Ooh, you must have been with men. You've got the logic down."

"Logic is logic, no matter which sex spouts it."

Katie took Erin's hand and kissed it. "I don't want to frustrate you. I really don't. I just believe this is right for me. You understand that, don't you?"

"Absolutely. I'm just giving you my view. And I don't want to give you the impression that I want to have sex just for release. I want to have it to communicate with you."

"In Braille?"

"No. With my heart." She flipped their clasped hands and brought them to her chest. "You're better at expressing things with words. I'm not as extemporaneous as you are. Sometimes, I have to think about things and ponder them a little before I'm sure what I think or feel."

"Yeah, I see that. And I'm sorry if I push you too much to tell me things before you're ready."

"That's fine. We'll learn how to accommodate each other. That's part of the fun of falling in love."

Solemn-faced, Katie looked into Erin's eyes. "Do you think you're falling in love with me?"

Slowly, Erin nodded her head. "I do. And as soon as you're ready, I want to tell you how I feel about you—with my body."

Katie took hold of the fabric of Erin's robe and pulled her closer. "You didn't learn that from a guy. That came from here." She patted the peach-colored fleece that covered Erin's heart.

⁂

The Delancy women had changed Brad's high school-boy room into a cheery guest room. Erin led Katie up to the room once they both started to yawn more than talk. "This is nice," Katie said. "Am I going to sleep in here alone?"

"I thought you'd want to."

"I think I do." She took Erin in her arms and hugged her close. "Thanks for telling me more about you." Lifting her head, she smiled broadly. "I love hearing about you and all of the things that make you tick."

"I hope you don't feel pressured about sex. I really don't want to do that. I'm just trying to be honest and say what I'm thinking."

"Mmm." Katie looked up at the ceiling and closed one eye. "I don't feel pressured, but I know you're ready. I hate to deny you something you're ready for, but—"

"I'm just trying to do what you asked me to do. I'm trying to tell you what's on my mind and what I'm ready for. That doesn't mean that you have to be ready at the same time. This won't work if we don't follow our hearts." Erin tilted her head and kissed Katie for a long time, savoring the sweetness of her mouth. "Sleep well."

"I will." Erin turned and started to leave the room, but Katie wrapped her arms around her from behind, whispering into her ear, "I think I'm falling for you, too. Hard. And fast." She felt Erin's giggle through her own body.

"Keep falling. I'll catch you."

Chapter Twelve

They spent the next morning at Erin's first-grade teacher's home, with Erin tending to her while visiting. On the way back to the car, Katie took in a deep breath of the sweet, clean spring air. "I can see why you like it here. It must be nice to live in a place where people take care of each other."

Erin came up next to her and took Katie's hand. "To be honest, you can slip through the cracks here, too. But Miss Blake is beloved. She gave a lot to the town, and people appreciate that. At our church, there's a sign-up list to make sure someone is with her every day. My mom takes her dinner every other week." She chuckled. "She'd do it every night, but she can only get on the schedule every two weeks. It's almost a competition now."

Katie pulled Erin close and leaned her head on her shoulder. "I think it's adorable. If I lived here, I'd bust my ass to make sure I was beloved." She grinned at Erin and winked. "I'd love to have people fighting over trying to please me when I'm old and frail."

"She is awfully frail, isn't she?" Erin asked, her expressive eyes betraying her sadness.

They got into the car, and Erin spent a moment mumbling under her breath to convince the car to turn over. "Ah," she said, when it stopped balking and coughed to life.

"How long have you had this car?"

"About a year. Why?"

"A year?" Katie shifted to avoid the spring that threatened to pierce her side. "Really?"

"Yeah. I didn't have one when I moved back. I couldn't afford much, so Butch at the garage bought this one for me at auction." She patted the dash. "Three thousand bucks. Not bad, huh?"

"For three thousand, it's very nice. Is this, uhm, is this really all you could afford?"

Erin's brows knit together. "I could have gone to thirty-five hundred, but I didn't want to. This one's been just fine. She doesn't like dampness, but she's great in the cold. Started up every time this winter."

Katie tried to hold her tongue, but she wasn't able to. "Do you get paid at all?"

Erin's smile was slow and easy, and she spoke thoughtfully, the way she often did when she was revealing something personal. "Yeah, but not much more than I got as a resident. I'd make more if I were teaching first grade."

Katie was obviously not willing to let the subject drop. "Can't schoolteachers afford their own apartments? I don't want to pry, but where in the heck does your money go?"

"I'm glad you don't want to pry." Erin snuck a very quick look to her right, showing that she was teasing. "I've spent most of my take home pay on the house. My mom has let a lot of things slide because she just didn't have the money. She makes a lot less than I do."

"Damn," Katie said, almost under her breath.

"I paid for a new roof and a new boiler this year. And we had to have some electrical work done. That stuff is expensive," she said with feeling.

"I know that. Owning an older home is like owning a boat. A money pit."

"Maybe I'll go take some classes at the county trade school. I could probably be a pretty good carpenter."

"You seem down. Wanna talk?"

"Sure." She pulled over, even though there wasn't another car in sight. "Where do you want to go? My house or somewhere else?"

"Let's go to Nashua and have lunch someplace nice. My treat."

Erin's face scrunched up in a way that made her look like a ten-year-old. "You don't have to pay for me."

"I want to." Katie put her fingers under Erin's armpit and tried to tickle her to no effect. "I make more for working less. Let's redistribute the wealth a little. Our own little communist system."

"I'm a firm believer in capitalism."

"So am I, but I want a nice lunch, and I don't want to worry that you're using your last dime to pay for your share."

"I could just have a salad," Erin said, grinning shyly.

"Drive, Cookie. We're going to eat well. We can argue about the bill later."

⌘

They were ensconced in a booth at a quiet Italian restaurant when Katie said,

"Now that you're not distracted, tell me how you're feeling."

Giving her a chiding look, Erin said, "You were the one who was distracting me. You've got to stop pinching and tickling me when I drive."

"You're fun to play with. You look so serious when you drive, with your lovely hands right on ten and two like they taught you in driving class. I can't help fucking with you."

"I thought following Mr. Gordy's directions would save my life, not endanger it."

The tone Erin used made Katie want to slap herself for teasing Erin while she was driving. Having lost half of her family to a car accident must have made her overly cautious. Trying to lighten the mood, she said, "I hate to break it to you, but everything they told you in school is total bullshit."

"Unh-uh." Erin shook her head. "I'll never believe Miss Blake lied to me."

Katie reached across the table and took Erin's hand, looking up, annoyed when their server approached and gave them a censorious look. "Yes?" Katie asked, meeting the man's eyes.

"I'd like to tell you about our specials." His expression was cold, and his small, closely set eyes glared at her.

In a conversational tone, Katie asked, "Would you rather we went somewhere else?"

"Pardon?" His eyebrows shot up in surprise.

"You gave us a disapproving look when you walked over. I assume that's because I was holding my girlfriend's hand. If you'd rather not wait on us, we'll go somewhere else." Even though her words were pointed, her tone was friendly and calm.

"We serve *every*one here," he said, acting as though he wished they didn't.

"I didn't ask if you *would* serve us," Katie persisted. "I asked if you'd rather not."

His small mouth pursed, and he said, "I'm happy to serve you."

He looked like he'd just eaten a lemon, but Katie seemed happy with his response. "Great. You can just leave the menus. We don't need to hear about the specials."

He placed the menus on the table and turned to walk away. Katie watched him, growling, "Don't fuck with me, prick."

Erin was leaning back in the booth, looking stunned. "Wow. Do you always do that?"

"What? Call people out when they don't give me a little respect?"

"Uhm, yeah, I guess that's what you did."

"Every time." She picked up her menu and tapped Erin's with it. "I hope it doesn't bother you 'cause I'm not going to stop. I never argue; I just make people admit their prejudice or back down."

"I don't do that," Erin said, not surprising Katie in the least.

"You look like you might prefer *I* didn't do that. Am I right?"

Erin couldn't stop herself from smiling. "Stop being so perceptive. It's like being under an emotional microscope."

Katie made her eyes wide and stared at Erin. "I can see inside you, Dr. Delancy. Deep, deep inside you."

"That's how it feels sometimes. It's hard to get used to."

Shrugging, Katie said, "I don't think I can change. I'm interested in your feelings. If you don't offer them up, I'm going to come digging for them."

"Well, I guess I could learn to be a little more open."

"Be open now. Tell me what you thought when I was calling our adorable little waiter on the carpet."

"Mmm, I'd have to say I thought you were being rude."

"Me?" Katie pointed at herself with her thumb. "He's the one who was giving us the fish-eye."

"Yeah, but he didn't say anything. He just looked like he smelled something bad."

"True. That's why I gave him the option. If he didn't want to wait on us, I would have left."

"That's hardly fair, Katie. He's not able to be honest. If he told you to leave, he might have gotten fired."

"One more slush-face out of my life." She slapped her hands together. "Mission accomplished."

"Right." Erin nodded forcefully. "You weren't really asking him if he wanted to wait on us. You were trying to humiliate him."

"Sure was." She looked so pleased with herself that Erin had to laugh.

"You're really unrepentant, aren't you?"

"Yeah, I am. I don't take shit."

"Okay, I don't think you should let people walk over you, but you could just get up and leave. You don't have to make an issue out of it."

Katie's eyes closed halfway, and her jaw worked for a few seconds as she thought. "I think I do. I do that because I'd get angry if I let someone disrespect me. Calling jerks out lets me maintain my self-respect. If I just slunk away, I'd feel like I'd done something wrong. And I didn't," she added pointedly.

"I like your self-respect. The waiter really was glaring at us, but I tried to ignore it."

"I can't. My way works for me."

"That's important, but I'd never do something like that." She looked at Katie for a moment. "You won't get upset if I don't follow your lead, will you?"

"Nope. If you don't mind if someone disrespects you, it's cool with me. But if someone disrespects me, I'm going to stand up for myself. Is that okay with you?"

"Yeah, I think so. This is probably the kind of thing we're going to have to reach an accommodation on."

"I can negotiate. I'm trained. By the way, I'll probably curse a blue streak if someone's rude to you. Just thought you should know." Katie blew Erin a kiss. "I like being able to talk about things like this without getting upset about them. I like how calm you are. You don't get your back up about things."

"Usually not. My natural demeanor is calm." She glanced at the menu and said, "Pumpkin ravioli for me."

"That was quick." Katie spent a few minutes looking at her menu, and when she looked up, Erin was smiling at her.

"I like to watch you look at a menu. I can see your eyes flitting across things and then coming back again. It's like you're thinking about each dish and how it'll taste."

"I am. Now tell me how you're feeling before I have to slap our waiter around again."

Erin shook her head, fairly sure that Katie would do just that if she was pushed. "I'm sure I'm down after seeing Miss Blake. She's going to die soon, and I don't want to have to sign her death certificate. I'd like to be one of the many mourners, not the attending physician."

"I think you're going to have to get busy and take some proactive steps. You're going to have to go to the people you contracted with and lay your cards on the table."

"That kills my appetite." She dropped her head. "They're the ones who insisted on making the contract so…"

"Unconscionable."

"No, that's not true. No one forced me to do this. I had other options."

"Don't think about it now. Let's enjoy our day and put business aside."

Erin tried to fix a smile on her face, but it wasn't very effective.

"Come on, now." Katie gave her a devilish grin. "I'm going to come over there and tickle you."

"I'm not ticklish, remember?"

Katie extended her hands and moved her fingers quickly. "You will be if I get my hands on you in public. You'll be giggling like a baby."

After lunch, they went for a walk along the Nashua River, another first for Katie. "It's lovely here," she said, taking Erin's arm and holding it to her body with both of her hands.

Erin slid her arm away and draped it across Katie's shoulders. "I want you to be closer."

"This is even nicer." She snuggled against Erin's body, smiling with contentment. "I fell a little more in love with you today."

"You did? Tell me why so I can do more of whatever it was." Erin giggled when Katie slipped her cold hand under her sweater to tickle her waist. "I'm not ticklish!"

"Then why are you laughing?"

"Because you're funny. You get a very cute look on your face when you tickle me. Now, tell me more about this falling in love. I'm very receptive to that."

"Well, I've known you were a generous woman, but I was so touched by the way you interacted with your old teacher today. I almost cried when you told her you needed to massage her feet to check on her circulation."

Erin grinned guiltily. "I don't think she believes that, either, but everyone needs to be touched. She smiles so serenely when I rub her feet."

"She loves you."

"I love her, too. She's almost like an aunt."

"I can see that." Katie noted the tears welling up in Erin's brown eyes. "I can clearly see what a loving woman you are."

Sitting by the river, Katie relaxed into the lounge chair she'd made out of Erin's body. "You're very comfortable. Not bony."

"No, I'm just bony enough to give my flesh some structure," Erin agreed, chuckling.

"You know what I mean. I'm all angles and sharp points."

"No, you're not. You have some very soft spots. I've rubbed against them." She laughed softly. "The day you came to pick me up to go to Killington, I almost drooled when I saw how your soft spots looked in that sweater."

"I changed three times to make sure I was wearing something that would catch your eye. I could tell you liked my…sweater."

"I barely noticed the sweater. Was I really obvious?"

"Yeah. Just like I planned. You're pretty easy."

"I don't have a lot of experience in this, you know. I'm a little slow sometimes."

"You're not slow at all. You're cute." She turned her head and nuzzled against Erin's face, waiting for a kiss. When she got it, she asked, "Do you know why you're falling for me? You *are* still falling for me, aren't you?"

"Yeah. No change there." Erin dipped her head and kissed all of the bare skin she could reach. "It's awfully fun falling for you, Katie."

"I know." She cuddled closer. "There's nothing better, is there?"

"Nothing I've experienced. I'm not going to try opiates, so I think falling in love will be a peak experience for me."

"I'm not into opiates myself. Liquor isn't an opiate, is it?"

"Not unless they've found a new chemical in it."

"Are you avoiding my original question?"

"About why I'm falling for you? No, I'm just thinking."

"Okay. I'll watch the river. Let me know. No hurry."

Erin watched the river, too. She let her focus soften and idly played with Katie's hands, stroking and manipulating them. She was quiet for a long time and then finally said, "I'm falling for you because of the way you live your life. I think you and I share a moral code."

Katie turned her head, smiling. "Not because of my tits?"

Chuckling, Erin said, "I love your breasts, but they're not your prime attribute."

"You haven't seen 'em bare. You might change your mind."

"Nope. I'm crazy mature, remember? You can't make me into a shallow woman that easily." She kissed Katie's ear, making her giggle. "But I don't mind having some nice accessories."

"I bet you'd have your hands on my accessories right now if we were at your house."

Slightly offended, Erin sat up straighter, seeking a little distance. "No, I wouldn't. You made it clear you didn't want to get too sexual. I don't want to torture myself, so I wouldn't do that."

"Ma-ture," Katie said in a singsong fashion. "I thought it was just because we were out in public."

"No, that's not it, but I wouldn't want to paw you in public, either. That's classless."

Katie burrowed into Erin, trying to reestablish their connection. "I think so, too. But I'm afraid that once I start, I'll have my hands all over you. You're so tasty-looking I won't be able to stop myself."

Erin gave her a squeeze and kept her arms tucked firmly around Katie while she set her chin on her shoulder. "That's a relief. I was beginning to think I was going to be chasing you all of the time. That's been worrying me."

"No worries there. I'll give you all you need."

"Turn around and kiss me," Erin said, her voice raspy and low.

Katie did, placing long, soft kisses all around Erin's mouth. She started to move against her, but stopped herself, consciously trying to ease the sexual tension that was flowing just beneath the surface. "We'd better stop," she said, looking into Erin's soulful eyes. "But I don't want to."

"That's progress," Erin said, grinning rakishly. "You've stopped *me* every other time." She kissed Katie lightly and then hugged her. "I hate always being the aggressor."

"Ha!" Katie rubbed her nose against Erin's. "You have no idea what you're getting into. But let me assure you that you won't be the only one starting the fire. I have never, ever been accused of having a low sex drive."

"That's one more thing I can add to my 'why I'm falling in love' list."

"It's a short list!" Katie laughed and then turned around, settling against Erin's body again. "So far, all you like is my character."

"Not true. But if I'm attracted to you—which I am—and you're a good person—which you are—and we've got the same life goals, everything else can be worked out. Right?"

"How do you know we have the same life goals?"

"Mmm, I can just tell." Erin giggled. "Not too mature, huh?"

"Not very, no. But you're young, so I'll give you a break. What are *your* life goals?"

"I haven't given a lot of thought to that, to be honest. I guess I want to marry, have a family, and try to do more good than harm. You know. Be a good person. That kind of stuff."

"Those are pretty good goals for coming up with them on the fly. You could save the world if you thought about it for a few minutes." She turned and kissed Erin on the cheek. "I think you're right. I think we have the same worldview. That's a good start. Now, how about this? What if my mother had to move in with us when she got older?"

"If you want her with us, I'm good with it. Same goes for your dad."

"No way. If you take my dad in, I'm leaving."

❧

On the drive home, Katie resisted the powerful urge to poke and play with Erin. Once she'd let herself acknowledge the pain that Erin had to feel at the mere thought of careless driving, she knew she'd never be able to do it again. She distracted herself from the tempting target by asking, "I've noticed how much more confident you seem now that we're officially girlfriends. Why do you think that is?"

"Confident? I didn't used to be confident?"

"Not with me. As soon as I told you we were dating, you started acting all skittish. Scared the hell out of me. But now you're back to normal. What gives?"

Erin looked bashful when she shrugged her shoulders. "I guess I was a little nervous. You know I don't have a lot of experience with dating."

Katie watched Erin drive, noting how avidly her eyes scanned the road and upcoming intersections. "Not with women, but you told me you dated men in high school and college."

"Yeah, I did, but it didn't mean a lot to me." She snuck such a quick look at Katie that she couldn't have seen anything. "It meant a lot to me that you liked me. I guess it made me nervous at first."

Katie rubbed her leg briskly. "But why did you get over your nervousness so quickly? That's what puzzles me."

"I guess…well, I guess it's the uncertainty that had me spooked. Your list of requirements sure didn't help." She smiled sardonically. "But once I figured out that your list wasn't as impossible to fulfill as I first thought, I loosened up."

"How do you feel now?"

"Good. Normal. More like myself."

"Really?"

"Yeah. I thought about what you said, and I believe that if things don't work out, it's because they shouldn't."

"And that makes you relax? That's funny."

"Yeah. At first, I thought you might cut me before you got to know me. Now I know that you'll give me a fair chance." With another very brief glance, Erin looked back at the road, smiling. "And that's what I'll give you. If we both try hard, but decide it's not working, that's life. As long as I know you're judging me on me and not some list, I'm good."

Katie patted her gently. "That's the first time you've said you might not choose me. That's good."

"Good?" Erin's eyebrow rose in question.

"Yes, it's not healthy to feel like I'm in charge. I'm not. This is about us—you and me. We're both in charge of deciding if we're getting our needs met."

"I am. Every time I look at your face, my needs get met."

"Mine, too," Katie said, leaning over to rest her head on Erin's shoulder.

≈

They returned to Erin's house at dusk, and after lighting a fire, they sat in front of it to warm up. Erin sat on a cushy floor pillow, and Katie took two of the pillows and lay upon them, resting her head in Erin's lap. "You know what would be fun?" Katie asked.

"Tell me."

"I'd like to look at old pictures. Do you have any albums?"

"Yeah." Erin nodded her head slowly. "We probably do." She smiled, but the smile wasn't her usual easy, gentle one. "Maybe we can do that later. I'll show you a picture of me tomorrow. How's that?"

"Funny. You'll say the same thing tomorrow and the day after." She looked up and met Erin's eyes. "Don't think you're leaving me in the dust, Ivy League girl. I get your little jokes. I'd just like to see what you looked like as a baby." Her eyes scanned the room, noting many mementos and objects d'art, but only one photo—the one of Erin's grandmother as a young woman.

"I'll ask my mom. She has some pictures around here somewhere."

"So, your mom's like you, huh? She likes to look forward?"

"Yeah." A little storm cloud passed across Erin's eyes. "I guess she does."

Like a slap, it hit Katie. Neither woman wanted to be reminded of her loss. It amazed Katie that Gail had been able to soldier on after losing not only her husband, but also her son. Gail obviously preferred to close the door on the past, as evidenced by her turning her son's room into a guest room and not having one photo of the young man displayed in the house. Erin had either adopted her mother's style or naturally shared it, but it was clear that she didn't want to look back, either.

Katie wrapped her arms around Erin and hugged her so tightly that Erin winced. "Sorry," Katie whispered. "I just had a massive need to hold you."

"No complaints. It's okay with me if I'm covered with hugging bruises tomorrow."

"I don't want to bruise you," Katie said softly, loosening her hold but maintaining contact. "I want to pet you and stroke you and kiss your pretty face. No bruises." She tried hard to keep her voice from breaking, unable to get the thought of a painfully young, grief-stricken Erin from her brain. "No bruises, baby."

≈

They talked for a long time, with the warmth from the well-built fire making their cheeks turn pink. "I'm about to melt," Katie said, fanning herself. "I'm going to go put on a T-shirt."

She started to get up, but Erin caught the hem of her slacks and stopped her. "Let's go sit on the sofa. It's cooler there."

Katie extended a hand and helped Erin to her feet. "I didn't want to complain, but these old bones were starting to ache. I can't sit on the floor for hours like you young whippersnappers can."

Erin put her arm around Katie shoulders and led her to the couch, where Katie propped herself up in the corner. Erin playfully poked and prodded Katie, trying to find a soft space for her to rest her head. "I don't always want to be the one to have to sit up like an adult. It's my turn to lie down to be petted."

"Come on, pup." Katie patted her lap. "Cookie's gone. You're my pup now."

"I knew I shouldn't have told you that's what Dr. Worrell calls me. Actually, I shouldn't have you anywhere near Essex. You'll know every one of my secrets."

Katie smiled down at her, her eyes expressing all of the tender feelings that welled in her heart. "I *want* to know all of your secrets." She stroked Erin's face, tracing the bones with her fingertips. "I want to know everything about you. You're the most fascinating person I've ever met."

Erin grinned, her eyes twinkling with amusement. "I *know* that's not true, but I know what you mean. You could spend the next hour telling me how you do your laundry, and I'd be mesmerized."

"This falling in love is sweet. I would have done it years ago if I'd known how cool it was."

Looking up at her, Erin asked, "How close have you gotten?"

"In retrospect, not close at all. I thought I was close about a year and a half or two years ago, but I think I just wanted to be in love. I really wasn't."

"What was missing?"

Katie slipped her fingers into Erin's thick, dark hair and drew them along its length. As the strands fell onto her lap, she said, "I'm not sure. I had a lot of discussions with myself where I tried to make a case for love, but I kept losing on the merits." She chuckled, looking at Erin to say, "That was a little lawyer humor. Don't worry if you don't get my jokes; I appreciate them enough for both of us."

"So, you really don't know?"

"All I know is that this feels like a whole new game. I've had discussions with myself trying to make a case against love, but I lose every one."

Erin's whole body twitched, and she stared at Katie, wide-eyed. "Why are you trying to talk yourself out of loving me?"

Soothingly, Katie continued to stroke and play with Erin's hair. "That's just what I do. I try to poke holes in my beliefs to make sure they stand up to scrutiny.

It's nothing to worry about, pup. Just my modus operandi."

"I don't do that. I just let myself feel. I let myself react and respond more often than I logic something to death."

"Tell me about your feelings. What was the first thing that made your sweet heart beat faster?"

Erin grinned sexily. "I'm sure I'm like every other lesbian who gets a good look at you, but that's attraction, not love. I started feeling like I loved you when I realized how much you cared about other people. You're a good person, and that attracts me as much as your beautiful face."

"It took me a long time to be able to read you. I was pretty sure you were attracted to me, but then you'd seem like you just wanted to be friends or… stepsisters." She made a face. "Blech!"

"I was a little up and down. I *was* attracted to you, but I'm sure that's not unique." Katie put her hand on her cheek, looking like she was surprised. "You *know* how pretty you are, Katie Quinn."

"But that wasn't what interested you, was it?"

"No, not really. Once I knew you were gay, I let myself think about what it would be like to be with you. That's when it got fun."

Katie looked down at Erin, her expression so sweet and welcoming that Erin forgot what she was saying. She was looking into Katie's blue eyes with a nearly vacant grin on her face. "Go on," Katie urged. "This is just getting interesting."

"Oh. Right. Well, I wasn't sure where you stood with the woman you were dating, or even if you were dating, since you were so cagey about it. And I was a little worried that you partied too much."

"I assume that doesn't mean you thought my social life was too interesting."

"No. I thought you might have a drinking problem."

"That would've scared you off?"

"Yeah, it would have. I'm pretty self-protective. I don't look for trouble."

"I think you're a little too self-protective. If you weren't, you would have been hooked up by now. But I'm not complaining."

Erin shrugged, looking a little embarrassed. "Maybe I am. I didn't know a lot of other lesbians in college, but that changed at Dartmouth."

Katie playfully pulled on a hank of hair. "I think some women might have contacted Erin Delancy, M.D., when word got out that she and Suzy were no longer."

"Maybe," Erin said, letting out a girlish giggle.

"How many? Come on, tell me."

"A couple."

"How many is a couple? Two?"

"Uhm, a couple of couples." Erin's cheeks were tinted pink, and she looked like she desperately wanted to change the subject.

"You are so damned cute, and I am so damned lucky that you didn't follow up with any of those Dartmouth girls."

"I like girls from Boston. Pretty ones with curly red hair and bright blue eyes."

"My hair is blonde, Erin."

"Yeah, it is, except when it's red."

"The Tierneys have red hair. The Quinns are blonde or brunette. I'm a Quinn."

"You should've told the Tierney's allele to switch off before it got imprinted onto your DNA."

Katie tweaked Erin's nose. "You can keep those big doctor words to yourself. I'm a Quinn. There's no Tierney DNA in here." She slapped her hand against her breastbone. "All Quinn, all the time."

Erin took Katie's hand and kissed it tenderly. "That's the other thing that had me worried about falling for you. I didn't want to get into the middle of anything between you and your dad. Given our parents' situation, you and I being together isn't the smartest thing, and I didn't want to risk that you were unconsciously using me."

"I guess I convinced you, right?"

"Yeah. You're not the kind of woman to date someone just to piss her dad off."

Katie smiled down at her. "I'm far too lazy to go to that much trouble. Besides, he's so easy to piss off that I don't have to try hard if that's my goal."

"We're going to have to work on that. The conflict-averse Delancy women won't be able to take too much strife."

"Then you two had better stay out of the way. When we're together, the fur flies."

"My mom will work on your dad, and I'll work on you. We'll all be one big, happy family."

"I don't think I want to be part of a family where the daughters are happy because they fuck each other silly."

Erin, looking wistful, said, "There's no better way to get silly."

Katie put her hands on Erin's shoulders and gave her a little pull. "Sit up so you can kiss me. We've been talking too long."

Eyes shining, Erin said, "I like it when you tell me what to do. It's a turn on."

"Then you're gonna be turned on all the time, you lucky devil."

"It's a turn on when it's sexually related. I'm not crazy about being bossed around on a routine basis."

"Oh." Katie put on a pout. "Then I guess you'll only be turned on some of the time."

Erin put her hand on Katie's chin and lifted it so that she could see the flames from the fire dancing in her eyes. "I'm turned on an *awful* lot. If I can't fall asleep right away, I think of how you looked the morning you picked me up to go skiing."

Katie laughed. "That sweater really pushed your buttons, didn't it?"

"Yes, but that's only part of it." She slipped her arm around Katie's back and pulled her close so that her warm breath was tickling pink lips. "I think of how clear and bright your eyes looked and how beautiful your hair was that day. When you're in the sun, it's so many different colors...of blonde," she added when Katie scowled slightly. "But what really stuck with me was how hard your nipples were." Katie's eyes widened in surprise. "It was cold out," Erin whispered, "and you didn't put your jacket on before you came to the door. Your nipples looked like little pebbles lying right under that green knit. I had an overwhelming desire to rip that sweater off you. That's what I do when I can't sleep. I think about your breasts."

The frank sexuality that flowed from Erin made Katie's mouth dry. Her voice almost broke when she asked, "And that helps you sleep?"

Erin kissed her, holding her tightly and probing her mouth for a long while. Katie was nearly panting when Erin released her fierce hold. "No. I think about how I want to kiss them and touch them and love them." Katie's head dropped back, and her eyes closed. Erin started to pepper her throat with kisses, murmuring, "I get so turned on that before I even know it, I'm touching myself. It never takes me long to come just imagining how fantastic it must feel to touch you." She laughed softly. "I've never gotten past your breasts in my fantasies."

Katie grasped Erin's hands and placed them on her breasts, squeezing her hands while she watched her pupils dilate. "Touch them," she begged. "Please."

Erin groaned with pleasure as her hands closed around Katie's tender breasts. She felt herself being pulled onto Katie's body as they began to kiss each other ferociously. Erin felt like she'd walked into a very hot kitchen on a very cold day. Warmth suffused their bodies, their temperatures skyrocketing. The heat prickled Erin's skin, making her itch. In a few heartbeats, the itch settled between her legs, where it quickly became a dull throb. Her clit pulsed with each beat of her heart, and she felt a little dizzy. She pulled away from Katie's ravenous mouth, but she could not, would not, let go of her breasts. She drew back and looked at them in her hands, feeling her head spin as she saw her fantasies become reality. Finally, she met Katie's eyes, and she knew. She knew they were making love.

Erin's heart started to beat so quickly that she could hear the blood thrum in her ears. Katie's eyes were burning when they met Erin's, and she slowly looked down to watch Erin squeeze and taunt her breasts. She smiled devilishly, murmuring, "That's it, baby. Make them yours." A whoosh of air left Erin's lips, something between a groan and a grunt. She began to shiver, her whole body shaking with desire. Katie's hands covered her trembling ones. "Whatever you want. Whatever you need." Their eyes met again, and Erin saw that Katie was not only giving her permission, she was asking Erin to make love to her.

In the blink of an eye, Katie's sweater was off, her hard nipples poking into the thin fabric of her insubstantial bra. Erin felt like her eyes were rolling around, unfettered, in her head. She was so painfully aroused that she thought she might pass out, but those fantastic breasts were right before her eyes, begging to be touched.

Without pausing to think, Erin grasped Katie under her knees and pulled her down the sofa, leaving her lying on her back. Erin sank to the floor, leaned over and began to kiss the flesh she could barely see through the filmy fabric. "You're so beautiful," she whispered reverently between kisses.

Katie stroked her hair, her body moving gently under Erin's tender worship. "That feels fantastic. Your mouth is so sweet."

Erin slid her hands under Katie and removed her bra. Staring at her body, she felt like a starving woman plunked down in front of a table groaning with a sumptuous feast. Katie's breasts held her in sway, but there was so much more. She bent to kiss her breasts again, but her hands started to roam, stroking and playing with Katie's body. She was lost in sensation, feeling lightheaded as her hands ran across pebbled flesh.

Erin felt a hand on her back, and then it slipped under her sweater to tickle its way up her spine. She mewed her satisfaction, her mouth too busy to utter a word. Katie tried to remove the sweater, but she was pinned to the sofa by Erin's body. She put her hands on Erin's shoulders and pushed, moving her only an inch. "Let me up, sweetheart. I have to be able to touch you, too."

Confused, with her mind barely functioning, Erin sat back on her heels and watched Katie get up and toss all of the cushions to the floor. She pushed the coffee table out of the way and created a semblance of a bed for them. Then she lay down and pulled Erin with her, smiling at how easy it was to control her.

It only took a second for Erin to reassert herself. Soon, Katie was on her back again, with Erin worshiping her body. But Katie had room to work now, and she was able to grasp Erin's sweater and pull it over her head. She feared she wouldn't get another chance, so she took the opportunity to unhook Erin's flesh-colored bra and slide it down her arms. A slight frown covered Erin's face, and she shrugged the bra off as though it were a fly, but when Katie's warm hands reached up and palmed her breasts, a look of wonder settled on her expressive face. Then she smiled and pushed her chest against Katie's hands. "That's so nice," she purred.

Katie grasped the waistband of her jeans and pulled as hard as she could. When she had the full, flushed breast over her mouth, she stroked Erin's back until Erin caught on and lowered herself onto Katie's waiting mouth. The groan Erin let out when her breast was enveloped by that wet warmth sounded as though she'd been kicked in the stomach. "Mmm," Katie purred, her eyes closing with delight. Erin looked down to see her nipple disappear into Katie's waiting mouth and moaned right along with her. The pounding in her clit was unrelenting, but the feelings that suffused her body when Katie suckled her were too fantastic to interrupt.

They took turns feasting upon each other. Back and forth they went, kissing, nuzzling, mouthing, and nibbling. Erin's arms gave out, and she collapsed onto her side, facing Katie. "I'm about to explode."

Katie slowly scanned Erin's body. Her cheeks were bright pink, as were her breasts and the hollow of her throat. Her eyes glittered with need, and a light sheen of perspiration glimmered around her hairline and between her breasts. She was so stunningly beautiful that Katie couldn't delay for another moment. She had to have her.

Forcefully, she grasped Erin and pulled her close. After several minutes filled with delicious kisses, her hand slid down between them, and she began to unbutton Erin's jeans. By the time the second button was unfastened, Erin was on her back, frantically pushing her jeans and her panties down.

"Shh, shh." Katie moved Erin's hand away. "Don't worry, sweetheart. There's no rush."

Shaking, Erin looked into her eyes. "I'm…I'm just so…"

"I know," Katie soothed. "I am, too. But don't you want to slow down and take our time?" She kissed Erin gently and brushed her hair from her face. "Don't you want to remember our first time?"

The confusion left Erin's face, and she smiled and then began to laugh. "We can remember it as the time I came before you got my pants off. Something to tell the kids."

Katie chuckled. "The kids don't need to know everything. This is just for you and me." She kissed Erin again and then again. "I'll never tell another soul about our lovemaking." She pointed to Erin and then to herself. "Just you and me, showing our love."

"I do love you. I love you so much, Katie."

Katie kissed her gently. "I love you, too." As the words left her mouth, she froze. Her eyes grew wide, and she whispered, "I really love you. I love you."

Erin gently touched her face. "Don't be frightened. I love you, too. I promise I do."

"But…this is so fast." Katie's whole body was shaking, and she'd grown pale.

"Too fast to make love?"

"No, no, too fast to be *in* love. I'm not ready. There's so much I don't know!"

"Shh, shh," Erin soothed. "Trust me. Trust us."

"You seem so sure." She grasped Erin's shoulders and shook her roughly. "How can you be so sure?"

The smile Erin gave her was so full of love and calm assuredness that Katie could feel her racing heart slow just a bit.

"I don't know. I just know that I love you, and I can feel how much you love me. That's enough."

"Are you sure that's enough?" Again, Katie held her so firmly that she left red fingerprints on Erin's shoulders.

"As sure as I've ever been of anything. I'm positive." She kissed Katie tenderly but briefly. "Absolutely positive."

Katie took in and let out a huge breath. She stared into Erin's eyes for a few seconds and then nodded. "Promise me you'll hang in there if we have problems. Promise me you won't give up."

"On my honor." Erin's eyes closed for just a second. "I'll fight with everything I have to hold on to you."

Katie threw her arms around Erin's neck and held on tightly. They lay together for several minutes, breathing in each other's scent. Finally, Katie pulled away and said, "Let me show you how much I love you."

Erin relaxed against the cushions and looked up at Katie. "I'm yours."

Deeply touched by the innocent, trusting gaze, Katie kissed Erin again and again, trying to convey in a kiss all she felt in her heart. With a glimmer of regret, she finally pulled away and settled herself between Erin's knees. She tossed the tangled clothing away and stroked the pale thighs that trembled lightly under her touch. "Don't be frightened, baby. Relax and let me love you."

"I can't stop shaking."

With a sexy grin, Katie said, "Then I'd better distract you. Take your mind off things."

Erin's eyes grew comically wide as Katie lowered herself to snuggle between her legs. "You're so lovely," she said, marveling at Erin's muscular legs and dark curls. She traced along her lips, puffy from arousal. "So remarkably lovely."

Erin's whole body shuddered, and she gasped when Katie's fingers touched her.

Meeting her eyes, Katie reassured her. "It's all right." She kept her eyes locked with Erin's as she parted her with her thumbs and lowered her head to taste her for the first time. Growling from the sensation, she murmured, "I could eat you alive."

Erin's teeth were nearly chattering she was shaking so hard. "Please," was all she was able to get out.

Katie dipped her head again and began to kiss Erin intimately. Shaking hands threaded themselves into her hair, but Erin didn't try to guide Katie's head. It seemed like she was just trying to center herself with the touch. Katie was so intent that she barely noticed Erin's hands. All she could see, feel, touch, and smell was the essence of Erin's body. Her tongue probed and delved into the heat, feeling like she was finally sated after a lifetime of searching.

Erin's body was a marvel, a feast for exploration. Katie couldn't get enough of any part of the experience. Her hands were on Erin's hips, holding her still so she could taste her again and again. She was ravenous for her and prayed the experience would never end.

When she slipped a hand between Erin's legs and probed her wet opening with a finger, Erin stiffened a little and pushed Katie's hand away. "Just your mouth," she begged. "Just use your mouth." A little puzzled, Katie complied, continuing to kiss, lick, and suckle at the glistening flesh. She lost herself in the experience, going deeper and deeper into a haze of desire. She wasn't sure how long Erin had been moaning, but the plaintive sounds finally reached her ears.

She looked up to see that Erin had risen up and was now resting on her forearms, her head thrown back in passion. Her nipples were so firm and red they looked as though they were sitting upon her round breasts. Her chest was covered with a pink glow, and her breathing was rough and labored. Katie tilted her head and sucked Erin into her mouth, working her clit over her lips and tongue. In moments, Erin was crying out loudly, and then her voice grew softer as she murmured Katie's name again and again. She collapsed onto the cushions, completely exhausted.

Katie stroked her body, feeling the heat flow from her. She wanted to hold

Erin in her arms, but the sight of her vulva in spasms was too fascinating to turn away from. She watched the pink flesh contract and expand until it slowed and finally stopped. Then she inched upwards until she and Erin were face to face.

That lovely face was damp and flushed, and Erin looked at her with barely open eyes. "I've never…" she began, but quickly gave up trying to speak. She merely shook her head, at a loss.

"I love you," Katie whispered when she shifted her body down to lie between Erin's shaking legs and rest her head on her belly. "I love you."

They rested against each other for a while, neither woman speaking. Katie satisfied herself by touching Erin everywhere, crawling up her body to watch her react to every sensation. When Erin thrust her hips to follow Katie's fingers, she was rewarded by having those fingers slip into her wetness again. For a long time, Katie played her, making her come with such ease that she happily thought they might be there forever, but Erin finally had enough. Weakly, she pushed at Katie's hand, almost missing it. "I can't," she moaned, her throat dry and her voice raspy. "I can't take any more."

"I think you can," Katie murmured into her ear, chuckling softly. "I think you could come all night."

"No, please, no." A small laugh bubbled up. "Don't kill me before I get to touch you."

"Oh, you're so smart." Katie kissed her loudly, making a smacking noise. "If I don't calm down, *I'm* going to come with my pants still on, and you'll tell our kids about it."

"I forgot you had them on. I also forgot my name. I'm glad you didn't need medical assistance because everything I learned in school is gone." She raised her hand and ran it over the top of her head. "Empty."

"I think you should snuggle up against me and rest for a while. Then I might be able to hold out for more than ten seconds when you touch me."

"I'd normally argue…" A huge yawn interrupted her. She gave Katie a satisfied smile and said, "A little rest is a good idea."

Katie thought Erin was asleep, and she started when she heard her soft voice say, "No one's ever made me come like that."

Confused, Katie asked, "You mean so many times?"

"Yes." She laughed so hard that her eyes squeezed closed. "And so forcefully. It's so different, Katie. Just so different."

"What do you mean?"

Erin turned to her, dark eyes burning with intensity. "We were both into it," she said emphatically. "You were right there with me. It was so intense. Everything was perfect."

"But you didn't want me to…" She trailed off, not sure if Erin would want to talk about the limit she imposed.

"Oh, that's just me. I've never been into that."

Katie sat up and rested her weight on her arm. "Really? Is there some reason?"

"No. I just don't like it."

Erin looked very comfortable, so Katie pressed. "That's kind of a big thing to take off your list. Have you tried it?"

"A little bit. I didn't ever do that when I was young, and now it's kinda distracting."

"Distracting? I've never heard it referred to that way. Are you sure nothing ever happened to turn you off?"

"No. I was incredibly naïve when I first started masturbating. I didn't even know I had a vagina." She chuckled, shaking her head. "It honestly never occurred to me to investigate."

"So, you started to masturbate and got into the habit of just touching your clit?"

"Yeah, I guess so."

"And you came without having anything inside, and now you don't want to change? Am I getting close?"

Erin smiled. "I'm sorry I don't have better reasons for some of the things I do. I'm like a dog. All instinct, no logic."

"Well, one thing's clear."

"What's that?"

"You've never been with a man. No guy would put up with that."

"Oops," Erin said, looking guilty.

"Why didn't you want me to know that?"

"Simple. I thought it might scare you off to know I only had one lover."

"Yipes!" Katie's eyes opened wide. "I didn't even think of that. You're practically a virgin."

With a charming level of childlike alarm, Erin said, "Nuh-uh! I had sex with Suzy. That counts."

Katie didn't comment, but her mind was busy thinking of the chasm between her sexual past and Erin's.

Erin watched Katie's face for a few moments. Tentatively, she asked, "You're okay with my lack of experience, aren't you?"

Katie forced herself to banish her misgivings and kiss Erin enthusiastically. "Of course. None of that matters, remember? That's the past, and that's not our thing."

Smiling shyly, Erin kissed her back, holding her tightly. They kissed for a long time until Erin started to work the button on Katie's slacks. She lifted her head and grinned, saying, "Even though I don't have a lot of experience, I'm pretty confident."

As Erin's warm hand slid across her belly, Katie said, "You look confident. You don't seem nervous anymore."

"I'm not."

Katie threaded her fingers through the dark hair that was obscuring her view of Erin's features. She pushed it back over her shoulders and looked into her eyes. "Why is that?"

"I guess I seemed really nervous earlier, but it was as much arousal as anything else. I've never been so turned on in my life." She scooted up to be able to reach Katie's lips. Once there, they kissed for a while, the excitement between them dimmed to a very small flame. "I've never, ever had an experience like that, Katie. Never. It was like a whole new thing." Her smile was so astoundingly lovely that Katie flung her arms around her neck and pulled her close, kissing her with abandon.

Katie seemed ravenous as she kissed Erin everywhere. Her face, her chest, down her arms. Then she blinked in surprise when she found herself lying on her back, looking up at Erin, who was grinning at her almost demonically. She wasn't sure how it happened, but her slacks were whisked away, along with her panties, leaving her naked and very ready.

There was no doubt that Erin was just as ready for her. With a quiet confidence that Katie hadn't seen often, Erin took over, neither asking for nor seeking permission to do as she wanted. And what she clearly wanted was to worship Katie's breasts.

Erin showed her need in every way possible. Katie had never been touched with such fierce determination and passion. It seemed as though her breasts were manna and Erin had been traveling, hungry, in the desert for years.

Katie was having a very difficult time thinking clearly. She was monstrously turned on, and watching Erin so greedily consume her made her almost frantic for release. She desperately needed to be filled, to have Erin enter her and ease the ache that thrummed deep within.

Both of Erin's warm, gentle hands surrounded one breast, squeezing it firmly while she suckled. Katie practically had to pry one of the hands off to guide it between her legs. Erin's mouth never left the swollen red nipple, but her eyes rotated to meet Katie's. "Come inside," Katie begged. "Fill me up."

Dividing her attention, Erin gently probed with her fingers while she continued to feast. Katie thrust her hips, willing Erin's fingers to enter her and quench her desire. She finally gasped out her satisfaction when first one and then a second finger slid into her. The tortured sound that left her lips was almost a gurgle, but it efficiently conveyed her pleasure.

Erin seemed to follow her lead, moving her fingers to keep pace with Katie's thrusting hips. But she was still focused on her breasts, almost frantically moving from one to the next, alternating between gentle kisses and voracious suckling.

Unable to wait for release, Katie slipped her hand next to Erin's, smiling at the groan of pleasure she heard from her when their fingers slid against each other amidst the moisture. Katie tried to press the palm of Erin's hand against her vulva, but the angle was wrong. So, she covered her own clitoris with two wet fingers and stroked herself until her climax tore a cry from her lips. For just a moment, she reached for Erin's hand and pushed it deep inside herself, holding it there while precious release surged through her body. Then she let go and forced her eyes to remain open to Erin's questioning gaze. She nodded and smiled when those warm wet fingers started to explore again.

As this new delight caught her attention, Erin finally pulled away from Katie's breast and moved down to rest her head on her thigh. She used her hands to explore and probe in the same way she had done with her breasts, but now she was wringing orgasms from Katie every few minutes.

Erin's fingers felt so delicious skimming across her clitoris that Katie was certain this was one of the peak experiences of her life and just as certain that the love of her life was providing it.

❦

Katie was still panting softly while Erin lay next to her, resting her cheek against her breast. "I must be getting old," Katie moaned. "A dozen orgasms and I'm ready for bed."

"Do you like that all the time?" Erin asked.

"What's that?"

"Do you like to have a lot of orgasms all the time?" She lifted up on her elbow and then tossed her head to compel her hair to swing back over her shoulder.

"Yeah, I do when I'm making love, but I don't usually make myself have multiples when I'm alone." She puckered up and said, "Kiss me with those lovely lips." Erin leaned over and delivered several soft, sensuous kisses. "When I'm making love, I get into a frenzy, and it's hard to stop."

"Yeah. That's a good way to describe it. When I masturbate, it's just for release, but making love with you brought up all of these feelings." She flopped down onto the floor, making a loud "thunk."

"Like what? Tell me more."

"When two people are involved, you make accommodations for each other. You know?" She looked at Katie again, as though she was seeking understanding.

"Sure. I wanted to crawl right up inside you, but I didn't."

Erin took her hand and kissed the fingers. "Maybe we can work our way up to that. I try not to be too set in my ways."

"We'll see. I haven't had enough time to test and see how set you are." She patted Erin on the side, making a slapping noise on her bare skin.

"Now that I can think clearly, I want to make sure you understand that tonight was life changing for me."

"It was for me, too, baby." Katie placed dozens of kisses atop Erin's head and face. "My life has changed because I'm in love. And even if we're not together forever, loving someone changes you."

"I think we're going to be together forever."

Erin gave her such a charming smile that Katie found herself nodding. "I think so, too. I've just learned to be cautious."

"You don't have to be cautious with me. You can trust me with your heart."

Chapter Thirteen

*W*hen Katie emerged from the bathroom, she was wearing Erin's robe. "I thought you slept in the nude."

"Are you crazy?" Katie ran her hands up and down her arms. "It's freezing in here."

Chuckling, Erin said, "We turn off the heat when we go to bed. We both like it cool."

"Cool is one thing. This is icy. I need some clothes to sleep in this meat locker." She moved to stand right in front of Erin, smiling playfully. "Unless you want to keep making love. You make me hot enough to compensate."

Resting her hands on Katie's hips, Erin smiled. "I can keep going. I've barely started on my long list of things I'm going to do to you before the weekend ends."

"Ooh, I knew there was a benefit to finding a young lover." She kissed Erin, making the embrace teeter on the edge between soothing and exciting. "You've got lots of energy. Like a sweet little pup."

"And lots of desire," Erin added, tightening her hold. "Lots and lots of desire." She started to walk towards the bed, pushing Katie along with her.

"Maybe we should save a little for tomorrow."

Startled, Erin met her eyes. "You're too tired?"

Katie turned and pushed Erin onto the bed, falling on top of her naked body. "I'm too tired to need any more loving, but I'm not too tired to give *you* some more."

Erin grinned up at her, looking like a child who knows she shouldn't accept another piece of candy, but can't help herself. "I just need a little more. It won't take long—"

Katie's kiss interrupted her. "You don't have to rush. I've got plenty of energy for you, sweet girl." As she spoke, her hand slid between their bodies, and she reached between Erin's legs, touching her silky skin. "It's so nice to touch you," she murmured, watching Erin's eyes flutter closed. "You're so soft and sweet and sexy." She shifted so she could better reach Erin and then stroked her gently, smiling when Erin started to pant. "That's my beautiful girl." Never faltering, Katie kept letting her fingers glide across the remarkably supple flesh, slowing down just enough to prolong the experience. Not until Erin gripped her hand and forced it to move more quickly did Katie whisper, "That's it, baby. Come for me. Come for me now." That was the release she needed, and Erin's lovely face contorted when her orgasm washed over her shuddering body.

"Better?" Katie whispered into Erin's flushed ear. "Can you sleep now?"

"Yes." Erin pulled Katie in for a long kiss. "As long as we can make love the minute we wake up."

"Just what I was planning." They kissed again, softly and gently. "I'll always remember this night. The first time I got to touch and taste all of your sweet body."

"You didn't get to half of me," Erin said, chuckling. "We've barely begun." She held Katie tightly. "Sleep now?"

"Yes. Sleep now."

Erin rolled onto her side, and Katie pulled the covers over them and plastered herself up against Erin's back.

⬤

Sometime during the night, Erin woke, uncomfortable and hot. She smiled when she realized the source of her discomfort. Katie was snuggled up behind her, both arms pressed against Erin's bare back. Erin could feel Katie's hands formed into fists, bracketing her spine. Her heart ached with the love that welled in her, but she couldn't stand to be so trapped. So, she got out of bed and went around to the expanse of space on Katie's other side. Just before she lay down, she took a heavy wool blanket from her armoire and placed it over Katie, tucking it around her snugly. Then she lay down and put a hand on Katie's back, hoping to maintain contact while keeping enough space to stay cool.

⬤

Once again, Erin woke hot and sweaty. She was about to throw off the covers when she heard a soft voice caress her ear. "Ready?"

"For what?"

"For this." Katie was lying behind her, and her hand slid down Erin's belly to rest between her legs. "Open up for me, baby."

Erin growled her happiness, opening her legs to Katie's searching fingers. "I've only been awake for five seconds. How can I be turned on already?"

"I think you've been dreaming about sex. Your body's ready for me."

Nodding silently, Erin stretched into the touch, moving her hips up and down so Katie could reach more of her. Once again, it didn't take long until her body demanded release. She pushed against Katie's hand, moaning softly as a quiet, gentle orgasm washed over her. Panting, she threw off the covers, exposing her heated skin to the cool morning air.

Katie took the sheet and fanned Erin with it. "Are you always this warm?"

"Yeah." She turned and faced Katie. "I have a feeling this is going to be a bone of contention between us."

"Could be worse. I'll just have to wear more clothes to bed."

Erin tugged at the peach fleece. "I'm sorry I was in such a haze last night. I should have gotten you some decent pajamas."

"This was good, but next time, I'm bringing a turtleneck and my silk long underwear."

"I'm sorry," Erin said, rubbing her arm. "I just get really hot when I sleep. I always have."

"So, no cuddling?"

"I love to be close when I fall asleep and when it's time to wake up, but I get too hot to stay close all night."

"Hmm, this is going to require a very big adjustment on my part. I love to suck the warmth out of my partner."

"We'll work something out. I'll wear less; you can wear more. If you like to cuddle, we'll figure out how to do it."

Katie put her chin on her fist, looking at Erin with an amused smile. "I've never been with a woman who didn't like to cuddle. Are you sure you're a woman?"

"I just like space. I guess I waited too long to be with a lover. My habits were entrenched."

Katie laughed softly, her eyes losing their sharp focus. "On the rare occasion my first girlfriend and I could be in bed together, we cuddled like a pair of puppies. That seems like part of making love to me." She met Erin's eyes. "Maybe I started having sex too soon. I still wanted to be in a litter."

"I think you were ready. You seem like a prodigy."

"I don't know about that, but I was ready. We spent all of our time figuring out when and how we could have sex. It wasn't until I went to college that we figured out we didn't really like each other all that much."

"That seems like an important fact."

"Yeah. Reality came crashing down when we didn't have to sneak around."

Erin gazed at her, watching Katie's eyes, not commenting.

"You're not going to ask me a thing about her, are you?" Katie finally demanded, giving Erin a push. "You don't even know her name or how old she was or how we got together."

"I'm interested in everything about you. If you want to talk about her, I'm very willing to listen."

"You're infuriating! You deserve a good bite." She leaned in, gripped a bit of loose skin on Erin's arm, and mouthed it. "What kind of woman doesn't want to cuddle and doesn't want to hear how I came out as a lesbian? I want to know everything about you, you incurious wench!"

Giggling, Erin said, "I told you I'm interested in everything about you, but I'm not going to probe into areas that might backfire on me. I'm interested in you, but not your sex life. That's private."

"Infuriating," Katie mumbled. "But smart, too. If you know that hearing details is bad for you, I'm glad you know yourself well enough to avoid it." She gnawed on her hand for a moment, growling. "But I don't have to like it."

"You certainly do not." Erin kissed her quickly and then slipped out of bed. "I can't believe you've captivated me so completely that I didn't even get up to pee yet." On her way to the bath, she said, "Don't go away."

"Leave the door open so I can bug you."

Erin quietly closed the door. "You can bug me with the door closed. We haven't been dating long enough to take all of our barriers down." She emerged a minute later, getting into bed quickly. "Now I'm cold. Still want to cuddle?"

"Come here, you big baby." Erin snuggled up to Katie's side and nuzzled into her chest.

"This is nice. Now we need to get busy making love. I believe it was your turn?"

"Correct." Katie lay on her back, looking at Erin curiously. "Will you tell me if there are any things you don't like doing? Or if I do anything to you that you don't care for?"

Erin laughed. "Yes, of course. I did that last night. I'm not averse to talking about myself, Kate. I just don't want to talk about my history with other people."

"Kate." She smiled warmly. "You've never called me that."

"You don't mind, do you?"

"No, of course not. I'm the nickname queen. You can call me anything you like."

"Uhm, we didn't talk about this before, since I didn't think it was going to happen so soon, but we should chat about safer sex."

Clearly amused, Katie nodded. "We should. How do I know where that vagina has been?" She reached down and tugged on Erin's curly patch of hair. "I had my mouth right there last night."

"I know," Erin said, looking abashed. "We really should have talked about this earlier. I'm a doctor, for goodness' sake."

"For goodness' sake," Katie mumbled, shaking her head. "I feel like I'm in bed with my great aunt."

"That's part of your family business I'm really not looking forward to hearing," Erin teased. "But I'm serious. This is important."

"I know." Suddenly, Katie's expression changed, and she looked angry. "Hey, was that why you didn't go down on me last night? Not that I minded, but it just occurred to me that you didn't even make a move in that direction."

"No, that didn't cross my mind. Really. I swear."

Erin looked so earnest that Katie couldn't help but laugh. "It's okay, pup. I believe you. Hell, I believe everything you say."

"I'm sorry if you thought I was worried about your history, Katie. I've just spent years learning how important it is—"

Katie cut her off by pinching her lips together. "It's all right. The last time I had a checkup, I had that new test for HPV. Much to my amazement, I didn't have any sign of having been exposed to it. I've never had syphilis or gonorrhea or had sex with a man or an IV drug user. Anything else?"

"No, no." Erin pursed her lips, looking distracted. "I should have that test. Even though I've only had sex with one person, she was with other people before me."

"I'm sure she was fine," Katie soothed. "Don't worry about it."

"No, I should have it. If you've avoided HPV all of this time, I don't want to be the one who gives it to you. Go wash your hands before you touch yourself." She started pushing Katie out of bed. "There's some bleach under the sink. You can make a weak solution—"

Katie pinched Erin's lips together. "Calm down, pup. You don't have the plague." She stood up and settled the robe. "I'll take a shower. Then you can worship me for a while."

"I won't move." Erin pulled the covers up around her chin and lay still. "Except to breathe."

"Be right back."

It took a while, but Katie finally walked back into the room, the ends of her hair a little damp and her cheeks pink. She was naked and did a little turn. "I'm clean and ready for inspection."

Erin held the covers up, welcoming Katie. "I thought you'd never get here."

They kissed, just beginning to stoke the fire that had ebbed. "I missed you."

Erin touched her intently, seemingly starved for her. There was a sense of purpose about her that Katie hadn't seen the night before. Erin acted as though she were on a mission—a mission to know Katie's body.

They wrestled briefly, giggling, while Katie tried to pin Erin down, but Erin was stronger, and she easily flipped Katie onto her back. Erin started to kiss her way down her belly, her dark eyes never leaving Katie's. When she reached the apex of her thighs, Erin paused for a few moments and then parted the neatly trimmed hair that everyone but Katie would have recognized as red.

Erin took her time, spending a little while gazing at the deep pink flesh before dipping her head to taste Katie for the first time. Erin's low, satisfied moan made Katie shiver, feeling as if she and Erin were sharing something intensely intimate and remarkably erotic. Even though many women had touched Katie just this way, she felt like this was a first for her—the first time she was sure of the woman who was lavishing her body with kisses, sure that Erin was the lover she'd been seeking most of her life.

Beautiful brown eyes sought out Katie's. "Is this good?" she asked, looking unsure of herself.

"Oh, yes," Katie whispered, gently stroking Erin's face. She was on the verge of tears, looking into those soulful, innocent eyes, seeing nothing but love in their depths. "You make me feel so loved."

Erin beamed, her dazzling smile making Katie's heart skip a beat. Erin rested her cheek on Katie's thigh for a moment, and then she tenderly kissed her, nuzzling deeper and deeper into her. She probed every bit of Katie's tender skin, finding spot after spot that had Katie squirming and breathing heavily. With tenacity, Erin learned all about Katie's body and her response to the tender ministrations. She took everything in—the aroma of her arousal, the texture of her skin, the way her body grew more heated as she got closer to orgasm.

Blindly, Katie reached down and grasped one of Erin's hands. "Inside," she panted. "Now." No sooner had Erin slipped a finger into her than she cried out her release, groaning throatily as Erin continued to lave her gently.

"So sweet," Katie murmured a few minutes later, touching Erin's head. "You are so very sweet."

Waiting just a few moments, Erin started to touch Katie again, licking her slick flesh until she pulled another orgasm from her shivering body. Erin seemed unable to stop, her attention unflagging as she changed her technique and tried various pressures and speeds, determined to love Katie until she was forcibly stopped.

It took a while, but Katie finally had all she could handle. She put her hand on Erin's shoulder and squeezed as she pushed her gently. "No more," she said weakly. "Have mercy."

Erin laughed, the gentle sound floating up to Katie. "I want more. A lot more."

"I need a break, sweetheart. Just a little one. Come on," she said, patting the mattress next to her. "Come up here and give me some kisses."

That did the trick. Erin pressed one last kiss onto Katie's glistening skin and slowly clambered up to join her. They kissed tenderly and quickly drifted off to sleep in each other's arms.

⁂

Katie woke from her short nap to hear a voice behind her ask, "Who's Dr. Wu?"

Chuckling, she rubbed her eyes and said, "I am."

"I heard people talking about Dr. Wu the whole night I was at your house. I thought there was really someone there named Wu."

"No, it's me. Why else would I have it tattooed on my back?"

"That was my second question," Erin said, tracing the tiny letters with a finger. "The tattoo of the…what is it, a harp?"

"Yeah. It's one of the symbols for Ireland."

"It's a good piece. The colors are really beautiful."

"I should use my tat to illustrate why you shouldn't be tattooed when drunk."

"You were drunk?"

"Not when I had most of it done, but I went in to have the shading done, and my friends talked me into adding my nickname. Bad mistake."

"You could have this part colored in," Erin said, running a fingernail over the letters.

"I had to get drunk just to have the shading done. I'm a wimp when it comes to pain, but I'll get around to it." She looked over her shoulder, meeting Erin's eyes. "Especially if you don't like the name."

"Doesn't bother me. Of course, I'm not the person who has to go around with 'Dr. Wu' tattooed on my otherwise lovely harp." She scratched at Katie's lower back. "Are you going to tell me why this is your nickname? It's not really obvious, you know."

"Oh!" Katie laughed. "I forgot." She scooted over so she could face Erin. "My buddies and I love Steely Dan. Do you know their music?"

"I don't think so."

"Oh, you probably do. I'll play their stuff for you. Anyway, we were in school, and Jimmy O'Herlihy was pissed about something. He kept insisting that I was bullshitting him. He finally said something like, 'Katie's lying! You can see it in her eyes.'"

"Go on," Erin said, trying to figure out where this was headed.

"One of the lyrics in this song 'Dr. Wu' is 'Katy lies, you can see it in her eyes.' Someone started singing the song, taunting Jimmy. That broke the tension, but for the rest of the night, Jimmy kept calling me Dr. Wu. I complained that I hated it, so, of course, it stuck."

"Ooh," Erin said, grimacing. "Did you really hate it?"

"No, I acted like I did because it was better than what I had."

"What was that?"

"Dutch or Dutchy."

"Because?"

"The Dutch boy with his finger in the dike." Katie rolled her eyes. "I was the only lesbian in my little group. They thought that was hilarious."

"It is kinda funny."

"Yeah, but I like Dr. Wu better. My ex got her nickname from that same album I think." She looked up, thinking. "Yeah, I think it's the same one."

Erin just smiled at her, not indicating one bit of curiosity.

Ignoring the fact that Erin hadn't asked for clarification, Katie said. "Her nickname was Buzz. The lyrics go 'She takes all my money, so I'm through with Buzz. She's not very funny, so I'm through with Buzz.' It was sadly appropriate."

"Wow. You and your friends really got a lot of mileage out of an album."

Katie slapped her on the shoulder. "Telling you she took all my money still doesn't make you ask about her?"

"Nope." Erin smiled contentedly. "Not gonna do it. I think you're just taunting me. I think you lie. As a matter of fact," she said, leaning over Katie, "I can see it in your eyes." She bent and kissed her until Katie stopped protesting and started to respond. Katie had just propelled Erin onto her back when a tentative knock at the bedroom door made them stop mid-gesture.

"Erin?"

Shocked, the women stared at each other.

The door opened a crack, with Erin crying out, "Busy!" while she scrambled frantically to pull the sheet over their bare bodies.

"Forgive me," Gail said, opening the door fully and entering. She was pointedly not looking in the direction of the bed, and her eyes were mostly shut. "I'm so very sorry. But Dan…your father…and I wanted to come take you…Erin…to church with us. We saw your…Katie's…car in front, and I wanted to just go on, but Dan…your father…wouldn't hear of it."

She looked like she was either going to be sick or cry, and Erin speedily climbed out of bed. She went into her bathroom and grabbed her robe, shimmying into it quickly. Katie had drawn the covers up to her chin, and she looked as uncomfortable as Erin had ever seen her.

Erin went to her mother and put her arms around her. "Is everything okay, Mom?"

"Oh, Erin," she sighed, leaning her head on her shoulder. "I'm so sorry for barging in on you. We have no right…" She trailed off, her voice breaking.

"Why did you come in? That's not like you."

"I know, I know." Gail took in a shaky breath. "I didn't want to talk to you through the door with Dan downstairs listening. I'm so, so sorry. I just wanted to talk to you in private."

"It's okay," Erin soothed. "What's going on?"

"Dan's upset. He won't leave until he talks to Katie."

In a flash, Katie was on her feet, throwing clothes on. Her hair was a jumble of curls, and she didn't bother with underwear, but she was mostly dressed in seconds. "You two stay here," she growled. "You don't need to get involved in his shit."

She stormed past Erin, hitting the stairs before Erin released her mother and darted after her. Catching her sweater, Erin pulled hard to make Katie slow down. "Not so fast. Come back here."

Katie turned and stared at her, amazed at Erin's tone and her assertiveness. "What?"

"Come back in and wait for me to get dressed. He can wait another minute."

"Erin, this isn't about you. He's mad at me. Let me handle him."

"Katie! Get down here right now!" Dan shouted.

"We'll be down in a minute!" Erin called out, staring at Katie with stunning intensity. Erin pushed her back into the room and closed the door. "He's obviously angry about our relationship. That involves both of us. Now, give me a minute to brush my teeth and comb my hair. I'm not going to talk to my mother's fiance looking like I just rolled out of bed. With his daughter," she muttered, going into the bathroom and closing the door.

By the time Erin came out of the bathroom, Gail was sitting on the bed looking ill, and Katie was pacing back and forth across the small room. Katie looked as though she was about to explode, and she whirled to stare at Erin when the bathroom door opened. "This isn't about you," she said, her cheeks flushed pink. "Believe me, this is just another incident in our long-running drama."

Erin went to her and put her hands on her shoulders, looking directly into her eyes. "We decided not to make love until we were sure we were in this for good." Her head turned, and she said, "I'm sorry, Mom. This is very personal, but Katie and I have to be on the same page here." Gail nodded, and even though she looked pained, she made no move to leave. Erin turned back to Katie and put a hand on her cheek. "We're in this together, Dr. Wu."

Involuntarily, Katie smiled. "Okay, Mad Dog. Have it your way, but I think you're gonna regret this."

Erin took her hand. "In for a penny, in for a pound." They headed for the stairs, neither one noticing that Gail wasn't behind them. As soon as they were halfway down, Dan glared at the pair, snapping, "Erin, you should go back upstairs. I want to talk to my daughter."

Not hesitating a bit, Erin continued walking, still holding Katie's hand. She didn't respond to Dan, which seemed to make him angrier. "Katie!" he shouted. "I want to talk to you alone!"

"I asked Erin to stay out of it, Dad. If you want her to leave, you're going to have to throw her out. Of her own house." She was wearing a hint of a smile, and she looked much younger than her age.

Dan's face was nearly the color of his hair. "Have it your way, you little smart ass."

Erin dropped Katie's hand and stood right in front of Dan. It looked as though she was going to chest butt him. "Just because Katie's your daughter doesn't mean you can talk to her that way. You're in my house, and we don't use that kind of language. If you want to discuss what has you so angry, feel free, but I won't tolerate disrespectful language."

Dan looked as though she was speaking a language he had never heard. He blinked his eyes slowly, backing up a step. "I didn't...I wasn't..."

"It doesn't matter," Erin said. "Let's just be civil." She took Katie's hand again and led her over to the sofa where they both sat down.

Dan didn't take the cue. He paced to and fro, anger flowing off him. He glared at Katie, who was giving him a half smile. "Erin won't think that smug smile's so cute when you use it on her."

"Maybe Erin won't deserve it. Maybe I had the sense to fall in love with someone who isn't a blowhard."

Dan started to reply, but Erin beat him to it. "Katie," she said sharply. "Why should your father be civil to you if you're just going to taunt him? Neither one of you is acting like an adult." Something caught her attention, and she looked up to see her mother coming down the stairs, dabbing at her eyes with a handkerchief.

Dan followed her gaze, and when he saw Gail, his voice gentled, and he said, "Honey, please wait upstairs. You don't have to get involved in this."

Gail looked from Erin to Dan, but Erin didn't say a word. Gail hesitated and then continued down the stairs. "No, I want to be down here. This affects all of us." She sat down in a chair behind Dan, her view of the action obscured every time Dan moved in front of her.

"It wouldn't have had to if Katie hadn't wormed her way into the family," Dan growled.

"Katie didn't worm her way anywhere," Erin said, her eyes flashing.

"You don't know her." Dan looked at Erin pleadingly. "I know she's told you I'm just an asshole, but I'm trying to stop her from hurting you. She's slept her way through all of Boston, and now she's going after you just to get to me."

"That's not true, Dad," Katie said, her voice remarkably calm. "Besides, even if I *had* slept with all of Boston, Erin's not interested in my past. And even though every move I make *does* revolve around you, Erin is mildly attractive, so it's not too horrible to be with her."

Her voice rising, Erin said, "Will you two please stop sniping at each other? You're the one who wanted to do this, Dan, so say what you have to say."

"Fine. You want the truth? Here it is. Katie hasn't had a girlfriend for longer than a month, and she's almost forty years old. She's out almost every night with her friends, and she's well on her way to joining the rest of the Quinns in the drunk tank. She's been picked up by the cops more times than I can count, and if it wasn't for me, she'd have a record." Erin's eyes widened a little, and Dan paused, seemingly letting his words sink in.

"She wouldn't have gotten admitted to the bar if I hadn't risked my job to make sure she didn't wind up with a rap sheet. She was a good kid, but she took a wrong turn." He glared at Katie with such anger in his eyes that Erin began to shake. "She still thinks she's in college, and that's not the kind of girl you are."

Erin's body shivered, and then she got up and stood tall, her arms crossed over her chest. She was clearly processing what Dan said, and everyone in the room stared at her, waiting for her to speak. "I think I'm starting to get a better perspective on why Katie tries to get under your skin. If you were my father, I wouldn't bother."

"What?" Dan's face grew redder.

"If someone makes it clear that he has no respect for me, I keep my distance. Of course, I wouldn't ask my daughter to drive up here from Boston to look after my farm if I thought she was such a degenerate, so you clearly do things differently than I would."

"Erin," Gail said, looking pained. "This really isn't any of our business."

"Yes, it is, Mom. Dan's made it our business."

"This is their relationship," Gail said. "Shouldn't they be the ones to resolve this?"

"Sure. That would have been fine. Preferable, actually. But when Dan and you drag us out of bed, it becomes my business."

"I told you I was sorry about that. Believe me—"

"It's fine, Mom. This had to erupt sooner or later."

"It's not fine," Dan said. "I don't want to talk about Katie like this. I swear I wouldn't have mentioned any of this if she wasn't playing with you. I didn't say one bad word about her before this."

"I must seem like a naïve fool to you, Dan, but I'm really not." Erin's voice was level and calm. "I don't jump into relationships, and Katie doesn't either. You'd know more about her if you took the time to converse with her."

"I never said she jumps into relationships. She jumps into bed, and then she moves on."

"If that happens, you'll have the satisfaction of saying you told me so." Erin sat back down, put her arm around Katie, and kissed her cheek. "But I'm betting you're wrong."

"People change, Dad," Katie said. "For Gail's sake, I hope *you* have."

"Knock it off," Erin said, anger flashing. "Stop digging at him!"

"All right, all right." Katie sank down in her seat, looking like a scolded child.

"This is getting us nowhere." Dan walked over to her and looked into Erin's eyes. "I'm sorry we came in. This is your house, and I shouldn't have barged in. I swear I'm only trying to protect you, Erin. I know how much your mom loves you, and I'm only trying to help."

"I'll take you at your word, but I don't need help in making decisions about my personal life. The only way Katie and I can get to know each other is by being together. Your opinions about her and her opinions about you are just that—your opinions. They aren't any of my business."

Dan sighed and then held up his hands in defeat. "Fine. I'm sorry for interfering."

"I think Katie deserves an apology more than I do, but I'm not sure either of you really wants to have a better relationship, so I'm going to stay out of it." She nodded towards Gail. "I *do* know my mom pretty well, though, and I wouldn't drag her to many of these kinds of encounters. She really hates being involved in confrontations."

With a pronounced chill in her voice, Gail said, "I can take care of myself, too, Erin. You don't have to talk to Dan on my behalf."

"Fine. I'll stop." She stood and started for the stairs, three sets of eyes watching her. "Then we're done. Katie?" She walked up the stairs, with Katie following close behind.

Katie closed the door behind them and wrapped Erin in a bear hug. "Are you all right, baby?"

"Yeah," Erin sniffed. "She just hurt my feelings. If she knew how to protect herself, she wouldn't have come into my room when we were making love."

"You're right. I think my dad's pushing her around, and I don't think she knows how to fight back."

"Maybe fighting isn't the answer."

Erin's gaze showed how weary she was, and Katie knew that this wasn't the time to debate tactics. She stroked Erin's hair, murmuring soothing, soft sounds into her ear. "Let's go back to bed and hold each other, okay?"

"Okay." They stripped out of their hastily thrown-on clothing and got back into bed. Erin snuggled up into Katie's warm embrace, crying a little at the pain she felt from the distance that had built up between her and her mother. "She *does* need my protection. Barging in here was ridiculous. I've never, ever seen her do anything so rude."

"That's good to know because I was going to call a locksmith and have a lock put on the bedroom door."

Erin snuck a look at her, seeing a completely neutral expression on her face, but after a second, Katie smiled warmly and gave Erin a soft kiss.

Katie kept stroking her, reassuring with her concern. "It's a statement about the health of our relationships with our parents that you're crying because your mom said she didn't need your protection and I'm not bothered by my dad calling me a drunken whore." She laughed wryly and bitterly.

"That's not true."

"What, baby?"

"It does bother you, but instead of letting it hurt you, you try to give it back."

"Nah," Katie scoffed. "I just love to bust his chops. It's in our DNA."

"I don't think that's true, but if it is, we're going to have trouble. You'd break my heart if you tried to get to me that way."

"Oh, baby." Katie kissed Erin's face, moving her light touch all over her flushed cheeks. "I'd never do that to you. It's just…how we've managed. It's us."

"Well, you two have exhausted me. I want to go back to sleep and start over again."

"My poor baby. I'm so sorry you had to get involved, but you made me feel very cared for, Erin. No one's ever defended me like you did today."

"I love you," Erin said, kissing Katie gently. "And I can't stand it when people nag each other. It's so unproductive and childish."

There was another soft knock on the door, and Erin looked like she wanted to throw something at it. "Yes?" she called out wearily.

"Honey?" Gail opened the door a crack. "May I talk to you for a minute?"

"Is it urgent? 'Cause if it's not, I've had enough talking for one day."

Gail didn't answer immediately, but when Erin didn't add anything, she said, "All right. Will you call me?"

"Sure. After Katie leaves."

"Okay. And Katie, I'm very sorry about today."

"Not your fault, Gail. He's a rock-head."

Gail didn't reply. She just quietly closed the door.

Katie nudged Erin with her shoulder. "Was what I just said snotty?"

"A little. You could have stopped after the first sentence, but it wasn't too bad."

"I'll try to be better. I really will."

"I hope you do," Erin said, sighing heavily before turning onto her side to get a little space.

Erin wasn't asleep yet, but she was very still, hoping that Katie would give her time to think about what had happened and cool down. She heard a sniffle and then another, and when she turned, she saw tears dripping onto Katie's pillow. "Of course it hurts," Katie whimpered. "He treats me like shit, and all I ever did was try to please him."

Erin gathered Katie in her arms and kissed her forehead. "Tell me about it," she murmured. "Talk to me."

It took her a few seconds to catch her breath, but Katie said, "I was daddy's little girl."

Before she could censor herself, Erin sputtered, "You were?"

"Yes. I was. I was five when Danny was born, and I spent every second I could with my daddy." She sighed shakily.

"Did that change when Danny…"

"No." Katie shook her head, her soft curls tickling Erin's nose. "We were rock-solid. Everything was great until he and my mom started having problems. When he moved out, I was furious. He abandoned us, Erin!" She turned, letting

Erin see the anger and grief still glowing in her eyes. "And then...and then..." she said, starting to sob again. "He sued my mother for custody...of Danny!" She cried so hard that Erin could hardly hold on to her, but after a long time, she settled down and caught her breath. "He left, and he took my brother. He destroyed our family." She buried her head against Erin's neck, disconsolate. "He even gave our dog away. Everything was gone." She started to cry so hard she began to hiccup.

"My poor girl." Erin kept patting her and rubbing her back until Katie spoke again.

"I was so mad," she whispered. "So fucking mad at him. I've never been so mad—before or since."

"Why did he leave? And why take your dog away? That doesn't make sense."

"Nothing made sense. He just did what he wanted. Like he always does. I came home from school and found Danny's stuff gone."

Confused, Erin asked, "What did your mom say?"

Katie shook her head. "Nothing. She was...well, she hid out in her room for a while."

"Was she depressed?"

"Yeah, I guess so."

"Who took care of you?"

"My aunt was right upstairs. She didn't leave me on the street or anything."

"Still," Erin said, "you needed extra attention, not less."

Bristling, Katie said, "I didn't blame her. What would you do if your husband kidnapped your little boy? If I was her, I would have done anything to get him back." The rage flowing from Katie was practically simmering.

"But she didn't do that?"

"I don't know what happened. I'm telling you, they both kept me in the dark. My dad just kept saying it was for the best, but it wasn't best for me and Danny!"

"So, you didn't feel like you could talk to him?"

"No! He wouldn't tell me anything. He does what he wants and makes everyone else deal with it. He and my mother never had a civil discussion about anything. They just yelled at each other, and then he did what he wanted."

"So, what did you do?"

"Do? What can a thirteen-year-old do? The only power I had was to refuse to see him, so that's what I did. I wouldn't have gone if the judge himself had put me in a car and driven me over there." Her voice was shaking with anger, and her eyes were steely in their intensity.

"Did you see Danny?"

"Yeah. My dad dropped him off every other weekend. He was so freaked out that he used to sneak into my bed and cry his little heart out. He had nightmares for years."

"Did it ever get better? I mean, it must have since you see your dad now."

Letting out another heavy sigh, Katie said, "Yeah. He came to my high school graduation, and we saw each other a little bit when I was in college. Things got a little better during law school, but we've never really healed. Obviously," she said, giving Erin a wry look.

"Wow. That was a long time. You honestly didn't see him at all for those years?"

"Not socially."

"Huh?"

A tiny smile curled the corner of Katie's mouth. "I ran into him professionally a few times."

"Professionally?"

"By getting into trouble when I was in high school."

"Oh. I was going to ask, but I was a little afraid. He made you sound like a thug."

"I wasn't. I never hurt anyone—except him."

"How did you hurt him?"

"Didn't you hear him still whining? I'd get into trouble, and the cop who picked me up would call him."

"And that hurt him? I'm not catching on."

"Erin, he was a captain. A big, tough, Irish captain from Southie. Having some patrolman call him to say his little girl was going down on some other girl in the backseat of a car was worse than finding out I was dealing crack."

Even though her words were serious and reflected some empathy for Dan, there was still a ghost of pleasure that Erin could detect in her voice. "Katie, I…I probably shouldn't get into this, but you've got to grow up about this stuff."

"What?" Blue eyes sparked with anger.

"I know this will make you mad, but you're playing a game with him. If you stopped playing, he'd have to stop, too."

"Okay," Katie said, clearly trying to hold her temper. "Explain to me how this is a game because it sure as fuck isn't any fun."

"I'm not saying it's fun, but you let him have these ideas about you. You don't even try to set him straight. Then you taunt him every chance you get, and he beats you over the head with the stuff he believes about you. Why do that?"

"I don't do that," she scoffed. "He's always spoiling for a fight. And he doesn't want to know me. He's too self-involved to care."

"Are you sure that's true? Are you really sure?"

"I think so." She shook her head roughly. "Yeah. I'm sure."

"Why don't you take a risk and try to be honest with him? Show him a little of your real self." She kissed her head while hugging her tightly. "Just try."

"I don't think it's worth it. He doesn't want to change."

Erin held her for a few minutes, trying to decide if she should say what she was thinking. She finally decided she had to. "Then stop seeing him. Cut your ties, and get on with your life."

A flash of panic showed Erin just how frightening the mere prospect of that was. "He's my dad. I can't do that."

"Sure you can. If you don't think it's worth it to be yourself, what's the point? Is it pleasurable to have a relationship with him that only consists of making each other angry?"

"It's more than that," she said, sounding very tentative.

"It doesn't look like it from my perspective. All I see is sniping and recriminations, and that can't be healthy for either of you."

"It's not." Katie was quiet for a minute, and then she said, "I don't know. I'll have to think about it."

"I don't want to pressure you. I just want you to be happy, and I can see how unhappy this makes you."

Katie nodded and then moved closer, letting Erin wrap her in a hug. They lay together for most of the afternoon, napping and holding each other, neither one having the energy to talk.

⤸⤹

The sun was setting when Katie tucked an arm around Erin's shoulders and asked in a shaky voice, "Do you still love me?"

Erin turned and searched Katie's eyes for a moment. "Of course I do. Are you feeling insecure?"

Katie's gaze shifted, and she seemed uncomfortable returning Erin's look. "No, of course not." She smiled, but it didn't look genuine. "I'm just fucking with you."

"No, you're not. You're feeling insecure, and there's nothing wrong with that. It happens to everyone."

"Not to me."

Erin laughed softly and gave Katie a squeeze. "I know it's not something you're used to, but I think it happens pretty frequently when you're falling in love. You've seen me running around like a long-tailed cat in a room full of rockers."

"Yeah," Katie laughed. "But you're not me. I'm immune to that stuff."

"Sorry, baby, but you're just a human, and humans get insecure. I hope you don't think my love for you is so tenuous that it'll fail because I'm not crazy about the way you and your dad interact."

"Well, I don't think it adds to my attractiveness. I know you don't like a lot of turmoil."

Smiling warmly, Erin said, "I think loving you is going to churn up my placid life, but it could use some churning up. It would be a deal breaker if you treated me like you treat your dad when you're angry, but I don't think you will."

"I never will, Erin. There's not much chance of you leaving my mother and taking my brother from me. That's pretty much what you have to do to really rile me up."

"I don't think I could get your mom. She seems pretty straight to me. But I might have a chance with your aunt."

Laughing, Katie said, "She's all yours, buddy. Although she'll break your rule about not dating women with a drinking problem."

"I was wondering about that. She seemed a little wobbly at your party."

"You heard my dad besmirching the Quinn name. He kind of has a reason to on the alcohol issue. That's one of the reasons I cut way back. I didn't want to run the risk."

"Is it a big problem?"

"I guess it depends on how you define 'problem.' My mom and my aunt get pretty lit when we have a party."

"Every time?"

Katie rolled her eyes. "You don't have to do an intervention. It just doesn't look good on an adult. Being drunk starts to look a little sad when you're over thirty."

"But your dad thinks you still drink a lot."

Katie blithely waved her hand. "He thinks what he thinks."

"No, baby. He thinks that because you used to, and he hasn't seen that you made the decision to cut back, and you haven't told him. You really can't blame him for thinking something that used to be true."

Holding her temples with the flat of her hands, Katie moaned, "You're making my head ache. I can only process so much in one day. I'm still stuck back in the 'Erin and I just made love for the first time' haze. It's not fair to try to shove more into this poor head."

"I'm sorry. This has been a pretty eventful weekend, hasn't it?"

"Yeah, and I wish all of the excitement had been centered right in this bed. I wanted to spend the whole day exploring you."

"I did, too. But there's nothing like a nice fight with your parents to drain all of the arousal out of a girl."

"Argh!" Katie grasped Erin and shook her. "I know I'll be hot for you the second I get home, and I probably won't get to see you until next weekend." She looked at Erin quickly. "I will see you next weekend, won't I?"

"Unless you move and change your phone number."

Katie chucked Erin under the chin. "Very good answer. You're a good girlfriend."

"I'm doing my best. I know I've still got a long way to go before I'll qualify to be Mrs. Kathleen Rose Quinn, but I'm working hard."

Katie grinned at her, charmed. "If this were a horserace, you'd be the heavy favorite."

⁓

Erin tried to make the weekend last longer by convincing Katie to have dinner with her, but the diner closed early on Sunday, and Katie begged off going to the next town. "I'd love to spend more time with you, but I'll want to eat something when I get home. I have some good things in my refrigerator, and I know they'll call to me whether or not I eat now."

"That's funny." They were sitting on the sofa in the living room, and Erin was absently playing with Katie's hair, making a long tendril straighten out and then bounce back into shape. "Tell me more about your eating habits."

"I hate to brag, but they're damned good. I went on a clean-living campaign when I cut down on my drinking. I convinced myself that fruits and vegetables were my friends. Now I try to use meat as a condiment."

"You'll have to teach me to be better. My instincts are all bad."

Katie reached under Erin's sweater and tried to pinch her waist, but even though Erin outweighed her, there wasn't much to pinch. "You've still got a few years to abuse yourself, pup. Enjoy it while it lasts." She put her hands on either side of Erin's face and guided her chin up so the light shone on her features. "You remind me of a beautiful pink rose that's just about to open. You're so fresh. I can just picture the morning dew on your soft, smooth cheeks."

Erin tilted her head and luxuriated under Katie's gaze, feeling sumptuously beautiful, but after a few seconds, a question clouded her eyes. "Have you always been attracted to younger women?"

Katie laughed, shaking her head. "All of the things I've hinted at, and that's your first question about my past?"

Grinning shyly, Erin said, "Yeah, and it's not really about your past. It's about your preferences."

"I can't guess why this matters, but you're the youngest woman I've ever gone out with. Well, that's not true, but the age difference between you and me is the greatest…I think. I'll have to check."

"Do you have a logbook or something?"

"No, smartass. I've always been drawn to older women. In the last few years, I don't think I've been out with anyone younger than me. One of them might have been more than nine years older, but I've never been out with anyone even three years younger."

"Interesting. I wonder why?"

"I don't spend a lot of time examining my motives. Didn't Freud say, 'An examined life isn't worth living'?"

"I think that was 'An unexamined life isn't worth living.'"

"Close enough." Katie leaned forward and kissed Erin's pink cheek. Then, unable to pull away once she breathed in her scent, she moved to her lips and started to explore. In less than a minute, they were nearly horizontal, frantically kissing each other, hands roaming wildly. The phone rang, and Erin jumped, clipping Katie on the cheek with her shoulder. "Ow!"

"Sorry, baby. I'm skittish." Looking guilty, Erin got up and went to the phone. "Hello?" She listened for a second and then said, "Uhm, yeah. That would be nice. Katie's going to leave soon, so having dinner would work." She made eye contact with Katie, who nodded. "I'll see you then, Mom. Okay, I will."

She went back to the sofa and said, "My mom asked me to apologize one more time for this morning. I can't imagine what your dad had to say to make her come into the room. Having a confrontation with somebody is probably her least favorite thing to do." She put her arm around Katie and hugged her. "I feel better when I hold you." Their eyes met, and Erin's smile was dim. "I hope she doesn't let your dad dominate her. That's not the kind of relationship she and my father had, and I know they were happy together."

"I wish I could reassure you, but I'm really not sure how he is. He and my mom fought like cats and dogs, but she always gave as good as she got. I've never really seen him interact much with any other women."

Erin started to speak, but she stopped herself. "I was going to ask you about his dating history, but that's none of my business."

"I think we'll do better if we focus on us, and now I think we need to focus on saying goodnight." She put her lips to Erin's cheek and stayed there, barely brushing her lips across the soft surface. "If that phone hadn't rung my head would be right…" She slipped her hand down Erin's body and settled it between her legs. "Here."

Erin put her hand over Katie's and moved it up and down. "If you liked being there half as much as I like having you there, we'd both have to quit our jobs."

"I've got some savings," Katie whispered, her voice full of desire. She forced herself to pull away and shivered as she sat up. "I am so damned attracted to you." Katie put her hands in her hair and fluffed it, settling it upon her shoulders. "I feel like a helpless little bee being pulled into you by your tantalizing scent." She lightly kissed across Erin's jaw. "I'm so tempted to dive in and drink your nectar."

"My poor mom has had a tough enough day," Erin teased, clearly trying to keep her head since Katie seemed about to lose hers. "Finding you and me on the floor like we were last night might kill her."

Katie stood up and stretched and gave Erin the grin she'd come to love. "My dad's seen worse, and it didn't even give him a heart palpitation. That I know of."

Erin gazed at her for a moment. "I'm not going to ask, and I'm not going to think about what might be worse. As a matter of fact, I think you conjure up things just to see if I'll bite. I think Katie lies. I can see it in those pretty eyes."

Katie slid her hands through Erin's hair and pulled her head forward. When their lips were almost touching, she said, "I don't lie about anything important. I love you, Erin, and you're the most important thing in my life."

⊚⊷

The pair had moved to the front door to say goodnight, and Erin was certain she would hear her mother's car, but with Katie's arms around her, she was soon lost in her kisses. Her mouth was open, and Katie's tongue was probing deeply when Gail started up the steps. Only her embarrassment compelled Erin to pull away and put one final, gentle kiss on Katie's swollen lips. "I love you," she said and then opened the door. "Hi, Mom." She draped her arm over Katie's shoulders.

"Hi," Gail said. She had a very fixed smile, and she looked as if she were in pain.

"I've got to go," Katie said. "I've got to be in court first thing in the morning."

"Drive safely," Gail said, clearly relieved that Katie was leaving.

"I will." She kissed Erin's cheek and moved onto the porch, mouthing, "Call me."

Erin nodded and closed the door. "Long day, huh?"

Gail took off her coat and hung it on the hook. "Very." She looked more like herself now that they were alone, but there was still a certain stiffness to her. "I don't think we have much in the refrigerator. How hungry are you?" She headed for the kitchen.

"Starving. I don't think we ate today." Erin paused to think. "No, we didn't get around to it."

Gail stopped and looked at her, but she didn't comment, turning and walking into the kitchen. She opened the door to the refrigerator. "I could make you an omelet. We have some English muffins I could toast up."

"That's fine. Actually, you don't have to go to that much trouble. I could just have an English muffin with some peanut butter."

Peering over the door, Gail asked, "Really, honey? I don't mind."

It occurred to Erin that her mother probably preferred being busy. "Okay. I'll have an omelet. Did you already eat?"

"We've been snacking all day. I think I'll just have a little orange juice." She smiled at Erin, looking relatively normal. "Making breakfast food makes me want a breakfast drink."

"That sounds good. I'll make the juice."

Neither woman spoke as they went about their tasks. Then Erin sat down at the table and watched her mother finish cooking. Gail set the plate in front of her, took a seat, and then took an appreciative sip of her juice. "This is delicious. Thank you."

"Thanks for cooking for me." Erin bit into her omelet, nodding with satisfaction. "Really good." She ate quickly, realizing how hungry she was as the first bites hit her stomach. Gail watched her, looking anxious once again. "What did you want to say this morning," Erin asked, "when you came back up?"

Putting her hands over her eyes, Gail moaned, "I've never been so embarrassed. Katie must think I'm a true busybody."

"If she did, she didn't say so." Erin took another bite, gazing at her mother while she chewed. "I think she attributes all sins to her father. So, you get a pass." She made sure Gail met her eyes before pointedly adding, "From her."

"I knew this was going to turn out badly." Gail slumped a little in her chair. "I truly wish you'd found someone without quite so many…complications."

"I'm sure you do," Erin said, clearly bristling, "but I'm not going to let a woman like Katie get away because you're involved with her father. Besides, I met her first."

Gail thought about that for a moment, then said, "But you didn't take up with her until Dan and I were engaged."

Erin saw the pained look on her mom's face and said, "I'm sorry that my being with her makes your life more difficult, but his relationship with her stinks whether I'm in the mix or not. I think being with a man who has a difficult relationship with his child is hard no matter what."

"It's worse in this case because Dan feels very protective of you."

Erin put her fork down noisily. "How stupid do you think I am? I know you think I'm naïve, and I don't have a problem with that, but I'm not stupid."

Stunned at the small, uncharacteristic outburst, Gail sat upright and covered Erin's hand with her own. "Why would you say something like that?"

"Because both you and Dan are treating me like I'm dense. I know I'm inexperienced, but that's mostly by choice. I've known what I was looking for, and I didn't want to settle for something less than my goal. Dan doesn't know Katie well, and you don't know her at all, but I can tell you, she's spectacular."

"You're right. I don't know Katie, but I think it's unfair of you to say that Dan doesn't know her, either."

"All I know is Katie's perspective, and all you know is Dan's perspective. We could both be completely wrong, but if I'm any judge of character, Dan doesn't know Katie."

"I think you're a very good judge of character, but even if she's as wonderful as you believe, she's so much more experienced than you are."

Erin leaned back in her chair, her eyes scanning her mother's face. "I have no idea what that really means. I think it's a codeword for something else."

"A codeword?"

"Yes. Given that we agree I'm rather naïve and inexperienced, why isn't it a positive choice to be with someone who's less naïve and more experienced? And why didn't you complain about Suzy's experience? Do you know how many people she was with before me?"

"No," Gail said, flustered. "I have no idea."

"The same is true for Katie. Neither you nor Dan nor I know how many women she's been with. And it doesn't matter if that number is two or two thousand. Just like it doesn't matter what Dan's number is. All that matters is that they treat us well and make us feel loved. If Katie learned how to love me by being with hundreds of women, I'm more than happy to benefit from their teachings." She leaned even further back in her chair and crossed her arms over her chest, practically glaring at her mother.

Deflated, Gail nodded. "I see your point. And I suppose that both Dan and I have been using 'experienced' as a codeword. I'm not sure how he uses it, but I worry that Katie is single because she wants to be single." She looked into Erin's eyes and added, "And that she wants to stay single."

"This is part of the 'you treat me like I'm stupid' syndrome. I thought to ask Katie about her intentions. As a matter of fact, she told me her intentions before I even knew we were dating." She got up from the table, crumpled her napkin, and tossed it onto her plate. "She wouldn't give in to my badgering her about sex until she was certain she was falling in love with me. So, if you're going to call either of us out about having loose morals, I'm your girl." She marched out of the kitchen, footsteps echoing loudly.

Gail jumped up and followed her, saying, "Erin, please, don't be angry."

"What's wrong with being angry once in a while? I have all the pop of an open bottle of champagne."

"You're just very mature. You always have been."

"I *am* mature, Mom, but I'm also flat. I've been tamping down my personality to fit into this town and into my job." Her voice rose as her cheeks gained color. "Being with Katie lets me act my age. She encourages me to be who I really am."

"What do you mean by that? You know I've always been supportive of your lifestyle."

Shouting, Erin let out, "I don't have a lifestyle! I have a life! And I'm not talking about my sexual orientation. I'm talking about my passion, or lack of it. Katie wants me to do what makes me happy, even if it's going to make a lot of other people unhappy."

Warily, Gail asked, "What do you mean? Who's going to be unhappy?"

"Essex. Especially the members of the town council. They're not going to like it when I tell them I'm going to break my contract."

❧

Katie muted the television and picked up her ringing phone. "Hi, there, Erin Delancy, M.D."

"Hi. You make me smile."

"I'm supposed to. I'm your girlfriend. So, how did it go with your mom?"

"It went all over the place." Erin tossed her legs over the arm of the sofa and braced the phone against her shoulder as she lay down. "I feel like I'm going through puberty again."

"I can't imagine where you're going with that line of thought. I just saw most of you, and you look like puberty is far behind you."

"Just the emotional aspects. I was snapping at my mom like the dickens, and I blurted out that I want to break my contract. It was weird. It's like I have no control."

Her voice softening, Katie said, "Maybe that's not such a bad thing, sweetheart. You're awfully buttoned-up for such a young woman."

Erin let out a stream of air that made her lips flap noisily. "Maybe. I actually said something like that when I was fussing at my mom. I know I need to be more genuine, but it's hard for me. It's scary," she added quietly.

"Oh, sweetheart. I'm sorry it's hard for you. I wish I could offer you some advice, but I have no idea what it's like to hide my feelings." She chuckled softly, and Erin could just picture her half-smile.

"I think you hide your feelings just like most people do, but you probably don't have much experience in keeping your mouth shut just to make other people happy."

"That's never worked for me," Katie agreed. "In the first place, I don't think it works. In the second, it's not my nature. But I think it is *your* nature, and I'm sure it's hard to change that."

"Thanks for understanding. My mom seems very perplexed."

"She probably is, especially if this has always been your style. Were you always this way?"

"I'm not sure," Erin said thoughtfully. "I don't have the best memory. I have a hard time remembering things that happened much before high school."

With a sick feeling hitting the pit of her stomach, Katie's mind flashed on a young Erin closing her mind to the pain of losing her father and brother, as well as shutting the door to the good memories. She could just picture a sweet little girl trying to keep her needs at a minimum, to help Gail make her way through the ocean of grief she must have been drowning in after losing her husband and son.

Katie's protective instincts kicked in, and she had an overwhelming urge to go right back to Essex and hold Erin in her arms. She tried to sound lighthearted when she said, "Kids are boring. I'm sure you didn't start to get interesting until you were in high school."

"I'm not sure I'm interesting yet," Erin said, chuckling. "I think you might be interested in me just to get free medical care."

"Darn, I hoped you wouldn't notice that I took one of your prescription pads."

Giggling, Erin chanted, "Katie said 'darn'...Katie said 'darn.'"

"Argh! I'm supposed to be a bad influence on you. You're not supposed to be a good influence on me."

"I like the way you curse. You look so sweet and angelic it's funny to hear those words coming out of your mouth."

"Which words are those, Erin?"

"I can see you batting your eyes at me, but I'm a Dartmouth M.D. And M.D. doesn't stand for 'me dummy.' I'm not falling for your trick so easily."

"I need to look for a dumber girlfriend. I think I made a critical error."

"No, you didn't," Erin said, her voice gentle and soft. "I'm really glad you decided to make me your girlfriend." She rolled onto her side and tucked her legs up behind herself, careful to move the phone so she still didn't have to hold it. "I wish you hadn't gone home. I miss you."

"I miss you, too. We have to find a way to move our cities closer together."

"Or just our bodies."

"Yeah, those are the important things."

"Hey, have you thought about what I should do if I can get out of my contract? My mom asked me, and I stood there like a dunce."

"Sure," Katie said immediately. "I've also thought about what you can do if you don't."

"Are you going to tell me before I do it?"

Katie laughed. "I might. If you're good, I'll give you notice."

"There's only one thing I really care about, and that's being with you as much as possible."

"Then we're on the same page, pup. That's number one on my list."

Chapter Fourteen

When Erin got home the next night, she was pleased and a little surprised to find Dan sitting on the sofa. "Erin's home," he called out when she opened the door.

"Oh, good." Gail looked out through the kitchen door. "Hi, honey. Dinner's almost ready. Are you hungry?"

"Of course. You know I'm always hungry for your cooking."

As Erin walked into the living room, Gail said, "No matter what people say, everyone loves to be complimented on her cooking."

"I don't have to fake it, Mom." She started to walk into the living room, but Dan was in front of her before she'd taken a step.

"I owe you a big apology. I lost my head yesterday when I saw Katie's car here. I'm very, very sorry for causing a scene and for getting you and your mother involved."

"That's all right." She slid past Dan and went to sit down. "We've all got to make some adjustments."

"We do." He sat down, too, and smiled stiffly. "I was surprised that Katie let you get involved. I've never known her to stop talking when someone tells her to."

Erin returned his smile, but didn't respond. After a minute, she heard herself lamely ask, "How's life at the farm?"

"It's good. Thanks to your mother, I'm able to step up my plans and put in enough plants to increase my capacity far beyond what I thought I'd be able to do. By the end of this season, we should be two years ahead of my projections."

The first thing to fly through her mind was Katie's warning about finances, but Erin couldn't bring herself to ask Dan for any details. Instead, she kept it light. "I'm impressed that you're so organized. It sounds like you really did your homework."

He looked at her with the intense stare she'd learned he used when talking about his business. "I put every dime I could get my hands on into this business. I can't afford to fail." A warm friendly smile settled onto his face when Gail walked into the room and sat next to him. "With your mother's help, I'm certain we'll be a success."

Fondly, Erin said, "Mom knows a lot about farming. If that was the only thing she had going for her, she'd be a good catch."

Dan put his hand on Gail's thigh and patted it familiarly. "She's got a heck of a lot more than that going for her. She'd be a great catch if she'd never seen a farm."

Surprising herself by asking the question, Erin said, "You haven't talked about when you're going to be married. Have you made any plans?"

Dan looked at Gail quickly, and she nodded. He said, "We've been kicking it around for a while now. We thought that maybe we'd do it on Memorial Day weekend. Most people have that Monday off, so it wouldn't be as hard for people to get here."

"Gosh!" She tried not to look as surprised as she was. "I don't know why, but I didn't have any idea you were in such a…I mean…I suppose I thought you'd have a longer engagement."

"We're not getting any younger," Dan said. He looked at Gail again, and Erin noted how much gentler his expression was when he gazed at her. "Well, your mother is, but I'm not."

Gail scooted closer and put her arm around his shoulders. "You're so silly."

Uncomfortable witnessing their comfort with each other, Erin said, "I'm going to get something to drink. Can I get something for either of you?"

"I wouldn't mind a beer," Dan said. "Do you have any?"

"We sure do." Erin went into the kitchen, not mentioning that she'd bought the beer for Katie. She went back into the living room when she'd gotten a glass of water for herself. Handing the beer to Dan, she sat down, hoping that someone else would lead the conversation.

༺✦༻

After a dinner that was thin on chit-chat, Erin went up to her room and Dan began to clear the table. "It's going to take me a very long time to get used to the way you two interact."

Surprised, Gail looked at him, eyes wide. "What do you mean?"

"When I tell Katie we've set the date, she's going to throw a dozen questions at me. Where will we live? Will you keep your job? What'll you do with your house? Etcetera, etcetera. She's like a machine gun."

"She just wants to make sure you're protected."

"Maybe. She's been on me to do a prenuptial agreement, but to me, that's like assuming you're going to get divorced." He smiled fondly at Gail. "We're *not* going to get divorced, but we probably should redo our wills."

"I don't have one."

"Then we'd better get busy."

On Friday night, Erin turned the corner onto Katie's street and broke into a wide smile when she saw her sitting on the top stair of her brownstone. Unable to stop herself, she started to jog, getting to Katie in a few seconds. "I would have run the whole way to see you sitting here waiting for me." She leaned over and accepted a long, warm kiss as Katie slowly stood, their lips locked together.

Reaching behind herself, Katie pushed the door open and pulled Erin inside, never breaking the kiss. The door closed, and Erin felt Katie's determined hand snaking between their bodies. In seconds, Erin's crisp blue shirt had fallen from her shoulders and was hanging down her back. She broke the kiss, laughing softly. "Now that's the kind of 'hello' I've been dreaming of."

Katie looked into her eyes, her longing for Erin showing vividly. "You're the one who wrote the short story. I'm just acting it out."

Growling playfully, Erin asked, "Are we going to act the whole thing out? I hope?"

"If you don't need to have dinner, I'm ready."

"I could stand to lose a few pounds. Let's go."

Katie took her hand and led her to the stairs. "On second thought…" She pulled the shirt from Erin's slacks and kissed her again, working her bra off while the kiss escalated to their bodies grinding against one another feverishly.

"You're very good at this." Erin was slightly dizzy from the rush of arousal, and she rested her forehead against Katie's while she caught her breath.

"I want you naked," Katie whispered sexily. "Totally naked and ready for me by the time we get upstairs." She worked at Erin's belt, looking into her eyes as she methodically undressed her. Slacks and panties pooled on the floor. Erin kicked them off and then shucked her loafers.

"I didn't wear socks." Erin smiled, looking a little woozy. "Saves time."

Katie led her up the stairs, her right hand palming and caressing as much bare skin as she could manage.

Erin was quivering with sensation, and she started to work on Katie's clothes as soon as they entered her bedroom. "First time we've made love at your house," she murmured, kissing Katie's now-bared breast.

"Not the first time I've wanted to." Katie dropped onto her bed, looking up at Erin with wanton desire. "The day after my party, I was almost a goner. You were so forceful. So decisive." Her grin was almost lecherous. "I was *so* hot for you."

"Was?"

"Am." Katie opened her arms, and Erin enthusiastically climbed on top of her. They wrestled on the bed with Erin finally managing to remove Katie's slacks. Katie wound up on top, giving Erin the opportunity to hook her thumbs into the waistband of her bikinis and start peeling them off.

Compliantly, Katie rose up on her knees and let Erin slip the panties down. Erin tumbled her onto her side, took the panties all the way off, and then dove in for another series of kisses. Katie was obviously feeling feisty because she started grappling again while still molding her mouth to Erin's.

They started rolling around on the bed, laughing and grunting with the effort. Neither was quiet sure of the purpose of the game, but they were each competitive enough to want to win. Erin was heavier and more muscular, but Katie was wiry and quick, making them fairly evenly matched. Each time Erin nearly had her pinned, Katie would squirm out of her hold and wind up knocking Erin off her knees. They fell onto the bed with loud thumps, expending a great deal of energy. After a good ten minutes of wrestling, Erin almost fell off the bed, rescued at the last second by Katie's quick hands.

As Katie tenaciously held on to her, Erin started to tickle her sides, making Katie laugh and tuck her elbows in to protect herself. Slowly, Erin slid off the edge of the bed, landing softly on the wood floor, panting. "I'm done."

Katie leaned over, smiling at the disheveled woman who returned her gaze. "I win."

Erin chuckled throatily. "I just got to wrestle with a really hot naked woman. I won."

"Come on up here, Mad Dog." Katie extended her hand, and Erin slowly got to her feet and then plopped down next to her, face to face. "That was hot."

"It was. I am." Erin grinned sexily. "Let's stop fighting and start doin' it."

"I knew you were a romantic. I could just tell." Katie wrapped her arms around Erin and yanked until she was on top of her. "Show me what you've got, you sexy thing."

"I can't tell you how nice it is to have a woman look at me like she wants me," Erin said, her voice catching a little.

Katie slowly and tenderly ran her hands up and down Erin's flanks, leaving a trail of goose bumps behind. "I want you so much it hurts. I ache for you." Her gaze was unflinching, filled with what was, to Erin, a wonderful mixture of certainty and desire.

Erin smiled despite the ache in her chest. She bent and wrapped her arms around Katie, holding on to her like a rare treasure.

❧

Erin bit into a crisp apple slice, nodding in satisfaction. "This is delicious."

"No, it's a Pippin." Katie handed Erin a slice of cheddar cheese. "Do you want any more crackers?"

"I think I've had enough. I don't want to get too full." She smiled, showing her teeth. "I have a lot of unfinished business to tend to."

Katie took the tray from the bed and put it on the floor. Then she carefully checked the sheets for crumbs, acting as though she couldn't hear Erin's laughter. "I let you eat crackers in my bed, but I won't let you leave crumbs. I have my standards."

Erin stuck her arms out and wiggled her fingers, urging Katie to join her. She didn't say a word, but her actions were so adorable that Katie jumped right back onto the bed and wrapped her in a hug. "You are so adorable! I never would've guessed that sweet, somber young doctor who patched me up would one day be sitting on my bed, naked, begging me to make love to her."

"I'm begging to make love to *you*." She cupped Katie's breasts in her hands and gazed at them lovingly. "I have to satisfy my need to have a breast in my mouth. Yours in particular."

Katie covered her nipples with her own hands. "I'm not going to be able to wear a bra next week if you don't calm down. You're voracious."

Feigning sympathy, Erin tried to pry Katie's hand off. "Let me kiss them and make them better."

"It's your kisses that made them tender. I'm going to have to get you a pacifier."

"If you can get turned on while I'm in bed sucking a pacifier, be my guest."

Katie grabbed her nose between two fingers and pinched it hard. "You are completely unrepentant!"

"I'm a doctor," Erin soothed, managing to push one hand away. She held Katie's breast in her hand and assessed it carefully. "It looks perfectly fine to me. A woman who's breastfeeding would trade with you any day of the week."

Slapping Erin's hand away, Katie tucked her hands into her armpits, completely covering her breasts. "I should hope so."

Erin shifted over and put her arms around Katie, murmuring into her ear. "After I leave tomorrow, they'll still be tingling. You'll be lying in bed and thinking about how it felt when I had your breast in my mouth and my fingers right here." Her hand trailed down and settled between Katie's legs, seeking entry. "You'll have to touch yourself. You'll just have to."

With a hungry growl, Katie lay down, pulling Erin with her. "Come inside me, you sexy thing."

Erin slipped inside, making Katie arch her back dramatically. When her ripe breasts were presented to Erin's fervid gaze, she was unable to resist, but she was much more delicate this time, limiting her attentions to the pale, flushed flesh, consciously ignoring the rosy nipples.

As she tended to do, Erin was soon lost in a reverie—seeing, feeling, touching, and tasting only Katie's body. Looking at the fire in Erin's eyes, Katie felt herself hurtling towards satiation, overwhelmed by the intensity of their connection. Her vulva thrummed with sensation, and she struggled to close her legs. "Mmm," Katie hummed, "Give me a minute, sweetie. Wait until I stop seeing double." She laughed tiredly. "Although two of you is a treat."

Erin moved up so they were on the same plane. With an expectant look, she asked, "Am I really doing what you like?"

The look Katie gave her clearly questioned her sanity. "I love you, Erin, but I don't love you enough to lie here for hours faking orgasms."

Giggling happily, Erin said, "That wouldn't work anyway. You have all the physical signs, and you can't fake those. I know you're having orgasms, but am I doing what you really want?"

"What I really want is to have you hold me and kiss me and love me. I don't have an agenda or a checklist." She raised herself up and rested on an elbow. Pushing her hair from her eyes, she said, "Why? Is there something you want that I'm not doing?"

Erin started to laugh, her eyes closing. "Are you kidding? Most sixteen-year-olds have done more than I have. If I had a list, you would have satisfied it while we were still lying on the floor at my house."

"I've been meaning to ask you about that. You don't mind talking about this, do you?"

"About sex? No. What do you want to know?"

Katie searched Erin's eyes, looking for any sign of discomfort. "I know you don't like to talk about your past, and I want to respect that, but there are some things that I can't quite figure out."

"Like what?"

Erin looked so guileless that Katie couldn't help smiling at her. "I was thinking about your disinterest or whatever it is about your vagina."

Erin laughed. "I'm not uninterested in it. It just hasn't gotten much attention.

I told you before, it didn't dawn on me to play with it."

Clearly puzzled, Katie said, "I didn't start playing with mine; other people did. But you gave me pretty clear direction that you didn't want me to touch you there. I've been worried about that."

"Katie," Erin took her hand and held it tightly. "I wasn't saying you weren't allowed to touch me there. I was just on the verge of orgasm, and I wanted you to keep doing what I knew worked. It's no big deal."

"So, you're not averse to my touching you there?"

"No, not a bit. You can touch me anywhere."

"Anywhere?" Katie's eyebrows popped up and down. "Are you sure that's your answer?"

"Get the KY and go for it." She stretched her arms and her legs out. "It's way past time I took the plastic wrapper off my body."

Katie rested her hand on Erin's belly and stroked it gently. "Are you sure? I don't want to make you uncomfortable."

Smiling impishly, Erin said, "That's why I want you to use KY." The serious look on Katie's face made her say, "Are you really concerned about this? I swear, I'm open to anything you want to do."

"I am concerned about it. I'm concerned because you don't seem into it. I don't want to touch you only for my pleasure. I want to do it for you."

Erin reached up and scratched her head with both hands. "Argh! What are you trying to get at? You want me to tell you that I'm going to enjoy something I haven't done. How can I do that?"

Stunned, Katie stared at her. "No one has ever put their fingers inside you?"

Erin's openness shut down immediately. "I thought we had an agreement. You said you wouldn't ask me about what Suzy and I did."

"I'm not! I'm asking if anyone in the world has ever touched you there. You didn't let guys do that to you?"

"No, I didn't." She lowered her eyes and looked a little guilty. "Boys didn't turn me on enough to go that far. I wasn't going to let them do anything I didn't want."

Katie chewed on her lower lip, trying to think of a way to ask questions that didn't upset Erin. Looking into her eyes, she consciously decided to give up. "I'm gonna take you at your word. If I can get my itchy fingers into a particular spot, I'll trust you to tell me if you don't like it."

Wrapping her arms around Katie and hugging her tightly, Erin said, "That's just perfect. And I promise I won't whine like every man does when I snap on a glove to examine his prostate."

Chuckling, Katie said, "I don't have a prostate, but I'm sure men wouldn't whine if having an exam felt like you're going to feel when I explore you, Dr. Delancy."

"I'm ready."

"No way. I'm gonna sneak up on you. Until then, we'll stick with the usual." She leaned over and started to kiss Erin, quickly and easily working her into her usual frenzy.

❧

Erin was dawdling on Sunday evening, trying to avoid having to get into her car and go home. She felt so content when she was with Katie that it was physically difficult to break their bond. "Hey, have you talked to your dad since the big fight?"

"Big fight?" Katie cocked her head for a moment. "Oh. At your house?"

Erin's mouth gaped open. "You've forgotten already?"

"No, no, it's just that I wouldn't call that a big fight."

Holding her hands over her eyes, Erin sighed, "Oh, my. You guys live in a whole different world."

Katie pried her hands away and kissed her. "We didn't specifically talk about what happened that day, but we never do. We just move on."

"Or fail to," Erin said. She held up her hand and added, "I take that back. You'll work on your relationship with him when you're good and ready. Did he tell you about the wedding date?"

"Yeah. That's why he called." She looked slightly ill. "Danny and I tossed a coin, and I have to tell my mom and my aunts. That's gonna be fun."

"What's your other aunt's name?"

"Ellen. She and my Uncle Mike live in Brookline. She's the baby."

"Does she share Eileen's love of your dad?"

Katie laughed. "No, she's relatively sane. Actually, for a Quinn, she's very sane. We'll have to go visit her. She'll love you."

They were sitting in the living room, cuddled together on the sofa. Erin put her arm around Katie and kissed her head. "I'm excited about meeting more of your family. Do you have cousins?"

"Yeah. Lots. Just three on my Mom's side, but nine on my Dad's. The Tierney cousins should all be at the wedding, even though they're getting less notice than they would of a snowstorm. What's the rush, anyway?"

"I have no idea. Your dad said a lot of people have Monday off, so it's convenient."

Katie gave her a sideways glance. "Your mom's not pregnant, is she?"

Laughing, Erin said, "That was my first thought, but that's really unlikely. It seems like they're treating it as a big party rather than anything formal. The only special thing they're doing is ordering a cake."

"They didn't send out invitations. Isn't that weird?"

"Yeah, it is to me. I guess they want it to be low-key. Almost like they're eloping."

"Is it gonna be in your church?"

"No. At your dad's house. My mom says they don't need any help, so it must be pretty simple."

Katie was quiet for a moment, and when she spoke, she looked a little sad. "Are you going to be in the wedding?"

"No. They aren't going to have attendants."

Lifting an eyebrow, Katie said, "Really? Aren't you a little pissed off about that?"

"No," Erin said, looking completely unfazed. "I wouldn't like it if she asked Mrs. Worrell or someone and not me, but if they don't want to have attendants, it's fine with me." She shrugged. "It's their wedding."

"I wonder what the locals think."

Chuckling, Erin said, "I'm not sure, but every time I go into the waiting room, Madge is on the phone. She hangs up as soon as she sees me, so I assume she's on rumor control—or dissemination."

"Well, if they were even ten years younger, everyone would assume your mom was knocked up. It's odd to rush to the altar."

"I agree, but as I said, it's none of my business. Maybe your dad just wants to make an honest woman out of my mom."

"Ugh. No offense, but I hate to think of my dad having sex."

"And you think I like it?" Erin's eyes were wide. "My mom hadn't been with a man in thirteen years. I assumed she didn't have a sex drive, and that was just fine with me," she added with a rueful laugh.

"I hope my mom doesn't get any big ideas about getting a man. I don't know if I could handle that."

"So you feel my pain."

Katie tossed her feet across Erin's lap and snuggled up to her. "Imagine how our parents feel about us. It must drive my dad crazy to think of my dirty hands running all over your innocent body." She snuck her hands under Erin's sweater and tried, unsuccessfully, to tickle her.

"It creeps me out to think of your dad thinking about my body at all—no matter whose hands are on it. Let's change the subject, okay? I'm beginning to feel nauseated."

"Ooh, I know something that'll make you smile. Opening day!" She jumped off Erin's lap and started to do a happy dance. Her enthusiasm was contagious, and Erin found herself clapping in time to Katie's gyrations.

"Woo-hoo! Shake it, baby."

"I've been told that after six or seven beers I'm quite a good dancer."

"I'm not in a hurry. Drink up."

"Not me," Katie said, tugging on a lock of Erin's hair. "You're the one who has to be drunk."

"Oh, that's different. I've never done that, but I guess I could have six or seven beers."

Katie stopped her dance and stared at Erin, mouth agape. "You've never been drunk?"

"No. Never."

Katie sank onto the couch, moaning, "I think my dad is right. My hands *are* too dirty to touch a pristine little jewel like you."

Erin wrapped her arms around Katie's waist and tugged her onto her body. They lay sprawled on the couch, nose to nose. "Your dad didn't say that. Your imagination did. Now you're having arguments with yourself."

Katie started to giggle and then laughed hard. "I crack me up. I was really insulted that my dad said that."

"See? That's what happens when you have such negative thoughts in your head."

"Don't go all new age on me. I hate that worse than country music."

"I'm not going anywhere on you. I'm just offering up an observation." She struggled to sit up with Katie's dead weight on her. Grasping the back of the sofa with both hands, Erin finally managed. "I should probably get going before I pull a muscle just trying to sit up."

"I can't help it. When I look into your beautiful eyes, I grow weak." Katie leaned heavily onto Erin's body.

"You were pretty peppy when you were thinking about the Red Sox game."

Swooning dramatically, Katie dropped onto the other arm of the sofa. "Thank God you didn't know me ten years ago. I had a tiny studio apartment in the Back Bay, and it looked like some total loser Red Sox geek lived there. My sister-in-law took me in hand when I moved here and said I had to start looking like an adult. I'm such a nerd."

"You're a Red Sox nerd. That's perfectly acceptable. Are you going to have a tiny little TV in your office tomorrow?"

Looking stunned, Katie stared at Erin. "I haven't told you about my tickets? The most important material goods in my entire world and I haven't told you about them?"

"You have tickets?"

"Yeah. We've had them since just after I graduated from law school."

"Season tickets?"

"Uh-huh. Matt Connolly's parents moved to California and Mr. Connolly was going to sell them to the highest bidder, but we convinced him to let us buy them."

"Who's us?"

"Matt and his wife Mary, Tony Giarmo, Rick Matthews, and me. They're awesome seats."

"Wow," Erin said. "Five tickets to every Boston game. That's awesome."

"Five? We don't have five; we have four."

"But you named five people."

"Oh. Matt and Mary flip a coin to see who gets to go to opening day. This year it's Mary."

"They flip a coin?" Erin asked, shocked.

"We've only got four. They pay for a quarter, so they get one."

"Is this a not-so-subtle way of telling me I'm not going to see you again until October?"

"No, of course not. We split them four ways for all of the games except the first, the last, and the playoffs. We have a whole system worked out so we each get the same amount of weekends."

"Does that mean you'll take me if I'm good?"

"No," Katie purred, giving Erin a very sexy smile. "I'll take you if you're bad."

⁂

The next morning, safely back in Essex, Erin called her mother. "Hi, Mom. I wanted to call to see if you had a good weekend."

"Hi, sweetheart. I called you before I went to bed, but you didn't answer."

"Yeah, I was driving home. I would have called you back, but you said you were going to bed soon, so I thought I'd call today."

"I'm glad you did. Did you have fun in Boston?"

"Oh, yeah. Very much. I love being with Katie, and it's nice to get away."

"I can imagine. It's probably more relaxing for you to go to Boston, even considering the long drive."

"You know, it is," Erin said. "Even though I don't care if people know about us, I don't like the scrutiny."

"I don't blame you. Sometimes, I wish Dan still lived in Boston. It's better now that we're engaged, but people still look at me like I'm a different woman. They have an image of me as a widow, and it seems to bother them that I'm interested in a man."

"You think you have trouble?" Erin chucked sardonically. "Coming out when you're the town doctor isn't going to be a picnic."

"You'll do that when you're ready. There's no rush at all."

"That's true. I have to remember that."

"Well, you'll do what feels right to you, but remember, if you tell anyone, you've told everyone."

"Kim knows, Mom. She has for years."

"Oh, of course she does. That's one way to know you can trust a friend. I've not heard word one about your sexuality, and I'm sure someone would have let it slip if you'd told even a few people."

"Oh, you'll hear plenty of words when I finally have to do it, but I'm going to hang on to my privacy as long as possible. It's kind of nice to have this just between Katie and me."

"Speaking of Katie, Dan tells me she's going to the game this afternoon. Dan's going to record it. Do you want to come over and watch it this evening? We could have hot dogs and Cracker Jacks."

Erin chuckled. "I'm sure you'll make some healthy form of both, but it still sounds good. I'll come over as soon as I'm through for the day."

⁂

Erin and Dan were both sitting in leather easy chairs, watching the game as Gail finished cooking. Erin was so involved she jumped when Gail touched her shoulder before offering her a plate. "I don't regret not replacing the television when it broke," Gail said teasingly. "You two are like zombies."

"It's Opening Day, Mom." Erin smiled up at her. "I'll be normal when the game's over."

"Oh, I'm used to it. Dan's always got it on. I've learned to tune it out."

"What?" Dan asked distractedly. "Did you say something, honey?"

"No, nothing important." Gail handed him his plate and he wrenched his attention away from the game momentarily.

"This looks great. You made French fries?"

"They're sweet potatoes, and they're baked, but it's nearly the same."

"Mom won't let your arteries clog up, Dan. You're going to have to sneak out for trans-fats if you want any."

He smiled at Gail, who was now settled on the sofa. "Your mom makes healthy food taste wonderful."

"She does, but I still need junk food once in a while."

Dan said, "I bet Katie and her buddies gorged themselves on every kind of junk they sell at the Fens today. Thank God there isn't decent parking around there. They have to take public transportation, so they're not tempted to drive drunk."

At first, Erin didn't take the bait. She'd decided to stay out of the Tierney/ Quinn affairs and let Katie stand up for herself when she was ready. But the way Dan so effortlessly assumed Katie would risk her own and others' lives got to her. "Katie doesn't drive drunk," she said flatly.

Looking a little surprised, Dan said, "You don't know her that well. She's been stopped more than once for D.U.I."

"Not recently," Erin declared, sure she was correct.

"No, not that I know of," he admitted. "But she should have taken you today. Aren't you upset she didn't offer?"

"No, not at all. We'll go sometime. I'm not in a rush."

"She seems to have a lot of friends," Gail said. "That will be good for you."

"Maybe." Erin shrugged. "Katie and I aren't alike in a lot of ways. She needs a lot more stimulation than I do."

"What do you mean by that?" Dan asked.

"I'd like a little more excitement in my life, but I don't need to go out all the time. I think Katie really needs that."

"How…how will you resolve that?" Gail asked tentatively.

"There's nothing to resolve. Katie has to do what she needs to be happy. If we wind up living together, I'll stay home and read if I don't want to go out. We don't have to be together every minute."

"That sure as hell wouldn't work for me," Dan said, his brow furrowed in a frown. "I wouldn't want my woman out carousing every night."

Erin smiled sweetly. "Pay attention, Mom. You're going to have to give up your regular place at the bar over at the Dewdrop Inn."

❦

The next morning, Erin overheard Madge on the phone. She hadn't been paying attention, but she heard her name mentioned and perked up. "No, I didn't know that," Madge said. "How many weeks has she missed?" There was a pause, and then she said, "I don't know why she's not going to church, but I'll find out. She tells me everything."

Chuckling, Erin went into the waiting room and sat down on one of the chairs. Madge quickly hung up and looked at her. "What's up, sweetie?"

"Not much. When's our next victim?"

"Not for twenty minutes."

"I think I'll go get a snack. Do you want anything?"

"No, thanks." Erin started for the door when Madge said, "Did you do anything special this weekend?"

Pausing at the door, Erin said, "Yeah, I went to Boston. My social life has really picked up since I met Katie. She's introduced me to so many new people." She smiled broadly. "I've always wanted to spend more time in Boston, and now I have a free place to stay."

"Oh, that's so nice!" Madge looked genuinely happy, and Erin had to acknowledge that even though Madge lived for gossip, her concern was real.

"Yes, it is. I'm much happier getting out and doing more things."

"You look happy. Maybe you'll meet someone and beat your mother to the altar."

"No, that's not going to happen. She's getting married over Memorial Day weekend." Madge jerked in surprise, and Erin went outside, knowing that the phone would be buzzing about the wedding, giving discussion of her life a brief reprieve.

❧

The following Saturday morning, Erin showed up at Dan's farm bright and early. Gail met her at the front door and hugged her enthusiastically. "I'm so happy to have you here to help out."

"I'm sorry it's taken me so long to offer."

"I'm making omelets," Dan called from the kitchen. "What kind do you want?"

Erin and Gail walked through the house to the kitchen. "Mom has you cooking?"

Gail put her arm around Erin's shoulders. "He's pretty well trained, isn't he?"

Giving her a fond look, Dan said, "She makes dinner for me every night. The least I can do is make breakfast for her on the weekends."

"That sounds more than fair to me," Erin said. "I'll take anything you're making. I'm not picky."

Erin and Gail sat down at the table, each with a cup of coffee. While he worked, Dan said, "Your mom tells me my roustabout daughter is in New York."

"Yes, she is. Along with about a dozen of her friends. I talked to her last night after the game. She was so hoarse I could hardly understand her." Erin laughed softly. "I hope she doesn't have to go to court next week."

Gail said, "I didn't know she was going with a big group."

"She does everything with a big group," Dan said. "Just like college."

"Not everything," Erin said. "On the weekends I've been in Boston, it's just been the two of us. But she does have a lot of friends, and I think it's very good for her."

"Even when she takes off with a bunch of them for the weekend?"

"Even then," Erin said. "Katie would go crazy if she was only with me. She needs variety."

"That's gonna get old," Dan said. "Nobody likes to be left out."

Refusing to be ruffled, Erin said, "There's a difference between being left out and opting out. Katie had it all worked out so that I could go with her. She was even going to pay for me, but I chose not to go."

Dan gave her a knowing look. "I can see why. It wouldn't have been any fun to sit in the hotel while they all went to three Yankee games."

Chuckling, Erin said, "She had tickets lined up from a scalper. I can't imagine how much the weekend would've cost her, but I just didn't want to go."

Dan's expression bore a surprising amount of pride. "That's one thing I've gotta say for my girl. Nobody's more generous. But I can see that you wouldn't want her to throw that kind of money around."

"That wasn't it. I genuinely didn't want to go. I like parties, and I like meeting people and having fun, but three days of it sounded like too much."

"Oh, boy, you're in for trouble. Katie's just getting started at three days."

"I don't think that's true, but it's okay with me if it is. I love being with her, but my love for fishing is just below being with her on my preference scale. If she wants to go to Mardi Gras for a week, I can easily occupy myself."

Dan had one eye on the cooking omelet, but he managed to spend a moment looking at Erin. "It seems like you've thought this through."

Gail reached over and grasped Erin's hand, laughing. "Erin thinks everything through. She doesn't have a rash bone in her body."

"Hey, I went to medical school. I just happen to know there isn't a rash bone."

"Well, I've said it before, but I'll say it again. You're just the kind of girl that Katie needs. I'm still not sure she's the kind you need, but you seem mature enough to decide that for yourself."

Without a touch of rancor in her voice, Erin said, "Thanks. I think I am mature enough to know what I need, and I hope you're right that I'm what Katie needs because I'm crazy about her."

❧

After dinner that night, Erin cleaned Dan's kitchen while Gail sat at the table guiding Erin as she put plates and utensils in their places. "I need some advice," Erin said. "I'm not sure what my first move should be, but I want to come up with an action plan for getting out of my contract."

"I was hoping you were going to ask where the vegetable steamer goes." Gail laughed nervously, got up, and went to the sink. She took out a clean dishtowel and started drying. "Just thinking about what you're going to do makes me nervous."

"I'm sorry, Mom. I hate that this affects you." Erin dried her hands and put an arm around her mother's shoulders, hugging her close.

"No, no, don't worry about that. I'm concerned about you, honey. It's going to be hard to talk to the people you need to speak with and not have everyone in town know. I've thought about this more times than I can count, and I don't know how to do it."

"Have you spoken to Mrs. Worrell?"

Gail turned and looked at Erin, clearly surprised. "Of course not. I haven't told a soul. But talking to Betsy and Tom is probably a good idea. When you're ready, we could make brunch for them some time after church."

Erin didn't move for a moment. She looked out the window over the sink, watching the fading sun illuminate the gentle hill filled with berry bushes. Nodding quickly, she said, "Let's do it tomorrow. I'm ready."

❧

On Sunday afternoon, Erin walked Tom and Betsy Worrell to the front door. "Thanks for spending so much time helping me think through my problems," she said. "You've both been a great help."

Tom Worrell clapped Erin on the shoulder. "I wish you loved the practice like I did, but it's not the kind of thing you can fake. If your heart's not in it, you've got to get out." He looked sad and, to Erin's eyes, disappointed.

She moved forward and wrapped her arms around him, smiling when he hugged her back. "It would be a lot easier if I did love it, but you're right. It's not the kind of thing I can fake." He patted her gently, and she moved back, wiping away a few tears she hadn't been able to contain. "I'll keep you both posted on how things go."

Betsy Worrell took Erin's hand and squeezed it. "We want what's best for you, honey."

"Thanks. That means a lot."

She walked them to their car and then sat on the stairs to the porch, thinking about the afternoon. After a while, Dan came out. "Mind if I join you?"

"No, please do."

They sat together in companionable silence for a few minutes. "This is a funny town," Dan said. "Everybody at that church knew how many weeks you'd missed and wanted you to tell them where you'd been. I still can't tell if people are interested or just nosy."

Chuckling, Erin said, "A little of both, but it does give you pause, doesn't it? I used to envy a friend I had in high school. She was Catholic, and since we don't have a Catholic Church, her family went to services in Greenville. I'm sure the people there kept an eye on them, but they could leave Essex and go anywhere they darn well pleased on Sunday mornings. I thought that was quite exotic."

"Well, after the sixth person asked you where you were for the past two weeks, I had to bite my tongue not to tell them it was none of their Goddamned business." He laughed softly. "But I'd hate to see your mom drop dead from shame on the church steps."

Nodding, Erin said, "That's a distinct possibility. Are you going to join the congregation?"

"Nah. I'm Catholic. I just wanted to go with your mom this time because I knew people would be yapping about the wedding."

"That was nice of you. And it was nice for me because people were more concerned with you than they were with my truancy."

"Darn near none of them are gonna be invited. What business is it of theirs?"

Erin patted his knee before standing up and stretching. "None at all, but that will never stop them from asking."

⟡

As soon as Katie got home that night, she called Erin. "How's my girlfriend?" she asked, her voice hoarse and rough.

"I'm very good. I missed you, of course, but I had a good time with our parents."

"Our parents. That sounds so weird, but I'm glad you had a good time. Have you done anything since the last time I talked to you?"

"That's only been…" Erin looked at her watch. "Two and a half hours. You've got to leave me unsupervised for longer than that if I'm going to get into any trouble."

"You don't really feel supervised, do you?"

"Not at all. I feel loved. And if I didn't make this clear earlier, I felt loved by Doctor and Mrs. Worrell. I know he's disappointed in me, but I also know he wants what's best for me."

"Try this on for size. I was thinking about this on the flight home. I'd like to schedule a meeting with the proper person and represent you."

"Represent me how?"

"I want to meet with someone from the city, and I don't think you should be there. Negotiations like this often get heated, and I think it's best not to have the client involved."

"Katie, I appreciate your offer, but I think that would just make them get their backs up. The men on the town council are a very conservative bunch. I think they'd feel a lot more comfortable dealing with me directly."

"I think you're right. That's why I want to be the one to talk to them. I don't want them to be comfortable, Erin. I want them to be off-kilter. Just like the Yankees' pitching was today. Woo-hoo! A big BoSox win!"

⁂

It took two weeks and some persuasion on Katie's part, but a meeting with the entire town council was finally set for the twentieth of April. The council's regularly scheduled monthly meeting was slated for seven in the evening, and they agreed to meet with Katie at six.

Erin had patients until seven, and she didn't want to attract Madge's attention, so she and Katie decided to meet at Dan's house as soon as they were both finished. Erin was pacing up and down the paths in the orchard when she heard Katie's tires crunch over the rocks in the long drive. Erin started heading for her, but Katie rolled down her window and called out, "Stay there. I'll come to you."

Reverting to her slow, considered gait, Erin laced her hands behind her back, looking mildly professorial. Her worried frown vanished, and her expression showed pure delight when Katie got out of the car. Katie looked pleased and a little surprised when Erin stuck two fingers in her mouth and gave her a loud wolf whistle. "This is fantastic," Erin said. "It's like having two girlfriends."

"You like the work duds, huh?"

"A whole lot. A whole, whole lot." Fascinated by the change, Erin studied Katie as she drew near. Her hair was the same as always, a beautiful profusion of curls that stopped just short of settling on the shoulders of a long, Asian-inspired dark-blue jacket. A few inches of a matching skirt and many inches of shapely legs were revealed beneath the jacket. As Erin got closer, she saw that the suit was made of silk and bore an intricate Chinese print. Katie was having a tough time traversing the plowed soil in her sling-back heels, and Erin held up her hands urging her to stop. "I'll come to you. You're going to ruin your shoes."

Smiling, Katie said, "Normally I'd take off my shoes and go barefoot, but this is a brand-new pair of stockings."

Erin reached for her and enveloped her in a hug. "Stockings?" she asked, her voice full of innuendo. "Do women wear stockings any more?"

"At work I do. I think it looks more professional, especially when I'm meeting with clients."

"What kind of stockings are they?" Erin asked, letting her fingers slide down Katie's thigh. "Like with a sexy garter belt?"

"Uhm, do you like garter belts?"

"Maybe." Erin pulled back and gave Katie a shy smile. "I've never really seen a woman wear one."

"Simple solution. Imagine you like them and imagine I'm wearing one."

"That's a good trick." Erin held Katie at arm's length and looked her over. "I can't tell you how fantastic you look."

Katie blinked at her, feigning innocence. "You're welcome to try."

"I'm not good at this, but it's like having a whole new girlfriend. I've never seen you in a skirt, and I've never seen you in heels." She moved back a few inches and let her eyes wander up and down Katie's body. "You look so adult, so sophisticated, so wealthy."

"Thank you. One of my friends used to date a woman who works at a very exclusive boutique. She and I are still friends, and she hides things for me right before they go on sale. I still pay way too much for my work clothes, but people judge your success by how you dress."

Eyes glittering with appreciation, Erin said, "You're the most successful woman I've ever seen."

"Give me a kiss, you sweet-talking woman." As Erin moved for her, Katie said, "Don't make it too enthusiastic. I'm sure our parents are watching us."

Erin was already zeroing in for her kiss, and after a brief buss, she pulled back and stared at Katie, clearly stunned. "What's wrong with me? You just went to the most important meeting of my life, and I haven't asked you about it!"

Katie hugged her tenderly. "You were blinded by my beauty."

Giving her the happy grin that always made Katie's heart swell with affection, Erin said, "That's 100 percent true, but I should be able to focus on two things at once. I'm surprised at this, but I can't read a thing by your expression or your demeanor."

"Don't ever bet against me in poker. You'll lose your shirt."

"Tell me!"

"I'm selfishly trying to keep you in a good mood for as long as I can."

Deflated, Erin gazed at her with hooded eyes. "Really bad, huh?"

"Not yet, but if I can guess what they're going to do, it's bad. They're going to get back to me by next week, but they weren't interested in discussing much of anything. I have to tell you you've been doing a very good job at convincing people you love your work because they were stunned."

"Well, I guess that's good."

"It is good, sweetheart." She put her arm around Erin's waist, and they walked together toward the house. "I'm very proud of you for being able to put your patients first."

"I always try to," Erin said soberly. "By the time I get around to thinking about myself, I'm usually in quite a fix already."

"I'd love for you to be able to put yourself a little higher on your list of things to think about, but I can understand it's hard to change."

"Yeah, it is, but I can do a lot if I put my mind to it."

"Let's try to have a nice night. The Sox are playing the Tigers, so maybe we can eat while we watch the game."

"I think that can be arranged. I'm not sure my mom knew what she was getting into when she agreed to marry a sports fan, but she's adjusted pretty well."

"You two were way too feminine before the Tierney-Quinns got to you. We'll have you both so androgynous you won't know how to put on makeup before long."

As they walked the rest of the way towards the house, Erin considered that this was the first time Katie had ever referred to her father and herself as any form of a team. It was a very small step, but one she considered important.

※

After she got home the following Thursday night, Katie called Erin. "Hi, there. The dingbat treasurer of your town council left a message for me this afternoon. He said they've reached a decision, and he'll inform me of it when we meet."

"You have to come up here?"

"Apparently so. I guess that's one way to discourage people from getting attorneys who aren't local."

"Why don't you just call him back and tell him he can talk to me? There's no need for you to drive up here, especially since we're planning on spending the weekend at your house."

"No, I don't want to do that. I'd much rather be the one they have to deal with. If there's any negotiating to be done, I'm in a better position to do it."

"It's possible they'll be nicer to me since they know me."

"Sweetheart, they didn't do you any favors with this contract. They played hardball with you, and that was with Dr. Worrell on your side. I went to give them the clear message that you're represented by counsel."

"Okay, you probably have a point. Maybe they'll tell you their decision over the phone."

"I've got an idea. I checked a couple of web sites and noted that this Saturday is the start of trout fishing in ponds. I know that's your favorite kind of fishing, so I thought maybe I'd come up there."

"You are the sweetest girlfriend. I know you looked up the fishing stuff just to have a reason to come up here and meet with the council members, and I really appreciate it."

"No, really, I want you to do what you love. We'll have fun."

"You're a very methodical woman. It's charming beyond belief to think of you sitting at your computer, trying to make all of these things work."

"No matter what the town council says, we're going to have fun this weekend. And that's a promise."

Chapter Fifteen

*E*rin jogged the last hundred yards to her home on Friday afternoon. She knew it looked a little funny, but when she saw Katie's car, she was unable to walk at her normal pace. When she opened the door, Katie was sitting on the sofa, dressed in a lovely cream-colored linen suit and drinking a beer out of the bottle. The discrepancy between the elegance of her clothing and the casualness of the beverage and its container struck Erin as very funny. She found herself laughing, even though her mother and Katie looked quite somber.

Katie stood up and smiled. Erin walked right into the hug she offered, and they embraced for a little longer than was probably polite. The way Katie held on to her clued Erin in to the results of her meeting. "I'm going to guess," she said as she pulled away, "that the council told me to shut up and get back to work."

Tapping herself on the nose a couple of times, Katie said, "We have a winner."

"We've been talking about your options," Gail said. "But we haven't come up with anything that will solve your problem."

Erin took in a deep breath and blew it out forcefully. She gazed only at Katie and said, "What are we going to do?"

Her voice sounded so sad that Katie was mildly shocked at the change from just moments earlier. From her plaintive expression Katie recognized her unasked question. "I'm not sure yet, but I *am* sure we'll figure this out." She grasped Erin's thigh and gave it a robust squeeze. "We'll figure out a way to be together. It's only about fifty miles from Essex to my condo. That's nothing." She snapped her fingers, looking supremely confident.

"That's a hundred miles. You've got to go both ways."

"Hey, those big brown eyes have those squalls in them. There's no need for that."

"I know," Erin said quietly. "And I know we can reach some solution when we're ready to live together. But I worry about having to do my job for the next eight-plus years. That's the part of this that worries me the most."

Nodding, Katie said, "I agree. I think the town council is being stupid. It's in their best interests to have someone who's called to do that kind of work, but they refused to listen to any of my points." She shot a quick look at Erin. "I've been kicking myself, thinking that I screwed this up for you. They really might have listened to you more than they did to me."

"I wouldn't have let you talk to them if I'd been confident that I'd have more success. You didn't push me into doing something I wasn't comfortable with. I know I seem pretty malleable, but I'm not when something is important to me. And this is very important."

"Thanks for saying that, but I'm still having second thoughts."

"You shouldn't. We're not close friends with anybody on the town council. To be honest, I think most of them are jackasses."

"Thank goodness! I was biting my tongue because I thought they might be your friends."

"There are a few cliques in town," Gail said. "We're not in the one that the politicians are in." She stood up and gave Erin a quick hug. "I'll leave you two to start your weekend. Call me if you need anything."

"We will," Erin said, not sure what her mother could provide, but glad for the offer.

They watched her leave and Katie flopped down on the sofa and tugged Erin with her. "Are you sure I haven't screwed up any relationships for you two?"

"Not a bit. Most of the people we socialize with don't care for the guys who run the town. They're...all I can guess is that they hate change."

"What kind of change? Not to be rude, but Essex doesn't look like it's changed in a hundred years."

"Oh, it has. It definitely has. Most people in town still consider my mom one of the newcomers."

Chuckling, Katie said, "I think a lot of small towns have that insularity. You have to be born there to be one of them."

"True. It's like that in the little town in Maine where my mom grew up, but there's a big difference between her town and Essex."

"And that's...what?"

"Boston."

"Boston? What's that got to do with it?"

"Essex is at the far end of commuting distance. Most of the people who've moved to town in the last twenty years work in Massachusetts. That never used to be the case. A lot of the old guard hates the new people and their big-city ways."

"Oh, I get it. They're not real New Hampshire people."

"Yeah, but they're also younger and not as dependent on the town. That's the biggest reason the council wanted to hire me."

Katie shot her a look. "Because of the new people?"

"No, because of the old-timers. They're the ones who don't want any form of change. There are dozens of doctors in a twenty-mile radius, and almost all of the new people go to doctors in bigger towns, but the old guard wants things to stay the same. There was a terrible fight when they decided to pay for my education. The newer people thought it was insane—which, in all truth, it was."

Stunned, Katie searched Erin's eyes, trying to get a feel for how she felt about this. "You were okay with that?"

"Well, I didn't like the arguing, but I wanted to be a doctor, and it was very appealing to have my education paid for. And Doctor Worrell really encouraged me. He believes the lifers should have the right to keep things our way for as long as possible."

"He's one of the old guard, right?"

"Yeah, in many ways. Born and bred in Essex. Fourth generation."

"Interesting," Katie said, her eyes partially closing as she nodded. "Very interesting."

Erin put her fingers on either side of Katie's knee, and squeezed. "I see that look, Katie Quinn. That's your 'that's stupid' look."

Katie laughed, her affection for Erin showing clearly in her expression. "I don't have a 'that's stupid' expression, and if I did, I'd never use it on you."

"I've seen that expression many times, and you always use it when you're thinking something you don't want to say. I can't imagine you don't want to say complimentary things, so I'm betting you're thinking I'm stupid."

"You're not being very creative here. I'm certain I have more emotions than praise and scorn, and in this case, I was thinking that I didn't really understand everything you'd just said. I'm gonna have to consider it longer, but I found it interesting." She stuck her tongue out insolently. "That's why I said it was interesting."

"What don't you understand? Maybe I can clear it up."

Katie pointed in her direction, a stunned look on her face. "You? Someone as stupid as...oh! Did I say that out loud?"

"You're so funny. Come on, spill it."

Katie's happy grin slowly dimmed. "I don't have a lot to say. Really. I was just having a hard time picturing you being in the middle of the argument, especially because you were so young."

"Don't get me wrong, I didn't like it. But as much as I don't care for the guys personally, I agree with some of their beliefs. It made sense to me to spend a couple hundred thousand dollars of the town's money to provide healthcare in the community. They really like the old style of healthcare. That's why they don't care how much I charge."

"Because the old-style doctor always has to live with her mom to be able to survive?"

"I see that sneaky little grin. And no, the idea wasn't to make sure I was poor, but they wouldn't have hired me if they thought I was mostly concerned about money."

"You're not concerned *at all* about money." It was clear she was teasing, and her gentle smile underscored that.

"Yes, I am. I make sure I earn more than the salary they pay me and Madge. But I don't do what a lot of people in private practice do and charge people two or three times what various insurance companies allow. I basically charge what the most common insurance allowances are. That way, the people without insurance aren't screwed. A doctor who is on her own could never afford to do that."

"Okay, I can see that. That fits with who you are, and I can see that you'd be able to tolerate the arguments if you knew you were doing something for the good of the town."

Smiling, Erin said, "Don't forget I was in Durham when all this was happening. I didn't come home to visit during the worst of it."

Dryly, Katie said, "I bet your mom enjoyed it."

"She most definitely did not. She never told me how she really felt, but I could tell she was very tense. Luckily, most of her friends thought it was a good idea. Our pastor was behind it, and most of the people in our congregation were. It was the younger families with no intention of using a local doctor who were most vocal in their dissent."

"I'm sure I'm not here enough to tell if there's any tension now, but everyone I've met seems really friendly towards you. Not that I blame them, of course. You're ridiculously charming."

"I know that's a lie," Erin said, laughing. "People are friendly to me, but I'm not charming. And there is still tension, but most of the new residents don't hang out at the same places the old-timers do. There isn't one young family in our congregation, and the diner is too down-market for them. My mom has more contact with the new folks than anyone because of the library. She was treated pretty poorly by the moms in the different kids' reading groups. Of course, I only know that because of Madge."

"Somebody had to take over when the city newspaper closed."

Erin acknowledged with a smile, "Gossip is the lifeblood of a small town. Madge definitely serves a function."

"I'm sure she does. But as for those dunces on the town council…"

"Feel free to cut them to ribbons. They mean nothing to me."

⁓

Even though she'd only had bad news concerning her commitment to the town, Erin practically skipped down the street on Monday morning. The weather had warmed up to a point where she needed only a poplin jacket, and the chirping birds made her smile. She flung the door of the office open, only to be greeted by a dour, chilly silence. Madge glared at her so balefully that Erin tentatively pulled back and considered turning and running. But the town was small, and Madge could easily find her before she got too far. So, she steeled herself, walked in and approached her obviously angry receptionist. "What's wrong?"

"I'll tell you what's wrong, Erin Delancy." Madge's eyes were burning in their ferocity, and her cheeks were flushed. "I've known you since you were in your mother's womb, and before this weekend, I would have considered you the last person who would have betrayed me. Obviously, you've had me fooled." She stood up and turned her back. Her shoulders were shaking when she marched toward the bathroom. Erin stared after her, dumbfounded, as Madge went into the room and slammed the door.

Resisting the temptation to stand outside and talk to her, Erin took off her jacket and put her lab coat on. She was sitting at her desk trying to get her stomach to calm down when Madge emerged. Erin hopped to her feet and went into the main office, calmly but determinedly guiding Madge into the office and closing the door. "Please tell me what I've done to make you so angry."

"I'm plenty mad at you, but not nearly as mad as I am at those Tierneys. I know they're behind this. Both you and your mother have had ideas put in your heads, but that still doesn't excuse you. You're a big girl, and you should know better."

The possible reasons for Madge's ire flew through Erin's head. She itched to question her, but knew that Madge would keep venting if she gave her the chance. As expected, Madge took a breath and continued. "No matter what those Bostonians have told you, no one appreciates having a big city lawyer come here and try to throw her weight around. Even though I thought Katie was nice, I've been worried about her influence. The fact that you've been going there to see her and her exciting life should have clued me in."

"I can understand your being angry with me. It probably feels like I'm betraying you by wanting to leave."

Madge's mouth pruned into a tense lump. To Erin's surprise, it looked as if she would cry. Clearly trying to control herself, Madge said, "Of course I don't want you to leave, but how could you do all of this conniving behind my back?"

Feeling sick to her stomach, Erin let her head drop into her hand and massaged her forehead. It honestly hadn't occurred to her that Madge would consider being kept in the dark the ultimate outrage, but in retrospect, it made perfect sense. Erin knew that Madge continued to work only for the benefits, and those benefits were being the first in town to know who was ill, who'd had a relapse, who was pregnant, and every other kind of news that a doctor's office generated. Ignoring something this obvious made her feel stupid and self-involved. "You're right," she said, meeting Madge's hurt-filled eyes. "It was incredibly selfish of me not to talk to you as soon as I started to feel like I was in the wrong job. I don't know why I didn't do that, Madge, but I'm truly sorry."

The truth is that Erin was sorry. She knew who Madge was, and she knew what was important her. Ignoring her had been a very big mistake, and Erin truly hated to hurt someone she cared for.

"Why did you ignore me? You know I only want the best for you."

Erin nodded, her eyes closed. "I know that. I know how much you care for me. It's not a good excuse, but my dissatisfaction dawned on me pretty slowly. By the time I gave voice to it, I felt trapped and needed to get out. Katie's used to negotiating with people, and she offered to talk to the town council for me. In my mind, we'd just talk about this and reach some form of agreement. I thought Katie was just opening the discussion."

Madge wasn't crying now. She puffed her chest out and put on her most superior look. "That discussion is closed young lady. This would've worked out very differently if you'd talked to me first. I've been playing Forte Fives with Millie Trotier for almost forty years. Pete and I went to school together. And if you don't have Pete Trotier on your side, you're done for."

"I know that," Erin said, hanging her head. "I just didn't think. I don't have any other excuse."

"You and your mother were different people before Dan and Katie got here. I know your mother's new to town, but you're a native. I expected more from you."

"We probably are different now, but Katie didn't talk me into anything. She just encouraged me to admit some of the things I've been hiding from myself."

Madge stood up and looked at Erin with what appeared to be a mixture of sympathy and scorn. "Well, you don't have any secrets now. Everybody in town will know by the end of the day. You'd better prepare yourself."

❧

Erin saw three patients before she had the opportunity to sit at her desk for a few minutes and ruminate on what had happened between herself and Madge. Her stomach had been in knots, and she knew she wasn't fully concentrating on work, something that seemed wrong to her on every level. She sat quietly, trying to think of a way to smooth things over when it slowly and fitfully dawned on her. Even though she'd known the older woman her whole life, she was now Madge's boss. And even though she understood that she'd hurt her, Erin wasn't willing to deal with temper tantrums at the office. That kind of behavior upset her, and when she was upset she couldn't focus on her patients. She consciously tried to quell the roiling in her stomach and called out, "Madge? Will you come in, please?"

Looking like a pit bull with a headache, Madge marched in, not even trying to hide her anger. "What?"

Erin forced her voice into its deepest register, afraid that it might break, ruining her speech. "I know you're angry, and I think I understand at least a little bit why you're upset." Madge opened her mouth, but Erin kept right on going, speaking over her. "But I can't allow you to chew me out. It's unprofessional and uncalled for."

Madge's eyes practically popped out of her head. She looked comically perplexed, as though Erin was speaking in tongues. Her mouth opened again, but Erin kept going, needing all of the momentum she could gather.

"I'd like to keep working together, but if you can't be civil to me and our patients..." She took a breath and felt all of her orifices clench. "You should retire."

"Are you firing me?"

"If you can't be civil—yes, I am."

Madge's shock quickly morphed back into anger. But she didn't say a word. She got up, eyes burning with unspoken rage, and walked out of the office, closing the door remarkably quietly.

Erin leaned back in her chair and felt the sweat chill on her back. She felt like her entire muscular system was in spasm, but her stomach was, surprisingly, beginning to feel better. She sat there and tried to relax, finding it easier than she would have guessed. When the bell over the door rang Madge calmly entered her office and announced, "Mrs. Delahunt is here," then turned and went back to her desk.

Erin wasn't at all sure that she'd done the right thing, but she felt a little spark of pride for her actions, and she went in to examine Mrs. Delahunt with a surprisingly clear head.

⁂

The stairs to her home seemed impossibly high that night. She was, for the first time, pleased to see Dan's truck in the driveway. She knew that having him and her mother at home meant a home-cooked meal and two friendly faces. Before she had the front door closed, Gail was at her side. "I can't imagine how bad your day must have been."

"I can't either, and I was there." Gail took her jacket and hung it up, while Erin shuffled into the living room and sat down heavily. "Do we have any wine?" She turned her head lazily towards Dan. "Hi. How was your day?" She let her head drop back to rest on the chair.

Dan and Gail exchanged worried looks. "My day was fine," Dan said. "But the whole town wasn't talking about me."

Letting out a soft laugh, Erin said, "Don't be so sure about that. More than one person complained that you and Katie have ruined Mom and me. People in town seem to think we're a pair of dunces just ripe for the pickings from a couple of city slickers."

Gail put a glass of wine in Erin's hand. "Dinner is ready, honey. Do you have an appetite?"

"Sure do. I stayed in my office during lunch just so I didn't have to talk to one more person about why I'm abandoning them. I assume this will blow over, but it's very tempting to take all of my vacation starting tomorrow."

⁂

Erin knew that Katie was at a baseball game, so she didn't bother calling her after Dan and Gail left the house. She felt both enervated and antsy, a bad combination for sleep. Nevertheless she got into bed early, but found her mind racing through the events of the day, replaying, in particular, her discussion with Madge. She didn't regret not taking Madge into her confidence, and also didn't regret dressing her down. She wasn't sure how that would play out in the long run, but she felt oddly confident that no matter what happened, she'd be able to handle it.

⁂

Erin woke up early the next morning, feeling oddly upbeat. Before she even turned the coffee maker on, she sat at her computer and summarized the events of the previous day for Katie. She knew that Katie would worry about her, so she made sure to linger on the fact that she was handling things and would be fine. She closed by saying that she knew they'd work things out together and that the problems in town were just a bump in a long road.

❧

As soon as she was finished with all of the critical items on her to-do list, Katie left work and took a cab back to her apartment. She changed into casual clothes and then packed a suit for work the next day. On the way out the door, she grabbed a couple pears, an apple, and a bag of pretzels, figuring that would be a good enough snack to get her to New Hampshire.

She was a little afraid of having Erin think she was smothering her, but she was so proud of her for standing up for herself she had to see her. It was as simple as that.

She'd managed to leave before traffic got too heavy, and knew she'd be there long before Erin got home from work. Nonetheless, she was surprised when she made the decision to go to her father's house.

After parking the car, Katie saw her father's bright-red hair shining in the sun. The earth was wet and heavy from recent rains, but she'd worn her favorite deck shoes, and they were easy to hose off, so she started to slog through the muck.

She called out to Dan before she reached him, and he whirled in her direction. "What's wrong? Is Danny okay?"

Katie put her hands up and made herself smile even though she felt like she had a knife in the gut. It had been many years since she'd dreaded every unexpected knock at the front door, but it all came back to her in a flash. Having a police officer in the family wasn't for the faint of heart. "Everyone is fine, Dad. I just came up to see Erin, and I knew she wouldn't be home yet."

He put his hand over his chest and patted it. "Oh, thank God. I wish to Christ I didn't worry about that kid so much. I thank the good Lord that you changed your mind about being a cop. I couldn't have stood to have both of you out there."

Her instinct was to tell him she'd changed her mind once it became clear he didn't love her anymore, but it felt as though Erin's hand was on her shoulder urging moderation. "I think I wound up in the right job."

His smile looked warm and affectionate. "I think you did, too. Every once in a while, I bump into one of the guys who ran you in when you were a kid. You should see the look on their faces when they ask how you're doing. I think they expect you to be a junkie." When he laughed, his eyes crinkled up, and Katie realized with a start just how much she resembled her father. "I tell them you're a partner at a big law firm. I always give them one of your business cards just so they don't think I'm blowing smoke. It's priceless," he said, laughing heartily.

"You...you have my business cards?"

"Yeah. Danny gave me some. I don't think I'll ever meet anybody who's putting together a big real estate deal, but just in case I do, I'm ready."

Stunned, Katie felt as though she might cry. Her father looked undeniably proud of her, something she had never dared to consider. She changed the subject, just to avoid feeling misty.

⌘

Katie helped Dan tend to his ever-expanding crop, the two of them working in near-silence for over two hours. The sun had dipped below the ridge of the barn, when he looked at his watch and said, "Gail will be here soon. I'd better go get cleaned up."

"You're still in the 'have to look good' phase? I thought that stopped once you were engaged."

He gave her a crooked smile and then started to gather his shears and other tools. "I'm not taking anything for granted. I've learned a few things over the years." He started to head back to the house, and Katie followed behind.

"To tell you the truth," he said, "I'm surprised you're here. I figured you'd keep your distance for a while after I charged into Erin's house like a bull moose."

She couldn't see his face, but he sounded remarkably thoughtful, a rarity. "You've done a hell of a lot worse."

Looking over his shoulder, he met her eyes and smiled. "We don't have to tell the girls all of the stupid things we've done in the past, do we?"

"Erin doesn't want to hear it, so I won't get the chance. How about Gail? Is she interested in your dark years?"

"Nah. That's ancient history. To tell you the truth, I don't even know her husband's first name." He laughed softly and said, "Those Delancy girls are a funny pair, aren't they?"

He started walking down the narrow row again, and Katie watched him carefully. She was briefly transported back to Southie and let her mind wander to the years she followed him around the town like his distaff shadow. He was a little beefier than he was then, and his shoulders didn't have the same square set, but she found herself mimicking his stride and the way his head seemed to stay level even as he walked over uneven ground. She felt like a child, and a sense of peace and serenity washed over her, the likes of which she'd rarely felt as an adult. There was something glorious about having Dan Tierney lead the way for you.

⊰⊱

Katie was sitting at the kitchen table when Gail entered the house. Holding up a beer in greeting, Katie said, "Welcome home. My dad's getting cleaned up."

Gail's smile looked a little forced, as Katie had noticed it often did when she and Gail were together. "It's nice to see you. Can you join us for dinner?"

"No. I'm hanging out until Erin's finished. She's gonna call me when she's ready to go. We're going to go out to dinner."

"Oh, that's nice." Gail sat down and primly folded her hands on the table. "We went to a nice Italian place in Manchester not long ago. Do you like Italian food?"

"Sure. I like just about everything."

"I can't imagine there's anything around here that you can't get at home, but this place in Manchester was good."

Smiling slyly, Katie said, "It's not bad here. New Hampshire has its charms."

"You couldn't…you wouldn't…"

"She wouldn't what?" Dan asked, coming into the room, his hair dark from the shower. He bent and kissed Gail's cheek.

"Hi," she said, looking up and giving him a full, warm smile. "I was wondering if Katie would consider moving here."

"Never," Dan said, laughing. "She's a Boston girl through and through."

"My dad's right on this one," Katie said, taking a sip of her beer. "I can't imagine leaving my family or my friends."

Quietly, Gail said, "Not even for Erin?"

Katie slowly shook her head. "Not even for Erin. I love her, but I know she doesn't want to keep this job. And I wouldn't make that kind of sacrifice to help her stay in this situation." She met Gail's eyes, her own unflinching. "Erin's going to have to step up and make some tough choices."

"But…" Gail looked up at Dan, then back to Katie. "Erin told me that you've promised that things will work out."

"They will." Slowly, but confidently, Katie nodded her head. "I know that Erin can gut it up."

"But what if she can't?" The skin between Gail's eyes puckered with anxiety.

"Then I've misjudged her." Katie reached down and took her phone off her waistband. She glanced at it, stood and clapped her father on his back. "Gotta go," she said, waving to a worried looking Gail on her way out.

⊰⊱

After their dinner in Manchester, Katie drove back to Essex, leaving the windows down to let the rich aromas of the country in. The night was still and humid, and Erin stood on the front lawn for a moment, tossing her keys in the air and catching them. The neighborhood was so quiet that the sound of the metal slapping her palm was surprisingly loud. "Why don't you park on the grass?" she asked. "Pete Trotier, the head of the town council, lives right down the street. He'd probably buy my contract out with his own money rather than have me trash the neighborhood up."

Katie saw from Erin's expression that she wasn't entirely kidding. "If we're gonna do it, let's do it right. A refrigerator, a couple of broken bicycles…we'll put the car up on blocks. There's no sense in making a halfhearted effort."

Erin put her arm around Katie, and they walked up to the house together. "It really touched me that you came up here today, but I promise I would have told you if I needed you. I'm trying to be more honest about my needs."

They went into the house and immediately went upstairs. Katie hung her garment bag in the closet and started to get undressed. "I wasn't going to come up because I could see that you had a pretty good perspective. But I called your office this afternoon, and Madge was a total bitch. For most of my drive, I was thinking of ways to insult her, her heritage, and the children I don't know she has. But then I thought I should try to act more adult, kinda like my much younger girlfriend."

Erin's eyes were dark, her tone low. "What did she say?"

Katie was a little taken aback, and she tried to make light of the encounter. "It wasn't what she said. It was what she didn't say. She was just cold. Normally, she's very friendly, and she kids around with me. Today, it was all business. To be honest, she seemed to take pleasure in hearing how befuddled I was."

Erin nodded her head slowly, looking less angry. "That doesn't surprise me. She's got a real mean streak. There are a lot of people in town who don't see me because of her."

"Why do you put up with that?"

"It's easier," Erin said, shrugging. "At least it *has* been easier. I've always wanted her on the inside spitting out than on the outside spitting in. But I'm getting spit on anyway."

Katie crossed the room and wrapped Erin in a rough embrace, rocking her to and fro. "It doesn't make any sense when you say 'spitting.' The word is 'pissing,' Dr. Delancy. 'Pissing.'"

"Okay." Erin gave Katie a sweet smile. "She's been urinating on me. Better?"

Katie squeezed her until Erin yelped. "You're incorrigible. Or is that corrigible? I have to coin a new word for a woman who refuses to use perfectly acceptable profanity."

"I'm not sure, but I think that's already a word."

"Fine." Katie held her and dotted her face with wet, sloppy kisses. "I have a perfect word for you. How about 'dork'?"

"That works." Erin smiled contentedly. "Let's go to bed and make so much noise the neighbors call the police. That might get me out of my contract."

"I planned on doing that anyway." Katie pulled Erin over to the bed and wrestled her down. "Having you stand your ground with Madge makes you even more tantalizing. A woman with guts is incredibly sexy." She hovered over Erin and gently kissed her. "I hope you're proud of yourself for not letting her shit on you."

"Nice image," Erin said, making a face. "I am proud of myself. And if she's outwardly rude to you or anyone else, I'll fire her. Period."

Katie looked at the determined brown eyes glittering below her and growled, her libido kicking into high gear. "Let's wake the neighbors."

❦

Erin was in her office the next afternoon when the phone rang. Without her usual jocularity, Madge called out, "Dr. Worrell on line two."

"Thank you." Erin hit the proper button and quietly said, "Hi. Did you get hit by the chill?"

"I was just going to ask you about that. She hasn't been that snippy to me since I wouldn't let her sister sit in the office during a two-week visit. She can make your day hell, can't she?"

"I'm not letting her get to me. I'm treating her the way I always do, but she's giving me the semi-silent treatment ever since I told her to be professional or quit."

"You what?"

Erin chuckled softly. "I couldn't let her ride roughshod over me. It's bad for my patients to have me riled up."

"You're more mature than I ever was. I'd sit in my office and sulk, trying to figure out how to make her get over whatever it was that had her riled up."

"Well, I don't have a clue how to do that, so I'm not going to try."

"I wish I had better news for you, pup, but I did some digging and found out why the town council has their heels dug in."

"Let me have it."

"They took out an insurance policy on you. If you default, they can make a claim and get all of their money back at once."

"Really? That doesn't seem fair. I would think the insurance would only be good if I was unable to do my job, not unwilling."

"No, they bought a good policy; it pays out for just about any reason if you don't fulfill your contract."

"Why did you say this wasn't good news? I'd feel much better if I knew the town wasn't going to suffer."

"No, the town will be fine, but you'll suffer. The insurance company will go after you with everything they have. They'd get a judgment against you in two seconds. You'd be paying them off for the next ten years, and your credit rating would be shot. I don't think that's the kind of thing you could even discharge in bankruptcy."

"I'd never do something like that. I don't dispute that I owe the money. I'd just like a way to be able to pay it back over time."

"I can understand that, but you're not going to have that option. I suppose you could talk to the insurance company and see if they would agree to a repayment plan, but it's probably easier for them to just get a judgment against you."

Erin let out a soft laugh. "I guess I'd better call my attorney. Thank goodness her rates are reasonable."

The next evening, Erin and Katie were on the phone for over two hours. "I really appreciate your spending so much time trying to get an answer out of the insurance company."

"I knew I was wasting my time, but I couldn't stop myself." Katie laughed, adding, "Sometimes, I'm a little too sure of myself."

"When I think about it, it makes sense that they can't tell you what they'll do until the city files a claim, but I was hoping for a little help."

"Oh, they know exactly what they'll do. They just won't tell us."

"You really think so?"

"I'm sure of it. They have a policy, and we won't be able to talk to anybody who has the power to change that policy. It's very hard to get to anyone of any real importance."

"So, I'm stuck, huh?"

"No, you're not stuck. You just have to make your decision based on the worst scenario."

"I know what that is," Erin said, sounding like a game-show contestant. "I default, the city collects on the insurance, and the insurance company hounds me for years."

"That's it. Could be worse. We don't have debtor's prison."

"Gallows humor is always appreciated. I have to remember to smile."

"You need to smile. I know it's hard now, but this will pass. This is only about money, nothing really important—like health or love."

"Good point. Uhm, would you think I was a total baby if I wanted to put this on the shelf for a few weeks?"

"I don't want to push you. I only want what's best for you."

"I know, I know."

To Katie's ear, Erin sounded unsure of herself and a little frightened. "Tell me what you're thinking. I can hear something funny going on in your pointed Ivy-League head."

Laughing softly, Erin said, "My head isn't pointed. And what I'm thinking is that no matter what happens, I'm going to be here for a while. And my mom is gonna be here for the rest of her life. I feel like I need to mend some fences. I'd really like to get Madge back on my side because that'll make any process go more smoothly."

"Do you really think that's true?"

"Yeah, I do. She's got a surprising amount of influence in town."

"Okay," Katie said, thoughtfully. "Let me ask you this. If you want to enter another residency program, do you just apply like you would for a regular job?"

"No, I wish it were that easy. There's a whole process in a matching program. It's a nationwide thing."

"Fine," Katie said, sounding businesslike. "Find out all of the details and fill out whatever forms you need to. It won't hurt you to know what your possibilities are."

"The timing could be better. The program only matches people to programs once a year. I just missed Match Day. It's in March every year."

"Well, that sucks. Can't you do it on your own?"

"Not for a decent program, and the programs I want are really, really decent."

"My little overachiever."

"That's me," Erin said brightly.

"And if you don't get accepted into an emergency medicine program, you'll what…?"

"I guess I'll stay in Essex."

"Pardon?" Katie tried to keep her voice from betraying her alarm.

"I'll be a berry picker at your father's farm. But I'm not going to be the town doctor. That phase of my life is just about over."

Katie let out a small sigh of relief. She'd been afraid to ask the question, worried that Erin would take the path of least resistance. But knowing that she had made up her mind made Katie feel almost giddy. "And my personal gynecologist," she said, giggling.

Erin chuckled, and Katie could just see the half-smile on her lovely face. "That's a given."

⟨⟨⟨⟩⟩⟩

Two nights later, Erin was at Dan's, helping her mother get dinner ready. Dan was sitting at the kitchen table, drinking a beer. "Do you want to tell Erin about our bad news?"

Erin's head snapped to the right, and she stared at Dan. "What bad news?"

He held his hands up. "It's not that bad!"

Gail put her hand on Erin's shoulder. "You seem skittish."

"Yeah, I guess I am. So, what's your not-so-bad news?"

Gail said, "We both feel so bad about the situation you're in. So, we went to the bank and talked to them about taking out a second mortgage on the farm."

Stunned, Erin's vacant gaze drifted from her mother to Dan. "Gosh! You two don't have to get involved like that. I got into this situation, and I can get out of it."

"That's good to know," Dan said. "Because we don't qualify for a dime. That little pipsqueak at the bank said he was surprised I got a mortgage as big as I got from my bank in Boston. He said a local bank wouldn't have been so generous." He snorted and took a swig of his beer, muttering, "Little prick."

Erin couldn't help smiling at Dan. Besides her gratitude at having him willing to mortgage his property for her, he looked so much like Katie when he so effortlessly cursed that she had to admit he, like his daughter, was pretty adorable.

⟨⟨⟨⟩⟩⟩

That Friday afternoon, Erin finished with her last patient, went into her office, and asked Madge to join her. Dutifully, Madge entered the room, but she didn't sit when Erin invited her to.

Refusing to let Madge's tactics sway her, Erin delivered the speech she'd been crafting. "I know you're angry with me, and as I told you before, I can understand why. But unless you're planning on retiring, we're gonna be together for a while."

Looking like she wanted to slap Erin, Madge said, "Are you asking me to leave?"

"No, but I don't want you to stay if you're not going to be happy here."

Snippily, Madge said, "Oh. So, only one of us can be unhappy, right?"

"Ideally, neither of us would be. I don't know what people are saying, but I think you know me well enough to know that I don't despise my job."

"Most people don't try to get out of a contract because they're too happy."

Erin leaned back in her chair and busied her hands by playing with a pencil. She was trying to appear calm and in charge, so she spoke slowly. "That's probably true, and I'm confident I'd be more fulfilled practicing another type of medicine. I think I owe it to myself to use all of my skills and talents in the best way. That's why I tried to open a discussion with the town council. But things got out of hand."

"So, you're not just going to up and leave?"

Erin shook her head, holding Madge's gaze. "No. I'd never do something like that. I love the people of this town, and I wouldn't consider leaving them in the lurch."

Madge stared at Erin with a withering intensity. "Do you promise you'll tell me before you make any more decisions like this?"

Before replying, Erin gave the matter the thought it deserved. She knew she would never talk to Madge about her personal life, but she thought there was a line she could draw and still be comfortable. "I promise I'll tell you before I make any final decisions about the practice, but I can't guarantee I'll tell you about every step on the road. I need my privacy."

Madge seem to consider that, and then she nodded firmly. She walked around to Erin's side of the desk, held out a hand and tugged her to her feet. She hugged Erin, squeezing her hard. "I can't protect you if you don't tell me what's going on."

"I know that, and I'm sorry. I'm really sorry."

Whispering into her ear, her voice raked with tears, Madge said, "I don't want you to be sorry. I want you to remember that I'm your friend." She let Erin go and wiped her tears while taking in a deep breath. "Now I guess I have to get working on making things better for your mother."

"My mother?"

Putting her hands on her hips, Madge glared. "Don't you two talk at all? Your mother's been hiding in her office ever since this happened. She didn't go to bridge this week, and I bet she thinks of some reason not to show up at church."

Sighing, Erin said, "I didn't know that. She'd never tell me anything that she thought would hurt me."

Madge ruffled Erin's hair. "Don't worry. Once everybody knows you're not going to leave, they'll stop talking."

Madge started to walk out of the office, but Erin called out clearly, "I didn't say I wasn't going to leave."

Stopping abruptly, Madge looked at Erin over her shoulder. "Do you have any plans to leave? Any *firm* plans?"

"No. Nothing firm. But I *am* going to leave."

"Maybe yes, maybe no." Erin watched her stride from the room, wondering if presidential candidates felt like she did when their handlers seemed to believe they were the ones running for office.

⁓

Later that evening, Erin arrived at Katie's and was delighted to see a blonde-red mass of curls floating above the stone banister. She couldn't stop herself from running down the block, surprising Katie when she skidded to a stop in front of her. Grinning toothily, she said, "I couldn't wait."

"What a good girlfriend you are." Katie stood up and put her arms around Erin shoulders. When she hugged her tight, the difference in their positions put Erin's head parallel to Katie's breasts.

Erin nuzzled her face into the cushy pillow. "Will you start wearing really high heels?"

"No, but we both have staircases at our homes. We can work something out."

"Are we going to do what we did last time? I really loved that greeting you gave me."

"We can if you want to. I made tentative plans for tonight, but I can cancel."

Erin pulled away and smiled up at Katie. "What are we doing?"

"If you want to, we're going to a bar to hear a band we like."

"I want to."

⁓

Three hours later found them at a bar in Somerville, listening to Irish music. The place was packed, but that gave Erin the opportunity to put her arm around Katie and speak directly into her ear. "I'm having a great time."

Katie pointed to the wine glass in front of Erin. "How's the Cabernet?"

"I've had worse. Not much worse…"

"That would have been my guess. The beer is great. Maybe you should change."

"No, I've had my fill. I've got a little buzz from the two glasses I've managed to force down."

"That's my girl." Katie slapped her on the thigh. "Forcing down swill is very wise. The good folks at AA recommend that."

The man to Katie's right leaned forward and said, "Are you having fun?"

"Definitely," Erin said.

"I had a feeling we'd see you around again. Katie barely let you talk to anyone at her party. That's a sure sign."

Erin smiled at him, nodding, but adding nothing.

Katie said, "You're wasting your time if you're trying to get her to ask you questions, Mark. She doesn't want to know about my past."

Mark's eyes widened dramatically. "Damn, Wu! Where do you find a great-looking girl who doesn't wanna beat you up about everything you did before you met her?"

Katie gazed at Erin with obvious affection. "Apparently, you have to go out of state."

❧

The next morning, Katie woke to the feel of Erin's body pressed tightly against her. A warm hand was delicately gliding up her thigh, and she could hear slightly elevated breathing in her ear. She stretched, pushing back against Erin, who immediately started slathering her neck and shoulders with kisses. "Somebody needs love, huh?"

"Mmm-hmm." Erin continued her tender assault, and now her whole body got into the act. She slid her thigh between Katie's legs and started pushing her hips up and down while her hand extended its range.

Katie looked over her shoulder, seeing Erin's bright eyes. "Let's take a shower together and have some breakfast first."

The look of disappointment on Erin's face was almost funny, but she didn't complain.

Katie got out of bed and extended her hands, helping Erin to her feet. She slipped her arms around her and hugged her while running her hands up and down her back. "Your needs aren't being denied, sweetheart. Just deferred."

"That's okay. I know I ask for a lot…"

Katie tapped Erin's mouth with the flat of her hand. "That's a ridiculous thing to say. Utterly ridiculous."

Looking abashed, Erin said, "I've never felt like this. I want you all of the time." She put her cheek against Katie's and hugged her tightly. "It feels like it might be too much."

"Are you worried about this?"

"No, not worried…" Erin said, her eyes darting away.

Katie gazed at her for a few seconds. Her expression was controlled and Erin couldn't guess what was on her mind. "I've been thinking about this for days, and it finally became clear to me during the seventh-inning stretch the other night."

Erin blew out a nervous breath, unable to keep from smiling at the thought of

Katie wracking her brain about something and having it miraculously revealed during a baseball game.

"You *do* have a list," Katie declared triumphantly.

"A list?"

"Yes. I told you I had a long list of girlfriend requirements and you said you didn't have one. But you do!"

"I do," Erin said dubiously.

"It's just a very short list. I think it consisted of only one thing, and that's whether I was going to be shut down sexually."

She paused dramatically, and Erin grinned at the look of triumph on her face. She'd learned that Katie had a way of pausing to let her points sink in, and she assumed that was a trial tactic she'd picked up. However she'd come by it, Erin found it adorable.

"So, even though you're generally not very assertive, you let yourself show me from the very beginning that you had a sex drive that needed to be taken into consideration. My guess is that you didn't really want to have sex the night of my St. Patrick's day party. You just wanted to make sure that you could tell me what you needed and I wouldn't shut you down."

There was another pregnant pause that allowed Erin to consider Katie's supposition. "Are you sure about that?"

"Yep."

Erin leaned back in the embrace and reflected on the enviable confidence that Katie showed in making this declaration.

"I don't, by the way, think you plotted this. I'm pretty sure you weren't even aware you were doing it. I think your fear of getting into a relationship where you weren't satisfied sexually overrode your normal reticence. But your normal reticence is on display this morning. That worried look on your face and your refusal to admit it seems much more in keeping with the woman I've fallen in love with. So, there it is. Chew on that for a while, and let me know if I'm totally off my rocker." She quickly kissed Erin and said, "I'm gonna go get breakfast."

Erin sat on the edge of the bed for quite a few minutes, considering what Katie had said. She lay down and covered herself with the quilt while she continued to ruminate. Even though she tried to focus on what Katie had said, thoughts kept darting in—images of the look on Katie's face when she was saying something important, the way she looked at Erin right before she kissed her, the almost conversational yet dramatic way she had of making a point. Before long, Erin couldn't keep thinking. She had to be beside her lover, even though she knew she was way behind on the race to analyze her own motives.

Chapter Sixteen

They sat at the breakfast bar in Katie's spacious, remarkably clean kitchen. Erin was munching away on a bowl of whole grain granola topped with blueberries and a banana, and Katie had chosen a blueberry banana smoothie. "This is just like eating at home," Erin said. "Nice and healthy." She stuck her tongue out and made her eyes cross.

Katie tapped her on the cheek. "That's because your mother and I both love you and want you to be healthy and happy."

"I'm gonna have to sneak out later for something lethal."

"Weren't those Buffalo wings at the bar last night lethal enough for the whole weekend?"

"Not even close. They satisfied my fat and grease needs, but didn't touch the sugar or chocolate requirements."

"Don't even think about bringing that stuff in here. If it's here, I'll eat it. I can only control my diet by abstinence."

"It doesn't bother you when I have things you don't choose to eat, does it?"

"Just a tiny bit. I'm jealous that you can get away with it."

Erin put her hand around her own thigh and then moved her hand onto Katie's. "There's about a two-inch difference between my leg and yours. I can't get away with eating junk. I just don't care if I'm a little overweight."

"You're not overweight." Katie playfully lifted Erin's T-shirt and ran her hand over her curves. "You're perfect."

"I have a bigger frame than you do, but even taking that into consideration, I'm probably twenty pounds heavier than you are. As I get older, I'm gonna have to be more careful."

"I love your body." Katie took a big sip of her smoothie, her eyes wandering up and down Erin's body with interest.

Smiling at the evident appreciation, Erin said, "And I love yours. I particularly love that you're not as flat-chested as many women with your build are." She wiggled her eyebrows, making Katie giggle.

"You can thank my mom's family for that. That's the first place I gain weight."

"Ooh…maybe another ten pounds wouldn't hurt."

Katie took Erin's hand and put it on her breast, moving it around while watching Erin's eyes dilate. "Have you always been obsessed with breasts?"

Erin shook her head, looking a little vacant and distracted. "No, not really. Yours are just…" She smiled at Katie, looking positively enraptured. "Awesome."

"You really weren't that into them before? I find that hard to believe."

A dark look flitted across Erin's face and disappeared quickly. "I never got to…" She looked away and Katie could see her try to adopt a genuine smile. "Yours are the first that have consumed me."

Katie contemplated her face for a few moments and said, "I am going to reveal my hitherto unspoken supposition that there were some issues between you and your previous partners that stopped you from doing quite a few things you wanted to do."

Puffing out a wry laugh, Erin nodded her head. "Artfully asked, counselor. True. My sex drive and my needs didn't always match my partner's. Things got in the way."

"Abuse?" Katie asked gently.

It took so long for Erin to answer that Katie wanted to shake her. But she forced herself to sit in silence, watching a storm of emotion flit across Erin's face. "I've learned that a person's sexual response can be massively affected by what others might not consider abuse. Little things can mean a whole lot. It's very, very subjective."

Katie reached across the table and caressed Erin's cheek. "For many reasons, I'm glad to say I haven't had any sexual experiences that I'd consider bad."

Erin's dark eyes caught Katie's and held them. "None? Really?"

"No, none. Have you had any bad ones?"

"No, but so many women have. I know you started having sex pretty early, and sometimes girls do that because they've been abused. I've been worried about that," she said, looking up and letting Katie see the doubt and concern in her eyes.

Katie slid off her stool so she could get a better hold on Erin. "Nothing bad. Nothing at all."

"I thought maybe the first people you were with were older and talked you into something."

Katie laughed softly. "Hardly. I didn't start dating older women until I was practicing law. Up to that point, I was always with people close to my age. No lecherous uncles, no grabby schoolteachers, no weird babysitters. Nothing."

Erin put her arms around Katie and squeezed her to the point of pain. She pulled back, looked into her eyes, and said, "Will you tell me about your first girlfriend?"

Katie kissed her, savoring the taste of the fresh berries. "After we make love. You've been very patient this morning. You need a reward."

❧

Katie tenderly stroked Erin's flank while she peppered her face with kisses. "Have you caught your breath, sweetheart?"

Erin smiled beatifically. "Yeah." Suddenly, her inert body leapt into action, and she pushed Katie onto her back and sat astride her. "I'm ready for you."

"I'm not finished with you." Katie sat up, put her arms around Erin, and then shifted their weight so they fell onto their sides. "Lie on your tummy for me."

Erin started to disentangle, saying, "Are you sure? A few minutes ago, you seemed like you really needed me to pay attention to a certain spot." She slipped her hand between Katie's legs and started to experimentally press here and there, watching Katie's face for a reaction.

Shivering, Katie grasped her hand and pulled it away. "I'm sure. Now, come on. Lie down for me."

Erin did as she was asked, lying face down on the bed. "Like this?"

Katie stretched out next to her and pushed Erin's more distant knee up. She adjusted her so that she was behind her, both of them partially on their sides. Then she snaked her arm under Erin's neck and held her tightly. "I've been thinking about ways to explore you," she whispered, "and this seems like the perfect day." Her fingers danced across Erin's back, down her side, and finally settled on her ass. "You've had a few orgasms, you're nice and wet and open, and I've got nothing but time."

Erin's body vibrated from her muffled laugh. "Go for it."

Katie's hand slid down an inch or two, and she started to circle Erin's opening deftly. She gripped her a little tighter, relishing the feel of controlling her body. Her finger slid inside so easily that Erin barely seemed to notice. But Katie noticed. Her heart started to race at the delectable sensation of being inside the woman she loved. Erin's slippery flesh caressed Katie's finger, and she found herself mouthing the smooth, muscular shoulder her face rested against. "So sweet," she murmured.

Erin let out a soft purr and pushed back against Katie's hand. "Nice."

"Yeah," Katie hissed. "Push against me, baby. Make it feel good."

Erin arched her back, making her ass press against Katie. "It does feel good. Feels sexy."

"Dance with me," Katie murmured, nipping at a pink earlobe. "I'll lead...you follow." She slipped another finger inside and hovered right at the opening.

Erin followed, pressing her body down to cover Katie's fingers. She mewed with delight as she began to pull away and press down again. "This is good."

Katie could feel and hear the pulse hammer through Erin's body. She pressed her ear against Erin's neck, thrilling to the way the beat steadily thrummed. "That's it, baby. Feel me inside you."

"Goooood," Erin crooned. "Feels so good."

Katie gripped even tighter, holding on to Erin like a drowning woman. "You're so slick and wet." Erin's incredibly resilient flesh clung to Katie's fingers like the softest silk. The sexy body writhed upon her, making her heart race. Every time she spoke, Erin contracted around her fingers, urging her on. "It feels so good to be inside you," Katie whispered hotly.

Heat radiated off Erin's body, and they moved against each other, their bodies slick with sweat. Katie curled her fingers just a little and gently applied more pressure. "Touch yourself, baby. Make yourself come when you're ready."

Erin pushed back, tossing her hair and making it cascade across Katie's face. She slid her hand down and in seconds gasped, "I'm gonna..." Katie felt her grip firmly and then still for just a second, before spasms rippled down Katie's fingers while Erin growled throatily.

Katie stayed with her, riding out the waves, experiencing the pure joy of Erin's body moving against her languidly. She kissed her back, her shoulders, and then tenderly lingered on her neck, tasting the tang of her salty skin. "I love you," she whispered. "I love you so much."

Erin panted softly, and when Katie slipped out of her she rolled onto her back and met Katie's gaze. Erin grasped Katie's warm, wet fingers and placed them against her clit and jiggled them. "More," she said, grinning. "I'm so turned on I could burst."

"I can keep up." Katie kissed her, probing her mouth with her tongue. "Anything you need, you sexy thing. Had enough penetration?"

Erin compressed her thighs, trapping Katie's fingers against herself. She shifted her hips a few times, the feeling so fantastic that she had to concentrate hard to speak. "Mmm, not necessarily. I have another spot you haven't been in. Want to keep exploring?"

With a surprised look, Katie said, "I'm up for anything once." She rolled over and started to open her bedside table, but Erin stopped her.

"Once? You don't…?"

"No. I never have. But I'm game. Really."

"I thought everybody did that." She studied Katie's face for a second. "No?"

"You've been reading too many sex stories," Katie said, laughing. "No one's ever asked me to play with her ass, but like I said, I'll do anything, and I do mean anything, once."

"No, no," Erin said, sitting up a little. "I just thought that was par for the course. I didn't want to be prudish."

"So, you don't want me to…" Katie slipped her fingers between Erin's cheeks and probed a little, giggling when Erin twitched and tried to pull away. "Might be fun."

"Let's save that. I don't have a need to do it. I was already girding myself to ignore how much bacteria live in my rectum."

"Ooh, now that's sexy." Katie made a face. "If you ever want me to touch you there, you can't refer to it as a rectum. That's a buzz killer!"

Now Erin's expression morphed into one of distaste. "Go wash your hand," she insisted, shooing Katie from the bed. "Go! Go!"

Katie started to laugh as she slid out of bed and went into the bathroom. "I've got to hand it to you, Mad Dog. You're a trooper. Most women wouldn't ask for ass play just to keep up with the lesbian Joneses."

"Just wash your hands. Get under the nails, too!" Erin called out. "Actually, do you have any bleach?"

Katie poked her head out of the bathroom. "I think I'll keep some surgical gloves in the bedside table just in case you ever do want me to go backdoor on you. Having to disinfect myself is a bigger buzz kill than your clinical descriptions."

❧

The next evening, they went to a bar located just behind the iconic left-field wall of Fenway Park with a few of the people from the night before and a few new ones. The place was crowded, but not overly loud. Most of the crowd was trying to watch the Red Sox game, which was being broadcast from several huge televisions.

Erin didn't sit next to Katie at first. She had decided to make an effort to get to know Katie's friends, so she moved around the group all night long. The game was almost over when Katie caught her eye and motioned for her to sit by her. Erin took her almost full bottle of beer and walked up to Katie. Erin smiled when she put her hand around the neck of Katie's bottle and said, "Yours is warmer than mine."

"I'm sorry you have to switch to beer to hang out with me. I know it's not your favorite."

"You've shown me the beauty of the first couple of sips of a cold one. And as long as I have a bottle in front of me, no one tries to buy me another." She grinned and gave Katie a kiss on the cheek. "Your friends are very generous."

"I missed having you next to me tonight. Are you bored already?"

"Not even a little. I just want to get to know everybody."

Katie looked longingly at Erin's lips. "Have I told you today what a wonderful girlfriend you are?"

"I think you have, but you can always tell me again."

"I'd rather take you home and show you."

Erin held her hand out and started to stand, but Katie grasped the waistband of her slacks and pulled her back down. "As soon as the game's over." Chuckling, she leaned over and said, "I told you I'm the biggest Red Sox nerd in the world."

The next evening, Erin started her usual Sunday night delaying tactics. "Maybe we should go for a long walk."

Katie looked at the clock. "I'd walk you home if I could, but it's eight o'clock, honey. You should get going."

With a charming grin, Erin said, "But I don't want to. I want to live here."

Looking into Erin's eyes for a few moments, Katie said, "I wasn't going to bring this up, since I'm just starting to explore it, but I know you like to think about things. So, you can think about this on your drive home."

Erin sat up straighter and said, "What is it? Is it bad?"

"No, of course not. Don't be so skittish." She put her arm around Erin's shoulders and pulled her close. "I'm trying to think of ways to make that happen."

"What?"

"Memory loss?" Katie tapped on Erin's head. "A way to have you live here."

"I think they'll find me. Insurance companies have lots of ways of tracking people down."

"The insurance company won't be involved if we pay the town what you owe them."

"True. What's your plan? Is it legal? It doesn't have to be. I'm getting more flexible." She smiled, looking so ingenuous that Katie had to spend a few minutes slathering her with kisses.

"It's legal," she finally said, "but those lips shouldn't be." She sat up and pushed her curls from her eyes. "I talked to a guy I know about refinancing. He says I can easily pull $200,000 out of my equity."

"You can't do that!" Erin jumped to her feet and stared at Katie. "You told me the payments on the money I owe would be thousands of dollars!"

"No, no, they wouldn't be. I could refinance for thirty years."

"What would the payments be?"

"Uhm…" Katie shifted and looked as though she was doing the math in her head. "I can't give you a firm number, but it would probably add around $1500 to my monthly nut."

"Gosh! What do you pay now?"

"That's not important. I can afford to do this. I really can."

Erin's head was shaking so fast she was making herself dizzy. "I can't let you do that, Kate. I just can't."

Katie stood and put her hands on Erin's shoulders, looking into her eyes. "Why not? It's just money. Your happiness is worth a whole lot more than money."

"Darn it." Erin put her head on Katie's belly and took a deep breath. "When you say things like that, I get woozy. I can't look into those beautiful eyes and think straight."

"I don't want you to think straight. I want you to let me take care of this. It's something I want to do."

Erin lifted her head and met Katie's gaze. "I can't. I just can't let you carry that kind of debt."

"You don't know how much I earn. I can show you my whole financial plan if you want me to. I talked about this with my accountant. It makes the most sense to do it this way."

"What do you mean?"

"Well, I've got a very healthy retirement fund, but he doesn't think I should touch that. Taking the money via a mortgage lets me deduct the interest, which makes it effectively cost less."

"I can't, Katie. I just can't. You'd be stuck with that mortgage for thirty years. What if I…I don't know…I could die."

"I'd take out life insurance on you. Believe me, Erin, I'd protect myself. I know how to handle money."

"You know how to give it away!"

Erin had worked herself into such a lather that Katie couldn't help but laugh. "It's okay. It really is. We'll have a contract outlining repayment in case you find a cuter girlfriend and break up with me. We can handle all of the details."

"These aren't details. This is a tremendous amount of money, and you're planning on being responsible for all of it! I really, really appreciate that you're willing to do this, but I can't let you." She held her tightly, rocking a little while she soaked up the security she always felt in her arms. "I have to find another way."

"There are only three ways of doing this." She pulled away and looked into Erin's eyes. "You keep doing your job for nine more years, you take money from me, or you take money from your mom."

"She already tried, not that I would have taken it anyway."

"No, not that. Your mom could sell your house and lend you the money."

"No, no, I don't think she wants to do that. She loves the house."

"I'm sure that's true, but she loves you, too, and you're worth more to her than a house."

Erin nodded, but she was clearly troubled. "I don't know what she'd do with it if I moved out. I guess I can ask."

"I think you'd better because I can't have you in Essex for nine years."

"I can't have me there, either." She sighed, feeling lonely, even though Katie was holding her in her arms. "Even if I hadn't met you, I'd have to quit. It's the wrong job for me and I took it for the wrong reasons."

⟡

It took Erin almost two weeks to bring up the topic of selling the house. She wasn't comfortable having the discussion in front of Dan, so she went by the library on a Thursday night—the night her mother worked late. Gail looked up, clearly surprised to see Erin walk into her office. "Hi, honey. On your way home?"

Erin gingerly perched on the edge of one of the side chairs, looking like she couldn't decide whether to sit or stand. "Yeah. I just finished for the day. Do you have a few minutes to talk about something?"

Taking a quick look her watch, Gail said, "I can close up now. Why don't you come to Dan's house, and we'll have dinner?"

"I'd like to have dinner with you two, but if you don't mind, I'd rather talk about this with just you."

A concerned and slightly anxious look settled on Gail's face. "Is everything all right? Is everything good with Katie?"

Sliding onto the chair, Erin took a breath while a warm smile covered her face. "Things are very good."

"You perk up just mentioning her."

A little embarrassed by her transparency, Erin nodded. "I guess I do. She's just so remarkable, Mom. She's one of the most thoughtful, generous people I've ever met."

"Well, that's one thing Dan has always said about her."

Erin didn't mention that Dan's compliments about Katie's generosity were usually backhanded. "He's right. She offered to refinance her apartment so I could pay off the city."

Gail covered her open mouth with her hand. "Oh, my goodness. That's remarkable!"

"I know. I wouldn't let her do it, but it was really an argument. She's very determined."

Gail smiled and met Erin's gaze. "That sounds like someone I know."

"Yeah, they're more alike than either one wants to admit."

"I'm proud of you for not taking the easy way out, even though I assume it was tempting."

"Not too much. I couldn't let her go into debt for me."

"That's because you've always been aware of how your actions affect other people. You've never, ever been a selfish girl."

"Don't be so proud of me until you know what I want." Erin smiled sheepishly and moved around in the chair, acting like the generous seat was constricting. "Well, I guess you can still be proud of me, but I *am* looking for an easy way out. Specifically, I wonder what you plan on doing with the house."

"The house?" Gail blinked a few times. "I don't have any thoughts of doing anything with it now. I want you to live there as long as you want to, honey."

"I appreciate that, Mom, but what if I were to move to Boston? What would you do then?"

"Oh. Right. That would be different." Gail picked up a pen and began to twirl it in her fingers. Her expression changed and became more pensive. "Milton just asked me the same thing when we talked about how my tax situation would change after I got married. Of course, I didn't tell him about you and Katie, even though I assume my accountant will keep my secrets."

"I think you can trust Milton, but I'm glad you didn't talk to him about Katie. I don't want people to blame her for my dissatisfaction with my job."

"Can I be proud of you for that?" Gail asked, smiling at her.

"Sure. So, what did Milton say?"

"I asked him if he thought I should sell the house, thinking I could give you the money."

Erin's heart started to beat faster, but she could tell from the look on her mother's face that this wasn't going to go her way.

"There are all sorts of rules and requirements for being able to sell property and escape paying gains taxes. Dan and I would have to be married for two years to qualify for a joint exemption on the house. So, with just my exemption, I'm only able to take $250,000 tax-free from a sale. I'd have to pay a hefty tax on anything over that. Milton suggested that I rent the house out if you're not going to live in it. There aren't many good rentals in town, and he thinks I could get about $2,000 a month for it. That would give Dan and me some reliable income, which we really need."

"That makes sense." She nodded, trying to keep the disappointment from her voice. "I know that's your only asset, Mom. I was just hoping that if you did want to sell it you could lend me the money to pay the city off, and I could pay you back over time."

"Honey, if you need me to sell the house, I'll sell it. I'm confident that we'll make a go of the farm and that I won't need my nest egg."

"No, Milton is right. If you can get monthly income out of the property, you have to do that. As a matter of fact, you should rent the house out no matter what happens. I'm sure I could rent a studio that would get me closer to Boston."

"I can imagine that sounds good to you right now. I can see how happy it makes you to spend your weekends with Katie, and you always seem more relaxed when you're going to her house."

"I haven't thought about it, but you're probably right. I know Madge wasn't the only person who assumed Katie put thoughts in my head about leaving. I get protective of her, and I don't want her to be seen around town too much."

"I think it's becoming more and more clear that my little girl is in love." Gail smiled at Erin fondly. "Who would have thought that we'd both meet our match from one berry farmer moving to town?"

"I wouldn't have put money on it, but I sure am glad it's working out this way."

❦

On the first Wednesday of May, Katie called Erin. "Our birthdays are coming up. How do you want to spend them?"

"Gosh, they are. How did it get to be May so soon?"

"You've been so deliriously happy that you lost all track of time."

"I can't, nor would I want to, argue with that. What are my choices?"

"We can do anything you want. Anything in the world. I want our first birthday weekend to be spectacular."

"Our birthday weekend? We're going to celebrate for a whole weekend?"

"Yep. Just because our birthdays are only two days apart is no excuse to slight either of us. We'll celebrate yours on Friday and mine on Sunday."

"The fifteenth is a Friday?"

"No, it's two weeks from today, a Wednesday. But you can't be here on Wednesday, so we have to move them."

"You're very organized, aren't you? It's good to be with someone who looks ahead and plans things."

"Oh, I plan things. To a fault."

❦

May the seventeenth, Katie's actual birthday, found the pair in Boston, celebrating Erin's. Erin had chosen a quiet celebration, and Katie had accommodated all of her wishes. It was eight o'clock in the evening, and Erin had just arrived. As usual, neither woman could restrain herself from offering a heartfelt, demonstrative welcome on the front steps of Katie's brownstone.

Erin looked up into Katie's bright blue eyes and saw them sparkling with happiness. "I don't know about you, but this is my favorite time of the week."

"Me, too. I wish you lived here, but then I wouldn't get the charge I get when I put my arms around you for the first time in five days. It gives me chills every time." She tilted her head and kissed Erin, both of them welcoming the touch, the smell, and the feel of the other. "Happy birthday, sweetheart."

Looking a little woozy, Erin said, "Best one I've ever had."

Katie took her hand and pulled her up so they were on the same step. "Don't let me off so easily. Make me work for some praise."

"Nope. If you ignored my birthday completely, this would still be the best one I've ever had. Falling in love with you has made every day special."

"You're about as sweet as a human being can be, Erin Delancy. I feel like it's my birthday."

"It is, you silly thing!"

Katie led the way into her apartment. "No, it's not. We've decided. Today is your birthday. Mine is Sunday."

"I think *you* decided that. I was happy to let the dates fall where they may. I'm crazy that way."

"You have to take charge of things, kid. Stick with me, and we'll get the calendar set up just the way we like it."

Erin put her arms around Katie and hugged her with bracing enthusiasm. "I'll stick with you no matter what. Every day we're together is a party."

"Let's go upstairs and get your party started. I want to get you into your birthday suit."

Beaming, Erin said, "I love birthdays."

❦

Clad in their birthday suits, Erin lay with her head in Katie's lap. She opened her mouth and accepted another sweet strawberry dipped in her glass of champagne. "I can't imagine a restaurant in the world that could make a better meal than we've just had."

Katie popped a strawberry into her own mouth and continued to massage Erin's face delicately. "I think there are one or two places that can beat cheese, cold cuts, and crackers, but there isn't any place with this kind of ambience. If there was…" She shook her head, unable to think of an analogy. "This champagne is making me silly. I'm really not used to wine."

Erin turned her head just enough to kiss the satiny skin on Katie's thigh. "I like you when you're silly. Of course, I like you when you're not silly, too. I just like you."

With a serious tone that had been completely absent before, Katie said, "What do you think? Are you in this for the long haul?"

"Huh?"

"Very eloquent."

"What are you asking?"

"Just what I said. Do you see yourself growing old with me? And if so, why?"

Erin turned just enough to be able to see Katie's face. It was clear she was being completely serious. "I can't imagine *not* being with you." She turned fully and met Katie's eyes. "You make me happy." Erin could see that her answer hadn't been sufficient, so she tried again. "This isn't what I'm best at, Kate. All I know is that if I wasn't your girlfriend, I'd want to be your best friend. I love you, but I also really like you. And I have a lot of respect for you."

Katie leaned over a little and wrapped her arms around Erin's neck, cradling her head. "Is that enough?" There was a hint of trepidation or fear or insecurity in her tone, but Erin couldn't pin down which it was.

"What more is there? Love and attraction and respect and friendship…that's everything."

Katie's grip grew a little tighter, and her skin felt cool. "But how do you know it will last? How do you know you won't get sick of me? How do you know you won't want other things? Other people?"

"I don't know how I know." She pulled Katie's arms away, turned over, and sat up so they were facing each other. Running her hands gently over Katie's face, she said, "I just know. There isn't a doubt in my mind."

"Are you old enough to know what you want? It was only a few years ago that you wanted to be the town doctor."

Erin nodded. "I can see why you think that's analogous, but it isn't. At least half of my decision to be the town doctor was based on finances."

"Half? Really?"

"Yeah. I wanted to be a doctor, and I didn't think it would make much difference where I practiced. I loved growing up in Essex, and I didn't want to be too far from my mom. When Doctor Worrell made the overtures, I jumped."

"But that was before you met Suzy, right?"

Erin shook her head quickly. "Not really. I didn't sign the contract until I got accepted to med school. Suzy and I were partners by then."

"Did she agree to live in Essex?"

Erin looked thoughtful as she considered the question. She wasn't entirely clear on the sequence of events, but she tried hard to line them all up. "I don't remember it being an issue. We were both going to med school, and having one of us get a free ride was more than either of us could have hoped for." She shrugged, looking a little at a loss. "You know how it is when you're fresh out of college. You think you can handle anything."

"Honey, that was only six years ago. It worries me that you were so sure then…"

Touching her lips with her fingers, Erin silenced Katie. "Six years is almost a quarter of my life. And it's almost my *entire* adult life. Suzy didn't protest, but I'll admit I let circumstances dictate too many things for me. And I don't think it's a secret that I tend to let things go along rather than cause trouble."

"That worries me a lot. I find myself lying in bed at night wondering whether you'll tell me if you're unhappy. I worry that you'll let things go until they're too far gone."

"No, I won't. I've had time to think about what went wrong between Suzy and me, and I won't let things like that ever happen again."

Looking almost frantic, Katie took Erin by the shoulders and demanded, "What did you learn? I have to know."

"Shh," Erin said, stroking her face with care. "Why are you so worked up?"

"I don't know," Katie said, looking abashed. "I guess I've been worrying about these things and they come out all at once when we're together."

Warily, Erin said, "Okay, let's clear some things up. Here's what I learned from being with Suzy. One: it's unfair to let things fester, and two: my needs are just as important as my partner's."

Katie's grip grew tighter. "Are you sure you've learned that? Are you positive you know that I'll do anything I can to make you happy? You just have to ask."

"Yes, yes, I'm sure. I thought I could wait for Suzy to come to grips with the things that troubled her and then we could go about being happy together, but it doesn't work that way. We had too many secrets between us, and that's a relationship killer."

Looking a little calmer, Katie said, "Why aren't you friends with her? You make it sound like you just drifted apart, but if that's true, you should still be friends."

"She doesn't want to be friends." Erin sat quietly for a few seconds, trying to make her scattered thoughts coalesce. "We finally broke up when I told her what I needed. I don't think I was asking for a lot, but some of the bigger things I wanted caught her by surprise."

"Things like sex?" Katie watched her face carefully, her eyes flickering over Erin's somber countenance.

Making a dismissive gesture with her hand, Erin said, "That was a small part. It was more important to me that she took the opportunity to work on all of the things that held her back. But she didn't want to, and I couldn't wait any longer."

"You're a very good woman." Katie put her arms around Erin and held her, trailing her fingers across her shoulders and back, soothing her.

"I hurt her more by hiding things from her than I ever would have being honest from the start. That's the biggest lesson I learned. She felt betrayed, and that's not something that you can get over easily."

"That's true." Katie pulled back and slowly her serious gaze melted into a compassion-filled half-smile. "I think you've learned a lot, but I'm really sorry you both had to learn it the hard way."

"I think that's the only way to learn."

Katie held her arms out, and Erin slid into her embrace once again. They shifted around until they were lying down, face to face. "I love you," Katie whispered. "You're the best birthday present I could ever imagine."

⁂

Hours later, Erin tried to tempt Katie into eating another piece of birthday cake. She swiped a bit of chocolate frosting across a nipple and then dropped her breast into Katie's open mouth. "How do I taste dipped in chocolate?"

Grinning, Katie smacked her lips. "Not bad, but you're better without any additions." She gripped Erin around the waist and flipped her so that she was looking down upon her. "What's your worst trait?"

"That is a very strange question, and it's being posed at a very strange time."

"Don't give me any delaying tactics."

"I'm not delaying. I'm just wondering what field that came out of?"

"It's your birthday. That's a good day to assess your life."

"My birthday was over twenty minutes ago. And shouldn't that be self-assessment?"

"Yes, but I can tell you're not going to do it yourself, so I'm helping." Katie grinned playfully and collapsed next to Erin. "Come on…"

"Okay. I guess my worst trait is my tendency to be lazy."

"Lazy? Really? I would have thought you'd say your aversion to conflict."

"No," Erin said thoughtfully. "I *am* averse to conflict, but I take it on when I need to."

"Do you really? Give me an example. What's the riskiest thing you've ever done?"

"Mmm, when I was an intern, I was assisting the head of general surgery when he was removing this guy's gallbladder. After he closed, he told me to come around to his side and check the guy's prostate."

"What's that got to do with a gallbladder?"

"Nothing. He said he thought women were tentative about examining men, and one way to get over it was to examine them when they were sedated."

"That's kinda weird."

"I thought it was more than weird," Erin said, her eyes taking on a steely resolve that Katie hadn't seen. "I refused to do it even when he tried to humiliate me. I don't think many people said 'no' to Dr. Baron."

"What happened?"

"We left the operating room, and when we were changing, he said he was going to make sure my attending knew that I didn't have the guts to be a good doctor."

"Damn!"

"Yeah, it was tense. But I didn't back down. I told him he was welcome to do whatever he wanted, but I was going to report him for trying to force me to examine a patient without consent."

Grinning, Katie put her fist out, and Erin touched it with her own. "Brass ones, Delancy! That was a great threat. Good move."

"It wasn't a threat. I *did* report him. What he told me to do was wrong, and I couldn't let that slide."

"Did he report you?"

"Not that I know of." She smiled ruefully. "He probably thought I was threatening him to get him to hold off, but I don't threaten. If I say I'm gonna do it, I do it."

Katie looked into Erin's dark eyes and said, "There's nothing sexier than a woman with fortitude." She latched on to Erin's mouth and proceeded to show her exactly what fortitude did to her libido.

Katie lay sprawled on her back, her hair a mass of blonde-red curls splayed across her pillow. She absently stroked Erin's head, looking down at her lounging peacefully between her legs. "How can you say you're lazy? Your tongue was moving so quickly there at the end that I thought you had batteries in it."

Erin's grin was proudly self-satisfied. "You liked that, huh? I think I'll save it for special occasions."

Wiggling her eyebrows, Katie said, "My birthday's coming up."

"It sure is." Erin flipped her hair over her shoulder and got to her hands and knees, slowly crawling up to lie next to Katie. "And if it's anything like mine it's gonna be the best one you've ever had."

The next morning, Katie fed Erin a bite of her cereal. "Do you like it?" she asked, watching her face.

"It's a little twiggy," Erin said, her nose wrinkling up. "Are there actually sticks in it?"

"No, silly. It's just high in fiber. Keeps you regular."

"Everything's good in that department," Erin said, rolling her eyes. "Why am I surrounded by women who want to keep me healthy?"

"Because you're so wonderful. No one can bear to think of the smallest thing harming you."

"I'll stick to my birthday cake." She put another frosting-laden bite into her mouth and smiled. "Nothing better than cake for breakfast."

"Where'd you get these habits? I know your mom only feeds you healthy meals."

"She's gotten worse—or I guess you'd say better—about that in the last few years. I had a normal childhood with sugar-laden cereal and chocolate milk. All of the good things."

"What would you do with our kids?" Katie's eyes were half-closed, and her gaze was intent. "What kind of parent would you be?"

"Are you sure you're not doing some sort of screening process for the CIA?"

Katie put her finger on the tip of the bowl of her spoon, acting as though she'd propel the contents into Erin's face. "I'm interested in you."

Erin took another bite of cake and chewed for a few moments. Her eyes roamed around the kitchen while Katie watched her. She finally said, "I haven't given a tremendous amount of thought to this."

"That's your standard answer," Katie teased. "Tell me about the tiny amount of thought you've given to it."

Smiling good-naturedly, Erin said, "I'd try to be like my parents were, I guess." She took another bite, her gaze idly gliding around the room again. "I'd probably lighten-up a little on the politeness issue, though. I think it's important for kids to be able to express their feelings, and that wasn't encouraged at my house."

Katie's expression immediately turned sympathetic. "You couldn't say that you were sad or hurt?"

"Oh, no. I could say any of that stuff, but it wasn't cool to be angry. Being respectful of adults was required, and it wasn't respectful to be angry."

"I think it's a priority to teach kids respect," Katie said. "My parents let me get away with way, way too much. I'd be much stricter."

"I didn't get away with *anything*, but I didn't really want to, so my mom must have done a good job. I don't recall being overly frustrated. There are just a few incidents I can recall when I was mad at her about something, and I didn't feel like I could say how I felt." She sat perfectly still for a few seconds and then added, "I think that's part of the reason I started to write. I could say anything I felt in my stories."

Fascinated, Katie asked, "How old were you when you started to write?"

"Not very. Maybe third grade. Somewhere around there. My characters were usually girls who did all of the things I was afraid to do."

"Wow! That's really young. No wonder your work is so polished."

"Do you really think so?" Erin was looking through her dark lashes, her head tilted down.

"Yes! I want to read everything you've ever written. I was blown away by the story you sent me."

"You didn't say that. I thought you were just turned on by it."

"That's part of it, but I wouldn't get turned on by poorly written sex. I have to be able to suspend disbelief, and I did that immediately with your work."

Erin grinned happily and bounced around on her stool. "Cool. That makes me happy."

"Finish that cake and take me back to bed, you sexy thing. I can't think of a better thing to do than make love to you all day."

"We've got to go to a certain someone's party tonight. Don't forget."

Katie checked her watch. "We've got about six hours to kill." She slid off her chair and took Erin's hand. "Making love to you is my kind of party."

⁂

That night at the birthday party, Erin watched Katie wade through a crowd of people, headed her way. Pleased, she saw that Katie was holding a laughing, kicking baby. "Cute, huh?"

"Very cute. Who is this beauty?"

"This is Shoshanna." Katie tried to hand her off. "Want to hold her?"

"Yeah." Erin stood on her tiptoes to look above the crowd. "Let me go wash my hands."

But Katie deposited the wriggling baby into Erin's arms. "Just don't put your hands in her mouth, you silly thing. Do you think you have diphtheria or something?"

"No, but I don't want to send her home with a virus."

"Loosen up, Delancy. I barely stopped her from licking my shoes. God knows what she's gotten into so far."

Laughing, Erin bounced the baby on her hip. Addressing her, she asked, "What have you gotten into? Are you eating shoes?"

"She has two older sisters, so her parents give her a lot of freedom. They've learned that they don't break that easily."

"She's really adorable. Nice name, too."

"Yeah. Joe and Leslie decided that their girls would take Leslie's last name and the boys would take Joe's. So, Shoshanna lucked out with Levi."

"What's Joe's last name?"

Katie chuckled. "There's a reason we call him Alphabits. It starts with an 'S' and ends in a 'ski.' The rest are all consonants."

Still talking to the baby, Erin said, "I think she's exaggerating, don't you? She does that a lot, you know."

"His name is Soberalski, for your information. And Shoshanna Soberalski is not a winning combo."

"Yeah, Levi wins that one."

"They agreed to raise the kids in the Jewish faith because Leslie's the last Levi in her extended family." She waited a beat and then asked, "Would you want to give our kids a religious background?"

Erin shrugged. "I haven't really thought about it, but I suppose I would. How about you?"

Looking stunned, Katie said, "What *have* you thought about? What religion you bring your kids up in is a big deal."

It was clear that Katie was irritated with her, but Erin wasn't at all clear what she'd done to merit that. "Do you get a little…irritable when you ovulate?"

Katie reached out and reclaimed the baby. "Shoshanna, will you tell Erin that no woman likes to be asked that question?"

"I didn't mean to be rude. I just wanted to know if there was some medical reason for your being irritable."

"Not everything has a medical reason. I'm irritated because these are big issues, and it worries me that you haven't thought about them. You say you see yourself being with me permanently. What if I want to raise my kids as Zoroastrians?"

More puzzled than ever, Erin said, "I don't know what that is, but if that's your choice and it means a lot to you, I'd be okay with it."

"Damn it! You can't give in about everything, Erin. You have to have your own priorities. Hell, I don't even know what church you go to. You might *be* a Zoroastrian!"

Katie's cheeks were starting to turn pink, and Erin could tell things were getting worse. The baby was starting to fuss from being inactive, so Erin took Katie by the arm and led her back to Leslie. Once Shoshanna was returned to her mother, Erin led the way outside. They started to walk down the street, with Erin holding Katie's hand. "What's got you so riled up?"

Frowning and looking grumpy, Katie said, "I'm not riled up. I'm worried."

"Okay, why are you worried?"

"It's the same old thing. I worry that you haven't given nearly as much thought to the future as I have. I worry that you haven't had enough life experience to make up your mind about some very important issues." She reached up and rubbed her temples. "It gives me a headache."

"I still don't get it, Kate. You seem to want some kind of full disclosure before you let yourself fall in love with me, but I can't give you that. Nobody can. Everyone changes over time, and being with someone changes you."

"Great! Now I'm worried that being together will change both of us in bad ways."

Erin couldn't help but chuckle softly. "I think I finally see why you've never been in a long-term relationship."

Stopping abruptly, Katie turned and stared at her, wide-eyed. "Exactly! It's almost impossible to find somebody who feels the same way I do about all of the important issues."

"No, it's not." Erin slipped her arms around Katie's waist and pulled her close for a hug. She didn't say anything for a while, trying to calm her through her touch. When Katie's tense body finally relaxed a little, Erin said, "You're confusing details with important issues."

"No, I'm not," she said insolently, trying to pull away. "People break up over religious differences all of the time. Joe and Leslie argued for two years before they agreed on their plan."

Erin held her tight and murmured into her ear, "You're over-thinking. The important issues are simple, sweetheart. Really simple."

"They can't be," Katie whined. "They just can't be."

"Yes, they are." Erin continued to hold and stroke Katie, now rocking her back and forth gently. "All we need are love and respect. Everything else will fall in line with just those two things." She pulled away a few inches and gazed into Katie's fearful blue eyes. "I love you, and I respect you and your feelings. If you feel the same about me, everything will work out."

"But there are so many other things! What if I'm into corporal punishment or three-ways or spending all of your money?"

"That's quite a leap from one to the other, but if we each respect each other, we can work it out."

"How do we work out a difference of opinion about three-ways?"

"Easy. Having a three-way would hurt our relationship and make me feel humiliated. If you respect me, you'd back off when I told you that."

Hesitantly, Katie began to nod. "That makes sense."

"We have to respect ourselves and each other and our relationship. If you can do that, you're ready to make a commitment."

"I can do that," Katie said, her lower lip quivering. "I just love you so much I'm terrified, Erin."

"Terrified of what, baby?"

"That you'll leave me or get tired of me or realize I'm not right for you."

"Why is this just one way? Why aren't you worried that you'll get tired of me?"

Katie hugged her so hard the breath was forced out of Erin's lungs. "Because you're the best girlfriend ever. I'll never, ever get tired of you."

"I feel the same way about you, Katie. You're endlessly fascinating. And stunningly attractive. Remarkably intelligent—"

Katie looked at her impishly. "Don't forget my sex appeal."

"That was next on my list. Don't worry, sweetheart. Your sex appeal is off the charts. You're hotter than the sun."

"Ooh, I like that. That's a good nickname, as a matter of fact. You can call me Sunny, and when people ask why, you can tell them how hot I am."

"No way," Erin said, smiling gently. "I don't want to let anyone know how fantastically wonderful you are in bed. I'd be beating men, women, and…more women off with a stick."

"I can't argue with you on that one. Now, let's go home and remind each other of how fantastic we are in bed. It's my birthday!"

Chapter Seventeen

*A*fter a few minutes of gentle prodding, Katie tugged the sheet off Erin's body. She ran her hand over the remarkably warm skin, commenting, "I don't understand how one seemingly normal woman can throw off so much heat." Not only did Erin not reply, she didn't flinch. Katie started to pat her butt gently, increasing the velocity until Erin finally showed a sign of life by rolling away. "Come on, sweetheart. We're gonna be late."

That seemed to do the trick. The shuttered eyelids finally opened a crack. "Late for what?" Erin's raspy voice asked.

"For breakfast. We've got to eat before the game."

With difficulty, Erin propped herself up, looking around the room like she wasn't quite sure where she was. She blinked a few times and pushed her hair from her eyes. "I'm really out of it."

Playfully tweaking her nose, Katie said, "You're not used to burning the candle at both ends. Your body seems to believe it needs eight hours of sleep."

Yawning and stretching, Erin said, "Nine. I need a lot of sleep."

"Oh, that won't work. It's a luxury if I get seven."

Erin tossed her feet to the floor, stood up, and stretched again. "I need my sleep. The worst years of my life were my residency. I vowed I'd never take a job where my sleep was interrupted."

"And you want to be in emergency medicine?"

Running her hands through her hair, Erin scratched her scalp while continuing to stretch. "Yeah. You just work your shift. You can't leave in the middle of treating a patient, but they don't tend to call you back in unless there's a big emergency. I've done my homework." Katie was watching her appreciatively, and Erin saw the open interest in her eyes. "You look like you want to go back to bed."

Chuckling, Katie put her arms around her and hugged her tightly. "You are so unconsciously sexy, and it really turns me on to see how unselfconscious you are.

I thought you'd be a little prudish, but you're anything but."

"I'm not prudish at all when I trust someone, and I trust you completely." They stood there for a few minutes, gently touching the other's bare body.

"How can you feel so normal now, yet be so hot when you're in bed?"

"I don't know, but I've always been this way. My mom says she could put me to bed with just a diaper on when I was a baby."

"I think that's a sign that we're made for each other. I can never get warm enough, and you can never get cool enough. I'll take your excess heat, and you can take my excess chill."

Erin leaned back in their embrace and smiled lovingly. "You let me know when you figure that system out. I'll be right here."

Even though Erin had been hard to wake, she was ready to leave before Katie. It was a lovely, sunny day, so she sat on the steps smiling and nodding to the passersby. She turned when she heard Katie close the front door, and a happy grin settled on her face. "It takes you a while to get ready, but it's always worth the wait. You look fantastic."

Katie twirled, showing Erin her complete ensemble. She wore a white Red Sox jersey, a short-sleeved red mock turtleneck, and a pair of navy blue shorts.

"Is that an authentic jersey?" Erin asked.

"Yep. Cool, isn't it?"

"It's got your name on it and everything. Whose number is this?" Erin traced the heavy lettering that had been meticulously sewn onto Katie's jersey.

Feigning outrage, Katie said, "I should break up with you just for not knowing that. It's Carlton Fisk's. Even the most casual fan should know that."

"I'm not much for numbers, but I love him. He's a New Hampshire boy, you know. Went to UNH for a bit."

"Not bad," Katie said, still looking suspicious. "Who was your favorite player when you were a kid?"

"Jim Rice," Erin said without hesitation.

"Oh, all right. You picked a good one." Katie took her hand and led the way down the steps. "You were on thin ice there for a moment, Delancy. When we get home, you can sign a petition I have to get him elected to the Hall of Fame."

Erin surreptitiously glanced in Katie's direction, wondering if she was being serious. When she saw the slight frown and level gaze, she gulped, realizing her own version of being a baseball fan might pale next to Katie's.

They arrived at Fenway almost an hour before the game began. Katie watched with delight as Erin enthused over every part of the experience. She'd never had tickets in the lower deck, much less within the base paths, and she was enthusiastically impressed. Danny and Stacy arrived close to game time, and they delivered ice-cold beers and hot dogs. Erin devoured her own, then made short work of half of Katie's, grinning guiltily as Katie dabbed at the mustard that lingered on the side of her mouth.

It was a picture-perfect day, and the Red Sox got off to a good start, managing to score in both the first and second innings. During the top of the third, Katie stood up and said, "Let's go stretch our legs for a minute."

Erin looked up at her, puzzled, but she got up. As she exited the row, she said, "Would you guys like another beer?"

"They're fine," Katie said, taking Erin's hand and practically dragging her up the aisle to the concourse. Once they got into the even more crowded area, Katie broke through the crowd like a woman on a mission. They walked all the way to the end of the concourse, past the last concession stand and restrooms.

"If we go up two levels I can show you where I usually sit," Erin said. Her smile froze when she saw an expression on Katie's face that looked like sheer terror. "What's wrong, baby? You look like you're gonna be sick."

Katie did, indeed, look like she was on the verge of vomiting. Her skin was clammy, and her face was devoid of its usual rosy color, leaving a fine spray of freckles standing out against her pale flesh. "I'm fine, I'm fine," she said, somewhat irritably, but Erin could see beads of sweat form across her hairline.

"Do you need to find a bathroom?"

"No!" She shook her head and then waved her hands nervously in front of her face. Biting her lip, she took Erin's hands and held them against her chest for a moment, letting her eyes close. Erin felt her take in a deep breath, and then Katie met her eyes and said, "How many outs are there?"

Confused, Erin searched the outfield and found the scoreboard. "Uhm, that was the third. Why?"

Katie stood behind her and put her arms around Erin's waist, holding on tightly. "Read the scoreboard."

"Okay," Erin said with trepidation. "Uhm, do you want the score or the batting order or what other games are going on right now? I don't know what you're after."

"Not the scoreboard. The message board." She was pressed up against Erin like a second skin, and she shook her a little in frustration. "The message board."

"Okay. The Roxbury Fire Department is here today. Girl Scout Troop 284 from Brookline. The Boys and Girls Club from Bangor, Maine."

"Not that stuff!" Katie's grip was tightening, and Erin was starting to feel anxious.

She quietly scanned the board as message after message flashed by. She had no idea why she was doing what she was doing, but she was certain it was important. Finally, she read a message that seemed to reach her body not through her eyes, but from the shafts of each hair on her head. Her scalp tingled as though an electric current had passed over it. The shock traveled down the back of her neck and continued down her body until even her feet felt mildly electrified. She had to pry Katie's arms away, but she managed as she turned to face her. Stunned, nearly speechless, yet bursting with joy, she felt tears in her eyes as she said, "Yes. Yes, I'll marry you."

Katie's viselike grip encircled her again, and they held each other as though they were about to be swept away by a raging sea. Erin wasn't sure how long they stood just like that, but she finally lifted her head and placed an achingly tender kiss upon Katie's quivering lips. "I'd give anything to be the first and last Mrs. Kathleen Rose Quinn."

"I love you," Katie said simply. Her eyes were wet with tears, and her skin still bore a ghostly pallor, but Erin had never seen a more beautiful woman. Katie fumbled in her pocket and finally pulled out a tiny glassine envelope. "Open your hand," she said.

Erin did, and Katie shook the envelope, causing a beautiful round diamond to drop into Erin's open hand. Puzzled, Erin said, "Is this…for me?"

"It is if you like it. I wanted to buy you a ring, but I wasn't sure what kind you would like. I have a friend…" She heard herself, and they both started laughing, but she kept going. "Whose father is a jeweler. I bought the prettiest stone I could find, but he said I could return it or exchange it for anything you like. You could get an emerald cut or a marquise or a sapphire or anything at all. I just want you to have something special. Something that you can look at and think of how much I love you." She started to choke up again, and now Erin held her tightly.

"I want this," she whispered. "I'll just carry it around in this little envelope and take it out a few dozen times a day."

Katie smiled at her and then kissed her gently. "I was thinking of making it into a ring. Would that be okay?"

"That's probably best." Erin opened her hand and looked at the diamond again. "Although…this is pretty cool."

Katie's smile was radiant as she took Erin's hand and started to tug her towards their seats. "There's a man on second. We've gotta get back." She handed Erin the small envelope and watched while she tucked it away safely. They started to walk back to their seats, being buffeted on all sides by the throng. There was a hint of uncertainty in Katie's voice when she said, "Was it totally stupid of me to propose at the baseball game?"

"It was totally cool."

"I thought it was cool," Katie said, almost to herself. "I've been thinking about doing it for years." She met Erin's eyes. "I just had to find the right baseball nerd."

"I'm your girl."

They finally made their way back to their seats. As soon as Danny and Stacy looked up, they both got to their feet and enveloped Katie in a hug. Then each of them hugged Erin, and Danny clapped her on the back. "Welcome to the family," he said enthusiastically.

"We're so glad to have you, Erin," Stacy said.

"How do you know she said yes?" Katie said.

"If she said no, you would've left by now. I know you, big sister. You would have stormed out of here, cussing all the way."

"I can't argue," Katie said amiably. "I wish I could, but I can't."

"I'll go buy us a round to celebrate," Danny said.

Stacy got up, too. "We'll be right back."

"Don't you want to see my almost ring?" Erin asked.

"We already saw it. Sorry," Stacy said, giggling. "Katie can't keep a secret."

Katie shrugged, grinning guiltily. "I can keep secrets from everybody but my family. And that now includes you," she proclaimed, tapping Erin on her nose.

∽

Both Erin and Katie were too excited to pay much attention to the game, but neither minded the distraction. Before the bottom of the sixth inning, Katie put an arm around Erin's shoulders and asked, "Do you mind if I kiss you in front of all these people?"

Erin grinned happily. "Not a bit." Katie leaned in and kissed her briefly but enthusiastically. Then she grinned at the cameraman, who was standing on top of the dugout, held her thumb up, and waved with both arms when the message board read, "She said yes!"

The sellout crowd broke into applause, and Erin sat, stunned, realizing the camera was still on them. People all around them realized they were on the screen, and many tried to crowd into the shot, slapping Katie and Erin on the back. As soon as the camera turned away, most people sat back in their chairs, but the buzzing continued. As people left their seats to go to the concession stands, they stopped by to offer congratulations.

In a daze, Erin said, "Was that on TV?"

"No. They don't telecast the stuff between innings, but if anybody you know was here today, you're going to get a phone call."

Warming to the idea, Erin said, "That's cool. I'm ready to take out a front-page ad to tell the world, but I should probably be polite and tell my mom first."

"I made sure to keep my Tuesday morning calendar light. I thought I'd come to Essex tomorrow night after work, and we could tell both of our parents."

Erin lit up. "That's great, but we have to go tell your mom and your aunt."

"They already know. They like the diamond, too."

Laughing at Katie's inability to keep a secret, Erin said, "You'd have a lot of explaining to do if I'd said no."

"One of the first things I learned when I started to practice was never ask a question if you don't already know the answer. I would have been the most surprised woman in town if you'd said no." She grinned toothily, and Erin couldn't resist kissing that happy, confident face.

❦

After a brief stop at the Quinn sisters' residence to once again display the quasi-ring and accept congratulations, they returned home. "I was going to drive back tonight, but I can't stand to leave my fiancé," Erin said as they pulled into the garage.

"I'd ask you to marry me every weekend to keep you here."

Erin just smiled and then took Katie's hand to walk around to the front of the building. Katie was exhausted, the lack of sleep from the night before mixing with the emotional tumult of the day. She stood on the front steps, almost too tired to go in. Erin sat and patted the step next to her. "Sit down with me and enjoy the evening."

"Do you want something to eat? I stocked up on a few things."

"Mmm, I can't think of anything I want…that you'd have," she said, grinning guiltily.

"You wait here. I need a snack." She ruffled Erin's hair as she went into the house. It took her a while, but Erin was very content sitting outside in the cooling, sweet air. Katie emerged, carrying a plate of strawberries, sliced kiwi, and a sectioned orange in one hand and a bowl containing a brownie and vanilla ice cream with hot fudge in the other. She bowed and handed the bowl to Erin with a flourish. "The first of many compromises I plan on making to make sure you're happy." She sat down and popped a strawberry into her mouth, savoring it as though it were the best thing on earth. "I just have to work on convincing myself that fruit tastes better than ice cream and brownies. It's going to be a struggle."

"Now I *know* you love me." Erin took a big bite and tried not to swoon. With her mouth full, she said, "It's so-so."

"Liar," Katie scoffed. "But a thoughtful liar."

"If I'm going to be a liar, I want to be thoughtful about it. Hey, are you sure you're able to come to Essex tomorrow and stay overnight?"

"Sure. If I have advance notice, I can usually switch meetings around."

"What about court?"

Katie blinked. "What about court?"

"It seems like you're always going to court. Aren't you?"

"For my job?"

"Well, yeah. Aren't you a lawyer?"

"Yes, but I've never been to court for my job." Her eyes brightened, and she nodded. "You're talking about my pro bono stuff. I go by housing court most Monday mornings. I supervise a bunch of young lawyers, and there's usually some emergency that came up on the weekend. If I go by on Monday morning, I can usually help them settle things before I go to work."

Erin's mouth was open a little, and she looked not only puzzled but embarrassed. "You supervise lawyers? Uhm, this is a heck of a time to admit this, but I don't know what you do."

Katie patted her knee. "This *is* a heck of a time to admit that, but I'll let it slide. Most people think they know what lawyers do, and they assume the details are complicated."

"Oh, come on! There's no excuse for my not asking you about exactly what you do."

Katie munched on a big slice of kiwi, grinning. "You have a point. Remember that we were engaged before you asked me what I did for a living. If you ever accuse me of being overly self-involved, I'm gonna pull this out in my defense."

"You're not self-involved at all."

"You say that now, but someday…"

"Nope. That's not gonna happen, but you'll have to wait and see. Now, tell me about your job."

"It's honestly boring if you're not into it. But I enjoy it, and I've pushed some deals through that previously would have gone to our mergers and acquisitions people."

"Huh?" Erin asked, staring at Katie with a complete lack of comprehension.

"Okay, it *is* pretty complex. Let's just say that real estate attorneys at my firm used to work on relatively small deals. Under ten million dollars. They limited themselves to fairly straightforward stuff. But about five years ago, I brought in a client who wanted to buy a big hotel. Since he was my client, I got to lead the team, even though the M & A people normally handle a deal like that. It was crazy complicated because the hotel was owned by a public corporation, but I fought to keep it."

"I have no idea what you're talking about, but I'm getting the impression that you're aggressive at work."

Katie grinned, showing her teeth. "You might say that. It was a two hundred million dollar deal, and I told them if they didn't make me partner before it closed, I'd never bring another one in."

"Gosh!"

"That's what they said, in other words. But they did it."

"I...I thought you were like the guy most people in Essex use to do real estate. I don't even know where your office is or how many people you work with."

"I'll take you to my office any time you want to see it, sweetie. There are just over two hundred attorneys in my firm, and about a hundred and fifty of them work out of the Boston office."

"Two hundred people!"

"No, two hundred attorneys. I think we have about seven hundred employees, but there are only twenty-five attorneys in the real estate section. I probably haven't met half of the attorneys in the firm. It's just too big."

"Do you like that?"

"It's fine. Working for a big firm gives you a name, and many people feel more comfortable dealing with a big-name firm. I don't have to work as hard to bring in new clients as I would if I were with a firm no one had ever heard of."

"You have to bring in your own clients? How do you do that?"

Katie laughed and shook her head. "Erin, I'm a friendly girl, but I'm also practical. The more people you know, the more often someone is going to refer a client to you. I've gotten more business from people I went to college with than you can imagine."

Erin stared at her dreamily. "You are constantly fascinating."

"You might not think that when we live together and I come home complaining about some REIT that's hit a snag and then proceed to bore you with all of the details."

"That's okay, honey. I'll sicken you by telling you about ghastly auto accident victims. We should even each other out."

Katie snuck a look at her watch. "Hey, we'd better get upstairs and watch the game."

"Watch it? We were at it."

"I know, but I missed half an inning when I was proposing. Let's go, let's go," she said, taking a compliant Erin's hand and leading her inside.

⁓

They managed to watch that afternoon's game on fast-forward so Katie was able to catch up on everything she'd missed. She was so engrossed that she didn't notice Erin slowly sink down into a horizontal position. "Are you tired?"

Erin gamely tried to rally. "No. I'm good." Her eyes blinked slowly, and she propped her head up with a folded pillow. "I want to make love to my fiancé."

"Do you mind if I watch the first few minutes of *SportsCenter*?" She urged Erin onto her side and started rubbing her back in big, lazy circles.

"No. That's fine."

Katie smiled down at her, knowing their lovemaking would have to wait for another night. She continued to touch Erin gently, even though the soft, rhythmic breathing confirmed that her fiancé was asleep. Just having her there and feeling her warmth made Katie nearly as happy as making love. She looked at the sweet, innocent face and felt her heart swell with the surety that this was the woman she wanted to spend the rest of her life with.

⁓

Erin was in the shower, humming a tune while she washed her hair. Katie stumbled into the room, her eyes nearly hidden by heavy lids, waved at Erin, and then turned for the door.

"Hey! Come back here and give me a kiss."

Dutifully, Katie turned and waited for Erin to open the shower door. Erin turned the shower head so the bathroom floor wouldn't get wet and then puckered up for a kiss. As soon as Katie's lips touched hers, her hand emerged and clamped on to the back of Katie's neck and pulled her into the steaming shower enclosure. She sputtered and blew the water out of her mouth, her eyes still largely closed. "Nice," she grumbled. "I go out of my way to give you a kiss, and you torture me."

Erin pulled her close and started to remove the dripping wet, heavy T-shirt Katie wore. She dipped her head and delicately started to kiss her way across the always-sensitive skin on the side of Katie's neck. "You let me fall asleep last night," she purred, her voice deep and husky. "I told you I wanted to make love to my beautiful, wonderful fiancé."

A small smile started to erupt, and Katie almost opened her eyes. "I don't think you went on like that, but you should have. Only a wonderful fiancé would let you fall asleep at nine o'clock."

Now that Erin had her naked, she dispensed some liquid soap into her hands and started to massage Katie's skin. She turned her around and worked on her back, letting her fingers probe into the long muscles. Katie held on to the wall and moaned in delight as Erin's strong hands woke every sleeping muscle fiber. "Ooh, you're good at this."

"It's easy to touch someone I love so much. My hands want to know every bit of you." She placed her mouth right next to Katie's ear and whispered, "I can't touch you enough. It's a craving I've never felt before."

Now a sunny grin had settled on Katie's face, and she turned her head to meet Erin's eyes. "Really?"

Solemnly, Erin nodded. "Really. I always felt tentative before. Like I'd go too far and ruin the whole thing."

Hearing the hurt in her voice made Katie's heart clutch in sympathy, but she didn't want to make too big a deal about Erin's little disclosures. It seemed that Erin felt comfortable revealing tidbits of information if she did so on her own, but she got her back up if Katie probed too much. "You can't go too far with me," she said, bringing the conversation back to the present. She grasped Erin's hands, held them to her body, and then felt her hips start to grind against Erin's belly. "You can touch me anywhere, anytime."

"That hardly seems possible. That's like telling me I can eat as much chocolate cake as I want. I'm afraid I won't know how to control myself."

Katie turned in her embrace and saw the tentativeness in Erin's eyes. "Let go," she said softly. "Don't worry about control. You think your needs are huge, but they're not, baby. They're just not."

Erin soaped up her washcloth and methodically started to clean Katie's body. She seemed to be thinking aloud, and Katie let her go, not interrupting her even when she was tempted.

"I was lying there last night while you were watching the recap, and it dawned on me that falling in love is so fantastic because you can…reinvent yourself. I don't have to follow the old rules with you. I don't have to walk on eggshells, hoping that I don't upset you. It's like…it's like I'm not walking through a bunch of land mines that can go off at any time." She put her hands on Katie's shoulders and looked into her eyes. "It feels so wonderful. I can't even begin to explain it."

"You're doing great," Katie assured her. "I understand."

"I couldn't play with Suzy. She was too guarded and too defended. I can't even imagine pulling her into the shower with me. She would have felt out-of-control, and she would have been quiet for a day or even two. Not mad…she didn't get mad. She just got quiet." She shook her head, sadly. "I think that's worse."

"You're right," Katie said. "Falling in love lets us both start fresh. We don't have habits or preconceived notions we have to follow. I want you to be yourself. Your true self." She put her hand on Erin's chest and looked into her dark, expressive eyes. "Tell me, show me what you need. If you can do that, I'll be very, very happy."

"That's all I have to do?" A playful smile accompanied her words.

"Well, a few more things, but the most important thing is that you tell me what you want. I can't guess. You've got to step up and put yourself out there."

"I'll try. I know it won't always be easy, but I'll try." She reached behind herself and turned off the taps. Wrapping Katie in a warm, wet hug, she stood there for a few minutes, letting the steam fill her lungs. "Right now, I'd give an awful lot to be able to make love to you. Holding you like this makes every nerve feel like it's firing."

Katie nuzzled her face into Erin's chest, breathing in her clean scent and letting the feel of her warm skin start to work its magic on her libido. "I don't think I can let you out of the house without getting my fill of some scrumptious doctor." Her hands were running up and down Erin's legs, making each follicle stand at attention. "I want to taste you," she whispered. "You are the most delectable woman on God's green earth."

Erin opened the door, letting the cool morning breeze chill their skin. She handed a towel to Katie and rubbed her own hair with another. "Let me comb my hair or I'll frighten my patients."

"Let me." Katie sat her down and took out the wide-toothed tortoiseshell comb that Erin carried in her toiletries bag. She started at the bottom and gently and carefully removed every tangle. By the time she was gliding the comb across Erin's scalp, she was being massaged by a pair of soft, strong hands. She could have stayed there all day, just grooming her lover, getting to know her intimately. But she realized Erin had a long drive ahead of her, so with regret, she took Erin's hand and led her back into the bedroom. She put a dry towel under her head to avoid soaking the pillows and then lay back and let Erin's fiery eyes glide up and down her body. She felt utterly ravished, as though Erin were consuming her with her heated gaze. Her eyes grew wide as Erin climbed on the bed and straddled her, sitting up tall and proud. She looked so confident and sure of herself that Katie wanted to swoon, but she stayed with her, meeting her eyes, showing her acceptance of anything Erin wanted.

What Erin obviously wanted was to kiss Katie in the most sensual, seductive way one woman's mouth had ever meshed with another's. Erin was bent at the waist, her beautifully formed breasts brushing against Katie's in such an erotic manner that Katie had to fight with herself not to throw Erin on her back and dive in.

Somehow, she controlled her urges, and let Erin express herself. The deep, lingering, wet kisses made her feel completely merged with Erin, and as she felt the muscles in Erin's back move, the feeling grew stronger and more corporeal.

As Erin lavished her with kisses, Katie felt their spirits join, and it struck her that this was what she'd been searching for. It wasn't lust. It wasn't just sex. It was the desire to share, to become more with Erin than she could be without her. It wasn't the merging of personalities she had been so fearful of whenever she'd been tempted to settle down in the past. This wasn't a merger. This was a way of enhancing each other, of growing stronger and more fully realized. This, she finally knew, was love.

Chapter Eighteen

That evening, Erin paced around her house, waiting for Katie to show up. She was so hyper-alert that she heard her car before it reached the driveway. She flew out the door, closing it behind her, ran up to the passenger's side, and got in as the car stopped. "Hi!" She leaned across and held Katie's face in her hands, gazing at her for a few moments before she kissed her. "How can the day go so slowly when I'm here and so quickly when I'm in Boston?"

"Time moves faster in the big city."

"So, your day went quickly?"

Katie gently rapped her head against the steering wheel. "Every minute seemed like an hour. My last meeting was a really important one, but I couldn't pay attention. I told my client I wanted to bring in one of my associates just as a learning experience, and I went out and grabbed the first warm body I could find and made this kid sit in on the meeting and write down everything that happened." She started laughing, finding the experience funnier in its retelling than it had been originally. "I'm not even going to bill the client for my time today. I'll have the kid bill his time and hope nobody asks why this stranger billed an hour."

"Gosh! Are you going to get in trouble?"

"No, sweetie. I keep really good notes, so I'll remember what happened. If the client asks who this kid was, I'll tell him the truth. Sort of. I'll tell him that I didn't want to double-bill since I did it to teach the kid something. I just have to find out the kid's name." She laughed again, rolling her eyes. "Are you ready to get going?"

"Past ready. I'm nervous!"

"Don't worry, I'll talk. After all, I'm the one who asked you." She sat quietly for a moment, turned her gaze to Erin, then said, "Could we talk for a few minutes? I'd like to sit on the porch and get a couple of things out of the way."

"Sure. Is anything wrong?"

"No, nothing's wrong. We just need to discuss a few things. People might have some questions that we should have answers for."

Warily, Erin got out of the car and went onto the porch, sitting on the top stair instead of a chair. She leaned against a post and said, "Do you want something to drink?"

"No. This won't take long." Katie looked surprisingly nervous, making Erin's heart race. Katie fidgeted a little, trying to get comfortable in the old wicker chair. "We didn't discuss timing, and I think that's something we need to clear up."

"Timing?"

"Yeah. When we plan on getting married."

"Oh!" Erin's face lit up in pleasure. "I've been saying that to myself all day. I'm getting married."

"We are. But I need for you to understand something." She got up and settled herself next to Erin, gazing deeply into her eyes. "I desperately want to marry you. But it doesn't make sense to me to get married when we don't live in the same city."

Erin noticeably gulped. "That might be a while."

"It might." Katie grasped Erin's hand and squeezed it until Erin winced. "I'll be as patient as I can be."

Speaking the words she could see forming in Katie's mind, Erin continued for her. "But there's a limit to your patience."

"I don't want there to be," Katie said, her eyes welling with tears. "But I think I'll start to resent you if you stay here for years. I want to live our lives together, Erin, and, to me, that means living together."

Quietly, Erin took in and let out a slow breath. "I understand."

"Do you truly understand? If you stay here I'd still love you, but I'd lose respect for you. And being married to someone I don't respect isn't—"

Erin squeezed her hand and made a "shushing" sound. "I understand. You wouldn't be the woman I've fallen in love with if you'd settle for seeing me on weekends."

"Not if you were here only because you couldn't make a tough choice. The situation would be different if you were following your dream or you had some obligation you couldn't get out of."

"Well," Erin said, smiling wanly, "I kinda do, but I'm not following my dream."

"I believe in you. I believe in you with all of my heart. That's why I asked you to marry me now, sweetheart. I wanted to show you that I'm in this with you—you just have to pull your own weight."

"I weigh a lot more than you do." The smile that curled the edge of Erin's mouth up was slow and sweet.

"And I love every ounce. Now let's get going if you still want to tell our parents."

"I do," Erin said decisively.

They got into the car and Katie started to pull out of the driveway. Erin said, "I've been thinking about my ring all day. I really want to get one for you, but I can't afford it right now."

"I don't need one. A wedding ring is enough."

"If I had the money, would you like one?"

"Maybe," Katie prevaricated. "We can revisit the subject when you're raking in the dough."

"Or making license plates in debtor's prison."

Katie was quiet for a moment, clearly thinking. "How about this? Let's agree on a setting and buy two of them so they match. My friend's dad can get me a cubic zirconium that will look like a real diamond, but won't cost much. Then, someday, if you feel the need, you could upgrade."

"Would you be happy with that?"

"Absolutely. Actually, it's kind of silly to buy a real diamond. We can spend your money on a nice vacation."

Erin gazed at her for a few moments, a contented smile settling on her face. "You know, one of your best traits is that you'd rather have a fake diamond and a real vacation. I'm like you are in that way, so why don't we trade my diamond in for a fake one?"

Once again, Katie seemed to give the matter her considered attention. "No, I like the one I bought. Besides, I want to throw this guy some business. He owns a nice piece of property in Cambridge that I'd love to develop."

"You know what's best, and I mean that sincerely." Erin paused for a moment, thinking. "We haven't discussed how we're going to do this. I'm kinda nervous about telling both of them at once."

Katie shot her a look, being careful to pay attention to her driving. "What would make you feel better?"

"Uhm…" Erin gave her a charmingly shy grin and said, "Could I talk to my mom first?"

"Sure. What do you want me to do? Should I just keep my dad busy while you two go for a walk?"

"Would you mind? I want my mom to be able to say whatever's on her mind, and she won't do that if you and your dad are there."

"Is that a good sign for people who are getting married in two weeks?"

"No, but that's her business. I know her, and I know that she'll just sit there and let your dad talk."

"You're probably right. You know, when I first met you two, I thought you were a lot alike, but now I think you're really pretty different. You're quiet and soft-spoken, but your mom's timid."

"Yeah, she is. I'm more like my dad in a lot of ways. He was quiet, but he didn't let anyone push him around."

"I'm glad you're more like your dad," Katie said, patting Erin's leg. "I hate to think of you letting people push you around."

"Well, I do tend to let things happen for a while before I take action, but I'm gonna try to work on that. The only way I can avoid making another mistake, like going to work for Essex, is if I'm sure I'm getting something out of a situation. I can't just do things because people want me to."

"Except for me," Katie teased. "It's perfectly all right if you let me run roughshod over you."

The gentle smile Erin gave her was so filled with love that Katie had to force herself to look at the road and concentrate. She just hoped they could get this announcement over with quickly, so she could get Erin home in time to make love to her even half as joyously as they'd celebrated that morning.

⌘

Since Dan kept farmer's hours, he and Gail had already eaten dinner and cleaned up by the time Katie and Erin drove up the long drive. Erin saw Dan at the window, and by the time they stopped, both he and Gail were outside. "This is a surprise," he said, looking a little nervous. "Is it a good one?"

"Yeah. Everything's good," Erin said. She got out, kissed her mom, and then gave Dan a hug that, she had to admit, she was beginning to feel comfortable with. Gail clearly hadn't quite figured out how to treat Katie, and she stood next to Dan and smiled expectantly when he clapped his daughter on the back.

"You two should have told us you were going to be around tonight. We could have had a birthday dinner for you," Dan said. "Did you just come by for your presents?"

"No, not really." Erin looked decidedly uncomfortable, and Katie put her hand on her lower back and gave her a little push. "Uhm, I have something I wanted to talk to you about, Mom. Could we…maybe walk around the farm for a bit?"

Gail looked to Dan, and Erin couldn't decide whether it was for approval or permission. She was glad when he returned Gail's questioning gaze with a neutral one, making her reply on her own. "Of course, honey. Now?"

"Yeah." Erin rocked back and forth on her heels, clearly nervous. "Now's good."

"Okay. I think there's enough light to take a spin around the canes." She gave Dan one more puzzled glance, and then she and Erin started to walk.

When they were out of earshot, Dan shoved his hands in his back pockets and watched them for a few moments. "What's that about? Erin looks like she's about to pee herself."

The comment was both accurate and unexpected, and Katie laughed. "She *is* nervous, but it's nothing bad." Deciding to go for broke, she said, "I asked her to marry me."

"You what?!?" Before the two small words stopped reverberating, his face had turned as red as a beet.

"I proposed." Katie's eyes started to narrow, and she stuck her chin out in the defiant manner that had never served her well with her father. "We're going to get married."

"Oh, crap!" He growled, running his hand over his hair, messing it. "I suppose you want to have a double ceremony on Memorial Day?"

"No," she said, her face growing hot. "We haven't discussed when we're going to do it, but you can rest assured that we won't do it here. We can really get married in Boston—almost like we're real human beings." Sarcasm was dripping from her words, and she nearly spit them at Dan.

"Great. That's just great. So, Erin can come home and catch you with another woman and have to divorce you."

Katie glared at him for a moment and then felt her chin start to shake. She couldn't bear giving him the satisfaction of seeing her cry, so she raised her voice and shouted out some of her hurt. "Why do you think I'm such a fucking whore? What have I ever done to you to make you hate me?" Eyes filling with tears, she ran for her car, fumbled wildly with the key, and managed to peel out of the drive, spraying him with dirt and gravel.

He watched her go, stunned by the sorrow and unshielded pain he'd seen in her eyes.

⊗⊗

Erin and Gail began to walk around the neat but still nearly bare canes. Erin had been going over in her mind what she would say, but now that it was time to produce, her mind was blank.

Gail was silent, but the anxious, furtive glances she kept stealing made it clear that Erin's silence was torturing her.

Finally, and a little inelegantly, Erin managed, "Katie and I made a big decision this weekend." She looked at her mother and saw that Gail continued to look frightened. Deciding she couldn't prolong the agony, she said, "We're getting married."

Gail's eyes opened as wide as Erin had ever seen them. Her mouth opened and closed several times, but no words came out. She grasped Erin's hand, and they walked for another few moments, the silence increasing the tension between them. She seemed to gather herself and finally said, "What exactly do you mean?"

Erin tried to stop herself from feeling hurt from the clear lack of excitement or even polite congratulations. She managed to pull off an expression somewhere between neutrality and happiness. "We're getting married. Legally married. You remember that we can do that in Massachusetts, right?"

"Right, right," Gail said, almost absently. "I was confused because we have civil commitment ceremonies here now. I thought that might be what you meant."

Her patience fading, Erin said, "No matter what you call it, it means the same thing." A derisive snort surprised both of them, but Erin didn't even try to cover. "I never dreamed of getting married when I was young, but if I had, I think one of the best parts about that fantasy would have been thinking about how excited you'd be for me when I told you. Good thing I didn't waste a lot of time on that." She wanted nothing more than to take off and find Katie, but she didn't have it in her to be so blatantly rude.

Gail grasped her hand more firmly, as if she could sense Erin's desire to flee. "Honey, you know how much I love you. There's nothing in this world I want more than your happiness, but you have to admit that this is rather sudden. You've only been dating for what, a month or two? You were with Suzy for years, and you never expressed any interest in having any kind of ceremony. This just doesn't seem like you to rush into something so permanent."

"It is me. It's exactly me." Erin could feel her cheeks begin to flush, but she didn't stop herself from saying exactly what was on her mind. "I loved Suzy, but it never occurred to me to have a commitment ceremony because part of me knew I wouldn't spend the rest of my life with her. It's completely different with Katie. I don't have any doubts about her, Mom. None."

"How can that be, honey? You only see her on the weekends. You can't possibly know her that well."

Her resentment building, Erin said, "You told me that you knew you'd marry dad by the end of your first date. Why are quick decisions okay for you but not for me?"

"I was just a girl! I didn't have any idea what it took to make a marriage. We dated for two years before he asked me to marry him, and we were engaged for a year after that. We didn't rush into anything."

Defiantly, Erin demanded, "Did you ever doubt your first impression?"

Clearly abashed, Gail shook her head. "No, I didn't, but that was just luck."

"If that's all it was, then I hope I get just as lucky. I don't think marriage is easy, but I've never met anyone I wanted to work with to make it a success—until Katie."

"How many people have you even dated? The only girl I know you've been with is Suzy."

"Suzy *is* the only other girl I've been with, but I've had other opportunities. I just wasn't interested in dating women I didn't see a future with. But when I'm with Katie, the future seems to stretch out in front of us for millions of miles."

Gail sighed wearily and then seemed to arrange a smile. "I wish you two would take it more slowly, but I trust your judgment." She blinked a few times, her dark lashes fluttering slowly. Her smile brightened and looked more genuine. "If you know this is right for you, you have my full support." She put her arms around Erin and hugged her tightly, soothing her and stroking her back when Erin's tears started to flow.

⁓

They took their time walking around the property. Erin's show of her vulnerability and her need for her mother's approval seemed to put both of them back on familiar ground. Erin chattered away, uncharacteristically regaling her mother with dozens of tales of Katie's near mythic status. It was dark by the time they returned to the front of the house, and Erin said, "Katie probably thinks we got lost. She'll never believe I was talking the whole time."

Beaming a loving smile at her, Gail said, "I love it when you tell me what's really in your heart. This is the nicest talk we've had in years."

"Katie's helping me open up. She's got her work cut out for her, but if anybody can do it, she can."

"From the way you talk about her, she can turn water into wine."

Erin giggled. "She'd turn water into beer. She hates wine." She opened the front door, and her smile froze and then vanished when she saw Dan standing at the window, his arms crossed over his chest, a look of bemused anger on his face. Erin dashed into the room and looked out the side window, seeing that Katie's car was missing. "What happened? Where is she?"

"I don't know."

Gail was now standing next to him, and she put her hand on his shoulder. "When did she leave?"

"A long time ago."

Erin reached into her pocket and took out her cell phone, but Gail stopped her. "She would have called you if she needed you. Hold on for a minute so you have some idea of what happened." Gail turned and looked at Dan, clearly waiting for an answer.

He seemed at a complete loss for words. "I don't know how it started. I never know how it starts. One of us says something stupid, and the other one jumps in. It happens so fast…" He looked at Erin with pain in his eyes. "I hate it. I can't tell you how much I hate it. I honestly thought things were getting better…" He walked away from her, looking disconsolate. In a few seconds, Erin heard the refrigerator open, and he came back into the room carrying two beers. Silently, he handed one to Erin.

Surprising herself, Erin opened the beer and sat down. She took a long pull on the bottle and reflected for a moment. "Do you remember anything?"

Dan nodded, looking almost humiliated. "The last thing she said was, 'Why do you hate me?'" He looked at Erin and then shifted his puzzled gaze to Gail. "How could she say that?"

Erin slapped her bottle down on the table and mumbled as she walked onto the front porch, "She said it because she believes it."

By the time the screen door closed, she'd dialed Katie's number. "Sweetheart? Are you all right?" she asked as soon as Katie answered.

"Sure." Her voice was too calm, too studied to fool Erin. "Same old shit. After a while, you get used to it."

"Where are you?"

"Your house."

"I'll be right there."

"Don't rush. I'm watching the game."

"We don't have a TV. Hey, how did you get in?"

"A spare key under the mat isn't the best burglar protection. You might want to upgrade your security system."

Erin couldn't make herself laugh. "I'll be right there," she said, and closed the phone. Gail and Dan were both staring at her when she opened the door again. "I'm leaving." She let the door close and was down the stairs when she realized she didn't have a car. Regretfully, she headed back towards the house, only to be met on the porch by her mother.

"This might sound crazy," Gail said, "but would you let me go talk to her?"

Erin blinked. "Why?"

"I don't think you could realistically call any of us impartial, but I love Dan, and I know how much he loves Katie. I might be able to give her some ideas about why he acts the way he does."

"If you have an opinion about that, why haven't you said anything to me? I've been asking you for months."

"I know, I know, and I should have talked to you earlier. Let me try to make up for that by talking to Katie now."

Erin's sighed tiredly. "Okay, if you really want to. But I'm going with you."

"Why don't you stay here and talk to Dan? I could be wrong, but he looks like he's in a place where he can listen."

"Just not to the person he *should* be listening to, right?"

Gail nodded. "That's probably true. It might be a complete waste of time, but it might also be worth the effort."

"Fine," Erin sulked. "I'll try to talk to him, but I'm not going to tolerate him cutting her down. She doesn't, in any way, deserve that."

Gail pulled her close and kissed her cheek. "I agree. Is she at our house?"

Erin nodded and then watched her mother dash down the stairs, leaving Erin standing there, not sure of what to do or how to do it.

By the time Gail's taillights were glaring in the distance, Dan was standing next to Erin on the porch. "Where'd she go?"

"To talk to Katie. I'm supposed to stay here and talk to you." She fixed him with her dark eyes, and she felt a frisson of pleasure when she saw him gulp.

"What…what is there to talk about? I already told you that I don't know what happened tonight."

Erin flopped down on the top step. "You've had many, many incidents like tonight. One of them must have made an impression."

"Do you want me to get your beer?"

She shook her head. "No. Katie has shown me that the first sip or two of a beer is really great. After that, I don't care for it. If they made two ounce bottles I'd be set."

Looking even more puzzled, he sat down next to her and took a long drink from his own bottle. "What happened tonight made a big impression on me." His voice was so strained and thin that Erin thought he might cry. "How could she think I hate her? What did I ever do to make her think that?"

"Oh, for goodness sake!" Erin glared at him, unable to hold her tongue. "How would you feel if the parent you idolized left home and chose to take your brother to live with him? How would you feel if your father chose his own happiness over keeping your family together? I'm astounded you can ask a question like that. You even gave her dog away! How was she supposed to understand all of that?"

"What? What?" He stumbled to his feet, staring at Erin. "That's what she thinks? She thinks I left so *I* could be happier? She thinks *I* was being selfish?"

"Yeah. That's exactly what she thinks, and I'd think the same thing if my father had done that."

He half-closed his eyes and pointed at her with the neck of his bottle. "Maybe you wouldn't have been such a hardheaded little shit! You might not have taken off and tried to walk home every time I brought you to my apartment. You might not have made the judge make *me* have a psychiatric exam before I could have visitation rights with her. Her mother was so Goddamned drunk that she ran over the fucking dog, but *I'm* the one who had to have my head examined." His anger seemed to drain from him, and he sat down on the stairs and leaned against a post. "Please, don't tell her that," he said, closing his eyes and dropping his head into his open hands.

"Which part?"

"About the dog. She doesn't need to know that."

"She told me she never went to visit you."

"Oh, she came to visit a few times. I had the scratches to prove it."

"Scratches?"

"It would've been easier to kidnap a kid. The first time she came over, one of my new neighbors called the police. They saw me dragging her in through the front door, and they heard her cussing me out. Once she saw that she could embarrass me by getting the police involved, she kept ramping it up."

"Yeah, she told me about some of the things that happened in high school."

"Every time I put pressure on her to spend time with me, she'd pull one of those tricks. I remember the first time I heard her drunken voice yelling out, 'Tell him his dyke daughter got caught giving head!'" He looked almost ill. "How could such a great little girl turn into such a hateful…" The dark look Erin gave him apparently made him reconsider his choice of words. "Young woman."

"What was she supposed to do?"

"She could have listened to me. She could've let me try to explain."

"Did you really try?"

"Hell, yes, I tried! But do you have any idea how hard it is to explain something like that to a little girl without making her mother the fall guy?"

"No, of course I don't. But couldn't you have…I don't know…let her know that you weren't punishing her?"

"How could I do that?" he said, plaintively. "I wanted to keep them together, but my mother wouldn't agree to watch both of them when I was at work. She flat-out refused to take Katie because Danny was easier to handle. I didn't have any choice."

"Darn," Erin said softly. "Her own grandmother didn't want her?"

"My mother was no saint. She would have blistered Katie's hide at the first sign of insubordination, but I wouldn't allow that. It's better that Katie didn't have to spend a lot of time with her. There could have been bloodshed," he said, smiling fondly. "You could never push Katie Tierney around."

"Do you ever think you should've stayed?" There was no censure in Erin's tone, and Dan, surprisingly, answered immediately.

"No, never. The best thing that ever happened to Betty was having to get a job. If I had stayed, she probably would have drunk herself to death, like her own mother did." He turned and gazed at Erin for a moment. "Like I worry Katie will."

Erin's formerly open expression closed tightly. "I don't want to talk about Katie. I've said too much already." She stood up. "I won't tell her anything you've told me, but I will tell you that she wants to have a relationship with you and she wants to know that you love her. If you won't gut it up and tell her that, you're not nearly a good enough man for my mother."

She started to walk away, with Dan calling after her, "Where are you going?"

"Home," she said, still walking.

"That's miles from here. Let me drive you."

"I'll be fine. I run this far all of the time."

❧

Gail knocked on the door before entering, even though it felt odd to do so. She smiled at the image of Katie, dressed in a T-shirt and a pair of shorts, her bare feet up on the sofa, her arms hugging her knees. A laptop computer was open and resting on the coffee table.

Katie cocked her head and asked, "What bet did you lose?"

Somewhat tentatively, Gail sat next to her on the sofa and saw that Katie had been watching a choppy version of the baseball game on the computer. "I didn't lose a bet. As a matter of fact, I had to plead my case to be allowed to come."

Releasing her legs, Katie swung them around and sat up straight. "Why did you want to?"

"I'm not sure. I just thought that I might be able to help."

"Help what?"

"Well, now I'm not sure what I was thinking," Gail admitted, coloring a little.

Katie smiled. "Now I see the resemblance between you and Erin. I'd never really caught it before."

"Yes, yes, neither of us is very verbal."

"Erin talks enough. She just doesn't *have* to talk. I like that about her. Actually, I like just about everything about her."

"She talked a lot about you tonight." Gail couldn't stop herself from smiling. "I doubt anyone has ever had a list of things he loved about me. You're a lucky woman." She put her hand on Katie's knee and looked into her eyes. "Erin is crazy about you. And if you're patient with her, she'll be the best partner you could ever hope to have."

Katie looked away and then let her eyes shift to a spot just short of where Gail sat. "I think she's the one who'll need the patience. I'm sure my dad has told you how difficult I can be."

"I've stopped paying attention to what your dad says about you." Katie sat up even straighter and looked at Gail curiously. "I finally realized that he doesn't know you well enough to have an opinion about you. I'm much more interested in Erin's feelings for you, and my daughter is a very good judge of character."

"Th…thank you," Katie said, trying to keep her tears from flowing. "I love her very much."

"I believe that. I don't think Erin would fall in love with someone if she wasn't absolutely sure she was equally well loved."

Katie sat back and let her head rest on the back of the sofa. "I'm worried about you being with him," she said, not bothering to mention her father by name. "I know he thinks I went after Erin just to spite him, but nothing could be further from the truth. It would be much better for me if you two didn't know each other."

"I can see why you'd think that, but I don't think you should let that worry you too much. Over time, I think you and your dad can develop a good relationship."

"Don't forget I'm almost ten years older than Erin. I don't have that long."

"I'm being serious," Gail said, smiling at Katie's joke. "I just think that you really have to take it slowly. If you and Erin can manage to live in Boston, I think that will help."

"Really?"

"Yes. Let him slowly get used to seeing you two as a couple. Over time, he'll see that you love her in spite of him, not *to* spite him."

"We can't live anywhere until Erin figures out how to escape her servitude."

The front door opened, and Erin scampered over to the sofa, throwing her arms around Katie with such force that she lifted her from her seat. "Are you okay?" she murmured.

"Yeah, I'm fine." Katie patted her back and then gently tried to disengage. "You're so hot. How did you get here?"

"Oh." Erin stood up and pulled her shirt away from her damp skin. "I started to walk, and then I ran for a while. One of my patients saw me, and after a long lecture, he gave me a ride home."

"Walk? Why didn't my father bring you?"

Erin saw Katie's face getting red, and she put her hands up. "I didn't want a ride. I wanted to clear my head."

"Is it clear?"

"Not really. What's going on here?"

"Your mom and I have just been talking about the benefits of you and me living in Boston."

Erin released her grip and turned to look at Gail. "Really? Why?"

"I just…" She seemed much less sure of herself now that Erin was home, and her voice trailed off to such a whisper that Erin wasn't sure if her mother had completed the sentence.

"Go on," Katie urged.

Gail moved around on the sofa, looking like she was trying to get comfortable. "I think you'd both thrive in Boston. Katie has a good social network and there's so much more to do."

Erin was sitting on the arm of the sofa, and she put her arm around Katie and tugged her close. "We both want that, Mom, but there's no way to have that happen without getting stuck with a lot of debt. That's not how I want to start our life together."

Katie smiled up at her and then turned back to Gail. "For the time being we'll keep doing what we've been doing. Going back and forth on the weekends."

"Oh, that will be hard for both of you. I'd hate to only see Dan on the weekends."

"Yes, it's hard," Erin said. "But I don't mind driving to Boston. It's so nice to see Katie that I'd go to Miami." She snuck a shy glance at her lover.

Katie chimed in, "I can do a lot of my work on the phone, I can come up here for three or even four day weekends."

"How often do you think that would be?" Gail asked.

"It's hard to say. I'd have to retrain some clients. But I could probably do it twice a month."

"Starting a relationship is hard enough when you're in the same place," Gail said. "Wouldn't it be better to have some debt?"

"Erin doesn't think so," Katie said. "And if she's not comfortable, I don't want to force the issue."

"I don't want this to be *my* decision," Erin said. "But I'm really uncomfortable with the thought of sticking Katie with a high mortgage payment. If she refinanced her apartment, she'd be stuck with high payments for thirty years."

Gently patting Erin's knee, Katie said, "Technically, *we'd* be stuck with them. And as soon as you start earning a good living, the higher payments won't be an issue at all. Actually, they're not an issue now. I can easily afford them and not alter my lifestyle."

Erin dropped her head, looking mildly chagrined. "I know, I know. I'm just really averse to having you be responsible for my bad decisions."

"With gas prices like they are you'll probably wind up paying as much to the oil companies as you would for the higher mortgage," Gail said. "Not to mention the toll driving that much can put on you. Your job is stressful enough, Katie. Wouldn't it be better to have Erin do most of the driving?"

Erin's gaze sharpened, and she looked at her mother pointedly. "Isn't *my* job stressful? It sounds like you don't want Katie to visit Essex."

"Honey!" Gail flushed and looked exasperated. "That's a ridiculous thing to even think. I want you to do what's best for both of you."

"There's something else going on. You're really making a case for us to spend more time in Boston, and that's not like you. What else is on your mind?"

Gail sighed dramatically. "It's just this town. You know how provincial the old guard can be. That's just another form of stress that you two don't need."

"You mean…because we're gay?" Katie asked.

"Yes. And Erin, you can say what you want, but if you felt entirely comfortable being out here, you would have told more people."

"I've wondered about that myself," Katie said. "But Erin claims she just likes her privacy about everything."

"Okay, it's more than just that," Erin admitted. "You know I don't like to invite trouble. If I can slide by, I do. But when I can't, I do what I have to do. I know a lot of people in town will be uncomfortable with my being gay. I know I'll lose some patients. I know Madge will make a federal case out of it—not so much because I'm gay, but because I didn't tell her. But everybody who matters to me knows. It won't be that big a deal."

"It's not just…random people in town who will have an opinion about this," Gail said. "When you make a public statement, it tends to affect everyone close to you."

Katie's cheeks were already pink, and her voice was rising in volume and timbre. "If you're referring to my father…"

"I didn't say a word about him," Gail insisted, her skin losing color as quickly as Katie's was gaining it. "All I said was that having people in town gossip behind your backs can be hard for everyone."

"What did he say?" Katie demanded. She got to her feet and glared at Gail, who was practically cowering. "Did he specifically tell you he wanted us to stay out of Essex?"

"I…I didn't say that, Katie. Please, please try to calm down."

"I'll calm down after I knock some sense into him," she snapped. "I'm so fucking sick of his homophobic bullshit!" She jumped up and headed for the door, grabbing her keys as she went. Erin stood to follow her just as Katie hit the front door. "Your car's in my way," she hissed. "Give me your keys!" Her laser-like blue eyes scanned the table near the entry, and she found Gail's key fob. Without another word, she grabbed it and took off.

Erin was so shocked it took her a moment to get her feet to obey the orders her brain was giving them. By the time she got to the door, Katie was in Gail's car, and the engine was roaring to life. "Katie!" she screamed, running after her. But her lover relentlessly drove down the street, leaving a sputtering Erin in her wake.

❦

Katie jumped out of the car while it was still rolling. She'd turned off the ignition, but didn't bother to put it in park. Luckily, the driveway was long and flat and the car came to rest just a few feet away. She burst in through the back door, stormed up to her father who was just getting to his feet, and slapped his chest with both hands, pushing the stunned man back onto the sofa. "What did you tell her?" Her eyes were wild, and she was panting.

"About the—"

"How did you convince her to do your dirty work? How did you manipulate her into telling us to stay out of Essex?"

"What? I don't know what you're talk—"

"Stop lying to me!" she screamed at the top of her lungs. "I can't stand it anymore! If you want me out of your fucking life, just tell me! I can't stand to be pulled back in and then shut out again. It's killing me!" She sank to the floor, her anger completely played out. "It's killing me," she sobbed piteously.

"Katie, Katie." He got up and went to her just as Erin and Gail stormed in through the door.

"What did you do to her?" Erin screamed, rushing into the room and pushing him aside with surprising force. "Katie!" She knelt next to her and gathered her in her arms. "Are you all right? Did he hit you?"

"Hit her? Why in the hell would I hit her? What in the holy Christ is going on around here?" He searched each face, but got nothing in reply.

"He didn't hit me," Katie said through her sobs. "He just wants me as far away as possible."

"What?" Dan cried. "That's bullshit! Gail! Haven't I been telling you how nice it's been to see Katie more often?"

She stared at him, not saying a word.

"Goddamn it, I have! Just the other day, I said I thought it would be great if Katie could manage to live in Essex. I think it'd be damned good for her to get away from some of those friends of hers."

Erin stared at him. "What's wrong with her friends?" She shook her head, trying to order her thoughts. "Did you really say that? Did you mean it?"

"Hell yes, I said it. I said it to your mother, who's standing over there acting like she's lost her tongue. Gail, tell Katie what I said."

Looking as though all of the blood had been drained from her, Gail mumbled, "I don't remember."

"What do you mean you don't remember? You didn't agree with me, but that shouldn't make you forget."

Surprising everyone, Gail turned and ran from the house. Erin helped Katie to her feet, and the three of them stood there for a moment, staring at each other blankly.

Finally, Erin spoke. Her words were soft, and she looked a little ill, but she spoke with certainty. "I think I see what's going on." She took Katie's hand and said, "We should go home."

Dan's voice boomed out. "Oh, no, you don't! Don't you dare leave if you know what in the holy hell is going on around here."

"I think you'd better ask my mother. She's the one who doesn't want us here."

Katie stared at Erin, dumbfounded. "Honey, why would you think that? Your mom loves you."

"I know she does," Erin said quietly. "You can love someone and not want to share your town with her." She looked at Katie, pleadingly. "Can we please go home?"

Katie turned and met her father's eyes, and in the second that followed Erin spoke again. "I changed my mind. I have to talk to her."

"I'll go find her," Dan said. With that, he went to the back door and exited.

Katie put her arms around Erin and squeezed her hard. "Are you sure? Are you sure it's your mom who doesn't want us here?"

"I am. And I'm just as sure that your dad *does* want us here. He loves you, Katie. I'm sure of it. He just doesn't know how to express it. He's a big chicken."

Smiling gently, Katie said, "If he heard you say that, he'd flatten you." She looked at Erin with what could only be described as childlike hope. "Do you really think he loves me?"

"I'm sure of it," Erin said, hugging her firmly. "I'm sure, baby."

The back door opened, and the younger women looked up from their emotion-filled hug. Dan had his arm around Gail and looked to be exerting the kind of force one would use to convince a cat to take a bath. "Gail has something she wants to say to you two."

"I'm sorry," she whispered. She cleared her throat and tried again. "I'm sorry I haven't been honest with you. I'm sorry that it matters so much to me."

Puzzled, Katie asked, "What matters to you?"

"What people in town think," Erin answered for her mother. "It's as simple as that, isn't it, Mom?"

"Yes," she admitted, tears streaming down her cheeks. "It's as simple and as complex as that."

"It doesn't seem that complex to me," Dan said. "If these lamebrains don't like it, they can lump it. I haven't met more than three people in the whole place who I'd give you a plug nickel for. It's the twenty-first century, for Christ's sake. What hole have these people been hiding in?"

"This isn't your home," Erin said quietly. "And other people's opinions don't affect you like they do my mom. That's just who she is."

"I know it's wrong," Gail said through her tears. "I want to be stronger, but it would torture me to have people talking about my sweet little girl behind her back. It would torture me." She walked over to Erin and put her arms around her. "I'm so sorry I'm not a better mother."

"It's all right," Erin said, patting her gently. "We'll get through this." She gave Dan a near-pleading look, and he picked up on it immediately, coming up behind Gail and turning her towards himself, whereupon she leaned against him heavily.

"I think it's time for us to leave now. Both Katie and I have to work tomorrow."

Dan nodded, giving both Erin and Katie a sad but encouraging smile. "We'll talk tomorrow."

Erin waved wearily, and she took Katie's hand as they went to the car. "Is it okay if I don't feel like talking?"

"Sure. We'll be home in a few minutes, and we can both collapse."

"No," Erin said, her voice low but clear. "This isn't our home. We're just visiting."

<hr />

Erin didn't say a word on the ride home. She didn't seem irritated, cranky, or even hurt to Katie's watchful eye. She did, however, seem flat, and after Katie watched her go into the kitchen and pour herself a glass of milk, she lost the control she'd been maintaining and started to speak her mind. "What's going on with you?" she demanded.

"Nothing." Erin shrugged and took a sip. "I think we should refinance your apartment and move in together as soon as we can."

"That's your answer?" Katie's hands were balled into fists, and her lips were pursed together tightly. "How do you feel? What's going on inside your head?"

Erin looked at her, clearly puzzled. "Why do you seem angry? What did I do?"

"For God's sake, your mother essentially told you that she wants you to move away just so she doesn't have to listen to people gossip!"

"Yeah." Erin took another drink. "I wasn't really surprised. It hurts, but I wasn't shocked."

"How many times will you let her do things like that?"

"I didn't *let* her. She's her own person. I can't change something so elemental about her."

Katie marched across the room and stopped right in front of Erin, who flinched a little. "I know you can't change her, but she has no motivation to change. If she can get away with treating you like that and not have any repercussions, why *should* she change?"

"She feels bad. I know she does. Those weren't crocodile tears. Why should I kick her when she's down?"

"There's a difference between kicking her and making it clear how you feel. You let her off scot-free. What will happen next time? What will happen at the wedding? If we come to visit, will you hide when we drive through town?"

"No, of course not," Erin said, showing a little irritation. "That's ridiculous. I don't hide. You know that."

"No, I don't. You can't have it both ways. If your mom's comfort is worth so much to you, don't you *have* to hide your sexuality? Don't you *have* to hide our relationship?"

"She doesn't want that." Erin's tone and the softness of her voice showed that she was losing her confidence. "She just doesn't want us to be really open."

"How do you know that?"

"Well, she's never said anything to me before…"

"She said an awful lot tonight. An awful lot." Katie's anger had dissipated, and she gently wrapped Erin in a hug. "It broke my heart to hear what she said to you. You're the best daughter a woman could ever have."

"She loves me. I know she does."

"I'm not denying that, but it's not fair that she can mistreat you and not even get her ass chewed out for it."

With a surprising amount of sarcasm, Erin pulled away and said, "That kind of thing works really well for you and your dad, doesn't it?"

Katie's cheeks started to color, and her voice got louder. "We don't tiptoe around each other like you two do, that's for sure."

"And you think what you do is more productive? Letting your dad think ridiculously hurtful things about you?"

"That's his choice," Katie said dismissively. "But I don't let him push me around."

"I'd rather take a punch in the face than have my mom think the things about me that your dad does about you."

"You'd rather take a second punch than tell your mom you were pissed about the first one she gave you!"

Erin perched on the arm of the sofa, looking at Katie like she was a complete stranger. "Why are you picking on me like this?"

"I'm not…oh, darn it!" She walked over to her and slumped into a seat on the sofa, resting her arm and head on Erin's leg. "I'm sorry. I just…I guess I…" She sighed. "Never mind. I shouldn't have said anything. I'm really sorry."

Absently letting her hand trail through Katie's hair, Erin said, "You've been thinking this for a while, right? That I should be more…forceful with her."

"No, not forceful. That's not how you are. But I do think you should stand up for yourself more. Your needs are just as valid as hers."

"I know that, and I *do* stand up for myself when I really need to."

Softly, Katie asked, "If you didn't need to tonight, what would have to happen to make you need to?"

Erin was quiet for a minute, still rhythmically stroking Katie's hair. "How did your fight start tonight?"

"What?"

"Who said the first mean thing? You or your dad?"

"He did."

"What was it?"

"It doesn't matter." Katie briskly shook her head.

"Yes, it does. What was it?"

Katie's voice was remarkably soft, but Erin managed to hear her. "He said I'd cheat on you and you'd have to divorce me. Oh, no, that was the second thing. The first was that he sarcastically asked if I wanted to have a double wedding with him and your mother."

"And you said?"

"I don't remember. Something snotty."

"Is that helpful? Is that the way to have a better relationship?"

"No." Katie's voice was almost a whisper.

"It sounds like we both need to make some changes."

"You first," Katie said, a derisive laugh bubbling up. "I'm older, and old habits…"

"Don't be that way. No matter what you think of her, I'm not going to shut my mom out of my life. And if she ever needs me to take care of her, I will. If that includes taking care of your father, I will." She stood up, and Katie was forced to look up at her to achieve eye contact. "If you can't agree to that, we'd better rethink getting married."

"You'd…you'd break up with me over this?"

"Yes," Erin said unhesitatingly. "I don't turn my back on the people I love because they disappoint me. I won't do that to you, and I won't do it to my mother." The look in Katie's eyes dropped Erin to her knees. "I'd never get over my broken heart, but I couldn't choose between her and you. I *won't* choose between her and you."

Katie gulped, stunned by the calm clarity Erin projected. "I'd never ask you to choose between us. That's unconscionable."

Erin put her hands on Katie's thighs. She looked deeply into her eyes and said, "You have to promise me that you'll try to show your dad who you really are. I'll be miserable if you're fighting every time we see them."

"I'll try. But you have to promise you'll try to make your mom share some of the load in your relationship. It will drive me nuts if you let her walk on you all of the time."

"I don't," Erin nearly whined.

"Yes, you do. You do anything to keep the peace, and that's not healthy."

After a few moments, Erin nodded. "Yeah, yeah, I do that." She slowly got to her feet and stood there for a bit, gazing at Katie intently. "Let's take a drive."

"A drive?" She looked at her watch. "Now?"

"Yeah. Right now."

⬦

A few minutes later, they pulled into the long drive at Dan's farm. Katie kept sparing nervous looks at Erin, but she didn't question her. The lights were on, and by the time the car stopped, both Dan and Gail were on the front porch, looking as if they were prepared for awful news.

Erin strode across the driveway and said, "Mom, I need to talk to you. Where do you want to go?"

"Uhm…" Gail turned to Dan, but her wide-eyed gaze wasn't returned, and she was forced to look back at Erin. "Is the kitchen all right?"

"Yes." Erin brushed past Dan and opened the door, waited for her mother to enter, and then followed her.

As they went into the room, Gail turned on the light and then sat on a chair, looking at Erin like she was expecting a beating.

⬦

Dan looked only slightly more puzzled by Erin's demeanor than Katie did. "What got into her?" he asked. "She walked out of here like a whipped puppy, and an hour later, she looks like the top dog."

The evening caught up with Katie, and she spoke without censoring herself. "I probably did." She was staring at the door, wishing she could be in that kitchen to support Erin. "I should have kept my mouth shut, but I was so damned mad at what Gail said to her…"

"Yeah. I can understand that."

That snapped her out of her reverie, and she turned to stare at him. "You can?"

"Hell, yes. You've got to stand up for the people you love."

"You…believe I love her?"

He gazed at her, pensively. "Gail's confident you do."

"Gail?" She felt her ire start to rise. "She's the one whose opinion matters? You've known me for a little bit longer, Dad. Maybe you could try to trust what I tell you."

"You?" His laugh was sharp and short. "You don't tell me anything."

"Gee, I wonder why that is…" She tapped her chin with her finger, acting like she was deep in thought. "I know. It's because you hate me."

"I do not!" He grasped her by her shoulders and held her tightly, his fiery eyes burning into her. Like a kitten held by the scruff of its neck, Katie's rigid body grew almost limp. She stood there quietly, gazing back at her father with her full attention. "How can you say I hate you?" he asked again, his voice softening a

Page 322

little.

She didn't even try to speak. She just looked at him, waiting for him to continue.

"Who are you?" He cocked his head a little, as if trying to see inside her. "I don't know you."

"You don't want to," she finally replied softly.

"Says who? I've been chasing after you for twenty years. Why would I do that if I didn't want to know you?"

"You don't want to *know* me." Her gaze shifted away from his penetrating eyes. "You just want me to do things for you. Like check your house when you're on vacation."

He loosened his hold and brought his hands up to rest lightly on the tops of her shoulders. "You told me to call you whenever I needed a hand. I thought…I thought you…" He moved away from her, half-turning his back.

Now that he had turned away, she seemed to gain energy. She slipped across the porch, staying in front of him. "You thought I what?"

He shook his head quickly and took another step away from her. "It doesn't matter."

"Yes, it does." She put her hand on his muscular forearm. "It matters."

Looking at her for a few moments, he let his guard fall and said, "I thought you might want to visit more often once I was up here. I thought you might want to spend some more time with me."

"You were in Florida!"

"I know that. But hell, I don't know. I thought you might get more comfortable coming here when I wasn't home." He saw the dubious look on her face and snapped, "It was just a thought. I couldn't figure out why you offered."

"I don't know why I offered, either. I just can't let go." She looked up and searched his eyes for a few moments. "Erin asked me why I don't just stop seeing you."

"Stop?"

"Yeah. Walk away and stop fighting once and for all."

"You'd do that?" He turned pale and looked almost frightened.

"No," she said immediately, her heart beating rapidly at the pain she saw in his eyes. "I was amazed she'd even suggest such a thing. So, I clearly don't want to drop you like a bad habit."

"Then talk to me," he begged. "Tell me about your life. Gail tells me I don't know you at all, but it's not that I don't want to."

"Why do you jump on me if you want to know me? I tell you I'm getting married, and you assume I'm doing it to get back at you somehow."

"That's what you've always done. I get...I don't know." He scrubbed at the back of his head, his eyes closed tightly. "All of the things you've done in the past go flying through my mind, and I start snapping at you."

"No kidding. You jump on me with both feet. It hardly matters what I say."

"I don't want to do that. It's just a bad instinct."

"I have bad instincts, too. Must be a Tierney trait," she added, showing a hint of a smile.

"Well, Gail is on me all of the time, telling me Erin wouldn't be with you if you're how you...used to be." The end of his sentence was far too equivocal for Katie, but the fact that he held out the possibility of being wrong about her was a little something.

"Erin says she won't be able to stand it if you and I keep sniping at each other."

"Same for Gail."

"I guess those are two good reasons to try to be more...what...adult?"

"Yeah. Being more adult would probably be good. It would be really nice if I didn't feel I had to force my way into your life. Twenty years is long enough."

She felt the all-too-familiar vein of anger being struck. "Well, it would be nice for me to feel like you don't hate me. Twenty years of that is enough, too."

Once again, he grasped her, but his touch was gentle, almost comforting this time. "I have never, ever hated you. Not for one single moment." He pulled her to his chest, and she could feel his racing heart. "I hated a lot of the things you did, but never you. Never. I swear." He pulled away, and she was astonished to see tears in his eyes. His voice grew raspy and broke as he continued. "You were my sweet, sweet little girl. My buddy. I missed you so much."

Like a long buried instinct, she slipped her arms around him and buried her face in his chest. "I missed you, too. Every day was..." her voice trailed off into a ragged whisper.

His arms tightened convulsively around her, and he tenderly stroked her back. "I tried my best to handle things, baby, but I screwed up. I screwed up a lot. I just...didn't know what to do."

She nestled further into his embrace, relishing his protective care, reveling in the sense-memory of the thousands of hugs he'd given her so long ago. Neither one spoke for several moments, but once the wave of feeling passed, they both grew a little uncomfortable with the intimacy. Dan pulled away, but kept his hands on her shoulders. "Let's try to listen to each other for a change."

"Okay. I promised Erin I'd try to let you get to know me. That's not gonna happen in an instant, but I'm willing to try if you're willing to stop jumping all over me."

"I'm more than willing. I'm Goddamned eager." He flashed his most charming grin, and she reflexively smiled back.

"I'm not going to go that far, but I promise I'll try. How's that?"

"Good enough for me." He wrapped her in a gentle, brief, emotion-filled hug. "I never knew how much I could miss someone who I saw all of the time. I used to go to the park across the street from your school just to see you outside at recess. I never stopped wanting you in my life, Katie. Never."

She cleared her throat and flicked a few tears from her lashes. "That's true for me, too. Maybe I didn't go about it in the most mature way, but the sentiment was there."

"Yeah. Having my phone ring all hours of the day and night to get you delivered home in a squad car wasn't my idea of closeness."

"I was a kid," she said testily. "I'm an adult now."

He smiled at her, letting himself take in the beautiful, mature woman who gazed up at him with such intense, intelligent eyes. "I can see that. Want to go see what the Delancy women are up to?"

"No, they'll come out here when they're done. I haven't heard any raised voices, which, in my opinion, is a bad thing."

He nodded. "They could both use a little of our temper."

"Yeah," she grinned wryly. "That would make life much more interesting."

⁓

Inside the kitchen, Erin sat down and put her hands on the table. "Katie and I are going to take out a second mortgage on her house. I'll pay off the city and move to Boston as soon as I possibly can."

"Honey, don't rush into this. I know that's not what you want—"

"I told you what I wanted to do, Mom, and you made it clear that you don't want us here. Don't act like that didn't happen."

Gail shrank back, her mouth opening in surprise mixed with outrage. "You said you understood!"

"I do." She stared at her for a few seconds, her gaze failing to hide the dark emotions that whirled inside her. "I understand all too well what's most important to you."

"You are!"

Erin's cold, strong voice reverberated through the room like a hammer hitting stone. "That's not true."

"It is! You're the most important person in my life." Gail was crying hard now, tears streaming down her reddening cheeks.

Erin's chin was set, and her expression was grimly determined. "I know you love me, Mom, but your peace of mind is worth more to you than mine is."

"It's not!"

"Your actions say that I'm right. That's all I have to go on."

Gail looked like she'd taken a mortal blow. "I'd do anything not to hurt you."

"That's not true, either. I'm sure you wish it were, but it's not. You had to know it would hurt me to try to manipulate us into spending our weekends in Boston."

"I wasn't manipulating—"

"Yes, you were. You tried to make us believe that Dan didn't want us here. What other word would you use for that?" Her glare seemed to be powered by an inner fire Gail had never seen.

"I want what's best for you. That's always number one in my mind. And being in Essex isn't best. You need to be in a big city where you can be yourself."

"That's for me to decide. I could be perfectly happy here."

"You know you'd have to put up with a lot of whispering behind your back. Why would you want that?"

Erin took in and let out a long breath. When she spoke, her words were pointed but quiet, and she fixed her gaze on the table. "I could easily put up with everyone in town talking about me. It would go away in time." Her chin lifted, and she locked on to her mother's pale eyes. "You're the only person in Essex whose opinion matters to me, and you've made it clear you don't want me here. That's why I'm going to do something that turns my stomach—have Katie bail me out of a mess I got myself into."

"I swear that I want you here! I just don't want—"

Rudely cutting her off, Erin said, "I know what you want, but you can't have it." She paused to make sure her mother was listening. "Once I move away, I won't hide. At all. I will tell anyone who asks that Katie and I are going to be married. So, you'll have to visit us in Boston until you're ready for me to be out."

"I need some time to get used to this, Erin. I'm surprised by your attitude. You've never—"

"Take all the time you need," she interrupted. "But I'm not going to change my position. Katie is my fiancé, and I'm as proud of that as anything I've ever accomplished." She paused and took a breath. "This is my home, but once I leave I'll never cross the New Hampshire border again without Katie by my side."

Gail stared at her, slightly in awe of this young woman, who looked just like the girl who'd left the house earlier that evening, but had clearly changed in a significant and wholly unpleasant way.

❧

Two weeks later, Erin and Katie stood on the steps of Katie's home, waving goodbye to the honeymooners. The day had been a whirlwind of activity, and both women were tired and emotionally drained from the ceremony. They sat down after Erin brushed the dust off the steps. "I'm so glad that's over." She leaned against Katie, then rested her head on her shoulder. "It was really nice of you to let our parents get married here."

"It wasn't a big deal. Your mom did most of the work."

Erin sat up and looked at her for a few moments. "I'm not talking about the work. I'm talking about your generosity."

"My dad paid for everything." Katie looked puzzled. "You know that."

Erin put her arm around Katie's shoulders and squeezed her. "I mean your spirit. That's the generous part." She kissed her cheek, relishing the feel of her soft skin. "It was very kind of you."

For the next five minutes, both women sat quietly, nodding at a few neighbors pushing strollers or being led down the street by toddlers. "How did it feel, having the wedding here?" Katie asked, reaching over to take Erin's hand in her own.

"Okay." There was a significant silence, then Erin added, "Not great."

"That's what I would have guessed."

Erin stretched and her back made a popping sound. "My mom probably created more gossip by moving the wedding here and dis-inviting everyone from Essex than she would have by having you and I in tuxedos acting as groomsmen."

"I don't look good in a tuxedo," Katie said, chuckling. "You might, though. One with a fitted jacket to show off your hips. Maybe we should consider that for our wedding."

"No way." Erin smiled at her. "I'm not going to wear a tux when you wear a dress. I still like the idea of both of us wearing dresses."

"I've never seen you in a dress before today." She pointedly ogled Erin's legs. "You were made for them."

"Thank you." She batted her eyes seductively. "Do I look remarkably different?"

"No, not really. Why?"

"I was hoping I could wear dresses to help hide from the process server who will soon be looking for me."

Katie slipped her arm around Erin's shoulders. "It's not too late to change your mind. I could get a second mortgage like that." She snapped her fingers noisily.

"Your debts would be paid."

"No. My mind's made up. I have to do this on my own. The city will be happy because the insurance will pay off, and I'll have a big, fat judgment against me that I'll pay off—eventually." She showed a good-natured smile when she said, "Getting Doc back for a while will soothe any bad feelings."

"For the people who liked him better than you."

"Can't have everything." She extended her legs and rotated her feet at the ankles. "Heels and comfort don't go together."

"Don't change the subject. How does it feel to invite someone to sue you?"

"Not good. Not good at all." She smiled, surprising Katie. "But everything has a cost. Being sued is nothing compared to being able to do what I love. With the woman I love," she added. "I was talking to your uncle, the lawyer, today. He was teasing me a little—like everyone in your family does, by the way."

"We're all comedians. What did he say?"

"He said he thought I should have waited to quit until we were married. Then you would've been on the hook for my debt." She leaned over until their foreheads touched. "I think you asked me to marry you when you did so you *would* be on the hook, you devious barrister."

"Redundant," Katie said, crossing her eyes. She pulled back and said, "You've got your dates wrong. You decided to quit before I asked you to marry me."

"No way."

"Think about it," Katie said, leaning in to kiss Erin as sexily as she could manage. She whispered against her lips, "Quit first, engaged later."

"What?" Erin asked, so easily distracted by a good kiss.

Katie placed another sizzler on her lips. "I asked you to marry me after you decided to quit."

"Right. Sure. Whatever." Erin's dark eyes were unfocused and half closed.

Katie kissed her lightly, while grasping her elbows to encourage her to stand. Then she opened the front door and guided Erin inside.

Standing right there in the vestibule, Katie slid her fingers into Erin's hair, sending goose bumps skittering up and down her body. Then she kissed her again and began to probe her mouth daintily with her tongue.

Erin pressed her breasts into Katie's, and writhed against her to increase the pressure. She came up for air after she started to feel lightheaded. "What were you saying?" she asked, taking Katie's hand to lead her upstairs.

As they walked, Katie tickled down Erin's partially bare back and then started to unzip her snug-fitting dress. "I was saying that I'm desperate to make love to you."

"Right. That's right." Erin's gaze was so lust-filled and vacant that Katie wasn't sure if she'd forgotten the conversation they'd been having. "I feel the same way." She stopped at the top of the stairs and grasped Katie with surprising strength. "I want you so badly," she whispered hotly and then started to mouth and suckle Katie's sensitive neck. "It's been so long since we've made love."

Even though every sensitive part of her was throbbing, Katie let out a laugh. "I know. We haven't made love since this morning."

Erin pulled away and fixed Katie with a remarkably intense look. "Let's never wait that long again." When Katie didn't reply immediately, Erin gripped her tighter. "Promise me."

Katie's first instinct was to laugh again, but Erin looked so serious that she stopped herself short. For a few seconds that seemed to go on and on, she let herself experience just how fantastic it was to have such an amazing woman desire her so ferociously. "I promise," she murmured before falling into another all-encompassing, love-filled kiss.

The End

Author Website

www.susanxmeagher.com

By Susan X Meagher

Novels

The Lies That Bind
Girl Meets Girl
Cherry Grove
All That Matters
Arbor Vitae

Serial Novel

I Found My Heart in San Francisco:

Awakenings
Beginnings
Coalescence
Disclosures
Entwined
Fidelity
Getaway
Honesty

Anthologies

At First Blush
Infinite Pleasures
The Milk of Human Kindness
Telltale Kisses
Undercover Tales

To purchase these books go to

www.briskpress.com